Other titles by the same author
available in paperback:

THE CHARIOTEER

MARY RENAULT

PANTHEON BOOKS, NEW YORK

The Library of Congress Cataloged the First
Printing of this Title as Follows:
Renault, Mary, *pseud.*
The charioteer. [New York] Pantheon [1959]
346 p.   22 cm.
I. Title.
PZ3.R2913Ch   59-8583
ISBN: 0-394-71480-6

Manufactured in the United States of America
6897

IT was the first time he had ever heard the clock strike
ten at night. If he had been asleep and waked to hear
the strokes, it would have been different, a small man-
ageable fragment broken off the unknown hugeness of
night, from somewhere in the middle. He would have
been a little uneasy, perhaps, in his waking solitude,
and, if he heard anyone stirring, would have found
something legitimate to call out for, such as a drink of
water. Only babies called out about nothing. The ten
months which had passed of his fifth year felt like at
least half his remembered life, and he was used to his
responsibilities.

Tonight was unique. Tonight he had not been to
sleep at all, and it was ten.

Seven o'clock was familiar and domesticated. With
luck and good management, at seven his mother might
still be sitting on the edge of his bed with an unfinished
story. Eight was unusual, and associated with trouble:
having been punished, or being sick. Nine was the wild
outpost of an unknown continent. Ten was the mountains of the moon, the burial-place of the elephants:
white on the map. He lay staring with round birdlike
eyes at the dim lapping of light on the ceiling, incredulous of the journey he had made alone.

Outside a man passed the house, whistling. The noise
had an absolute foreignness, like the note of a jungle
bird. It had no link with humanity; it was simply a
mysterious feature on the face of night. Somewhere, so
far off that in the daytime one never heard it, a line of
railway trucks was shunted together. The metallic
clangs, melancholy with distance, not quite harsh and
not quite musical, made a loose chain of sound, then
stopped inconclusively, leaving the ear suspended and
waiting.

If one sat up as long as an hour past bedtime, except
on Christmas and birthdays, one would be ill. Laurie,
who had had this explained to him many times and ac-

cepted it as incontrovertible fact, inferred from it that after three hours, one would probably die.

Separated from life by this vast stretch of solitude, he would not have been surprised to find himself dying any minute. But first an angel would come. Grannie, who had been in heaven for a year, was the only one personally known to him, so it would probably be she. Laurie didn't remember her very well, and thought she would have altered a good deal. She would pick him up out of bed (Grannie had had cold hands, he remembered), and fly with him out of the window, up to heaven. He looked at the space between the curtains. The sky was vast, empty, and quite black.

Last time he had seen Grannie she had been in bed, thin and yellow and absent, with a sweet sick smell. He pictured her thus, wearing her embroidered flannel nightgown with the addition of wings; then as a younger lady like the other angels, with long golden hair floating behind her and a thinner nightgown, just like all the rest. Neither of these pictures soothed, nor—and this was the worst—wholly convinced him. In this enormous vacuum, he felt a crack open in the warm pearly shell of belief. He knew that dying was being fetched by the angels and taken to heaven; but, suddenly and terrifyingly, he could no longer feel it. What he felt was that it would simply grow darker, not only in the room, but also inside him; and that his mother would not be there.

A wave of despairing terror seized him. A known fact had become real to him for the first time, that sooner or later everyone died; not only old people like Grannie, but Laurie, Laurie Odell, I. He sat bolt upright in bed, a point of protesting, passionate identity in echoing space.

The room *was* darker. He looked at the night-light, sitting in its saucer of water on the bedside cupboard. Was it really lower, or was he beginning to die? No; the flame was little and round, instead of long and pointed; it always got darker then. He craned over, and looked into the pool of clear wax cupped in the paper shell. It was deep and still, and through it, at the bottom, he could see a glittering square of tin. This was very interesting; it was also strange, and different, like everything else tonight. His especial things were on the cupboard-top beside it: the blue and gold cap from a broken fountain-pen of his father's, a knob of pink quartz which had been the head of one of his mother's hatpins once, a piece of green bottle smoothed and frosted by the sea, a big glass marble with a red and blue twist in its middle. He wasn't allowed them in bed since the quartz had slipped down while he slept and made a sore place on his leg. He remembered this; but everything was different tonight, lawless and wild; if he were dying, he must have at least one of them with him. The pen-cap was the newest and most dear; his father had given it him only a week before. With the desperate courage of an invested garrison making a sortie, he jumped out, snatched it up, and curled back again, still alive.

As a traveller beset with wild beasts and fighting a fever has no time to think about the causes that took him abroad, so Laurie had almost forgotten what it was that, aeons ago, had first kept sleep from him. *"Tais-toi; voici l'enfant."* He still had the animal's ear whose vocabulary is in the pitch, not the words. The pent-up vehemence of his mother's caress, to herself a comfort and release, had been to him a great breach blasted in the walls of heaven, letting in the terrors of empty space. Something was going to happen. He did not expect to be told what it was, any more than a dog expects to know why the trunks are being got out, or for how long, or if he will be going. He had gone about dumbly, aching with secret fear and avoiding his father; for as surely as he knew that something was going to happen, he knew it was his father's fault. His mother, a fastidiously truthful woman would have denied with the dignity of affronted innocence that she had given the child so much as a hint of her wrongs; but to him she seemed to have declared in the clearest language that he was her only solace and the last refuge of her violated trust.

During his approaches and retreats he had heard snatches of the conversations his presence had interrupted. He knew that his father had done something

3

wicked while he was away from home. He was often away, covering things (it was not so very long since Laurie had first understood that his father was a newspaperman and not a kind of upholsterer). Laurie loved and admired, without respecting, his father. They were too often in trouble together, for making a mess without clearing up, or being late home from their joint expeditions. Laurie knew that his father had to obey his mother just as he had, under penalty of exile from love. Even though the exile was brief and symbolic, it was still the worst punishment he knew. Now that his father had committed some mysterious, unforgivable sin, he felt his own security still more vulnerable, and in the whole huge unknown world there was no relief for his fears, since she, the source of all safety, had appealed for protection even to him. Tonight, when she tucked him into bed, her face had looked as it had the day Grannie died; and he had listened dumb and uncaring to St. George and the Dragon, though it was his favorite tale; he knew that nothing was safe. Now, his fears confused with the stuff of bad dreams and frightening stories, he had gone so far into danger that he had forgotten how it all began.

Then suddenly rescue came, a step on the stairs. It was his father's. In the relief of hearing it, he forgot all associations except the old one of laughing reassurance. He sat up in bed, but the feet passed, and when he called it was too late; they had gone on to the door of what had in the last few days become Daddy's Room. But he knew by the sound of the door that it hadn't shut properly. Suddenly he was filled with the conviction that all his terrors, like so many before, had been evolved out of his own head and could be dispersed for him, returning him to the eternal verities of warmth and safety. For this his father was better than anyone; he took things easily, and whether he decided to answer a question or not, never rebuked one for having asked it. The landing was dark outside; it took him a few minutes to drum up his courage. Then he jumped out of bed on the side nearest the night-light: a compact, hazel-eyed little boy, with the beautiful gold-red hair that darkens at the end of childhood, and the redhead's thin skin which stays for life, bleeding too quickly and showing sooner than others the stigmata of pain and of fatigue.

The passage perilous of the landing was relieved by the crack of light from the door at the other end. Laurie padded up to it, and looked in.

His father was packing. This was no new sight to Laurie, who had often helped pack; yet he knew, at once, that it was different. Not only had his father got down the big suitcase that he used only for going abroad, not only was every drawer open and the cupboard as well, but there was something different too about the way his father stood and moved. As Laurie looked, he took a file of papers out of a drawer, flipped it through, took out a few sheets, and tore up everything else the file contained. The pieces he threw down in a corner, on the floor, and simply left them there. Laurie had never in his life seen a grown person do this. He went in.

He was halfway across the room before his father noticed. He had picked up another file, and now turned with it in his hand. His face altered. There was something startled in it, shocked and strained. This frightened Laurie. He knew he was committing an enormity by being out of bed in the middle of the night; but he knew too that the look in his father's eyes was not adjusted to his offense. It was private and personal. It recalled the unknown fears of the day.

"Hello," said his father, staring at him. "What do *you* want?" He spoke quite kindly; but the feeling of difference grew.

Laurie made the emergency known at once. "I can't go to sleep."

"Never mind." His father drew his thick dark brows together; his eyes glancing at his wristwatch looked narrow and blue. He said absently, "It's not eleven yet."

Laurie perceived that his father didn't think he would die. But this fear had dropped away of itself as soon as he entered the room. The fear which returned in its place had, for all its doubtful shape, a dreadful solidity.

"Daddy," he said in a tight, casual voice, "where are you going?"

"Now look," said his father quickly, "this is no time at all to be running all over the house. You'll catch cold. Straight back to bed now and not another word out of you. D'you hear?"

"Yes," said Laurie slowly. The cold was striking through his pink-striped flannel pajamas. He waited for his father to pick him up and carry him back to his own room. But his father stared at him in silence for several seconds, then said in a quick, different voice, "Away with you, now." He began to smile at Laurie, but that was worse, for the smile had something wrong with it. Suddenly his father turned away, and began throwing things into the suitcase from the bed.

At this moment the undertones, the gradual gathering of some days' uncomprehended dread, coalesced for Laurie into a terrible certainty. He didn't attempt to speak. The absolute impotence of childhood crushed him like the weight of the pyramids. His throat swelled; his face, squared like his father's under his mother's hair, grew crimson; the first silent tears burst out, followed by the first, most painful sob. The pressure rose in him, working toward the raging rebellious grief of the man-child who seeks in sound and fury for the strength of a man.

"Mother of God!" said his father. All other considerations swamped momentarily by dread of the approaching noise, he caught Laurie up into his arms, and smothered the convulsed face against his shoulder. The unfamiliar words and the rough gesture increased Laurie's panic. He tried to scream, and, when his father held him more tightly, fought him, rigid, seeking space to thrash about and open his lungs. Dimly sensing this need, his father slackened his grasp, which now felt firm and reassuring. Laurie's screams sank to sobs, to hiccups; he was quiet. Father and son gazed for a moment, with an equal anxious uncertainty, into one another's eyes. Laurie gulped softly, his throat swollen from crying; and his father's hard grip softened into tenderness. He freed one of his hands and began to ruffle Laurie's hair. "Sure," he said softly, "it's a terrible thing then, so it is."

The door opened wide. Laurie, looking over his father's shoulder, saw his mother standing on the threshold.

"Michael!" she said quietly. "Oh, how could you?"

Laurie's father said, "He woke up and came in."

There was a pause. Still held in his father's arms, Laurie looked around and saw his parents confronting one another. With a sense of profound shock, which altered the meaning of everything, he realized that his mother didn't believe his father was telling the truth.

So dreadful a misunderstanding couldn't last for more than a second. But, when he looked at his father's face, he perceived that his father was accepting it. In some larger, unknown way beyond Laurie's scope, the accusation had struck him home. He didn't argue. He just lowered Laurie gently down, and set him on his feet on the floor.

As the firm, warm, supporting strength withdrew, Laurie was seized with a panic sense of insecurity and loss. He rushed blindly forward, sobbing, into his mother's arms. Now all was familiar, immutable, sure. Cozily patted and smoothed, he pushed his wet cheek into her shoulder, and felt the final, absolute reassurance of her soft breast. Dimly he was aware of footsteps, and of a door shutting. When he looked up again his father had gone.

Tucked into bed with the rabbit hot-water bottle, a fresh night-light lit, he cuddled his mother's hand, testing the favor and privilege he had sensed already. Tonight she wouldn't say, "I must go and get dressed now, darling. I'm going out with Daddy." Tonight and always she belonged to him. His mind felt beaten and aching, he would soon be sinking into exhausted sleep; but he knew also, with a triumph too profound to recognize itself, that after all it was he whom she loved the best.

"Go to sleep now," she said, echoing his thought. "Mummie loves you. Mummie will always be here."

He said drowsily, "Mummie. When I'm ten, will I be grown-up?"

"Not quite, darling."

"When I'm grown-up, I'm going to marry you."

"No, darling, but never mind. You'll always be kind to Mummie, won't you, and never do anything to make her cry?"

He pressed his flushed cheek against her hand, feeling its familiar shape, and the warm hardness of her rings. A vast and beautiful emotion filled him. He said, "I won't ever be unkind, Mummie. I promise faithfully"; repeating it to make the beautiful feeling last. She stroked the curls back from his forehead. "That's my darling boy. Now you must go to sleep. Shall I tell you St. George again?"

He said, "Yes, please," to keep her beside him, but he only half listened to the familiar words. He had made, as he lay looking at the night-light's quivering circle on the ceiling, a strange and solemn discovery. It had come to him that no one would ever look from these eyes but he: that among all the lives, numerous beyond imagination, in which he might have lived, he was this one, pinned to this single point of infinity; the rest always to be alien, he to be I.

". . . So when St. George had untied her, he said, 'Why have they left you all alone?' And the princess said, 'They were too much afraid of the dragon to stay with me, they ran away.' Then St. George pulled out his sword, and he said . . ."

She paused, because this was the line on which Laurie liked to come in. But he had fallen asleep. After, when the passage of years had confused his memories of that night and overlaid them with later knowledge, what he remembered best was having known for the first time the burden, prison, and mystery of his own uniqueness.

He never saw his father again.

2

IN the dense sunlight, an inkstain on the table showed up in impasto, an iridescent peacock green. Between it and the window suspended dust shaped the path of the light; Laurie, who had written nothing for five minutes, wondered why of these seemingly weightless particles some should elect to rise and others to fall. It was like Jacob's Ladder. He had moved around the table once already to get the sun out of his eyes. Even its refracted heat was making him drowsy; and the ink, flowing incontinently from his warmed pen, made blots on the page. He shook his nib over the linoleum, yawned, pulled his brows together, and wrote *"Julius Cæsar* shows that Shakespeare understood politics, but saw them chiefly as a field for the study of human . . ."

Unable as always to remember where the *h* came in "psychology," he reached for the dictionary. It offered its usual distractions to a mind already relaxed. "Pedant," he read with approval, "(It. *pedante,* a schoolmaster) *n.,* One who makes a show of learning, or lays undue stress on formulae; one with more book-learning than practical experience or common sense."

A lullaby sound of distant cricket floated with the dust in the heavy air. The study furniture, deal dressed with a dark toffeelike varnish, its wounds explored by the light, looked weary, loveless and revealed. Laurie, to whom it was the emblem of luxury and prestige, balanced his rickety chair on one leg, listening to the creak of its strained joints with a vague affection. He was timelessly, cozily bored. The muted sounds were like those that filter through to a sickroom during a placid convalescent doze, pleasanter than the exercises of recovery for which one pretends to be eager. Summer cradled him, the lap of a kind nurse whose knitting-needles click in the rhythm of sleep.

"Psychology," he wrote, rousing himself. "Cassius, for example, is a familiar type, whose temperament modern science links with gastric ulcers." He paused on this, wondering whether the English master would guess it had been inspired by the science master, or, if he guessed, would care. Rather than be at the trouble of erasing it neatly, he decided to take a chance. He inked a groove on the table, turning it into a miniature canal.

A yelped "Owzat?" came from the cricket-field; the

9

quiet flowed back and closed. The thought of the work he would have to do next year gave flavor to the moment's unpressed ease. His mother had already begun telling him not to worry himself into nerves about the exhibition for Oxford; she had been alarmed by reading a newspaper report of a boy who had hanged himself, it was thought from this cause. Laurie had given suicide, its ends and means, the abstract meditation proper to sixteen; but, as he had assured her, he didn't feel drawn to it. He took the exhibition seriously, knowing that if he failed she would make economies to send him up without it; but mainly he wished to prove that one could do these things without getting in a panic.

He had been too young when his father went to fear economic changes; and in fact there had been none. Mrs. Odell had been a beloved only child, and her parents, though they had thought her marriage in every respect beneath her, did not allow her to suffer for her mistake in any way they could control, either during their lifetimes or afterwards. Laurie knew his mother's side of the story so well that on the thinking surface of his mind it was the only one. His father had been dead for ten years now; pneumonia, helped by acute alcoholism, had taken only three days to finish him off. His family responsibilities had seemed to sit on him lightly; but, detached from them, he had gone downhill with the steady acceleration of a stone loosened on a cliff.

Laurie was used to the idea that his father had been a bad lot. It did not consciously disturb him, since he had been brought up, for almost as long as he could remember, to think of himself as wholly his mother's child.

A clock struck; it was later than he had thought. If he didn't get the thing done, there wouldn't have been much point in staying in to get the study to himself. As it was, Harris or Carter might be back any time now.

The subject of the essay was "Compare the character of Brutus's dilemma with that of Hamlet." In his private mind, Laurie thought poorly enough of both. In Hamlet's place he wouldn't have hesitated for a moment; and Brutus he thought a cold, joyless type, with

10

his moral searchings in the orchard. Not thus, in Laurie's view, should a cause be embraced. If it were worth anything, it would come down on you like a Pentecostal wind, not the better but the only thing; it would sweep you up. "Over thy wounds now do I prophesy ..." That, he felt, should be the stuff; though all that calculated demagogy afterwards was revolting. He gave up the effort to express this. "Portia," he mentioned coldly, "is the ideal Roman wife."

He disposed of Portia quickly, and counted the pages he had filled. One more, written large, should get him by. He got up to stretch, and strolled to the window. The pitch-pine sill on which he leaned was plowed and seamed with boot-marks; this was a ground-floor study. The window had the social as well as the practical functions of a front door. The actual door served as a kind of tradesman's entrance, for junior boys, cleaners, and the Housemaster.

A straggle of boys carrying towels was crossing the grass from the baths. Laurie watched them idly, smelling the dry summer scents of earth, piled mowings, and wallflowers from the Head's garden out of sight. The sense of a wasted afternoon suddenly oppressed him; he craved for the water, but it was too late now, the House's time had run out. Depressed, he was about to turn away when he noticed young Barnes, noticeably isolated as usual. Peters would have been coaching him again, if, thought Laurie, you liked to call it that. It was a pity about Peters. The inter-school cups came in all right, but he shouldn't be let loose on these wretched little twirps, bawling them into a panic and then telling the world they were scared of the water. Barnes, poor little runt, probably thought himself a marked man and it was giving him a bad start in the House. Peters always seemed to crack down extra hard on these pretty-pretty types, who after all soon grew out of it if you let them alone.

By falling behind the others and edging sideways, Barnes had come within a few yards of the window. He looked horrible, Laurie thought; furtive and squinting, as if he had been caught pawning the spoons. It was worse, somehow, than if he had been grizzling.

Laurie had no theories about the dignity of man. He assented cheerfully to a social code which decreed that he should barely acknowledge Barnes's existence, except as a featureless unit in a noxious swarm. Something, however, seemed to him to need doing. He leaned half out of the window. Laurie never considered his own compromises. His methods of defying convention were as a rule so conventional that they passed unnoticed by most people, including himself.

"Hi!" he bawled.

Barnes turned, with a hunted start. When he saw who it was, he registered a modified relief, mingled with awe and a paralyzed hesitation lest someone else might after all have been addressed.

"You!" shouted Laurie. "Whoever you are." Only the prefects, whose job it was, were supposed to know their names. Barnes came up to the window.

"Barnes, J. B., please, Odell."

"I want a chit paid at the shop. Do it straight away, will you?"

"Yes, Odell." Barnes gazed up at the window, like a dog on trust. He had a face like a Spanish madonna with steel spectacles. When frightened he had a heavy sullen look; the contrast between features and expression was more unpleasant than ugliness. At the moment, a strained vacancy made him classic. Laurie felt in his pocket for the coppers and the chit.

"Stand on one leg or the other," he said encouragingly. "You look as if your pants were wet. Of course, don't let me keep you if they are."

At first overwhelmed by this condescension, Barnes presently essayed a kind of grin. Mixed with its servility, traces of gratitude, humor, and even intelligence appeared. He looked almost human, Laurie thought.

"Here you are. And don't lose it."

"No, Odell."

"Hi, stop, you've not got the chit yet, you fool."

"Sorry, Odell."

"Have the baths shut?"

"Yes, please, I think so, Odell."

"Curse. I meant to get over. What was that extraordinary roaring going on?"

"I don't know, Odell. Mr. Peters was coaching."

"Oh, ah. I didn't know he used a megaphone now."

A flickering smile, in dread of presuming, appeared on Barnes's face like an anxious rabbit ready to bolt back down the hole.

"The thing with Peters, once you're on the board, is just to carry on as if he wasn't there. He likes that really, you'll find. It soothes his nerves."

Laurie, a steady but unsensational performer at other games, was the House's white hope at swimming and was expected to get his School colors next year. Barnes said, "Yes, Odell," with an expression of almost inert stupidity. The awe of this heavenly message had stunned him. Laurie observed it with approval; it was no good if encouragement made them fresh.

"Here's the chit. And you can take this bottle back." The bottle was a gratuity. There was a penny refund on it.

"Oh, thanks very much, Odell."

Barnes sprinted off, with a new animation. Laurie, looking after him, felt a warmth at the heart which he hastened to shed. A little drip like that. Perhaps he reminded one of dogs, or something. Dismissing Barnes from his mind, he was about to get back to the essay again, when Carter appeared outside. Luckily Laurie had the last paragraph in his head.

Carter climbed in, leaving two more scratches and some fresh dirt on the sill. He suffered from the disability of being already almost six feet tall, and not having caught up with it. Even his voice hadn't finished breaking. Laurie's had settled quite firmly, but he ran to compactness and was still at the five-foot-seven mark. You could see by his build that five-foot-nine would probably be about his limit. He had to look up to Carter to talk to him; to the onlooker, this had a somewhat incongruous effect.

Carter uncoiled himself from the window. He had to use the arts of a contortionist to get through it; but he would have shunned the eccentricity of using the door. "Now, now," he said, jerking his head toward the receding Barnes. "You want to sublimate, you know. Collect antique doorknobs, or something."

"It's too strong for me," said Laurie movingly. "I can't get him out of my head. Those long eyelashes. Would he look at me, do you think?"

Carter followed this up, but rather half-heartedly. He was not the only one to find Laurie's conversation disconcertingly uninhibited. The innuendo, more generally approved, was apt when it reached him to be smacked into the open with the directness of a fives ball. Lacking in some social instinct, he seemed never to know the difference.

"He's the worst drip we've had in years," Carter pursued. "And anyway, it's hardly quite the moment, when you come to think."

"Think what of?" Laurie put his feet on the table and rocked the back legs of his chair.

"You don't mean you've not heard?" Carter had so far been only at the receiving end of a sensational stop press. He dashed into it headlong. "Jeepers is happy at last. He's really found something. This is the stink to end all stinks for all time. There's going to be hell let loose in this House by tomorrow."

Laurie brought his feet down with a clump, and shoved back his chair. "Look here," he said. "No, this is getting not to be funny. He'll turn this place into a loony-bin, before he's done. He ought to be analyzed. Doesn't he ever think about anything else?"

"Shut up and let——"

"How for heaven's sake did he ever get given a House? Know what Jones II told me? Jeepers went down to the bogs yesterday and threw a school blazer over one of the doors, and sat locked in there all the time the changing was going on, to see if the conversation was pure. It's too bad he's got such big feet."

"Well, that's nothing to——"

"Nothing is it?" said Laurie, whom something had rendered perverse. In this mood he was apt to become Irish. His brogue, however, was of literary origin, consisting of stock phrases carefully acquired. The Celtic period had set in about eighteen months ago; he had even gone through a phase, till stopped, of spelling his name O'Dell, and had opted out of the O.T.C., which was theoretically allowed but almost never done except by boys with rheumatic hearts. At about this time, his mother had been receiving attentions from a retired colonel; but, in the end, nothing had come of it.

"Sure, then," he continued, "it's more than enough for me." Forgetting about it, he dropped back into English. "If Lanyon weren't the best Head the House has had in years, the place would just be a sewer. I can't think how he sticks Jeepers without going nuts."

"Well," said Carter, triumphantly getting it out at last, "he won't have to much longer."

Laurie stared, abruptly sobered up. Presently he said, "Why not?"

"Because he's due for the sack, as soon as the Head comes back from London tomorrow."

"*Lanyon?*" Laurie sat with empty face and dropped jaw; turned; stared at Carter; saw that he meant it. "Whatever for?"

Carter shrugged his shoulders, expressively.

"Look," said Laurie, "if this is a joke, I've laughed now, ha-ha. Is it?"

"Far from it for Lanyon, I should think. They say he's shut up in the isolation ward in the sicker, and they're only letting him out to pack his room."

There was a short silence. Presently Laurie said slowly, "Jeepers ought to be in a strait waistcoat. Is he drunk, or loopy, or what?"

"Personally," said Carter, with some reluctance, "I think Lanyon's cooked. It seems Hazell went to Jeepers about him."

"*Hazell?* Hazell, did you say? Don't make me laugh. Everyone knows Hazell. Hazell, I ask you. They never ought to have sent him to a proper school. He ought to be at one of these crank places where they run about naked and have their complexes gone over every day. Hazell, of all things. Good Lord, Lanyon only keeps an eye on him because he's such a misfit and people were giving him hell. No one would be surprised if Hazell came down one morning saying he was Mussolini, or a poached egg."

"He may be a drip, but he isn't absolutely ravers. You know that go of religion he had last term. When he had that rosary. You know. I should think now he's had a go of this Buchman thing, where they confess everything in public. Anyway that's what he did. Not in public, pity he didn't, he could have been shut up. Then afterwards he got cold feet, and went bleating off to Somers, I don't know why Somers, to confess he'd confessed. So everyone knows now."

"Hazell would confess to anything. It's a thing people have. When there's been a murder, dozens of loonies write up and confess to it. It's well known. I bet he didn't confess to Lanyon, anyway."

"He asked Somers whether he ought to, Green says."

Laurie got up abruptly from the table. He knew the feeling, though he hadn't had it for years: exalted, single-minded rage. Laurie was all for moderation, as people can be who have learned early some of their more painful capacities. It had become an accepted fact that nothing ever ruffled Spuddy. He had enjoyed this reputation, so inwardly reassuring, and made the most of it. This was different. He felt, suddenly, the enormous release of energy which comes when repressed instincts are sanctioned by a cause. Down Hamlet, up Antony. Over thy wounds now do I prophesy.

"Something," said Laurie, "has darn well got to be done about this."

Carter looked uncomfortable. Laurie's tacitly acknowledged position as a leader of public opinion had been founded not on spectacular escapades, which in real life are often a nuisance, but by a quiet positiveness and a knack of settling other people's quarrels without getting involved in them. This irrational incandescence wasn't in the contract. "Well, but——"

"Well, but what? At our age where d'you think we'd be if our people were poor? Doing men's jobs and belonging to unions and sticking together. If we were in a mine or something, and a chap got the sack who didn't deserve to, we'd call a strike till they reinstated him. Well—this is worse."

"Yes, well, but——" Carter looked increasingly uncomfortable; there were times when Spuddy seemed not to see where to stop. "I mean, when miners strike they state their grievances, don't they, and all that?

You could hardly jump up in the Day Room and make a speech about this sort of thing."

"Why on earth not, if Lanyon can be sacked for it? That's how people like Jeepers get away with what they do. It's playing into his hands."

"Do wake up, Spud." Earnestness and embarrassment made Carter's voice leap from the lower register to a cracked alto. "You know perfectly well you're just talking for the sake of it. How could you possibly go making a b.f. of yourself in front of the whole House? If you run around talking about strikes, they'll think you've been reading a boys' comic or something. And if you did manage to start anything, it would only raise the most appalling stink. And this is about the last House that can afford it."

"But we can all afford to sit tight while Lanyon gets kicked out of the back door in a whisper. After all he's done pulling the place together. How many years since the last time this House put up a Head of the School? No one remembers. You make me sick. Will you come in if the others do?"

"What others? They'd think you were nuts. Half of them wouldn't know what you were talking about, even."

"Oh, yeah? I'll bet you ten bob, if you like, there's not a living soul in the place who wouldn't know. All Jeepers' tactful little talks about clean living. You can spot the clean livers afterwards, beetling off to ask whoever's got the dirtiest mind they know what it was all about. It would just about serve Jeepers right."

"But that's not the *point*," said Carter helplessly. "It wouldn't *get* anywhere. And it wouldn't do Lanyon any good. Anything but, I should think."

His will kicked impotently at Laurie's obtuseness. He propped his big-jointed, awkward frame against the mantelshelf with a knobby hand, and rubbed a patch of acne on his chin. He was of an age to find male good looks mentionable only by the way of a joke, and in respect of one's friends not at all. Only pressure of circumstances made him admit even to himself that he thought Laurie strikingly handsome. Carter, who would come into a fine presence in a few years' time, did not

17

perceive that Laurie had merely escaped, or got over early, the more unsightly physical disturbances of adolescence. Between now and, say, eighteen, he would be at the climacteric of his looks, such as they were. The auburn lights in his hair were darkening already, and their copper would dim to bronze. His coloring would lose its vivacity; he would remain clean-looking, no doubt, with hair of a pleasant texture, soft and crisp; on the strength of his mouth and eyes, people would describe his face vaguely as nice. Carter could hardly be expected just now to consider this prospect.

"I mean," he said, doing his best within the limits of decency, "when a row starts in a House they always get to know who's at the bottom of it. If they didn't think you were bats, they might think——"

"Shut *up*," said Laurie, who had not been listening. "I'm working something out. Oh, boy, I've got it!"

"Now look here, Spud." The telepathic message which Carter was straining to convey was, "Lanyon likes you, and other people have noticed it if you haven't." But Spud must know this, he wasn't a fool; since he would talk, it seemed, about anything, why couldn't he think? "Now just calm down and——"

"Shut up and listen. This is what we do. A protest meeting's not enough, you're right there, what we want is more of a sort of psychological war. Now the whole thing about Jeepers is that he's terrified of scandal. It's himself he has cold feet about, really, and his job. So that's where we hit him. We'll just all go along to him in a body and say the whole House is immoral, one and all, and we've come to confess like Hazell did. Then he won't sack anyone, he'll fall over himself to hush it up. Even if it got to the Head, *he'd* have to hush it up. He might sack Jeepers, and good riddance too. It's foolproof. It——"

"Oh, *really*, Spud. For heaven's sake." Overwhelmed, Carter struck for the first time the *basso profundo* of his adult voice. A moment's partial enlightenment touched him, eluding his terms of speech. He recognized a paradox: the surface acceptance of unimagined evil, the deep impenetrability of a profound innocence.

18

"The trouble with you is, you don't know what you're talking about."

"Oh yes I do; it's absolutely sound psychology. They couldn't sack Lanyon without sacking the rest of us, and they can't sack a whole House without ruining the School. And as for Jeepers, it serves him right. The way he puts ideas into people's heads, nothing that went on here would astonish *me*."

Wouldn't it? thought Carter to himself. Perhaps other people too were a little bit careful what they told Spuddy. "Seriously, how could you possibly expect people to stand up and say——"

"What *of* it? Everyone's immoral. It's immoral you doing my maths, or me doing your French prose. We can't help Jeepers' one-track mind."

Emergency had inspired Carter to psychological tactics of his own. "You know what he'll think it means, so it's a lie; you can't get out of that."

"Yes," said Laurie at once. "But then it's a lie about Lanyon too, so it cancels out. You know, in Euclid: then A equals B, which is absurd, Q.E.D."

To Carter this offered for the first time some promise of reason. "Well, that might be all right if'—touched by a sudden loss of confidence, he swallowed quickly—"if we were certain it *is* a lie about Lanyon. I mean, we don't *know*."

Laurie, who was sitting on the table, didn't get up. He looked at Carter with no conscious effort at annihilation. He simply felt what his face expressed, that the world was a meaner place than he had supposed, but that one got nowhere by making a fuss about it. Carter withered; he felt rubbishy, a mess of poorly articulated bones in an unsavory envelope. He said, "Of course, I don't mean to say——"

"It's all right," said Laurie, with unconsciously devastating quiet. "I'm sorry I said anything. My mistake. I should forget all about it if I were you. I'll manage on my own."

He went out, through the window. It might have been more effective to use the door; but he didn't want to be effective, merely to be rid of Carter; and the very transparency of this fact completed his effect.

Laurie took a turn around Big Field, and, finding it was almost teatime, bought a bottle of lemonade at the tuck shop and half a dozen buns in a bag before setting out again. These he took to a retreat of his behind a haystack, slightly out of bounds, where he spent the next hour or so planning his campaign. By the time he turned homeward, shadows were lengthening on the grass. He wished he could do it all now, before he started to cool off. When one started to think of difficulties, they cropped up. But there was prep to finish, and Harris, who would be in the study by now, to be rallied to the cause. A pity Carter would have had time to get at him first.

As he walked the last lap to the House, Laurie realized sinkingly that the last of his effervescence had subsided, and that from now on only stone-cold will-power would push him through. He wished, for the first time in nearly four years, that during the next hour the School could be burnt down.

From the study window he heard Harris saying, "Get your eyes seen to. Odell's there."

"Oh, I'm sorry, Harris." The small boy at the door took a nervous step into the room. "Please, Odell, Lanyon says will you see him in his study, please?"

"What, now?" drawled Laurie with the calm convention expected. For a moment this summons—which usually meant trouble of a disciplinary kind—only struck him as embarrassingly ill-timed. It wasn't till the fag had gone that he saw Harris looking at him, and Carter at the floor. There was a dragging silence where the usual pleasantries should have been.

Laurie remarked casually, "What the heck does *he* want, I wonder?" and, as no one answered, went out into the corridor. For this purpose it was in order to use the door.

At the foot of the stairs, surrounded by dark green paint of the resistant kind used in station waiting rooms, he stood still. This, he knew with a certainty exceeding all the other certainties of the day, was the most awful thing that had ever happened to him in his life. Carter must have told someone, and somehow . . . The palms of his hands felt sticky and cold. He had

20

been prepared to face Jeepers, even the Headmaster. He had been ready for anything, except this.

From the moment of conceiving Lanyon as a cause, there hadn't been much time to contemplate him as a human being; perhaps because the thought of him in any kind of equivocal or humiliating situation was so improbable, and indeed hardly bore thinking of. That Lanyon might be grateful for the campaign on his behalf was the last thing Laurie had contemplated. Lanyon would never so compromise his dignity; it would be a sufficient gesture if he ignored the episode. Head prefects didn't thank people for starting riots in Houses; on the contrary. And no Head of any House had ever stood for less nonsense than he. It was an academic question whether anyone would get fresh with Lanyon twice, for no one, as far as Laurie knew, had tried it once.

As he began, draggingly, to mount the stairs, Laurie's dominant wish was that he were not too senior to be beaten, which would have been quick, simple and relatively unembarrassing.

He had got to the door. His footsteps must have been heard by now; there could be no more procrastination. He knocked.

"Come in," said Lanyon briskly. At this point Laurie ceased to feel any awkwardness. Fright had swallowed everything. Concerned only not to show it, he walked in.

Lanyon was sitting in his armchair, doing something with a pen-knife to a propelling pencil. He looked up. He was slight and lean, with dusty-fair hair and eyes of a striking light blue which were narrowed by the structure of the orbit above, giving him a searching look even when he smiled. He wasn't smiling.

"Oh, yes," he said. "Odell. Shut the door."

Laurie shut it, feeling sick in the pit of his stomach, and waited. The length of the wait was always proportioned to the offense; but he was past measuring time. Lanyon made some further adjustment of the pencil, screwed down the lead, shut the knife and put it in his pocket. As always he was extremely neat, his hair brushed and recently trimmed, his shirt looking as if he

21

had just put it on. He had spent last year's summer holidays working his passage to Iceland and back in a trawler, and had recently been accepted for a projected research expedition to the Arctic. The biggest toughs in the School, when they stood against Lanyon, looked muscle-bound or run to seed. Lines of decision showed around his eyes and mouth; at nineteen, he was marked already with the bleak courage of the self-disciplined neurotic. Laurie, who was in no state to be analytical, only thought that Lanyon looked more than usually like chilled steel. Suddenly it seemed certain that the prevailing rumor had got garbled in transit, and almost certainly didn't even refer to Lanyon at all. Laurie waited as if at the stake, clenching his lower jaw.

Having disposed of the penknife, Lanyon looked up again. His light eyes raked Laurie, coldly, from head to foot.

"They tell me," he said, "that you appear to be going out of your mind. Is there anything you want to say about it?"

"No, Lanyon," said Laurie mechanically. He could have feigned noncomprehension, but with Lanyon one didn't try anything on.

"Had it occurred to you," said Lanyon evenly, "that if anything needs organizing in this House, the prefects are capable of seeing to it without any help from you?"

"Yes, Lanyon." Laurie looked, for relief, away to the work table in the window. It was very tidy, like Lanyon himself.

"Of course, the prefects are only used to routine work. If they ever decide to get up a revival meeting, or some other form of mass hysteria, no doubt they'll ask for your expert advice before they begin."

Laurie said nothing. His gaze fell from the work table to the wastepaper basket standing under it.

"Do you often," Lanyon asked, "have attacks like this?"

"No," said Laurie. The wastepaper basket was full. It would have been overflowing if the contents had not been rammed down. The mass of torn papers stirred in his mind some dimly remembered sense of dread.

"Well, another time"—he could feel a hard blue

22

stare tugging his own eyes back—"if you find your exhibitionism getting too much for you, I suggest you join the Holy Rollers, and give yourself some scope. You don't want to waste your gifts, merely landing one school in a mess it wouldn't live down in ten years."

"I'm sorry, Lanyon." But Laurie was hardly aware of speaking. He had seen, among the papers, the torn boards of the cloth-bound notebooks only issued to the Senior School, in which permanent material, the indispensable stuff of exam revision, was kept. There were three or four of them, probably more.

"Don't stand there like a dummy." The compressed snap in Lanyon's voice was more alarming than a shout. "Do you realize you've been behaving like a dangerous lunatic, yes or no?"

"Yes," said Laurie. To his own amazement he added, "I suppose so."

Lanyon rested his hand with the pencil on the arm of the chair and leaned forward slightly. His eyes looked like chips of blue enamel. "You suppose so?" he said softly. "You *suppose* so?"

"Sorry," said Laurie quickly.

"So I should hope." Lanyon leaned back again, looking as if he had just brushed off some dirt and supposed it had been worth the trouble. In the slanting light from the window, the lines around his mouth were deepened to hollows. "Very well, then. When I have your word there'll be no more of this nonsense, you can go." There was a pause. Laurie swallowed; it seemed to him that it must be audible across the room. "Well? Have you got softening of the brain, Odell? You heard what I said."

Pushing his voice up through his throat, which felt as if it were lined with sandpaper, Laurie said, "I'm sorry, Lanyon. I'll give my word if—if it isn't true about you leaving."

"*What* did you say, Odell?" Lanyon stared at him, level-eyed. This time, though he felt as if the back of his neck would crack, Laurie met it without looking away. "Have you gone completely crazy? Who the hell do you think you are, standing here when a prefect sends for you and asking me questions about what I'm going to do? You need to see a doctor, I should think."

"I'm sorry, Lanyon." Laurie felt he must sound like a cracked gramophone record. "I know it's cheek. I'm sorry. Only I can't promise if I don't know."

Lanyon put the pencil away and stood up. He had the whippy, dangerous spring of a bent rapier let go.

"For your information, I shall probably be leaving sometime tomorrow. Is that enough for you? And if I don't have your word within one minute, I'm going to lay you out cold, here and now, and you'll spend the time between now and then in the sicker, and that will settle that. Well?"

He could do it, Laurie thought, with one hand tied behind him. It would probably be too quick to hurt very much. The odd thing was that whereas he had entered the study almost paralyzed with fright, now he was hardly frightened at all. His admiration for Lanyon had soared to the point of worship. This is the happy warrior, this is he whom every man in arms would wish to be.

"Have you taken that in?" Lanyon asked. "Because I mean it."

"That's all right." Laurie's voice was suddenly clear and free. "You've got to, I see that. But you can't actually kill me, so it won't stop me for long."

Lanyon took a step up to him, as if he were measuring his distance. Laurie very nearly threw up his fists by instinct. No, he thought, Lanyon couldn't be found fighting in his room after all this, besides he very likely wouldn't hit so hard in cold blood. He was just about right now for a straight one to the point of the jaw. Laurie hoped there was room enough behind for him to fall without hitting the door or something. One couldn't turn to look. There was time for all this because it took so long for anything to happen. Lanyon must be hoping he'd crack up yet and save having to do it. He felt, standing like this, eyes front, that he had never really seen Lanyon before. His face was a clear light even brown, toning with his dusty-fair hair. There was a little triangular scar, old and colorless, on his forehead above the left eyebrow. His mouth was tight

24

and straight, a horizontal line between two verticals. His eyes fixed Laurie, stilly.

He stepped back.

With a spent force in which sounded the flaw of a desperate weariness, he said, "You *bloody* fool."

Laurie had reached a pitch of tension where no inhibitions touched him. The frame of convention, with its threats and its supports alike, was broken. He was left, a single-handed individual, to take things as they came. "I can't help it," he said. "If you're leaving, somebody's got to cope. I know I'm not a prefect, and if Treviss and the others were doing anything, that would be all right. Only they won't, I know what this House is when it comes to something like that, they've been got down like everyone else." Lanyon was looking at him, quiet, almost relaxed, incalculable, but now for some reason unterrifying. Laurie went on with a rush, "It makes me sick, the way people will let anything by, even something like this, sooner than come into the open about—anything you're supposed not to."

"I see," said Lanyon. "And tell me, what makes you so cheerful about coming out into the open yourself?"

"I don't know. Well, somebody's got to. It stands to reason Jeepers can't be let get away with this."

"Mr. Jepson to you," said Lanyon mechanically.

"Mr. Jepson. Sorry. It isn't only even that it's not fair to you. It's not fair to the House either. Till this year, it's been going down ever since Mr. Stuart left. Jeep—Mr. Jepson can't even see how you've pulled the place together. You *are* the House really, everybody knows that. He doesn't seem ever to notice the things that really matter, the feeling in the place, and giving the new people a start. You know the sort of thing that was thought to be smart here before you took over. Peterson and that lot. Jeepers hasn't a clue. He's all taken up with the moral tone. There wasn't any moral tone when Mr. Stuart was here. The place was just normal."

"Quite the budding analyst." Laurie knew suddenly that he had been talking too much, too loudly, and too long, to someone who was very tired. "So you think that Mr. Jepson has an anxiety neurosis, due to being oversensitive to a certain weakness in the system he represents."

"Yes," said Laurie recklessly.

"In view of which, you're proposing to take on the whole foundation of society single-handed. My strength is as the strength of ten . . ." He gave a tight little smile, which went out quickly. With a change of tone he said, "You're an orphan, I take it?"

"No," said Laurie. "It's only my father who's dead."

"Your surviving family," said Lanyon carefully, "will be putting down the red carpet, I suppose, when you go home expelled in a couple of day's time?"

Laurie said nothing. He had a sudden, horribly clear vision of his mother's face.

Watching him, Lanyon said, "Yes, it's about time you woke up."

"I could explain," said Laurie dully. He tried, desperately, not to imagine it.

"Oh, don't be a fool. Admit it's washed up, and let's finish with this nonsense. You're wasting my time, I've got a lot to do."

Suddenly Laurie's exhilaration returned. It was worth it; anything was worth it. Tomorrow could take care of itself.

"No," he said. "You're Head of the House, and you've got to stop a row if you can. But the House isn't bound to stand by and see them do this to you and do nothing about it. We'd look like a lot of worms if we did. It doesn't matter what happens. It just isn't fair."

"Isn't it?"

Laurie noticed that he had got the pencil out again, and was screwing the lead up and down. He seemed absorbed in this. It made Laurie feel as if he were confronting a vacuum. He wondered if he were meant to go. But one always waited for explicit permission. "Of course it's not fair," he said. "It's crazy."

"And being such a good psychologist"—Lanyon pushed down the lead more firmly—"you feel sure that a poor helpless type like myself will naturally let himself be expelled for something he hasn't done, unless people like you dash up with a rescue party?"

A bright ray of hope shot up in Laurie's mind. How

26

absurd not to have thought that Lanyon could look after himself; and why should he confide his plans to his inferiors? So long as it was going to be all right ... but he wished Lanyon would look up. "I only thought," he said to fill in the pause, "it was a thing the House ought to get together on."

"So I gathered." Lanyon raised his eyes. The hard, blue shine had gone. They looked tired, almost gray. "Let me see; is it Cambridge, or Oxford, you're going to sit for?"

"Oxford," said Laurie, now quite at sea.

Lanyon leaned an arm on the empty mantelshelf: the room, Laurie realized now, was stripped almost to the bareness of vacant possession. "Yes," he said unemotionally. "Oxford, of course. You ought to fit in well there. It's the home of lost causes, so they say."

There was silence. In the last ten minutes, Laurie had almost exhausted his capacity for taking in new experience. He knew what he was being told, and it seemed now that he must have known for at least some seconds beforehand. But he had reached a full stop. He couldn't make it mean anything.

"Too bad, Spuddy." Lanyon smiled, it seemed from a long way off. "You'll have to hang the shillelagh up again."

At this point, in one of those moments which seem crucial only because they complete long, hidden processes, a man disappeared: a right-thinking, crisply defined, forcible person, rather dogmatic and intolerant in a decent, humorous way; the nearest in succession of Laurie's potential selves. A usurper moved in, all unaware of himself, concerned only with his sudden perception of the fact that Lanyon's steady gaze was being held up with tightened muscles, like a weight. At the higher-barbarian phase of adolescence, it comes as unwanted, dismaying news that the gods feel pain. But it seemed to Laurie that something had to be done, and no one else was here to do it. All the rest would have to be thought about later.

"All right," he said. "I'll promise not to do anything, if you like. But it's not because I feel any different, or ... I mean I'd as soon do it now as ever. Sooner."

Some change in the quality of the pause made him lose the thread of what he was saying. He finished. "I don't think things ought to be let happen like this."

"You don't think at all." Lanyon paused a moment, blankly. Then his eyes seemed to relax. Slowly a perverse and charming smile, unfamiliar to Laurie, lifted the ends of his mouth. "Your spontaneous reactions are going to land you in a lot of trouble, if you don't look out."

"Are they?" said Laurie vaguely. Instinct caused him to keep some sort of conversation going; if someone had asked him a second later what he had said, he couldn't have answered. So this, he was thinking, is what it's all about, all Jeepers' snufflings and fidgetings, all that bated breath. In a mingled exaltation, pride, and sheer consuming interest, he smiled back into Lanyon's eyes. Scarcely aware of continuing the unheard, instead of the heard, conversation, he said, "Jeepers is just a dirty old man. People like that don't know."

"Do you?" asked Lanyon, watching his face.

"Anyway," said Laurie, "I do now."

Lanyon seemed about to step forward; and Laurie waited. He didn't think what he was waiting for. He was lifted into a kind of exalted dream, part loyalty, part hero-worship, all romance. Half-remembered images moved in it, the tents of Troy, the columns of Athens, David waiting in an olive grove for the sound of Jonathan's bow.

Still watching him, Lanyon made a little outward movement. He paused, and drew back.

"To give them their due," he said, his voice suddenly light and crisp, "dirty old men know one or two quite material facts. Incidentally, they're quite material facts themselves."

Laurie listened with his eyes. This time there was no need to answer.

"You'll be taking this study over yourself," said Lanyon in a businesslike way, "in course of time."

"Who? Me?" said Laurie, startled.

"Obviously. Who else is there? I expect Jeepers will give you a frank little talk the first evening of term. Watch him carefully while he does it, and you'll learn a

28

lot. It's not very edifying and rather a bore. However. Oh, just a minute."

He turned and went over to the wooden book-box that stood in the window. Instinctively Laurie followed him, and looked over his shoulder. Lanyon straightened abruptly; his light, fine hair flicked across Laurie's cheek.

"Get out of the light: d'you mind?"

"Sorry."

"I'm just looking for something. Oh, yes, here it is." He stood up with a thin leather book. The spine said *The Phaedrus of Plato*. Laurie hadn't got much beyond selections from Homer. He thought Lanyon, in this practical mood, was bequeathing him a crib.

"Read it when you've got a minute," said Lanyon casually, "as an antidote to Jeepers. It doesn't exist anywhere in real life, so don't let it give you illusions. It's just a nice idea."

Laurie was strongly aware that as he took it their hands had touched. He said, "I'll always keep it. Thank you."

"It's a pity you and I couldn't have talked a bit sooner."

Laurie looked up from the book. "I wish we had."

"Well," said Lanyon briskly, "it's too late now."

Laurie continued to look up at him. With a feeling of great strangeness and astonishment he knew that they were no longer the head prefect and a fifth-former, but just two people in a room.

"Is it?" he said.

Lanyon sat down on the edge of the table, looked at Laurie, and shook his head. "Spud," he said quite gently, "you mustn't be difficult."

Laurie didn't answer. He felt like someone who tries to read a book when the pages are being turned a little too quickly.

"I've been watching you," Lanyon said, "for a long time. You're on the way to being something, and I don't know what, not for certain. So I'm not going to interfere with it."

"I don't know," said Laurie slowly. "I feel as if you had already."

Lanyon smiled at him and he had to look down.

"That's only because you don't know what it's all about. Look, if you want to know, one reason why not is because it would mean too much. To me, too, if that's any satisfaction to you. Anyway, no. Too much responsibility."

"I can take my own responsibility. I'm not a child."

"That's what *you* think. Stop making such a bloody nuisance of yourself."

"I'm sorry."

"It's all right. You'll see the point of all this later."

Laurie turned and looked out of the window. He couldn't think what had come over him. Lanyon had taken it pretty well.

From over by the fireplace, Lanyon said, "No good getting ideas, Spud. It doesn't get you anywhere. It's all just a myth, really."

Presently Laurie said, "What are you going to do? After you leave, I mean?"

"Merchant seaman." He spoke with the effortless-seeming decision he might have used on a matter of House routine. "I'm going straight down to Southampton tomorrow."

"Are you all right for money?" It was strange to feel so natural about asking Lanyon a thing like this. "I've got about a pound I could lend you."

"No, thanks. I can get a ship quite quickly. I know a man who'll fix me up."

"Oh," said Laurie flatly. "That's all right, then."

"We ran into each other. He's not so bad. I don't know him very well."

Suddenly they had come to the end of all that there was to say.

"Well, I'd better finish packing," Lanyon said. He looked at Laurie, telling him to go. Laurie stared at him, mutely; but there wasn't anything one could say. Lanyon said, briskly, "Take these lists on your way down, will you, and pin them on the board. The usual order. You know how they go."

"Yes."

"That's all, goodbye. What is it, then? Come here a

moment. . . . Now you see what I mean, Spud. It would never have done, would it? Well, goodbye."

"But when can we——"

"Goodbye."

After a moment Laurie said, "Goodbye, Lanyon. Good luck."

"I don't believe in luck," said Lanyon as they parted.

3

THE two lines of beds converged in a neat perspective on the desk at the end. The crude design on the cotton counterpanes was shrill and unfaded, hard reds and blues on a buff ground. The deal lockers, the low beds, even the prefabricated walls were new. New things were everywhere; it was only the men in the beds who looked shabby and worn. None of them were old, and many were no older than Laurie, who was twenty-three; but they had had a good deal of hard use.

It was ten minutes to eleven of the Sister's morning off, which began at ten-thirty. As usual she was still there, giving last reminders to the Charge Nurse, who as usual resented it.

"Don't forget that Major Ferguson is doing the sequestrectomy *after* the arthrodesis."

"No, Sister."

"And do see that there's no muddle about the injections, this time."

"Yes, Sister."

Laurie, overhearing this, unstrapped his watch; later he might get drowsy and forget. He pushed it across the locker to Reg Barker, who said, "Uh-huh," and put it on. They always looked after each other's on operation days.

The Sister said, "Oh, and Nurse. I want Wilson moved out of the side ward for today, and Corporal Odell put in there when he comes back from the theater. He was very noisy coming round last time." Two of the men exchanged grins and her back stiffened.

"There," said Reg Barker to Laurie when she had gone. "Put in solitary. That'll learn you, Spud."

"Suits me," said Laurie, who had had this joke in every way. "I'll get a bit of sleep."

"Sleep! *We* know. Mind, now, I'll be listening. Minute I hear a woman scream I'll be there. You watch out, Spud, she might be more oncoming when she gets you alone."

"Comment? Pardon?" Laurie stifled a sigh. Charlot hated to miss anything. None of the nurses spoke French, so they had put Laurie next to him to interpret. His father and three brothers had been killed by machine-gun fire in the boat after their fishing smack had been bombed. Charlot, the sole survivor, had been picked up unconscious, drifting with the corpses. He had been shot in the spine, and after three months and two operations was still in plaster from chest to hips. His legs were paralyzed; Major Ferguson thought that it was functional. So now Laurie explained to him what they had all been laughing at, as brightly as he could. It gave Charlot the chance to try out some of his English vocabulary; Laurie wasn't the only one to give him lessons.

"Now, boys," said the Charge Nurse, "I don't need to ask if that was a dirty one; I can tell by the sound. Odell, have you used the bottle yet?"

"I can go through, Nurse; I'll look after the leg."

"Don't you dare. If you think we've got time to prep you again at the last minute. Ask for one when you have your injection."

"I was wondering about my X-rays, they don't seem to be here."

"Oh, yes they are, they're on the desk. I know what you are, reading your notes and getting half-baked ideas. Shakespeare says a little knowledge is a dangerous thing."

"Sorry, Nurse."

"That put you in *your* place," said Reg. "Time you was kipping down, ain't it? They going to fix the knee so you can bend it, this time?"

"I can now, a bit."

"Ah," said Reg with foggy tact. He changed the subject. "You was supposed to be done first. They ought to be more careful, drawing it out how they do."

"Oh, well. When we were lying out on the beach we wouldn't have minded swapping for this."

Reg replied in the conventional way, which was to mill over a number of old grievances. No one discussed what he had really felt; they took it out on other things. They were an extremely touchy society, but most of them were aware of it.

What with one thing and another, Laurie felt as touchy as anyone that morning; but he was anxious not to let it loose on Reg, to whom he was bound in a kind of blood-brotherhood. The stretcher party had dumped them side by side on the Dunkirk beach, and they had had time to get used to one another. Laurie had had two shots of morphia inside an hour, which removed apprehension to some extent but seemed hardly to touch the pain; so it had sometimes been a relief to know that Reg was then totally blind. The bomb which had splintered his arm had mildly concussed him, and his eyelids had swelled and stuck together. He was sure he had lost his eyes, and, the concussion having destroyed his inhibitions, begged loudly to have a bullet put through his head. It was months since either of them had referred to this even obliquely; but now Reg said, "I wonder I didn't do you when you shoved me eyes open. If I could have found me rifle I'd have done for you sure. Set me mind at rest, though, that's a fact."

"I'm starting to forget half of it now. All for the best."

"Never been able to think how you moved that far."

"Dope. Doped to the eyes."

"Well, here's another coming for you now. Be turning you into a flipping drug fiend, this rate."

Laurie rolled up his sleeve. The ice-cold evaporation of the spirit, the wasplike sting of the needle, once more set his teeth on edge. When the nurse had "settled" him, he ran his eye over the paraphernalia on the locker-top: enamel vomit bowl and cloth, tongue

33

forceps and spatula. The absence of the notes and X-rays fidgeted him. There was a new nurse on and they might get forgotten. Well, she would probably not resent being reminded as the Charge Nurse would. She hadn't minded his shaving the leg himself while she was called away from the screens. One glance at her face had assured him that she wouldn't shave it far enough up, in which case Major Ferguson, who gave no marks for modesty, would make her sorry she had ever been born a country vicar's daughter or whatever it was. It was a job for an orderly, but the whole place was in a chronic muddle.

He ought to shut his eyes now and give his sedative a chance. He wished he could cure himself of fighting drugs and anesthetics, since this only seemed to make it worse. The Night Nurse, a comfortable person, had said that nurses were far too busy on operation days to listen to all the rubbish they heard, which meant nothing anyway and all sounded alike. Laurie, who had no great sense of his own importance, was very ready to believe this; but it never quite reassured him.

Seeing him move restlessly, Reg said, "Doing you this late, you could have had breakfast."

"Hell, don't remind me. They can't help it here, it's all fixed in the theater."

"Post's late today. Heard from Madge yesterday, though."

"She and the boy okay?"

"Had a bomb in the next street. That's the nearest yet. She'll have to go to her auntie in St. Albans. I keep telling her. Don't know what makes her so obstinate."

Laurie, who had met Madge Barker several times, thought he could guess. Lest his face should hint at this, he got down into the bedclothes.

"That's right. Get yourself some shut-eye. And when they do you, you watch yourself and don't get fresh with no officers, 'cause you'll have to meet them again, see, you won't be lucky like you was on that ship."

Laurie smothered the conversation with a sleepy-sounding grunt; this reminder came at the worst possible time for his self-confidence. He could remember very little about the crossing from Dunkirk; he had lost

34

a good deal of blood by then, since they couldn't keep a tourniquet on all the time, and had had some more shots of morphia. Barker, who was seeing by then as his swollen lids contracted, had told him a little. Laurie only knew that the ship was small and crowded, and that sometimes his life had seemed to be going out on a cold wave of nausea. Once, returning to himself for a few minutes, he had looked up to find a bearded face peering into his. It hung there persistently saying something and asking questions he felt too ill to deal with. Dimly he reflected that he was filthy and unshaved, and that his leg felt like some extraneous decaying mess. This attention was very flattering and suddenly, weakly funny. His inhibitions must have been at their lowest; for he remembered giving a wry kind of smile and saying, "Sorry, dearie. Some other time." The face had disappeared rather quickly; he couldn't remember seeing it again. Luckily, Reg Barker had his own version of this story. "Old Spud was a one coming over. The captain took a look at him to see he was still alive, like; and old Spud was that far gone, he took him for some tart and give him the brushoff. Chap with a mucking great beard and all. Laugh!"

A fuzzy dullness was creeping over his brain. He recognized the effects of morphia and atropine, being too old a hand not to have found out by now what the syringe contained. Resolving not to doze off, he lay staring at the ceiling. He was in a punt on the Cher at Oxford, lying on cushions and looking up at the leaves. Between the willow banks he saw Charles swimming toward him. "Come along," said Charles, "the water's absolute heaven. You know you can swim really." "Perhaps I can," Laurie told him, "but I don't want to. It's not allowed, I'm having an operation."

The theater trolley came squeaking up to the bed; the orderlies said, "What, you again? Watch after the towels, Sid," and lifted him onto the cold, taut canvas. He was aware of it all but it couldn't have mattered less. They went out through an unwalled covered way, roofed with iron, to the theater. Here was the anesthetic room with the awkward ledge in the doorway. The previous operation was still going on; one of the orderlies went, the other whistled between his teeth and looked out of the window. Captain Hodgkin, the anesthetist, came out masked and gowned, holding a big syringe. Laurie thrust out his arm.

"Well, Odell, back again. How's it been?"

"Coming along, sir, thanks."

"Good. Clench your fist."

The vein inside the elbow corded and stood out. The needle went into it. "Count."

"One. Two. Three. Four." Nothing was happening. "Five. Six." Nothing. "Seven ... Nine. ..."

The trolley beneath him ceased to be palpable. He floated, soared. The doors of a forgotten home opened to receive him.

He was being lifted and put down. They were putting him on the table. They hadn't given him enough, he wasn't under; they would start to operate if he didn't tell them now. He struggled with a sore throat and furred mouth. His knee felt sore; good God, they must have begun.

"Hi." It came out like an animal grunt.

"All right," said a girl's voice. "Keep quiet. It's all over."

He opened his eyes; he was back in bed. "Sorry," he said. "Silly. Always do this. Awfully sorry. So damned silly."

"Sh-sh. Go to sleep again."

"Sorry to be so silly. Do excuse me."

"It's all right, but you ought to be resting."

"Don't worry about me. I know you, you're the new one. So sorry to be a bother. What's your name?"

"Nurse Adrian. Don't talk now."

"Good night."

He shut his eyes, but opened them again.

"Nurse."

"Yes?"

"You're staying with me, aren't you? You won't go?"

"Not if you're quiet and don't get excited."

"No, really, Nurse. I'm not excited at all. I just think it's so very good of you. I don't deserve it, you know. If you knew all about me, you wouldn't be good to me like you are."

"Hush, you've had an operation, you *must* keep quiet."

"I'm always having operations. I'm quite used to it. Don't go back over there. I want to hold your hand."

"Sister says you've got to keep still."

"She doesn't understand. You see, you see it's important. You don't think I'm like that, do you?"

"Of course not, it's just the anesthetic."

"Going through a phase is different, I mean people do. It isn't anything. You never met Charles, did you?"

"Please try and settle down."

"It was the people he knew, awful people you'd never have believed, it was that, really. Can I have some water?"

"You've just had some. Only a sip."

"Thank you. There was a man at school, that would have been quite different, you may not understand that, but it would. But he had too high ideals, I can't tell you now, it was all wrong the way they treated him, of course I never saw him again. So please don't think I've ever done anything that would make you not want to sit here with me. You don't, do you?"

"Of course you haven't. It's only the ether upsetting you. Is your leg hurting much?"

"It always hurts a bit. Just don't think about it. I should like to kiss you and I think that speaks for itself, don't you?"

"You're talking rather nonsense and it's only making you tired."

"I suppose you wouldn't kiss me, just quickly?"

"Sister wouldn't let me sit here if I did, I should have to go."

"People don't understand, do they? I'm sorry, Nurse."

"It isn't your fault, it's only the ether. I think I'll ask if you can have a sedative now."

A light crossed his eyes. The blackout was up; it was the Night Nurse leaning over him with her torch.

"Hello, Odell. Feeling better now?"

"Oh, hello, Nurse. Yes, thanks. What time is it?"

"Nearly one."

"Good Lord, is it? I say, I do hope I've not been making a row."

"Not since I've been on. We'll put you back in the ward in the morning."

When she had gone he shifted his leg cautiously on the pillow, moving it from the hip. It felt tender and aching, and the joint seemed stiffer than ever, but then the bandage was tight. Major Ferguson would be doing a round tomorrow; one could ask him, perhaps.

All being well, this was his final operation. In a few weeks' time, someone would write in the ward report book, "Returned to unit for discharge: Odell. Admitted: So-and-So." They would remember him, perhaps, as long as people remember one of the bit parts in an old film. Exit a quiet, tidy patient (except on operation days). Enter, somewhere else, a young man with a lame leg and an unanswered question. Statistics gave this new character something like fifty years' expectation of life. Laurie reminded himself that it was two in the morning; he drank his malted milk, wriggled down in the pillow and shut his eyes.

The river flowed gently under the hanging willows; the sun shone slanting through it, lighting up dark streaming weeds along the bottom, warm umber mud, and golden stones. The fish slipped by, sly fine shadows among the other shadows of water and weed. The afternoon sun felt warm along his side. He raised his arms and dived, straight and clear; came up, shook his eyes free, and with long, easy strokes swam into the sunny waters upstream.

Eight days after his operation they had still not told him anything. The morning of Major Ferguson's round had come again. It was the most detested event of the week; for the staff, because he expected the punctilio of a large teaching hospital to which the resources of the place were unequal; and for the patients because for an hour or more they would be virtually on parade, unable to move from their beds, smoke, or talk.

Laurie's knee had been cleaned and dressed, and a cheap gauze bandage put on which could be cut to save ninety seconds of Major Ferguson's time. There had been opportunity for a good look. The upper half of the scar had been reopened; it was thick, purplish, deeply indented, and smelt of pus. Two red rubber drainage tubes stuck out of it. Below that it was almost healed; but that was where the kneecap had been shot away and the ragged skin cobbled over. From there a long, deep, jagged scar went plowing down nearly to the ankle. He had got over feeling sick when he looked at it. Sometimes it had been a struggle to hide this ungrateful reaction. He had been told often enough it was a miracle he should have the leg at all.

There seemed, he thought, to be a worse flap than usual today. Every nurse was doing the work of one junior to herself; and now for the first time he noticed that the junior of them all was sweeping the floor, a job normally finished hours before by the wardmaid. It was the young Nurse Adrian: he had been a little shy of her since the operation, which he felt to be selfish since she was probably much shyer. It was high time to be making an effort.

"New job for you, Nurse?" he ventured when she got to his bed.

She gave him her open, schoolroom smile. (A bumpy tennis court, he thought; red-hot-pokers in the border, and a few cobby old trees with a hammock they call the orchard; a pensioned-off gun-dog who sits in with Daddy, and a wire-haired terrier you couldn't show, but a good listener.) "I do wish these beds had wheels, I can't get behind them properly."

"Where's the maid, off sick?"

"No, they've left."

"What, not all of them?"

"Yes—oh, I'm *so* sorry, I hope that didn't jog your leg. They thought it was too isolated."

"Oh, they *did?*" said Reg Barker. A walking patient, he saw a number of small fatigues coming his way. "That's too bad, that makes my heart bleed, that does. I been in some isolated places too, and so's Spud here. See, Spud, that's how mugs like you and me waste our lives. That's what we ought to have done, packed it in and gone to the pictures. We wouldn't be no trouble to anyone then."

39

Neames, who had been in a bank in civil life and was dignified, said, "From what I hear, Nurse, there's been a good deal of mismanagement over staff conditions here."

"I wouldn't know about that," said Nurse Adrian correctly. She hurried on. Everyone in earshot, except Charlot, settled down to a solid army grouse.

"Quiet, everyone, please," said the Charge Nurse. A clump of white coats had appeared in the doorway.

Laurie stubbed out his cigarette, moistened his lips, and waited. They would start on the other side and take more than half an hour to reach him. The thing was to be prepared for the worst; and at once he imagined Major Ferguson saying, "Well, Odell, I think we can get you back the full use of that leg. A few exercises and some massage . . ." The scene presented itself to him with vivid clearness, like a landscape before a storm.

He had no entertainment to pass the time, except the slow procession across the ward. There was a different lot of students. They came out from the large City Hospital at Bridstow. The pink young man at the end was a new one. Crowded out from the case under discussion, he was running his eye idly along the opposite line of beds. His glance lingered on Laurie; slid away with a flick of his light eyelashes; slid back and lingered again, cautiously, as a fly settles. Laurie, whose nerves were strained, began to be irritated. In heaven's name, he thought, why so shy? Every second man in this room, on a modest estimate, must have wiped out at least one of his fellow creatures; with the gunners it might run into scores for all they know. That poor little devil with the white eyelashes, with any luck at all, will probably save enough lives to balance the book. But because something holds him back from reproducing himself in time for the next holocaust, here he is peering out at us from under a flat stone. Cheer up, darling, after all you might have invented a bigger and better bomb and got a bloody knighthood. . . . At this point the young man looked his way again. Rapidly, Laurie caught his eye before

40

he could disengage it, and gave him a deliberately dazzling smile. As he had confidently expected, the young
man went crimson, and merged himself deeply in the
throng. I do hope, thought Laurie, he won't decide
later to write me a little note. But no, I don't think he
puts much in writing. To a nunnery go, why wouldst
thou be a breeder of sinners?

From long practice on mornings like this, he and
Reg had perfected an almost soundless speech like
that of convicts at exercise. Reg said, "Know that
guy?"

"No. Made a mistake."

"I'll say. Proper sissy." But the Sister had turned.
He pretended he had only leaned over for a drink from
the locker-top.

The clump of white coats moved sluggishly on,
clotting around each bed like ants around lumps of
sugar.

"Morning, Odell."

Laurie sat at attention, a little lopsidedly because of
the cushions under his leg. "Good morning, sir."

"Leg more comfortable now?"

"Yes, thank you, sir."

"Much drainage still, Sister?"

"Very little now, sir."

"I'll see it, please."

The Sister folded back the clothes, snipped the bandage, and lifted the dressing off with forceps. Major
Ferguson peered down with simple pleasure, like a gar-
dener at a choice rose. Laurie got his question ready;
his hands felt rather cold.

"I think you saw this man after his first operation,
sir."

The question died on Laurie's lips. He had noticed
for the first time, on the visiting surgeon's shoulders,
the tabs of a brigadier.

". . . and comminuted patella," Major Ferguson was
saying. "The fractured ends of the femur were exten-
sively exposed and penetrated with gravel and so on.
The osteomyelitis responded remarkably well to sulph-
onamides, but, as you see, we had to open four times

41

in all to remove various sequestra, and about a month ago we began to feel he'd probably be better off without it. However, the callus started to look more promising, and the question then was whether amputation would be justified by the increased mobility he'd get from an artificial limb."

"The knee's completely ankylosed, is it?" The brigadier sounded like an intelligent player discussing a chess problem.

"No, sir, we managed to give him a flexion of about twenty degrees, and that decided us to leave it, combined with the fact that we've reduced the shortening to just about an inch. The repair of the quadriceps . . ."

Laurie sat at attention, eyes front. After the blow had reached him through the swathes of technical jargon, he had suddenly remembered the pink young man lurking somewhere at the back. It stiffened his pride, which the two specialists had made to seem nugatory, a trivial reflex like a knee-jerk. Laurie schooled his face, for the necessary minutes, to a wooden noncomprehension; and soon he was alone again, half hearing the exchange of Charlot's patois and the surgeon's public-school French. Then he slipped down in bed with the caution of a criminal, lest the counterpane should be disturbed and some nurse come to straighten it. Luckily this fear was a kind of distraction; soon he was able to blot his eyes on the sheet and come to the surface again.

Reg was maneuvering a book in front of his face, signal of a wish to talk. Suddenly Laurie felt a great craving for simple, platitudinous sympathy. He turned around, and held a paper up too.

Reg said, "Had a letter from me dad today."

"M-m?" The doctors had worked over the next few beds quickly; they were nearing the door. Laurie realized a delayed impression which his tension had excluded before, that all day Reg had been rather like an actor gagging to cover up. "Your dad all right?"

"Dad's okay. Me better half's gone off the rails, that's all."

Laurie remembered the letter coming and the long silence after. An awful sense of inadequacy appeared

42

ahead of him, like a gulf into which he would have to step. He murmured, "Things get garbled. Gossip and so on."

"Gossip?" Reg's coarse-grained forehead puckered down the middle, so that the reddish hairs of his eyebrows met. "She's gone to live with the mucker, and she's took our boy."

"Bloody shame," said Laurie, desperately trying to make emphasis do the work of sense. Madge Barker was a dumpy, bosomy girl with a dusty, mouse-colored parting in her platinum hair, which she wore shoulder-length, emphasizing the shortness of her neck. Her real-good-sort façade was not so much false as slovenly, like a cover flung over an unmade bed. She looked at every man she met as if there were only one thing she wanted to know about him, but her speech was terrifyingly genteel. Laurie detested her.

"Boy's turned six now," Reg was saying. "Kids that age understand."

"They'll give you custody." Thankfully Laurie accepted the side issue.

"Who'd I get to look after him? 'S not just the kid."

"No, of course. It's hell."

"You're right," said Reg, and fell silent. But Laurie felt a heavy certainty that he was waiting; for sympathy, for fellow feeling. He felt like a man who has strolled empty-handed into a famine area.

"She can't be worth it. Treating you like that." But, he thought immediately after, perhaps she was, perhaps he ought to be urging Reg to understand, to win her back.

"Too true she's not. But it's one thing to know you been a mucking fool, it's another to learn sense." His face reddened. A shiny rim began to form along his lower lids.

"You know, my father wasn't faithful to my mother. She minded a lot at the time, but she's all right now."

"It's not the same for a woman. That's their lot, and nature made them to stand it. But a man's nature's different."

"Is it? It's bloody hell, Reg, I know. I'm terribly sorry."

43

"Her sister's a good girl. Looked after the mother and got passed over like. Our dad would have rather I'd picked Ireen, I know. But she hadn't the life in her that Madge had." He snatched a handkerchief from the pillow and blew his nose.

"If she got sick of all this would you take her back?"

"No. Never." Reg swallowed convulsively. "I couldn't never go with her again, thinking of how she'd been with him." He swallowed again; there was a pause. "But I'd never get used to no one else. She was one of those that know what a man needs—I used to think she only learned it thinking of me." Suddenly he turned over with his back to Laurie, and held up the book close to his face.

"Goodness, they *have* left you in a mess." It was the Charge Nurse with the dressing trolley, making the bandages good. The doctors had been gone some minutes. The nurse bandaged the leg and straightened the bed, tutting mildly. He lay looking at the ceiling, wondering whether to tell his mother by letter or wait till she came.

"*Qu'est-ce que tu as, Spoddi?*" He turned to meet Charlot's kind, vague eyes. Here was someone who could be told without bothering Reg. If he could tell just one person it was all he wanted. He said in French, "It's only something the doctor has just said about my leg—that it will always be stiff, and shorter than the other, and that all my life I shall be lame."

"That is bad," said Charlot slowly. "That is a wicked thing." Suddenly a spasm of extraordinary violence convulsed his face. "The filthy Boches. Animals. Pigs. . . ." Laurie could only guess at the next few words. "When the war is over we shall split the gullets of these assassins. All . . . all——"

"Oh, I don't know. If you hanged the lot of them it wouldn't put back an inch on my leg."

"The world knows what they are. They are——"

"Yes," said Laurie soothingly. "Yes, I know." He had been forgetting the Germans, and was ashamed of his lack of tact.

"You're having your stitches out soon," said a shy,

44

cool voice beside him. "I heard Major Ferguson telling Sister."

It was Nurse Adrian. He looked around, smiling. The emotions of the anesthetic were still tangled in his consciousness; he felt at once that it was she all the time whom he had really wanted. Her hand, resting on the locker, looked cool and slim, with nice bones.

"You'll be up again before long," she said. "What's the matter, is it aching?"

"Not much, thanks." He looked at her again, longing to speak; but he could only think of things too simple to say. "I shall always be different," he wanted to tell her; and some part of his mind expected that she would say "No," and everything would be changed. "It only aches on and off now," he said, to fill the pause which already she might be noticing. She had none of that awful knowingness; one could take one's time with her, hesitate, and she would only be grateful. "Different?" she would say, surprised. "But of course you're not."

"I'll ask Sister for some A.P.C. for you," she said.

"No, really, it's all right." As she stood looking down at him in kind anxiety, he saw what his own trouble had hidden before, that she was dog-tired and harried to death. Strands of her fair hair were slipping down damply under her cap; her face was shiny like a schoolgirl's after hockey; the inside of her hand was soggy and rough, she must have been scrubbing somewhere out of sight. She had the air of giving up appearances and expecting nothing. He remembered that both the maids and the nurses had always seemed to have a full-time job, and there were no maids today.

"Thanks all the same," he said, "but it's gone off now, it feels fine." On a sudden impulse, because she looked plain and didn't deserve to, he added, "Seeing you must have cured it."

"Silly," she said offhandedly; but she gave him a quick, shy smile as she went on to the next locker.

"Now then, Spud," said Reg, suddenly reappearing. "At it again. Ought to be ashamed. Here, I never asked you, what did the old man say about your leg? He was going on long enough."

45

"God knows," said Laurie. "It was just Greek to me."

They put Reg into an airplane splint next day. It supported his arm outwards on a level with his shoulder, flexed at the elbow. Learning not to knock people down as he passed them gave him an occupation. He wrote Madge a long letter. Laurie had his stitches out, and was allowed up. This was his fourth convalescence; there was nothing to it, except that, as usual, he found when he used the crutch again that his arm muscles had gone soft. The stick would come later; he had only graduated to a stick once before.

In the evening, when he came back to the ward from the kitchen where he had been washing up, he was pleased to notice still more progress in Reg. Not only was he not sitting alone, but he had a grouse. It was plainly a stirring, public, and noisy one. His face looked a healthier color already. He was sitting on the end of Neames's bed. Between Reg and Neames there was always something of a class war; so Laurie realized the grouse must be serious, and he had better be in on it.

"Hello," he said. "What's cooking?"

"What's cooking? Eh?" Reg wheeled round, so that Neames had to duck to dodge a scythelike sweep of the splint. "Cor, Spuddy, you wait till you hear. This'll kill you, this will. Listen to this. Who d'you think they're sending up here, to do for us 'stead of the maids?"

"German prisoners?" guessed Laurie. Unlikely as it seemed, he could think of nothing else proportionable to Reg's fury.

"Oh, come on, wake up, Spud; what Jerry prisoners do we get? Only the Luftwaffe boys. And God's truth, I'd rather have a bunch of them. They learn them this Nazi stuff in the schools, they don't know no better, they've been had for suckers but they done their duty the way they see it, same as us. Not like these creeping-Jesus, knock-kneed conchies."

Laurie took it in. He whistled.

"C.o.s? God, that's going to be a bit embarrassing."

"Embarrassing?" said Reg sharply. He usually covered up Laurie's social gaffes, but this was serious. "Too true it is. Embarrassing for them, the muckers."

"One way to look at it," said Neames, making what was evidently not his first speech in the debate, "they're mouths the country's got to feed. If they're kept in prison producing nothing, who foots the bill? We do. Now here we have the nurses wasting half their time on cleaning, and everyone's comfort going by the board. No fraternization, that goes without saying. But no obstruction. That's what I suggest."

Reg snorted. "Got it totted up like the petty cash, haven't you? After all we been through, if I was to see one of them muggers coming up with a soap and flannel to wash *me,* I'd smack it acrost his face. Don't worry, we'll soon have them out of here."

There was a growl of assent from the meeting behind him. Laurie listened in mounting depression and dismay; his imagination flinched from the series of excruciating little dramas he saw approaching. He said, "You know, they did some pretty fine ambulance work in the last war, right in the line."

"Ah," said Reg, "that would be the Quakers. Not that I hold with them, but that's a proper religion, what they've been brought up to, same as what the Catholics are."

"But if——" began Laurie. His knee, which had been aching dully, like a sprain, had begun to ache fiercely, like a burn. Growing cross, he said, "Don't look now, but it's supposed to be our religion too, when there isn't a war on."

"If you'll excuse me saying so, Odell, you're apt to be a bit too easygoing. Suppose we had Hitler here, and all our kiddies brought up to worship Valhalla and inform on us to the Gestapo. What about religion then?" Laurie perceived in Neames's sallow face the old stresses of a fierce struggle and hard victory; it gave him, for a moment, almost distinction.

"Yes, that's a point. Still——"

"Good old Spud," said Reg with sudden awkward kindness; he had recognized the signs of pain and fatigue around Laurie's eyes and mouth. "Argue the case for Jack the Ripper, *he* would."

"What are you men doing still up?" The Sister, expecting trouble, had scented it from afar. "I know you've been helping outside, Odell, and thank you, but get along now. Barker, you've been here long enough to know the rule about sitting on beds."

Laurie's leg felt worse before it felt better. He lay trying to forget it, thumbing the pages of a dog-eared magazine. The unshaded electric bulbs revealed mercilessly the cement floors, the wooden lockers with their day's burden of ash, orange peel, paper, and foil.

Reg Barker, returning from a trip to the lavatory, jerked the thumb of his good hand at the outer door. "Them sods has moved in."

"Which?" asked Laurie vaguely. "Oh, yes. Have they?"

"Just been out and seen them come up in a truck and move into the maids' block. Proper lot of pansies, too."

"Go on, Reg, it's been dark for hours, you couldn't tell if they were Zulus."

"Wait till tomorrow and you'll see, then. Same as what they will."

"You know, Reg, let's face it, we're all a bit on edge here. We can do to take things quietly, for our own sakes."

"Then why do they have to send the muckers here, as if we hadn't got no feelings?"

"God knows, and some zombie at Whitehall. Still, why make it worse?"

"You know, Spud, it's right for once what Neames said, you're too easygoing by half. Why should they get away with it? Sitting safe on their backsides at home and taking our jobs." A dark flush rose in his forehead. "There's women that fall for that smarmy sort," he said, "if they can talk posh."

"Did you say taking our jobs? They're welcome to mine in the kitchen. I say, Reg—before you get into bed, would you mind asking Sister if I can have some A.P.C.?"

"Knee playing up?" Reg leaned forward; the shape of his splint made him look as if he were preparing a savage blow. Anxious creases divided his brows.

"Nothing much. You were right, though. I did mess about on it a bit too long."

"They got no business to have put you on that kitchen fatigue. I said all along."

"Someone's got to, with all you lucky people in arm splints."

"Well," said Reg with vicious emphasis, "from tomorrow on, those muckers can do it. *And* like it."

Laurie looked ingenuously up at him. "So they can. I shan't be sorry, I must say."

It was not one of his good nights. He was awake till the Night Sister gave him medinal at two. This sent him soundly off; so that a touch on his shoulder, waking him to light and clatter, filled him with impotent outrage. Dimly aware that the offending hand was not a nurse's, he burrowed into the pillow and growled, "What the bleeding hell is it?"

"I'm sorry. If I can just take your temperature."

Sudden recollection jerked Laurie awake. He looked up into a lean, austere face with a short grizzled beard. There was no doubt that the beard had a chin under it.

"Excuse my language," he said uncomfortably. "I was half asleep." He suppressed what he had meant to say; tomorrow would do. This was silly, for he might have known Reg would never let it pass.

"He don't have it taken mornings," said Reg promptly. "He gets up."

The man withdrew his thermometer from Laurie's arm. "Then I've waked you for nothing. I'm extremely sorry. I won't do it again."

"It's all right. I never sleep much after the work starts."

"Go on," said Reg, more in sorrow than in anger. "Day before yesterday you slept till the breakfast come round, you know that."

The bearded man as he passed on gave Laurie a slow smile which seemed, oddly, both sophisticated and good. He went on to Charlot, to whom he spoke in fluent idiomatic French. Reg said, in a hoarse whisper, "Here. What's he doing here? You're not telling me *he's* still military age. Nor anywhere near."

Laurie looked again. "No, of course. He must be a good fifty. Perhaps it was all a mistake."

He looked along the ward. Another man, wearing a coarse, gray cotton coat like the first, was pulling out the beds one by one to sweep. No, thought Laurie with sinking spirits, this one wasn't over age. He was a small man, with a small licked-down mustache, and looked about twenty-six. Eager conscientiousness informed his every movement. Chapel type, Laurie decided; and thinks damn is pretty serious swearing. This really is going to be rather hell.

"Proper little pipsqueak," hissed Reg.

"Doesn't look as if he'd pass a medical," said Laurie hopefully.

"Go on. Course they're c.o.s. It's written all over them. Search me what the old boy's here for, though."

Laurie glanced after the bearded man, now several beds away. Neames, looking straight ahead, allowed his temperature to be taken as if by an automaton. The next bed was Willis's.

Willis was a towheaded youth, whom Neames had early christened the Missing Link. He had never seemed to resent this, though he was quarrelsome by nature; Laurie deduced that he didn't know what it meant. Willis always made him feel uncomfortable. One felt he should have been given a choice at the outset, whether or not to be born. It must have taken generations of conditioning to breed him, in some dockside warren neglected by angels and the borough inspector.

Reg said, "Watch this, this'll be good."

"Willis gets up," said Laurie. "He's only got to say so. What the hell did they send them here for, this bloody Government'll lose us the war."

It was often quite hard to hear what Willis said, even when he was not chewing. It was the prevailing hush which carried his voice along the ward.

"You can take that —— thing away, and put it where the —— monkey put the —— nuts. I don't want none of you ——'s touching me."

The c.o. replied as if to an expected social commonplace. "I expect not, it's awkward for both of us. Still, we'll have to get on with it, I suppose."

50

"You —— off and get on with it somewhere else. See?"

"This is a lot of silly bull," said Laurie. He sat up, and reached for his crutch. But the little c.o. had just pulled out his bed from the wall where it was, and he couldn't reach it.

"I say, Reg." But Reg had hitched his dressing-gown over his shoulder, and was shuffling down the ward.

"Here," he said to the c.o. "Didn't they give you no list of the men that gets up?"

"No," said the c.o. with a friendly smile. "I ought to have asked for it."

"You only want it mornings. Evenings they take them all round, barring the chaps out on passes. I reckon that's soft, not giving you no list. Asking for it, that is. Here. You turn that paper over and I'll give you one now. Save tempers all round, that will."

When they had finished he turned around. "And when you done your funny number, Willis," he said over his shoulder, "you remember there ain't been no comfort in the ward since the maids went, and if this lot's transferred there won't be none again. What you want them to do, go through the whole flipping war without working?"

Just then Laurie's bed moved. The little c.o., having swept behind it, was putting it back. His face confronted Laurie over the end of it, as he shoved earnestly with all the force of his thin arms. Laurie said encouragingly, "Next time give me that crutch first, then you can have the pram without the baby."

"Oh, beg pardon. Yes, of course." With helpless concern and irritation, Laurie saw that he had blushed to the ears. Perhaps he thought his physique was being sneered at. Suddenly Laurie felt that, early as it was, his nervous system had had enough. He would get away for a bit, he thought, before he lost his sense of humor over some trivial annoyance. He was not allowed to dress yet, but with luck the bathroom might be free.

The lavatory was too filthy to linger in—no one could have scrubbed it since the maids went—but he was lucky with the bath. Although he couldn't get into it properly because of the dressings on his leg, at least the water was hot. The window was steaming up; he opened it; an apple tree in a cottage garden looked faintly gold against a cool blue autumn sky, and he caught the smoky tang of sun on frost-caught leaves.

Behind the noise of the taps, the jerry-built hut echoed with every thud and bang of the morning work. He could hear someone scrubbing the floor just outside, and whistling quietly. The whistling stopped almost as soon as he turned the taps off. The last notes had sounded like a phrase of Mozart, but he had probably imagined it.

As he dried himself, the sun went in behind a cloud; easing himself slowly and stiffly into his pajama trousers, he got a waft of watery haddock from the kitchen. Just another day, he thought. He put on his dressing-gown, reached for his crutch, and opened the door into the lobby.

The cement floor outside was wet; a voice said quickly, "Look out for the bucket."

Before he had seen around the door, some instantaneous reflex caused Laurie to say "Oh, thanks very much" in a conversational, instead of an automatic way.

He came out. In the open doorway of the lavatory, the boy who had been scrubbing the floor sat back on his heels and smiled.

Laurie stopped in his tracks, balanced himself between the crutch and the bathroom doorpost, and smiled back. Well, he thought after a moment, one can't just stand grinning like a fool. "Hello. What was that bit of Mozart you were whistling just now?"

The boy put down his floorcloth, wiped his hand on the seat of his trousers, and with the back of it pushed the hair away from his eyes. It was fairish, the color of old gilt. He had a fair skin which was smoothly tanned, so that his gray eyes showed up very bright and clear. He was working in old corduroy trousers and a gray flannel shirt with rolled sleeves.

"I'm not sure," he said. "I was thinking about something else." Fearing perhaps to have sounded unsocial, he smiled again.

52

Laurie had become touched with a feeling of panic, like someone confronted with a locked door and a strange bunch of keys, none of which may fit. He said with a jerk, "I thought it might be the Oboe Quartet in F Major." This simply happened to be one of the few he could identify by name. The boy said in a willing way, "It might have been; it's one I'm very fond of" and stirred the cloth in the bucket, sending up a clean bleak smell of carbolic.

"Was it this bit?" Laurie said. He tried to hum a few bars of the first movement. The boy sat with a listening expression; at the end he said with serious courtesy, "Yes, it probably was that bit," and then, as there began to be a pause, "Have you ever heard Goossens play it?"

"No. Only on a record. Have you?"

"Only the record."

There was another pause. The boy started to work again, though not in a dismissing way, and moved his bucket into the lavatory doorway. "This is a bit of a dreary job for you," Laurie said.

"Here. Move that mucking bucket, you lazy——, d'you think we've got all day?" Laurie hadn't heard Willis coming up behind them.

The boy had started a little, but repressed it quickly; he moved the bucket, civilly but without apology. Willis stepped forward to pass it. There was a kind of forced clumsiness in his gait, a crude preparation for knocking the bucket over. Laurie swung out on his crutch and, silently, caught Willis's eye. It was a look he had not tried on anyone since his last year at school, but apparently it still worked. Willis's face slumped soggily, seeming to mirror a defeated ancestry as long as Banquo's line of kings. He went inside and slammed the door. It was over in seconds.

The boy stood up. Laurie could see that he was shyly, but doggedly, working up to something. "That was very kind of you. But it will have to come out sometime, if that's how he feels. We have to cope with all that ourselves, I mean. It's the least we can do, after all, isn't it?"

The brush with Willis had fortified Laurie's self-confidence. "Well, to you it probably seems to be your business; but to me it seems to be mine. I have to live here."

"Have you been here long?"

"Oh, I more or less crept out of the woodwork, I——"

The face of the bearded man came in at the door. He looked at them with kindly detached interest and said briskly, "When you've finished in there, Andrew, will you take the swill bucket down to the main kitchen? They'll show you there what to do with it." The boy looked up, smiled with casual but affectionate ease, said, "All right, Dave," and bent to his scrubbing again.

Andrew, thought Laurie; the name slipped into place like a clear color-note in the foreground of a picture. Mechanically he stepped aside as the lavatory door opened; Willis came out and went off without a backward glance. "Andrew what?"

"Raynes. But we don't use surnames much."

"Are you Quakers? Sorry, I'm never sure whether that's rude or not."

"Oh, it stopped being rude about 1700. We mostly say Friends."

"Here," said Laurie suddenly, "you washed all that before." He looked past Andrew into the open door. "Stop that. Leave it just as it is. I'm going to fetch him back and rub his face in it."

Andrew, busy with the cloth, said over his shoulder, "Well, I can't stop you. If you think it'll do any of us any good."

"This is my show. Just leave this to me."

"Look. This man's had nothing since he was born but his two hands to work with; and he's given one of those. You can't expect him to welcome us with flowers. Give him a chance."

"Willis," said Laurie crisply, "is suffering from a self-inflicted wound, caused by gross incompetence. He fumbled a grenade in the practice pit. It killed his instructor, a very good man who was decorated in the last war, and he's never shown the slightest sign of giving a damn. I shouldn't waste any beautiful thoughts

54

on Willis, if I were you." They stared, with very mixed feelings, into each other's faces. Suddenly Laurie laughed and said, " 'I saw the 'potamus take wing, Ascending from the damp savannas——' "

Andrew laughed too; his teeth showed clear, like his eyes, against the tan. He backed out of the doorway and Laurie saw that the floor was clean again.

"You'll hear me called Spud about the place, but actually it's Laurie. Laurie Odell. I'd give you a hand with that, but this strapping's a bit tight on my knee."

"I can see Dave's face if I let you."

"That chap with the beard?" Jealousy breathed on him, like the first shiver of sickness. "Who is he exactly?"

"Well, he's just Dave. I mean, nothing officially. He did a lot of this work in the 1914 war. He's voluntary now, of course."

"Do you like him a lot?"

"Oh, I've known Dave a long time."

Laurie saw that the last patch of floor was nearly finished. "If I only had my gramophone here, we could have had some Mozart, sometime." He tilted his shoulder against the wall; the crutch felt a little shaky. "I've got quite a bit of Tchaikovsky, ballet music mostly. It's all right when you feel like it, or don't you think so? I read somewhere once, Tchaikovsky was queer."

He seemed to wait hours for the upturned face to change; but the pause was in his own imagination, as he realized when Andrew said with mild interest, "Was he? I hadn't heard. He was never actually shut up, surely?"

"No, it never came out. Though I believe——" He saw his mistake, and with a painful jolt caught himself up just in time. "Not mad, you know. Just queer." He waited again.

"You mean a bit ... Oh, yes, I see." Andrew wrung out the cloth in the bucket. "I find all Russians slightly mysterious, don't you? Perhaps if one met more of them."

Laurie said yes, that was the trouble, probably. He leaned heavily on the door-jamb; he had been standing too long. He hoped that Andrew wouldn't look up for a minute; he knew that with these cold turns he went sensationally white. It would pass off, it was all a matter of will-power. His brain felt drained and light; he thought: If he's seen it in the Bible and guessed what it meant, that's about as much as he knows.

Andrew stood up and tipped the dirty water into the lavatory. "I must do the swill," he said, and paused. "I say, you do look tired. Let me see you back to bed before I go."

"God, no. I'm officially up. I'm all right. Are you detailed to this ward from now on?"

"I don't know yet, we're just filling in till the lists are done. Thanks for coming to talk to me." He colored suddenly. Laurie saw why: he had let down the side, he shouldn't have thanked a soldier for talking to him, as if he belonged to something that had to apologize for itself.

"Thanks for putting up with me, under your feet. Goodbye."

"Goodbye." He moved to the door, with young pliant awkwardness, swinging the bucket. Laurie said quickly, "Oh, by the way——" but it was too late, he had passed into the clatter of the corridor and didn't hear. The clank of the bucket sounded for a moment, receding. Laurie's armpit felt wrenched by the pressure of the crutch; his arm was numb, and his leg had started to ache again. The breakfast trolley, with the haddock, was being wheeled into the ward. He followed it. There was nowhere else to go.

4

LAURIE signed his letter to his mother, and reread it. He used to write her rather good letters once, he remembered. "Major Ferguson went over the leg the other day. He says it will always be a bit stiff, and I shall have to wear a thick sole on my shoe or something." She knew already about his discharge, so there had been little more to say. He went over her last letter again, looking for something that would give him another paragraph; but the best he could find was that the vicar still felt the loss of his wife very much, though it was a year now since her death. Desperate for material, Laurie added a short postscript in which he said he was sorry to hear this.

He sat staring at the letter on the writing-pad, and imagining it rewritten.

Darling Mother,

I have fallen in love. I now know something about myself which I have been suspecting for years, if I had had the honesty to admit it. I ought to be frightened and ashamed, but I am not. Since I can see no earthly hope for this attachment, I ought to be wretched, but I am not. I know now why I was born, why everything has happened to me ever; I know why I am lame, because it has brought me to the right place at the right time. I would go through it all again, if I had to, now that I know it was for this.

Oddly enough, what I feel most is relief, because I know now that what kept me fighting it so long was the fear that what I was looking for didn't exist. Lanyon said it didn't, and after meeting Charles's set I thought he was probably right. If it hadn't been for him I might have fallen for all that, and missed this. I wish I could thank him.

You may think I have been rather quick to decide I am in love . . .

He looked up from the page, and then back to it, in an absurd fear that something of all this might have become stamped on the paper. For the first time, now, the secret between them had shape and outline; it would be real when she sat by him at her next visit.

She had been very good to him since he had been wounded. He had wished for her sake he could have got his commission first. There had been hints, and he had already been recommended for sergeant when the great confusion descended; but she had never reminded him of his folly in throwing up the O.T.C., though she had been against it at the time. He had always felt that his best wasn't good enough for her. Now there was this. But after all, however orthodox his sex life might

57

have been, he knew they would never have discussed it; the mere thought would have shocked her to death.

His imagination wrote on:

. . . to decide I am in love. But he is a clear kind of person, about whom one has to think clearly.

He moved his hand across the letter, as if to brush away the invisible words, and sealed it up.

Suppers were finished; the loose ends of the day's work were tied off. Laurie's meditations returned, growing somber with night and weariness. He limped on and on through a darkening maze without a center.

"'S matter, Spud? Tired?"

"Bit. Sorry."

"Get you some A.P.C.?"

"Later, I think. Thanks, Reg."

The ward lights were turned off, leaving only the yellow pool by the Sister's table, and the glow of the radio dial. The star program of the week was on: a cinema organist, who played request numbers for the Forces, chosen by their people at home. Laurie was tired, and his stomach for this kind of thing was queasy at the best. He got down into the bedclothes, and tried to sleep. The Sister gave the report, added her afterthoughts, and went off duty. Nurse Sims, the Night Nurse, stepped forward with decision to the radio table.

"Have a heart, Nurse," said someone as usual. "Suppose there was a request for one of us?"

"The B.B.C. always sends a——"

". . . And now," said the radio, its inhuman geniality becoming tinged with a manly pathos, "I have a rather special message for Lance-Corporal Reginald Barker, who is a patient at . . ." Not so much the name, as the ward's electrified hush, roused Laurie from his apathy. Beside him Reg, who had just got into bed and had been reaching down for something in his locker, lay frozen in that position by shock. Among all this Laurie had missed a phrase or two. ". . . to forgive and forget. And she hopes that this lovely melody will recall happy honeymoon days, and bring you both together again. So here it is, for Lance-Corporal Reginald Barker—'Souvenirs'!"

The organist did Reg proud. He used the *vox humana* in the first half, and the *vox angelica* in the second. It was like sugar with warm treacle sauce.

Laurie crawled down into the bed. No one could very well suppose him to be sleeping, but there seemed nothing else one could do for Reg. In the Dark Ages, he thought, they only cropped your ears, or branded you in the forehead, or stood you in the pillory. They hadn't the resources of civilization.

All activity in the ward had ceased. The man on the other side of Charlot was trying to explain the situation to him in five well-chosen words helped out with mime. At the bottom end of the ward a young man with a passable tenor had begun to croon expressively (filling the merciful gaps in Laurie's memory) the words of the song.

The first essential, Laurie thought, would be to see that Reg didn't put his razor under his pillow and cut his throat during the night. He peeped out cautiously from under the blanket, but Reg's head, as he had expected, was turned the other way.

> *I count them all apart,*
> *And when the tear-drops start,*
> *I find a broken heart among my souvenirs.*

It was over. A low buzz of comment quivered through the ward. Nurse Sims stared at the radio, lastingly defeated; she would never be able to turn off a request program again. Laurie turned on his side, the side facing Reg. One could take delicacy too far; it didn't help to make a man feel like a leper.

Reg turned round. It surprised Laurie vaguely that he didn't attempt to hide his face. His lower lip was trembling. Tears welled from under his sandy lashes.

"I'll send her a wire tomorrow, first thing. I never knew she felt like that."

He fumbled for his dressing-gown, hitching it blindly over his splinted shoulder. While Laurie was still searching for a reply he had gone down the ward. In

59

his wake the buzz rose to an eager, satisfied muttering. If one could have turned all the lights on suddenly, Laurie thought, there would have been applause.

He lay back on the pillow, the only one not running over with gossip and sensation, the odd man out.

The clink and rattle of mugs on a trolley sounded beside him. The nurse usually came around at this hour, putting water on the lockers for the night. He turned over.

"Please, Nurse ..." His voice stopped. It was Andrew with the trolley.

The forms, the shadows, the colors in the ward magically regrouped and changed. The pool of light on the Sister's table had for the first time mystery beyond its rim.

Andrew pushed the trolley up quietly. He was wearing old, white tennis shoes. The light shining sideways on his hair made it look fairer and brighter than in the day. Shadow made the structure of his face emphatic, the eyes deeper-set, the mouth firmer. He looked more resolute, and at the same time younger. When he smiled, as he did immediately he saw who it was that had spoken, it seemed to Laurie almost frighteningly dramatic and beautiful.

Whispering as everyone did after lights-out, he said, "Now I know where to find you. Did you think I was going to leave you out?" He came with a mug and stood it on the locker, pausing, his fingers around the handle.

"What are you doing here, so late?"

"I've just gone on night duty. General orderly."

"But have you had any sleep?"

"Oh, one hardly would the first day." He lingered, with a curious lack of awkwardness, like a well-mannered child who assumes that, if unwanted at present, he will be dismissed without ill-feeling. Laurie at once found his mind a helpless blank.

"What about the man next you?" Andrew said. "He'd like some water, wouldn't he?"

"Yes, please." In a moment he would be gone; Laurie saw "Good night" forming already on his face.

"That's Reg Barker's bed, we came off the beach together. Have you heard what happened tonight?"

"No." Andrew came back easily. There was a kind of trust behind the surface attention in his face. Laurie saw suddenly that it wasn't the too-easy trust of people to whom everything has always been kind. Thankful that whispering would hide anything odd in his voice, he told the story.

Andrew said, his eyes looking grave under their shadowy lids, "Well, if he loves her."

"After that?" Like someone touching the edge of a sleeve by stealth, he said, "Could you?"

"I expect, you know," said Andrew, "he only had room for just the one thing."

It was the morning of visiting day. Walking patients sat on the edges of their beds, polishing their brass. Supplies of hospital blue had not even yet caught up with the sudden Dunkirk demand upon a stricken commissariat. Many of them had arrived in rags, some half naked, or draped in the wayside gifts of shocked civilians; and few of them had not retained from this experience some traces of a savage, primitive humiliation. Even now those who got up were often dressed partly in items of uniform taken from the dead, and Laurie had asked nobody where his trousers came from.

Matron had just arrived, and done a round. She came poking into the ward, her petticoat showing slightly, defensively frigid; she had been promoted beyond her dreams and it had been a Nessus' shirt to her. Homesick for her little country nursing home, she peered down the line of beds, noting with dismay how many men were up and at large, rough men with rude, cruel laughter, who wrote things on walls, who talked about women, who got V.D. (but then one was able to transfer them elsewhere). She was wretched, but her career was booming.

"Sour-faced old bag," said Reg as she disappeared.

"I suppose . . ." began Laurie vaguely; but the feeling of pathos he had just experienced, meeting her slightly bulging, frightened eye, defied communication. He applied himself to the job of darning Reg's socks.

61

"God, Reg, I can get my fist through this one. It'll be the most awful cobble. Why the hell don't you let me do them when they start to go?"

"Here, you leave it, I'll wear odd ones."

"No, I can get it together." He had invented a kind of blanket-stitch for this purpose. "When's she coming? First bus?"

"That's right." There was a tacit understanding between them that the recent breach should be admitted, but not discussed. "Your mum coming 'sarternoon?'"

"That's right," said Laurie, trying to sound flat and unexcited.

He had been allowed to dress today, for the first time since the operation. He was getting about briskly now; the stage of transition between crutch and stick had been reached. They had measured him already for a surgical boot.

Presently he slipped out of the ward, and into the square between the huts. He stood on the dirty grass enclosed by the asphalt, sown with coarse weeds and empty cigarette-cartons; the sky shone with the warm, yet delicate and tender blue of early autumn, a huge cumulus towering in it. At this hour, toward midday, it was almost certain that Andrew would have gone to bed. There was just the faint possibility which had become the mainspring of Laurie's morning. In the afternoon, when the whole of the night staff was sleeping, the tension relaxed; this, if Laurie would have admitted it to himself, was usually the happiest time of his day.

The usual people were coming and going in the square. Watching the traffic, Laurie got little pointers to the degree of acceptance the c.o.s. had achieved. A sergeant from another ward, a lonely schoolmaster whom his wound had balked of promotion, was frankly and enjoyably chatting with the bearded Dave. A nurse stopped one of the others, to discuss briefly but amicably some current job. A private from Ward A, whom Laurie didn't know, observing this conversation spat noisily in the grass. Another soldier offered him a rather awkward "Good morning."

Reg was back in the ward, supervising Derek's preparations for lunch. Derek, the little man with the licked-down mustache, had become Reg's protégé. Willis had soon found Dave and Andrew unrewarding subjects; but this shy and earnest little creature was the ideal victim. Laurie had interfered now and again; but Reg, pricked by the memory of snobberies in his home neighborhood, had found Derek's refinement as irritating as his name, and decided that a bit of toughening-up wouldn't hurt him. This attitude had changed mysteriously on a day when Reg's arm was replastered, and Derek had the tricky and painful job of cutting the old plaster off. This was done in the privacy of the bathroom, and Reg had never volunteered any information about it, except once to say to Laurie that, in his opinion, Derek's growth had been stunted by always taking other people's troubles too much to heart.

Thinking about these things in a general way, Laurie became aware of a thin, tinny warble, the hospital's Imminent Danger siren. There had been no big daylight raids hereabouts, so, though officially everyone out of doors was supposed to take cover, in fact a few extra people came out to scan the sky.

Presently there was the deep contrapuntal hum of many engines together, and in the broad square of sky between the roofs the dogfight appeared: small black plane after small black plane, weaving and circling. At that distance the motion looked joyful, like a dance of gnats. Then in the fresh sky one of the Spitfires turned away out of the battle. It glided for a while, then seemed to slip sideways. Something broke off from it; it fell over and over, like a toy thrown by a child from a high window, and disappeared behind the roofs. Nobody spoke. One of the nurses, who had an Irish face, made the sign of the cross.

But the Messerschmitt which had shot down the Spitfire had been engaged at once by another. Suddenly the German plane leaked a dribble of smoke, there was a silent flash, then as the sound overtook it, the explosion. A scatter of black shards fell at leisure. The battle passed out of sight, the planes catching the sun in silvery flashes as they turned, pretty and brisk as minnows in the high clear air.

A little mounting cheer ran around the group in the

63

square. The Irish nurse, waving at the voided sky, looked as if someone had given her a present. Laurie was cheering too, his pent-up emotions escaping thankfully in the general release. Then on the outskirts of the group he saw Dave. At first his face seemed almost expressionless, till one looked at his eyes.

"Here," said Reg in the ward, "whassup with you, Spud? You look properly cheesed. Have done for days. Trouble at home?"

"No. Oh, I don't know, Reg. One thing and another."

"Leg's been a long time. Playing up and that. Bound to lose patience, stands to reason." He looked as if he were anxiously balancing a large handful of tact, without quite knowing where to put it down.

"It'll never be up to much: I heard Ferguson say so."

"Ah," said Reg. He had evidently tried to strike a note of surprise, but without much success. He rubbed the back of his head. Laurie realized that Reg had been anticipating this moment, trying to prepare consolation in advance, worrying about it. "Well, Spud, what our mum used to say, you never know if them things is meant. What I mean, say that one missed you. Advance ten paces, stop another one; might have been your head. See, you never know."

"No," said Laurie. "That's right. You never know."

"Cheeses you off, though. You know, Spud, what I reckon, do you more good than anything? Start to go steady. Meeting all the girls you must have, college and all, bound to have one marked down, don't tell me. Eh?"

Laurie bent quickly to hunt for something in his locker. "Well—sort of, I suppose."

"Ah. Well, Spud, only way to look at it, if she loves you, won't make no difference. If not, better off without her. Can't get away from that, can you?"

"No. That's right—I've never said anything to her, matter of fact. I don't think it would work. I'm going to forget all about it."

"Ah. One thing you got to remember: let it run on too long and it's got you, see? That's where the trouble

64

starts. Well, it's nice your mum coming up today. Takes you out of yourself. Getting the news from home, and that."

"Yes. I've been bloody awful company lately, Reg. I'm sorry."

"Ah, nark it. Here, you get used to that stick soon as you can, we can pop over on the bus to the pictures."

Laurie found himself counting the hours till his mother arrived. He thought of her coming with inexpressible comfort although, if challenged, he could not have told anyone what he trusted in. She loved him; but she was apt to offer or withhold her love in a system of rewards and punishments, as she had during his childhood. He scarcely concealed from himself the fact that what she called looking on the bright side was what he would have called wishful thinking in anyone else. But among his own uncertainties, all these settled attitudes of hers gave him a sense of stability and rest. In the deep places below his thinking, she had kept the old power to make Providence seem a projection of herself; if she approved, it too would approve and reward him. Now he had committed himself to courses which only lunacy could have supposed her to sanction; yet instinctively he still transposed into this different medium the basic lessons he had learned at her knee: own up to what you do, never break your word, never hurt anyone's feelings unless there is something or somebody to be defended; always kick a banana-skin off the pavement, someone might slip on it and fall.

Even now, as he waited for her at the outer gate, he dreamed of a kind of undefined, tacit understanding, misty at the edges, like an old-fashioned photograph.

She always picked him up in the car that brought her; they drove back to the nearest small town, had tea, and talked till it was time for her to catch her train. Waiting in the usual place, he saw the old blue-and-gray bus arrive, the visitors struggle up with their parcels. In the gangway Madge Barker moved slowly along, wedged in the crowd; impatient it seemed for reunion, she began making arch little signals to Reg through the window. But after all, Laurie never knew how Reg received his prodigal; for, just behind her, his mother was standing on the step of the bus.

Laurie limped forward to meet her. He was using a stick for the first time out of doors; the shortening of the leg, without the crutch to swing on, now made itself felt with brutal insistence. She would know, this time, that it wasn't going to alter.

She hadn't noticed him yet, however. A fellow passenger, a clergyman, was helping her down, and she was thanking him. She had on a travelling coat of soft gray wool, which made her look a little plump, and a new little pale blue hat. Her auburn hair, fading while Laurie's had darkened, was turning sandy-and-silver; but it would be exquisite when it was white, silky and pure. The hat was younger than those she usually wore, but it suited her.

"Well, my *dear*." She kissed him, smelling of fresh face powder and eau de cologne. She always gave him the illusion that he was tall, from the way she put her hands up to his shoulders. "How *nice* this is, dear, to see you really walking again, and so *much* better than last time."

For a moment he was hurt, as sometimes before when she had retreated into optimism leaving him to face reality alone; but he had worked through all that long ago. "Yes," he said. "What happened, couldn't you get a car?"

She had made a little warning face. Then he saw that the clergyman who had handed her off the bus was standing almost at her elbow. He was carrying something. It was Laurie's portable gramophone, which he had asked her to send by train.

Somewhat to his surprise, the clergyman returned his glance promptly with a smile. It was the kind which insists on the adjectives "frank" and "manly," even from those by whom they are not much employed. He was big-boned and tall, over six feet; the gramophone dangled like a light parcel from his big red hand.

Mrs. Odell turned from one to the other of them; Laurie saw her go a little pink before she smiled.

"Laurie, dear, you *did* meet Mr. Straike, didn't you, just before the war?" Laurie remembered that if he had

66

been to church he would have been greeted in the porch after the service. Mr. Straike was smiling in what Laurie felt to be a professionally tactful way.

"I don't think we've actually met to speak, have we, sir?" He was full of the bewildered courtesy one extends, as compensation, to people for whom one is wholly unable to account.

Mr. Straike held out his hand in a big, sincere gesture; Laurie, balancing awkwardly, had to change his stick to his other side in order to respond.

"I've heard so much about you that, like your mother, I felt the introduction to be almost superfluous." He turned the frank smile on Mrs. Odell.

Planning instant escape, Laurie remembered with helpless embarrassment the gramophone. By no possible effort could he manage it himself. Unless he were to watch his mother carrying it, this inexplicable person would have to walk up to the hospital with them.

"Which of the men have you come to see?"

"Only this one." The difference of height seemed to give Mr. Straike's smile an avuncular quality. A five-shilling tip would hardly have taken Laurie by surprise. He felt faintly sick; but nothing would happen, he was getting stronger every day.

Mrs. Odell spoke quickly, as if to forestall awkwardness even before it had time to exist in her own mind. "Wasn't it *good* of Mr. Straike? I was telling him the other day how worried I was in case the railway people broke your gramophone, you know with all these *temporary* porters, and he insisted on coming *all* this way with me to help carry it."

She smiled at him. It was a special smile, which had been Laurie's exclusive property ever since he could remember. To see it used, so easily and as if already by habit, upon a stranger, gave him the emotional counterpart of a violent kick in the stomach. At almost the same moment a trailing end of the smile rested on him, in a delicately admonishing way. A scrap of her last letter came back to him. One must be nice to this man, he had been recently bereaved. A new, dreadful thought ran through Laurie like cold steel. He felt that he must get away, if only for seconds, to collect himself. But common good manners, and his lame leg which made an elaborate business of everything he did, held him to the spot like a ball-and-chain. He looked at Mr. Straike, to whom it seemed his feelings must by now have been delivered in stark nakedness: but Mr. Straike was looking manly, modest, and deprecating, and murmuring something about its being a privilege.

"It's very good of you," said Laurie, speaking his lines like a well-trained actor in an air raid. "You really shouldn't have; a battered old thing like that could have taken another kick or two. Shall we go up to the ward, then you can get rid of it?"

His mother, he now noticed, had a record album under her arm. It raised his spirits; his imagination in a brief idyllic flight listened to Mozart with Andrew in the woods. He took it from her and saw at once that it wasn't the one he had asked for, or even one of his own at all.

His mother said, with a defensiveness which made her sound faintly reproachful, "We didn't bring any of your *classical* records, dear, they'd be *sure* to get scratched in a place like this; and besides, Mr. Straike said he felt certain they wouldn't be popular with the men. And he was a chaplain in the last war, so he does *know*."

Mr. Straike acknowledged this with a short modest laugh. "Something they can sing." He spoke like a kindly uncle explaining his small nephews. "You can't go wrong with a good chorus. Your mother and I brought ourselves up to date and made a little expedition in search of the latest."

Laurie could see that he ought to look into the album. Managing his stick with difficulty, he succeeded in doing so. The records were, indeed, the latest song-hits. There wasn't one of them that the Forces' Radio hadn't been plugging three times a day for the last month. "That's marvellous," he said. "Thank you so much."

"They're your mother's choice," said Mr. Straike, gallantly surrendering the credit. "I think you'll find they make the party go better than Mozart. After all,

68

these lads leave school at fifteen, one must temper the wind to the shorn lamb, ha-ha."

"They want to be taken out of themselves," said his mother, gently making everything clear.

Laurie said yes, they did, of course. The pause that followed was broken by Reg greeting Mrs. Odell as he passed with Madge on his arm.

"That's the man I told you about, whose eyesight Laurie saved." Once she had taken to herself an impression of this kind, no subsequent explanations ever shifted it. Laurie had long given this one up. "Is that girl his 'young lady,' dear? Do try and warn him not to marry her. Oh, *is* she? Oh, I see. Well, girls of that class are often *so* unfair to themselves. I expect under all that make-up she's really quite a nice little thing."

Laurie found a glance being shot at him from the corner of Mr. Straike's eye. He gathered from it that his mother was a pure, generous woman, while he and Mr. Straike were men of the world making their own little reservations. As soon as he had looked away from this glance without response, Laurie knew that a line had been crossed. Some events are crucial from their very slightness; because circumstances have used no force on them, they are unequivocally what they are, test-tube reactions of personality. Between Laurie and Mr. Straike there began to weave the first fine filaments of a dislike mutually known.

As they walked up the path to the wards, Mr. Straike kept them entertained with a humorous account of how they used to detect malingerers in the base hospitals of Flanders in 1916.

The patients' tea was being served as they arrived. Lacking transport there was nowhere else to go but here. Laurie guessed by now that his mother had foreseen Mr. Straike's chivalrous insistence on paying the car fare, which ordinarily she and Laurie would have shared together. (He wouldn't consider it really necessary, either, and through all his protestations this would somehow appear.) Now, the trolley arriving, both the others insisted that Laurie should not miss his tea. He assured them he wasn't hungry, knowing the inflexible rule against treating visitors; there was no getting

69

around it, since there were only just enough cups for the patients themselves.

"Nonsense," said Mr. Straike bluffly. "You take everything that's going, my boy, it's the only way in the army, *I* know, ha-ha. Just have a word with the nurse, and tell her to rustle up a cup for your mother too. Tell her she's come a long way. *She'll* understand."

Laboriously, Laurie explained about the crockery. Mrs. Odell looked understanding, Mr. Straike surprised and reserved. Laurie felt forced to add that half these people had come from the other side of England, and it would cause hurt feelings if exceptions were made. Everyone agreed to this, leaving Laurie with a damp sense of ineffectuality. He offered his mother a drink from his own cup, the accepted practice, and collected it from her, firmly, before she could suggest passing it on. Embarrassment, damp and penetrating as a mountain mist, settled upon the party.

Laurie had always known in his inmost heart that there were times when, if his mother couldn't have her cake and eat it, she would convince herself that someone else must be to blame. A bitter conviction told him that this time it wouldn't be Mr. Straike.

Conversation, however, had to go on. Mrs. Odell had brought as usual the local gossip for Laurie's amusement. She enjoyed being very slightly shocked by his comments and making womanly, reproving little exclamations. Laurie found Mr. Straike's reaction to this as exactly predictable as if they had known one another for years; so he listened with Sunday-school brightness, saying, "No, really?" from time to time. The footnotes were provided by Mr. Straike. It seemed to Laurie, who was admittedly prejudiced, that their manly humor was not of the kind that is inspired by good nature.

For the first time, the clock's approach to his mother's hour of departure was a signal of relief. At the last moment Mr. Straike withdrew, as he put it, to "explore the place." Laurie had almost risen to show him the way, but suddenly saw in his face a conscious tact. Laurie and his mother were being left alone to exchange their little confidences. Their awareness of this, combined with feelings, for which there would be no time to find words, of mutual reproach and remorse, made this the most clammily tongue-tied interval of all.

Laurie watched his mother gathering her umbrella, her bag, and gloves. In the perky blue hat, with its soft feather curling into the soft hair, and the fluffy coat, she looked like a plump ruffled bird, dainty, timid, a little foolish, full of confused tenderness and of instinctive wisdom from which, too easily, she could be fluttered and scared away. His throat tightened; he wanted to take her away and cherish her as if she were about to die. But the bus was due in a few minutes, and now they were all walking out toward it.

Just as they were leaving, the tea trolley came back for the used crockery. This time, little Derek was pushing it instead of the nurse. Mr. Straike's nose went up, like a pointer's.

"Who," he asked in a loud aside, "are all these healthy-looking young men in mufti I keep seeing about the place?"

A wave of rage, the piled flood of the afternoon, broke in Laurie's head. He did not trust himself to reply.

"Medically exempt?" asked Mr. Straike. Derek had been passing at the time, and must have heard.

With the cold ingenuity of repressed violence, Laurie gave a prudishly reproving shake of the head. "Male nurses," he hissed. Mr. Straike said "Urhm." Laurie indicated his mother with a glance, and pointedly dropped his voice. "Can't very well discuss it here. Some things"—he paused, with heavy-handed delicacy —"women can't be asked to do."

"Quite," said Mr. Straike. "Urhm, quite." He ran a finger round the inside of his collar. Laurie found himself indulging an absurd self-righteousness, just as if it had been true.

They walked with the crowd down the iron-roofed cement path. Laurie felt his hatred and anger like a sickness. He no longer wanted to justify or fulfill them, only to clean them out of him and be quiet. He looked at Mr. Straike, who was gazing straight before him, grave, judicial; he had a digestive look, as if he were assimilating something, adapting it to his metabolism, settling it in.

"Well, dear, aren't you going to say goodbye to me?"

Laurie saw that the bus had arrived, and people were streaming into it. His mother had come up to him, and had had to touch his arm before he had seen her. He met, defenseless, the reproach in her eyes.

Back in the ward, Neames and another man were playing chess on a locker. Laurie stood and watched the game till he realized he could not retrace it by a single move. His knee had got worse; little Derek, who always knew without being told when someone was in pain, got him a dose of A.P.C. He turned down his bedcover, sat on the bed, and tried to read. If one ceased the pretense of doing something, one became at once conspicuous, a man thinking, naked to public speculation.

"Well, Spud, how's life?"

"Oh," said Laurie, "hello, Reg." For a moment, too full of himself, he expected to be asked what was up; then he remembered. "How was it? All right?"

"You said it." Reg was, he could see now, very much moved. His face was pink, his eyes bright; he fidgeted with the things on Laurie's locker, moving them unseeingly here and there. "Sometime, Spud, I'll tell you a bit; mean to say, you'd be the first. How it is, I dunno, talk about a thing and the feeling of it goes off, gets more ordinary like. Haven't felt like that for, oh, going on seven years. Well, just take a turn round the block. See you later."

The flowers had been arranged in jam-pots, the cakes and sweets crammed into lockers, the locker-tops wiped over; the disorderly invasion of the visitors left no material trace. The evening dressings had started; but Laurie's was done only in the morning now; it was nearly healed. The A.P.C. had helped the pain. If he changed the stick for the crutch, which they had left with him for a few days longer, he could escape for a little while. He even knew of somewhere to go.

Once out of the gate, he turned off the main road into a lane. A short way down was a rose hedge, with a little white gate. Inside the gate was an old brick path, bordered with lavender. A few late bush roses, yellow and red, were crisped with frost at the tips; but they looked rich, and faintly translucent, in the pale-gold light of the September sun. As Laurie approached the green latticed porch of the cottage, the door opened, and a little birdlike old woman peered out. She had on a brown stuff dress with a high lace neckband in the fashion of thirty years before; her wide black straw hat was trimmed with cherries made of glazed papier mâché. Laurie said, "Good evening, Mrs. Chivers."

"Evening, sonny. I always know *your* step. Have you come to sit in the garden, then?"

"If you're sure you don't mind."

"All of our boys are welcome any time. That's what I told the officer, right at the beginning." Laurie had never been able to identify the officer, and was even doubtful about the war. "There's one or two nice Victorias ripe on the trees. You know the eating apples. Don't you go taking the cookers, now, they'll gripe you."

"No, I won't. Thanks so much."

"You eat all you can pick, sonny. Fruit's good for the blood. Back in the trenches, you won't get it fresh, I know that. If the good Lord had meant us to take our food out of tins, that's how we'd find it growing. The Creator knows best. Wait a minute."

She popped back into the shadowy parlor, like a bird into a nesting-box, the cherries on her hat clicking dryly together. "Here you are, sonny," she said returning. "And when you've read it, pass it on to one of the other lads."

He thanked her, and took the tract. He had had this one before, though she had several varieties. They were all of a lurid evangelical kind, trumpeting Doomsday and exhorting him to wash his sins in blood. Laurie had seen, felt, and smelt enough blood to last him some time, but the paper and print had a fragrance of age about them. He was the richer for her zeal; it had caused his comrades to shun the old lady, as in the fourteenth century they might have shunned the local witch. No one came but Laurie, and it was his only sanctuary. He always missed it badly over operation times. Mrs. Chivers, however, had never noticed his absences.

The orchard ran beside the house, and continued behind it. He paused to knock down an apple with his crutch from his favorite tree, and picked his way carefully through the long pale grass, in which early windfalls were already treacherous to the foot.

Beyond the oldest of the apple trees, too gnarled to bear, the bank grew lush; the stream ran over a gravelly shallow, then tinkled down a foot-deep fall of stone. On the far side of the stream was a row of beeches. Already the breeze, passing under them, raised a whisper from the first crispings of the autumn fall.

Laurie lowered himself down gingerly by a branch. There would be sun, still, for the best part of an hour. He loosened his battle-blouse and felt the gentle warmth on his face and throat. The jagging of worry was smoothed in him; his unhappiness became dark and still. Tomorrow and next week kept their distance, dimmed by the huge presence of time, love, and death. He felt that kind of false resignation which can deceive us when we contemplate trouble at a moment of not actually experiencing it. This tranquil solitude seemed to him like loneliness made reconcilable by an act of will.

A foot rustled in the beech-mast across the stream. He didn't want his peace disturbed; he sank deeper in the grass and pretended to doze. A voice said, "Why, Laurie. Hello."

Laurie said, "Hello. Come over and talk to me." He felt, evident as the sunlight, a great shining inevitability, and the certainty that something so necessary must be right.

Andrew took off his socks and shoes, and paddled across. Sitting beside Laurie, he worked his bare feet into the grass, to get off the mud. Now he was here, Laurie could think of nothing to say. Andrew on the other hand seemed to have gained assurance. As he stretched against the grass, his eyes, narrowed against the bright sky, reflecting its light clear blue, he looked at home in the place, freer, more sharply defined. "You *have* found yourself a private Eden, haven't you?"

"It isn't private," Laurie said. "Everyone's invited;

74

but only the serpent comes." He produced Mrs. Chivers' tract.

Andrew rolled over on his elbows, skimmed the first page, and remarked, "I always think one of the world's most awkward questions is 'Are you saved?' One's more or less forced to sound either un-co-operative and defeatist, or complacent beyond belief."

"I think I said one can only hope for the best; but she seemed to think it rather evasive."

"Well, what else could one say? I should like to take my shirt off; would it upset her?"

He rolled it into a bundle and put it behind his head. His body was slim, but more solid and compact than one would have thought, and very brown, with the tan deepest across the backs of the arms and shoulders, as it is with laborers who bend to their work. His hands, which were structurally long and fine, were cracked and calloused, and etched with dirt which had gone in too deep to wash away.

Laurie, who had been some time silent, looked up from the tract he had seemed to be reading. "I suppose the polite comeback would be 'No, but I should like you to save me.'" He flipped the paper over quickly. "Do you believe in hell?"

Andrew, who was holding a frond of fern against the sky, said, "Well, I should think your opinion would be the one worth having."

At twenty-three, one is not frightened off a conversation merely by the fear of its becoming intense. But intensity can be a powerful solvent of thin and brittle protective surfaces, and at twenty-three one is well aware of this. Laurie looked around at the pale gentle sunshine, the ripe fruit mildly awaiting its passive destiny, sleeping around the life in the core.

"Don't ask me," he said. "I'm just a do-it-yourself amateur. Boys! Get this smashing outfit and make your own hell. Complete with tools and easy instructions. Not a toy, but a real working model which will take in your friends and last for years. Or isn't that what you meant?"

"Yes, I suppose it is. I'm taking advantage of you,

you see, because you give me the chance. What's the joke?"

"Nothing. It's the sun in my eyes. Go on."

"Oh, it's just that you could tell me so much I ought to know; but I don't know if you want to think about it any more."

"No, it's all right." Laurie pulled a long tassel of field grass and slid the smooth seeds off the stem. "Carry on, what is it?"

"Well, for instance—when it started, did you have any doubt about what you'd do?"

"No, I don't think so. I mean, of course, I thought the whole thing was a bloody muckup and ought to have been prevented. But then it just seemed something that had happened to one, like getting caught in the rain." Now for the first time he realized how important it had been not to admit any alternative to the hard, decent, orthodox choice which need not be regarded as a choice at all; how important not to be different. "Probably," he said, striving for honesty, "I didn't think too much in case it got awkward. I can't remember now. Of course, one had other sorts of doubt. What would become of one, not just that sort of thing"—he jerked a quick thumb at the crutch half buried in the grass—"but what one would turn into, how one would make out. You know."

"Yes, of course. Has it been like you thought?"

"No, not really. Months of boredom, followed by a sort of nightmare version of one of those ghastly picnics where all the arrangements break down. One thing, it shakes you out of that sort of basic snobbery which makes you proud of not being a snob. On the other hand it doesn't alter your own tastes, I mean things like music, and however you look at it the people round you don't share them, and when you feel less superior it seems you feel more lonely. Except in action, of course, which is what one's there for but for me it didn't last very long."

"You've got a sense of proportion out of it, though you didn't say that."

"It's a very limited one, I assure you."

Suddenly Andrew sat up, and clasped his bare arms

around his knees. His face had hardened with some inward resolution. He was looking straight before him; his profile, firm, intent, and for a moment absolutely still, had a clear austerity imposed on a latent sweetness, which seemed to Laurie unbearably beautiful. As he looked away Andrew turned around. "We can't go on like this, can we?"

"Meaning?" said Laurie. His heart gave a racing start that almost choked him. The sky, the water, the fine leaves through which the late sun was shining, had the supernal brightness which precedes a miracle.

"You know what I mean. What about *your* question? Am I afraid to fight? After all, you've got a right to know."

Laurie couldn't speak for a few seconds. The lift and the drop had been too much. Then he remembered how silence might be taken. "Good God, what bull, I've never thought of it. Anyway, if you were you wouldn't bring it up."

"Why not? It would still be just as important. Actually, of course, the answer is I don't know. It's not a thing you can know in theory. I wish I did know for certain, naturally one would rather have it proved. But that only matters to me. I mean, the rightness of a thing isn't determined by the amount of courage it takes. It must have taken a lot to assassinate Abraham Lincoln, for instance."

"Fair enough. I should think more crimes have probably been committed by chaps with inferiority complexes trying to demonstrate their virility, than even for money."

"Well, about six months before the war started I went off walking for a week to think about all this. It was rather a shock to the Friends that I could have doubts, but they were wonderful about it, especially Dave. I thought all around it. I thought there might conceivably even be some circumstances when I felt it was right to kill. If I knew whom I was killing and the circumstances and the nature of the responsibility. What I finally stuck at was surrendering my moral choice to men I'd never met, about whose moral standards I knew nothing whatever."

"Yes, I know; but in Napoleon's day if you wanted to cross the Channel in the middle of the war and talk sensibly to the enemy there was almost nothing to stop you. Even in 1914 they had the Christmas Truce and it very nearly worked. Nowadays we're all sealed off in airtight cans and there's nothing between war and surrender. You can't convert a propaganda machine."

"'Machine' is journalese." Often in his concentration he made statements whose brusqueness he didn't notice. "Inexact terms like that are part of the war psychosis. People are never machines, even when they want to be. You have to start somewhere."

"Only an awful lot of innocent people are going to suffer meanwhile."

"I know," said Andrew. "That's the whole crux, of course." His blue eyes stared at the moving water. "One could say, which is true, that war's such a boomerang it's impossible to guarantee anyone's protection in the long run. We went into this to protect Poland, and look what's happening to the Poles now. But that would really be side-stepping the issue. It's a very terrible responsibility, or it would be if one had to take it without help."

"Whose help did you ask, then?" asked Laurie rather coldly. He had not been pleased by the introduction of Dave's name a few minutes before, and jealousy made him stupid. Andrew's meaning broke on him, devastatingly, a second too late.

"Sorry," he said with difficulty. "I really am a clod. Have you been a Quaker—a Friend I mean—all your life?"

"I'm not a very good one; please don't judge the Society by me."

"Your people don't belong, then?"

"No, they've always been soldiers."

"God! This must have been difficult for you."

"Not compared with a lot of others. I'll tell you about my father sometime; but now I'd rather talk about you."

Laurie sat for a few moments collecting his thoughts. Presently he said, "I never can put these things very well. But I suppose, though it sounds cockeyed, I don't fancy the idea of a State where your lot would all be rotting in concentration camps. I know you'd be ready to go there and I suppose that ought to alter my feeling, but it doesn't, so there you are."

"It should," said Andrew. His face had stiffened and the light in it was gone. Now he looked just a stubborn boy with good bones and a brown skin.

Laurie took the point. He saw how it is possible to idealize people for one's own delight, while treading on their human weaknesses like dirt. "Look," he said, "get this straight. I'm not trying to put you under an obligation to the army for defending you, I'm not so bloody unfair. You haven't asked to be defended, you don't want to be, and I suppose it makes me your enemy, in a way, as much as Hitler is. I'm only trying to explain how some of our lot think."

"Nothing could make us enemies," said Andrew in a rush. Laurie didn't look around, in case his happiness showed in his eyes. Andrew said with sudden awkwardness, "I'm sorry to be so adolescent. It was what you thought, of course. Sometimes one can get one's mind straight but one's feelings take longer."

"You're telling me," said Laurie smiling. But he mustn't indulge this private humor, he thought, it was far too dangerous. He said briskly, "I thought you wanted to ask me about the army, or something."

Andrew paused hesitantly, trailing a foot in the stream. Laurie watched with a moment's sharp envy his relaxed body unconscious of its own ease. The knee had started a cramp, from the evening chill and lying in one position; he moved it stiffly and carefully when Andrew wasn't looking. "I can guess what you want to ask anyway. Have I killed anyone and how did it feel? Well, my answer's as good as yours. I don't know. Any half of us will tell you the same. Our lot fired, and some of their lot died, that's all. It encourages loose thinking, like you say. Funny thing, though, when you think, all those murder trials before the war, people coming for miles to stare at a man merely because he'd killed just one human being. And then overnight, snap, homicides are much commoner than bank clerks, they sit around in pubs talking boring shop about it. 'Oh, by the way, Laurie, how many men have you killed, approximately?' 'Honestly, my dear, I was so rushed, you know, I couldn't stop to look, a couple perhaps.' Have an apple."

They bit into the glossy winesaps; on the sunny side of the fruit, the clear crimson had run below the skin and streaked the crisp, white flesh.

"You see," said Laurie presently, "it's all a muddle, nothing clearcut."

Andrew didn't answer. As soon as Laurie turned he looked away, not furtively but rather shyly. During his last term at school, when it had seemed to be a fairly generally held view that he hadn't made too bad a job of the House, Laurie had sometimes caught the tail-end of looks like that. But this time it seemed too much that it should be true, and he dared not believe in it. He put his head back in the grass, watching its fine stalks laced against the sky. The world was full of a golden undemanding stillness. Even the wretchedness of the afternoon now seemed only the gate that had brought him to this place. But this reminded him to look at his watch; it was time to go.

Andrew got up first and held out his arm smiling, managing to make it seem a light-hearted gesture like that of children who pull each other up from the ground for fun. Laurie had observed sometimes in the ward how his tact would conquer his diffidence. His grip was firm and his rough hand had a kindly warmth in it. He had remembered to have the crutch ready in the other hand before he pulled.

As they walked back through the orchard the grass was deep green in the twilight; but across the stream the tops of the beeches, catching the last sun, burned a deep copper against a cloudless aquamarine sky.

"My gramophone's come," said Laurie. "But——" He stopped, because the door of the cottage had opened, disclosing a square of dusky lamplight against which Mrs. Chivers stood sharply black and animated, like a figure in an early bioscope. She still had her hat on.

"Hello, Mrs. Chivers," said Laurie. "We're just

going. Thank you so much. This is a friend of mine, Andrew Raynes."

Mrs. Chivers came nearer. As she left the lamplit door she grew three-dimensional again. Her little face, yellow and creased with wrinkles as if the skin had been wrung out and hung over the bone, peered up at them, bright-eyed.

"Young man," she said, "why aren't you in khaki?"

Laurie gazed at her blankly; it was as if one of the ripe apples had proved, as one bit it, to contain a bee. Andrew said seriously, "I'm a pacifist, Mrs. Chivers, I belong to the Friends."

Mrs. Chivers looked up under her hat, rattling the cherries; she stood no more than five feet, and had to tilt the brim to see them. "Take shame to yourself. I've heard of that. Friends, indeed. A big strong lad as you be, I wonder you can look your friends in the face. It's all foretold in the blessed Scriptures, Battle of Armageddon, that's what our lads are fighting. Conscientious, I never heard such stuff."

"Mrs. Chivers," said Laurie when he could get it in endways, "Andrew's a friend of mine. He's doing war work, you know. He's all right."

Ignoring him, she thrust her head out at Andrew, like a furious little wren. "And mark my words, young man, if you come here talking your wicked nonsense to this dear wounded boy of mine, and trying to make him run away from the war, I'll write to Lord Kitchener myself about you. *He'll* know what to do."

"I won't hurt him," said Andrew gently. "I promise you that."

"I should think not indeed. Get away with you out of my garden, it's no place for the likes of you. Now, sonny, that's enough, I'm ashamed of you speaking up for him, and you in the King's uniform. Run away home, the pair of you. I've no patience."

The orchard smelt of September and early dew; the grass in the deep light was now the color of emerald. A blackbird, the last awake, was meditating aloud in a round, sweet whistle. Everything had the colors of farewell.

Andrew was walking ahead, but when he noticed

81

Laurie's awkward haste behind him he waited, surrendering his breathing space: Laurie reflected that being a cripple involves special kinds of social finesse, which only come gradually. "I'm terribly sorry," he said.

"No, I ought to have thought, it's being with you that makes me forget. I shouldn't have come in and spoilt all this for you."

"She'll have forgotten by tomorrow." They had come to the tall yews by the gate; it was very old, and flakes of paint and rust came away as he touched it. He had said the sensible thing and it would be wise to leave it there. The huge bulk of the yew trees was like dark-veined malachite against the bronze-gold sky. He was filled with a vast sense of the momentous, of unknown mysteries. He did not know what he should demand of himself, nor did it seem to matter, for he had not chosen this music he moved to, it had chosen him. He smiled at Andrew in the shadow of the yews.

> *"They looking back, all th' eastern side beheld*
> *Of Paradise, so late their happy seat,*
> *Wav'd over by that flaming Brand, the Gate*
> *With dreadful Faces throng'd and fiery Arms . . ."*

Andrew put his hands on the top of the gate and swung it open. His face had a solemn improvising look. He said,

> *". . . They hand in hand, with wandering steps and slow,*
> *Through Eden took their solitary way."*

Laurie went through the gate, out into the lane. Two great horses, ringing with idle brass, were being led home, their coats steaming in the cool. He felt absolute, filled; he could have died then content, empty-handed and free. All gifts he had ever wished for seemed only traps, now, to dim him and make him less. This, he thought with perfect certainty, this after all is to be young, it is for this. Now we have the strength to make our memories, out of hard stuff, out of steel and crystal.

The steam of the horses, a good strong russet smell,

hung on the air. Sailing in a deep inlet of sky off the black coast of an elm tree, the first star appeared, flickering like a riding-light in a fresh wind. Andrew walked beside him silently.

An eddy of air in the quiet lane brought back like an echo the stamp and jingle of the horses, a shake of the bridle and a snort.

... Let us say, then, that the soul resembles the joined powers of a pair of winged horses and a charioteer. Now the horses and drivers of the gods are of equal temper and breed, but with men it is otherwise. ...

For the first time in months, he had remembered the dirty little parcel done up in newspaper at the back of his locker. It had contained the things saved from his pockets after Dunkirk, when the clothes had been cut away. A pocket-knife; a pipe he had been trying to get used to; a lighter; and the book Lanyon had given him seven years ago, with a brown patch of blood across the cover, and the edges of the pages stuck at the top. At different times he had tried the knife, the pipe, and the lighter, found them ruined, and thrown them away. The book had looked done for, too; but it was still there.

5

LAURIE was anxious to get the gramophone out of the ward before it was noticed; he had not forgotten that a former patient had been accustomed to play his against the radio. Under cover of night he passed it to Andrew, who received it with joy; the c.o.s had had only one gramophone among them, and it had broken down. Laurie apologized for the records; but this proved to be quite unnecessary. A few days later the hospital rang with a new and sensational scandal: eight nurses had been found by the matron in the orderlies' common-room, dancing with the orderlies.

The news soon got to the wards, where it divided opinion as decisively as the Dreyfus affair. The hard core of animosity centered on Neames; his cold resentment, which had seemed temperate at the outset compared with noisier indignations, had outlasted them all. Willis was surprisingly tepid. As for Reg, he was anti-matron before anything else. He spent a happy day imputing to little Derek unimaginable excesses; but these two understood each other perfectly.

It took Laurie some hours of unobtrusive intelligence work to learn that Andrew hadn't been there. He enjoyed this relief till the evening, when they met, and it turned out that Andrew had merely left before the matron's arrival, being due on duty.

"It's very interesting," he said, fixing Laurie with his candid gray eyes, "very primitive, you know. Subconsciously they feel we're a biological loss and ought not to have women or propagate ourselves. John in the kitchen said that was sure to happen, but as a matter of principle we shouldn't submit to it."

Laurie needed a moment or two to recover from this. "But did you want to have any of them?"

"Oh, not *literally*." Andrew looked amused. "I have hopes for John, I must admit; but it's much too early to say anything."

"Who did you dance with?" asked Laurie, who had just ordered himself to change the subject.

"Most of them, as far as I remember. I danced with Nurse Adrian twice."

"Did you find plenty to talk about?"

"Yes, we talked about you." Andrew smiled, and settled his head back on his arms. "We were in favor of you," he added sleepily. He had only just got up.

They sat on a bank scattered with old beech-mast. Through a gap in the bronze trees, across the stream, the apples of Eden could be seen, blandly shining. It was like Limbo, Laurie remarked.

"Who is Limbo supposed to be for?" asked Andrew. "I can never remember."

"The good pagans, to whom the faith was never revealed. Such as Plato, I suppose; Buddha, Socrates,

84

Confucius, and so on. A sort of eternal consolation prize."

Laurie settled his back into the slope, and lit a cigarette. The stream sounded different from this side, mixed with the dry whisper of the beeches. After a few minutes he said, "How would you feel about your mother marrying again?"

After a pause Andrew said, "I don't know. I daresay I shouldn't have cared for it, really. Now, of course, I feel I should be only too glad, if it meant she was alive."

This caused the inevitable awkwardness and apologies; but a little later he made no difficulty about talking. He had been born into one of those army families where every second or third generation throws off a sport, a musician perhaps, or a brilliant agricultural crank. Andrew's father had served with distinction through the First World War, and had gone to Germany with the Army of Occupation. Peace had not been signed and the blockade was still on: an undisciplined habit grew up among the Allied troops of giving away their rations to the match-limbed, potbellied German children. An Order of the Day had to be issued about it. In the following week Andrew's father, about whom no one had noticed anything odd except a certain taciturnity, resigned from his regiment, arranged his affairs at home in a family atmosphere of shocked silence, joined the Friends' Ambulance Service, and went back to Germany again. There, some months later, he met and married Andrew's mother, a lifelong Quaker; they continued working together until she became pregnant. While she was in England awaiting Andrew's birth, the unit, which was by now in Austria, went to deal with a typhus epidemic. Overworked and under par, Andrew's father got the disease, and in a couple of days was dead.

Dave had known both his parents, Andrew said. In fact, Dave was almost his only living link with his mother. He had been in charge of the unit, and it had been to Dave that Andrew's father, in a more or less lucid interval of fever, had dictated his will.

At this point, Laurie was shocked to find his mind

85

centered entirely on the unfair advantage this start had given to Dave, who, Laurie thought, on the strength of all this seemed to have assumed almost proprietary airs; there must be something behind it. But Andrew had noticed his lapse of attention, and evidently feared the story was becoming a bore. He dried up, and it took a couple of minutes to get him going again.

He had been brought up as a Quaker by his mother, to whom, obviously, he had been passionately devoted. If half he said about her was true, she had been an exceptionally gifted saint. When he spoke of her Laurie saw, as he had never seen in him at other times, a strain of fanaticism. She had died very suddenly when he was twelve, leaving no relatives who could do with him. His paternal grandmother, however, had been more than willing. It had been anguish to her all this time to see their good stock running to waste. She had treated him with kindness, and in her way with tact, never slighting his mother's memory except in the daily implications of the code she taught him. The uncle and aunt, to whom he was passed on at her death a couple of years later, were less tactful. They had tried to send him at fifteen to the family school, which prepared for the army; he had refused to go there; they had insisted; Andrew had written the headmaster a letter which had caused him to turn Andrew down as an unsuitable entrant. There had been a shattering row about it, during some stage of which Andrew had appealed to Dave whom at that time he hardly knew. Dave had turned up, only to be insulted by the uncle and shown the door; but from that time onward, Andrew had kept in touch with him.

Throughout this crisis, Andrew seemed to have behaved, according to the view one was inclined to take of it, with rocklike integrity or mulish obstinacy; in any case, with determination much beyond his years. His face became a different shape when he spoke of it; incongruously, one could now trace the soldier forebears in the set of his jaw. Laurie gathered that during the row something had been said about the mother which Andrew, if he had forgiven it, couldn't forget; but he never told Laurie what it was.

They had sent him in the end to a moderately progressive school, where he had enjoyed the term and dreaded the holidays. Then his call-up papers had arrived, heralding an explosion fiercer than any that had gone before. He talked of this less easily and Laurie could see that he was still raw from it.

But for the war, he said, changing the subject, he would have been going up to Oxford this autumn. The college he had been entered for was just across the road from Laurie's, and they reflected solemnly on the fact that they would have missed one another by a matter of a month or two. Quite likely, said Laurie, they would have run into each other somehow or other. Andrew smiled, and said yes, it seemed that they were meant to meet. Laurie lived on these words for the next two days.

The week after, Laurie's own mother wrote to him, announcing her engagement to Mr. Straike. There is only one kind of shock worse than the totally unexpected: the expected for which one has refused to prepare.

He was still staring at the open letter when he heard Reg creaking and breathing near him, minding his own business with that heavy tact which invites a confidence. Suddenly Laurie craved for those kind flat feet trampling down the sharper edges of his misery. He looked up.

"Cheer up, cock," said Reg in a leading voice. "All the same in a hundred years."

"That's right. Not so hot now, though."

"How's that, then?" Reg sat down beside him on the bed.

Laurie told him the news. He did not canvass Reg's views on Mr. Straike. When Reg said politely "No kidding?" and then "Bit unexpected, like?" there was perfect understanding between them.

"Mind you," said Reg, "it's a nice position for her. Nice house and that, too, I daresay."

Laurie thought of the red, damp Gothic pile of the vicarage, its high, heavy rooms and horrid little lancet windows. He and his mother had lived in their seventeenth-century cottage almost since he could remember.

For the first time he realized that this too would have to go.

"Never told you, did I," said Reg, "our dad nearly got caught, seven year it must be going on for now. Girl young enough to be his daughter. Never forget him bringing her home to tea. Only had to look at her. Well, I mean, you don't know how to put it, like, to your own dad. Then my brother Len found out she was in the family way by a chap at his works. He had to tell the old man then. Proper broke him up, for a bit; and poor old Len, he didn't like to show up at home for a couple of months; missed his birthday and all. Well, one thing, you got nothing like that to worry about with your mum. 'S all aboveboard and that."

"Oh, yes. I think he was keen to get it fixed up before I got home."

"Ah. On the artful side. Not after your mum's money, you don't reckon?"

"She hasn't got much. It would help, I suppose."

"Well, one way to look at it, you do know who he is. Not one of these fly-by-nights, mean to say. Mind you, Spud, it's partly just the idea, like, and you get used to that. Still, got to face it, home's not the same. Here, Spud. No offense and that, but this girl, now; I wouldn't let her slip off the hook, not if I was you."

"Girl?" said Laurie, taken off his guard.

"Come off it, now, you told me about her only the other day."

"Oh, that. I don't think that will ever come to much."

"More fool you, excuse me saying so. Be better off with you than someone with two good legs what kicked her with them Saturday nights, wouldn't she?"

"I suppose so."

"Right, then. That's how you want to keep looking at it."

Laurie agreed to do so. Meanwhile, there was his mother's letter to answer. After tearing up two versions which read too revealingly, he urged quite simply a pause for consideration. He sealed, stamped, and addressed it, with a heavy sense of its ultimate uselessness.

The only other person with whom he discussed the news was Nurse Adrian, whom he met at the village post office when he was posting the letter. On the spur of the moment he invited her to tea at one of the rickety tables in the postmistress's garden, and told her all, or nearly all, about it. It was pleasant, he found, to see her listening, her bare brown arms with their soft down folded on the table, her brown little face, under the straight flaxen hair looped back at the side, looking honest and troubled. At the end she said, "I'll tell you something if you like I've never told anyone. When Bill, he's my brother, he's a prisoner of war now, when Bill was engaged two years ago to Vera, who of course is now my sister-in-law, and she really is a terribly nice person, she got pneumonia. I was lying in bed one night and my thoughts were sort of running on, and suddenly I woke up and *looked* at them, and I realized I'd been planning for when Vera was dead just like one might for the holidays. And she'd always been *perfectly* nice to me, even when I was in the way. Yet I knew I'd been wishing her dead, can you believe that? So, you see, if a person who's had such terrible thoughts can get over it, and I *have* got over it, you're bound to get over it before long."

He saw her looking at him with sudden anxiety; after this confession she was clearly prepared to see him turn from her with loathing. Without thinking much about it he leaned out and patted her folded arms.

"Get along with you," he said. "You know perfectly well if anything had really happened you'd have jumped into the river to pull her out." Her unguarded eyes looked at him across the crumby little table, in admiration and relief. In them he saw himself reflected, a man, protecting, lightly lifting the burden. It did not seem to him specially ironic. His loneliness had preserved in him a good deal of inadvertent innocence; there was much of life for which he had no formula; it had never even occurred to him that he involved himself in various kinds of effort which, by ruling a few lines around himself, he could have avoided.

She gazed at him with respect, and presently asked his opinion on the probable course of the war. Silly little dumbbell, he thought; but he could not analyze his affectionate amusement. The fact was that he found her a refreshing relief, and was already cutting and fitting himself a special personality to oblige her. He could be no more than three or four years her senior, but it felt like fifteen. Ever since he grew up he had been unobtrusively avoiding girls, whom secretly he imagined to be applying subtle and sophisticated tests to him, and observing the results with hidden scorn. Watching her off, he thought that she wore slacks well, as if she didn't think about them; she had the right kind of shoes, and moved from the hips. He smiled and waved, and, as he turned away, wondered what the brother was like.

Back in the ward, with the radio blaring "Roll Out the Barrel," the thought of his mother came back to him, burning with all its implications deeper and deeper in; whole vistas of the future, as he reviewed them, suddenly becoming consumed and blowing away. He longed for the evening which would bring the relief of telling Andrew.

"Been out?" said Reg as they waited for supper.

"Not far. It's nice outside. Warm."

"Sharp frost this morning. Nice now, is it?"

"Yes, nice out of the wind."

"Here, Spud. No offense and that."

"Uh?" Laurie went deep into his locker after a cigarette.

"Well, see, Spud, I know how it is. No one here can't say you ever done any highbrow act. But what I mean, these lads come along, college boys like yourself, reading literary books and that. Well, stands to reason, ordinary, you have to keep a lot of your thoughts to yourself. I watched you when you didn't know it, time and again."

Laurie came crimson out of the locker, where he longed to remain. "Christ, Reg, the bull you talk." They sat, not looking at each other. Laurie knew his protest had been too weak; it should have been something more like "What would I want with that bunch of sissies?" Why, he wondered, was it the people one held

90

in the most innocent affection who so often demanded from one the most atrocious treachery?

"They interest me," he said, doing his best. "You can't help wondering what's at the bottom of it, whether they just don't like the idea of getting hurt, or what. Well, having seen a bit of them I don't think it's that. It may be with some of them; but not this lot."

"Ah, go on, Spud, don't tell me you've been this long working that one out. I could have told you that, first day they come here. I watched them, I never said nothing. Not even Neames don't think they're yellow, no matter what he gives out. It's just the idea, like, that gets him. Same as what it does me, and that's a fact."

"Fair enough, so it does me in a way. But as people, you know——"

"That kid that does the ward at night, the young one, properly took to you, hasn't he?"

"Me?" said Laurie. He went back quickly into the locker again. "Can't say I've noticed it specially."

"What I'm getting at, Spud, you want to watch it. No offense."

"Come again?" said Laurie into the locker.

"I mean the law," said Reg with deliberation, "that's what I mean." He paused to push back the wet shreds into the end of his cigarette. " 'Course, Spud, if you can talk some sense into him, good enough. But if he tries to start in on you, that's where you want to watch it. Because that's an offense. Seducing His Majesty's troops from their allegiance. High treason, that is. Got to look out for yourself in this world, 'cause no one won't do it for you."

"That's right," said Laurie. He took a long steadying draw on his cigarette. "I appreciate it, Reg. Don't worry, I guarantee that if any seducing goes on it'll be done by me." He held his breath. Look out you don't cut yourself, Reg had once said.

Reg said, approvingly, "Ah. That's more like it. That's all a lad like that wants, someone to make a man of him."

After a restless night, he was awake in time for the six o'clock news. It seemed to him to contain more than the usual number of euphemisms and it occurred to him that fresh ones were steadily being coined, which met with less and less resistance. One by one the short bloody words, which kept the mind's eye alive, were vanishing: a man-killing bomb was an anti-personnel bomb now. He remarked upon this to Neames, who was standing beside him.

Neames hitched his dressing-gown, giving Laurie a hard sideways glance. The two of them were always getting involved in arguments; but, as the only men in the ward who acknowledged the rules of logic in debate, they put up with each other for the sake of conversation. "Morale's a munition of war," Neames said.

"Morale's just another blanket-word. What does it mean? Courage, or bloody-mindedness, or not asking awkward questions, or does it mean whatever we're told it means from day to day?"

Neames's dressing-gown was a faded purple; it made his rather sallow face look yellow. He hitched the girdle again. "I'm afraid that's too intellectual for me," he said. "You'd better talk to your friends about it." He turned his shoulder, and walked away.

Laurie felt a little sinking jolt. He remembered, now, seeing last night the little group gathered around Willis in a corner. Luckily, Andrew had been in the next ward, and hadn't heard.

He was still thinking about it while he made Reg's bed. Reg couldn't do it for himself, and patients whose beds were made by the staff had to be waked an hour earlier. Feeling a twitch on the opposite side of the blanket, he looked up expecting to see Reg back from the bath; but it was Dave, who must have come early on duty as he often did. He made beds with mechanical efficiency, like a trained nurse. When he caught Laurie's eye he smiled without speaking. Often as he worked he seemed occupied with his own thoughts.

"I can manage, thank you," said Laurie politely. "I expect you're busy."

"Not for the moment," said Dave. He flicked back a corner expertly, flattened it, and tucked it in.

At the end of the ward, Andrew came in pushing the breakfast trolley. He steered it carefully around the center table at the bottom of the ward. As soon as this tricky bit was done his eyes came over toward Laurie as they always did. This time he felt rather than saw it, for he did not look. He was rather slow with his side of the bed, and Dave had to wait, which he did very patiently.

As they moved up to the top end of the sheet, Laurie looked up. He said, "You're one of the organizers, aren't you?"

"Not exactly, but I won't split hairs if there's anything I can do." Dave picked up the pillow and slapped it into shape.

"It's nothing much really." They shook out the top sheet. "But the other day I was talking with one of your people, getting his angle and so on. Afterwards someone said it could have landed him in trouble, treason or some nonsense. I suppose that's just a lot of—— I mean there isn't anything in it?"

Dave mitered a corner. "I suppose," he said easily, "that would be Andrew."

"Yes. Yes, Andrew Raynes."

"I doubt whether Andrew would say anything technically treasonable. He knows the rules. He didn't urge you to desert, for instance, or refuse to obey orders?"

"Oh, God, no. He just explained things."

"Well, knowing Andrew, I should say the position probably is that you could make trouble for him if you wanted to, but it would depend on you."

"Seeing I started it, that's hardly likely."

"That's what I thought."

Laurie picked up the counterpane on which ugly stencilled flowers, in a hard red and prussian blue, wound around a black trellis. Studying this pattern carefully, he said, "I suppose he told you more or less what we talked about."

"You won't find he's like that." Dave moved the center fold more to the middle. "I remember his saying some time ago that he found you easy to talk to. I didn't warn him to be careful; it didn't strike me as being necessary."

"Well," said Laurie, "thanks." There was a curious moment in which the small space around the bed contained two different kinds of silence. It was broken by the rattle of the breakfast trolley behind them. As they turned Andrew looked from one to the other, his pleasure in their amity as plain as print.

Over his bacon and tea, Laurie felt that the only comfort would be found in full-time, party-line nondeviationist hatred. One could warm oneself with a good thick hate by shutting all the windows and doors; but he knew, unfortunately, beforehand, that the snugness would not last, and the fug would drive him out into the cold again, gasping for air.

About a week later, on the day when Reg was liberated from his airplane splint, Laurie got his surgical boot.

He was sent into the Sister's office to try it on. There it was, with an ordinary boot for the left foot all complete; black, shiny, hitting the floor with a clump. He had not foreseen that the design of the upper would be quite so ugly, nor the sole so thick, but after all, a cripple's boot was a cripple's boot. Perhaps after the war . . .

"Comfy, son? Because now's the time to say. You've got to live with it, remember."

"Yes," said Laurie. "I know." He felt sure the bootmaker's man had meant well.

Out in the corridor he clumped stiffly up and down: it felt heavy and seemed to shift the weight to a different muscle which was unused to it; but it was pleasant to walk again without a sideways lurch. It was going to be a bit tiring at first, but this was an adaptation he would have every day of a lifetime to make. In a few years it would be like spectacles to a myope, he would only notice its absence. He walked on, toward the ward, getting ready the bit of clowning which would ease him over his entrance. One might as well learn to laugh it off, because this was not transitional like the crutch or the stick. This, henceforward, was Laurie Odell.

He walked in, ostentatiously not using the stick, twirling it like a drum major.

For the day of this event he had a firm date with

94

Reg of several weeks' standing. He could in fact have applied for a cinema pass before, but the airplane splint had made Reg as awkward in crowds as an antlered stag, and Laurie had waited with little enough impatience; he and Andrew took it for granted now that they would meet every evening unless something prevented it.

The bus got them into town just at opening time, a party of six. Reg and Laurie stood drinks, in honor of their emancipation. Then a civilian, who was several drinks ahead, insisted on standing pints all round, and on the strength of it decided to make a speech. He had a fine carrying voice, which reached to every corner of the bar.

"What do our lads ask?" he demanded, repeating it several times, and then pausing to savor the respectful silence. "Not a medal. Lads like these two here"—he made a large expanded gesture at Laurie and Reg—"they don't ask to go up to Bucknam Palace and shake King George by the hand. They don't want no disabled badge to wear, they don't need it. Anyone only got to look at these two lads, he can see for himself. And what do they ask, that's what I ask you? What do they ask? Only a square deal, a square deal for rich and poor alike. . . ."

He turned to harangue the crowd on his other side. Laurie pulled at Reg's sleeve. Reg gave a swift repining glance at the froth halfway up his mug, and nodded. They slipped out. The pale street of sky above the blacked-out shops reflected a dim glimmer on the oily wet street below.

"Got away before the collection," Reg said.

"That's right."

"Funny, how some chap'll get stinking in a pub, and if he carries on in that certain voice, no one don't listen no more than if he was talking Dutch."

"I suppose not."

"Know how I look at it, Spud? Got to get used to people. Sometime we all got to. Mean to say, if it's not one thing it's another. Take some other chap, say. Got trouble at home, maybe. Silly muggers sticking their oar in, only making it worse. See what I mean?"

"Yes, I know, Reg."

"Well, then. What I mean, they say put yourself in the other chap's place. But what I reckon, it's more of a knack, see, and not many people got it. Now you got it, Spud. You got it more than anyone I know. So stands to reason, you expect it back, that's human nature. Well, you're out of luck, Spud, that's all. That's life and you got to face it, may as well face it first as last. See what I mean?"

"Ah, cut it out, Reg, it was just for laughs. Let's drop in somewhere and have the other half."

"Over the road's a nice one. Quiet."

As they stepped onto the opposite curb, a cloud of warm scent steamed over them, mixed with the smell of cheap fur.

"Hiya, fellers." The voice was fake Hollywood, spread thinly over urban Wessex. "Where's the big hurry? Remember us?"

"Ah?" said Reg noncommittally. He peered into the gloom. Laurie felt a swift nudge and realized that the pause had been for appraisal rather than identification. He knew that Reg's marriage vow was, on his side, intact; what this meant to his conscience was unknown, but Laurie had a good idea of what it meant to his self-respect, and as a talking-point. All this Reg was prepared to offer up in the cause of taking Laurie out of himself. He suspected that the sacrifice wasn't looking to Reg absolutely intolerable. Embarrassment robbed him momentarily of all presence of mind.

"You guys still fond of dancing?" the girl said.

Reg took a step backward. "Pardon me," he said formally. "You're making a mistake, Miss. Me and my friend haven't had the pleasure. Got to be going now. Good night."

"Ooh! La-di-dah!" the second girl emerged from the shadows. She was very young, seventeen at most. "Don't be soppy. No need to dance for a good time." She giggled.

It wasn't fair, Laurie thought reluctantly, to leave it all to Reg. "Sorry, girls," he said. "We're on our way to a date."

At the sound of his voice the first girl diverted, suddenly, her attention from Reg to him. He was enabled to see in the gloom the pancake make-up on her bad skin, and the large generous mouth painted over the little mean one. Their eyes met. Then she swung around on her three-inch heel.

"Oh, come on, Doreen, what you waiting for? Sorry, boys, I'm sure. *You're* all right, so long as you got each other." She tittered shrilly. "Bye-bye, both. Enjoy yourselves."

Slowly, as he steadied his mind, Laurie became aware that Reg was swearing. He was making a speech to the vanishing girls on the lines of "state the alternative preferred, with reasons for your choice."

"Steady on, Reg," he said. He managed to keep his voice even, but knew he could not look at Reg even in the blackout, so didn't try.

"Lost me temper." Reg fell into step beside him. He, too, looked ahead. "Dirty-minded little cats. Make you sick. Well, we missed a lovely evening with those little bits of sunshine. *And* how. Lucky you made up your mind quick, Spud. I reckon you're a better picker than what I am."

The film of the evening was all singing, all dancing, and in Technicolor; so Reg had taken for granted from the first that there was no other possible film to see. The rest of the hospital contingent was all there too. Laurie was glad to get inside; in the queue his leg suddenly started to ache very badly. It must be the boot, because the pain was in a different place. He supposed it would settle down in a few days. Meanwhile he tried to forget it by attending to the film. The star was young, and highly groomed to resemble in face, figure, and range of expression a pin-up in *Esquire*. Laurie could feel the men around him soaking her up through the pores. She was the perennial *eidolon*, the clean pampered harlot, the upper-class luxury article, reduced in some magic bargain-basement to a price within each man's means. The music had occasional moments of narcotic charm; it was relaxing, when not too loud, like a warm bath with colored bath-salts. Laurie's mind withdrew, after a time, to a middle distance behind his eyes, where he thought about Andrew.

He solved no problems, nor attempted it; he made no plans. He was twenty-three: he received infinite consolation and joy merely from the contemplation of Andrew's being.

They were about halfway back when the first of the sirens went. First came a single deep moan; then the mounting, ragged chorus of inhuman howls and wails. The bus was old and noisy, and one could not hear whether planes were about; the usual lugubrious voice announced that one was following them home. Shortly after this, when they were nearly there, a new sound began: the tinny warble of the Imminent Danger siren, which always sounded different after dark.

Laurie shoved at the bus with his will, urging it on. Every minute he waited to see fire spring up beyond the hedges: he imagined the bus arriving to find a rescue squad at work, a covered stretcher passing. "All the men okay. Only one casualty. The night orderly, Raynes. . . ." They reached the gates without incident, two or three minutes later.

As they walked up the covered way, shrapnel rattled like flung stones on the iron roof above them. Something emerged from the background of night noises, a kind of throbbing in the air, a sensation more than a sound at first, then the rhythmic bumbling of a bomber's engines, getting nearer. A small isolated battery, not far off, began to cough and bark; a searchlight fumbled about among the stars, fingering patches of cloud and dropping them and fidgeting off again.

A couple of nurses whom he knew were on the bus; though he was good for little more than moral support, it seemed kind to escort them back to their hut. As he returned toward the ward he saw that two more searchlights were flicking around. The plane was buzzing now like a fly caught on a windowpane; the guns kept swatting at it. A big lump of shrapnel came rattling and scraping down a nearby roof, and fell just beyond him; he stepped back under cover again. Suddenly a tiny silver cross glittered in one of the beams overhead. At once all the others swooped over and closed in. The pursued mote made for another bit of cloud, like a bird for a bush; they lost it again, but the guns banged more

98

eagerly. It was then, as he looked down for a moment to rest the back of his neck, that he saw Andrew standing out in the grass, unsheltered, looking up.

"Hello, there," Laurie said. "What do you think you're doing?"

"Hello," said Andrew. He walked toward Laurie, but didn't come under the roof. Laurie limped angrily over the rough grass toward him.

"For the Lord's sake, come in out of there."

"I will in a minute. I couldn't see properly." Laurie could see his face now. He was smiling. His fair hair, in the glimmer of moonlight, had a faint pale shine. He glowed dimly like a memory or a ghost.

Of all that Laurie felt there was nothing he could release but anger. He gripped the handle of his stick and pushed it viciously into the earth. "You bloody fool. Do you want a chunk of shrapnel in your brain? If you have one? Christ, are you deaf, you can hear it now."

Andrew said, good-humoredly, "You go to bed, or Nurse Sims'll be after you. I'll come in a minute and tuck you up." There was something different about him, elated and defiant, like a schoolboy breaking bounds.

In a controlled voice Laurie said, "Don't they issue you with tin hats?"

"There's a couple hanging up somewhere. Don't they you?"

"Why should they? We've got sense enough to take cover."

"What are you doing messing about here, then?" said Andrew gaily.

The guns bickered again, but the shrapnel went somewhere else. Then they heard the bomber coming back. It sounded lower, and one of the engines was cutting, Laurie thought.

"That plane's been hit," he said. "Listen to it. It's just about due to unload everything it's got left. Are you half-witted or what?"

"I don't suppose that roof would keep out much of a bomb, do you?"

The faint light from the sky caught the outlines of his face, his loose, thin boyish shoulders. He looked intolerably vulnerable and unsecured. Laurie's tension suddenly snapped. "Oh, don't be so bloody pleased with yourself. If you'd ever been under fire you wouldn't think it so funny."

There was a moment's silence.

"I'm sorry," Andrew said. He walked past Laurie onto the covered way. Laurie swung around on his stick and limped after him. "Good night," said Andrew. He began to walk off.

"Come back," said Laurie breathlessly. He reached out, almost losing his balance, and gripped Andrew's shoulder. They faced each other in the almost black shadow beside the deserted office hut.

"For God's sake, Andrew. What do you take me for? You know damn well I didn't mean it like that."

"The more fool you," said Andrew in a flat strained voice. "You ought to have."

"I was in a hurry to get in, that's all. We're a bit of a jittery lot, you know."

Andrew looked around at him. "You can afford that. I shouldn't bother."

"Oh, hell. Look here——"

A bright moving illumination had fallen on the huts, around each tuft of grass wheeled a black swinging shadow. Andrew ran out, and paused; Laurie checked a stumble with a hand on his shoulder. They looked up. A streaming torch was crossing the sky above them, in a steep path like a comet's. It passed out of sight beyond the roofs. There was an instant when the light went out in perfect stillness; the ground under their feet shook with a heavy jar; last came the detonation. The plane must have had most of its bombload still on board.

Laurie let go of Andrew and said, "Well, that's that." Doors began to open in the wards; nurses and patients peered out. Now, finding nothing (the guns had stopped, the searchlights dispersed), they all went in again. "Not bad," said Laurie, "for a little popgun like that."

Andrew didn't reply for a moment or two. Then he said, "How many men do those bombers carry?"

"I don't know. I suppose six or eight." There was

silence again. This diversion was a reminder to him of all separation. Blindly he resisted it. "Hell, that was self-defense if anything could be. If they hadn't been stopped, they might have wiped out a block of work-ing-men's flats by now, or the children's ward at the City Hospital. Wouldn't you have been sorrier about that?"

Andrew turned around and looked at him, mutely and painfully, searching for words. At last he said, "They were dying up there. If they had innocent blood on their hands it was worse for them to die. I ought to have—I was just thinking about myself."

"It's a filthy business," said Laurie awkwardly. "I don't say it isn't."

"You showed me up to myself," said Andrew slowly. "You've got the decency of your own convictions. And you've the courage of your convictions, too."

"Oh, come off it, relax. So've you, we all know that."

"No," said Andrew looking away. "I haven't the courage of mine, not always. I thought so. But I didn't know then what it meant."

"Andrew. Andrew, look here. If you only knew what I really——"

There was the sound of a door opening. "Odell! Are you out there? Odell!"

"Coming, Nurse. Shan't be a minute. If there's any-one who ought to be——"

"Do come along at once, Odell, *please*. I'm trying to get the ward settled."

"Sorry, Nurse, I'm on my way. Look, Andrew my dear——"

"I must go in too. I shouldn't be here. I'll walk with you."

"She's only fussing; no one'll settle till the All Clear. Silly bitch. All this is my fault, you'd have been all right on your own."

"That doesn't arise."

"I don't——"

"Well—I was waiting for you. I saw you taking the nurses back. I——"

"*Odell!* If you don't come straight in I'm going to re-port you."

"Yes, Nurse, coming. Andrew, we must——"

"You must go, she meant that."

"But——"

"Please. I'll be seeing you in the ward."

As he went in he heard the thin, steady shrilling of the All Clear.

Laurie looked up from his home letter to say, "Don't you wish your name was Gareth, Reg?"

"Eh? Wish it was how much?"

"Gareth. That's what my stepfather-elect's called. I suppose he was conceived with Tennyson in limp suede sitting on the po-cupboard."

Reg coughed repressively. Habit had made of the standard nouns and adjectives in his own vocabulary something merely conventional, like italics or points of exclamation. He sometimes found Laurie's conversation highly obscene, and would have voiced his disapproval to anyone he had liked less. "Comes from Wales, I reckon. I had a girl called Gwynneth once. Have a Gold Flake. Ah, come on, got the best part of a packet left. Chap in our unit was called Jutland Jellicoe Clark. Course, being called Clark, that was a help to him. Always got called Nobby, barring when anyone wanted to nark him."

"I might try Uncle Nobby. I've got to call him something."

"You want to go careful at first with a parson. Nice day, today. Lovely the trees look, now they've turned. We always took our holiday August, to get the social life. Never knew it got so pretty. Evenings it gives you the pip, though. Makes you miss home, and that."

"Yes," said Laurie. He remembered how, in other autumns, he and his mother had roasted chestnuts, sitting on a sheepskin rug before the fire.

"Afternoons is the time, though. Lovely it is then."

"How's Madge keeping?" asked Laurie quickly. He was afraid Reg was about to suggest a walk, and today he felt that at any cost he must get away alone.

The declining sun was ripe and warm. Hips and haws shone like polished beads in the hedgerows; the damp mats of fallen leaves had a smoky, rusty smell.

102

There was a bridle-path running between brambles, and a stile he had taught himself to manage. It was all right when no one was about.

The blackberries tasted of frost and faint sun and smoke and purple leaves: sweet, childish, and sad. Soon came the wood, with light edges of coppice, full of birds, and birches beyond; the golden leaves shook like sequins against the sky. Presently the path opened into a field of stooked barley. Along its border he found his old place, a smooth bank running up to a big elm. He lowered himself down, carefully. It had been a long pull up and the knee had hurt him, but it was worth it.

He hadn't been here since two operations back, before he had met Andrew. The barley had been standing in the ear then, dipping and shivering silkily under the running breeze. It was caught now, its fancies were ended. He had brought, he remembered, Herrick to read.

The sun slanted deep into the wood, making hidden birds sing softly. The touch of autumn struck from his youth that cosmic sadness, which time will tame like the bite of spring. Under the pale sun, beauty and fate and love and death ached through him. After a while he sighed, and took out his book.

He found that the sea water hadn't soaked in beyond the notes at the back. The front cover unfortunately recalled the butcher's order book which his mother used to keep, fastidiously, apart from the others; but though the tops of the pages were stained, they parted easily, and inside they were clean. He turned them to and fro, remembering other places where he had read them: in a punt moored to a willow by Magdalen Bridge, on a packing-case behind a Nissen hut; and the first time of all, in a sunny clearing with a stream running through it, a short way from his home. It had struck him with religious awe to find Phaedrus leading Socrates almost, it might have been, to the very spot. The spreading tree, the green bank to lean on, the water cold to the foot: nothing had been wanting, except the votive offerings and the shrine. "Give me to be beautiful within,"

103

Socrates had prayed, "and for me let outward and inward things be reconciled together."

Laurie turned the pages gently; they separated at the top with a crisp little sound. He found the part he was looking for and smoothed it open.

... and so it is with the followers of the other gods. Each man in his life honors, and imitates as well as he can, that god to whose choir he belonged, while he is uncorrupted in his first incarnation here; and in the fashion he has thus learned, he bears himself to his beloved as well as to the rest. So, then, each chooses from among the beautiful a love conforming to his kind; and then, as if his chosen were his god, he sets him up and robes him for worship. ...

Laurie looked up at the barley; if any of the beautiful and ruthless Olympians had owned him they had lost him, he thought.

... and this striving to discover the essence of their proper god, by tracing him in themselves, is rewarded; for they are forced to look on the god without flinching, and when their memory holds him, his breath inspires them, and they share his attributes and his life, as far as man can enter godhead. And for these blessings they thank the loved one, loving him even more dearly ...

Laurie put down the book and folded his arms behind his head. He was not analytical enough yet to have discovered that there are certain loves, and certain phases of love, which bring perfect happiness only in their pauses and intervals, as water grows clear when one's progress has ceased to stir it.

... and it fills the soul of the beloved also ...

As he read on, a cock pheasant made easy by his stillness came picking within a few yards of his feet.

He is in love, therefore, but with whom he cannot say; he does not know what has become of him, he cannot tell. He sees himself in ...

The pheasant, startled, burst up almost into Laurie's face and whirred away; but he scarcely noticed it.

... he sees himself in his lover as if in a mirror, not

knowing whom he sees. And when they are together, he too is released from pain, and when apart, he longs as he himself is longed for; for reflected in his heart is love's image, which is love's answer. But he calls it, and believes it, not love but friendship; though he too——

"That book must be good," said Andrew. "What is it?"

Laurie felt his heart jerk like a shot deer. An uncontrollable reflex, as he sat up, made him slap the book shut and lean his hand on it.

"Good Lord, Andrew," he said breathlessly, "you made me jump half out of my skin."

Andrew came out of the wood behind him, from the footpath he had forgotten.

"Well, I needed that to make me believe you weren't cutting me on purpose. You looked too absorbed to be true."

Something in his voice made Laurie look up at him. His air of ease had not come easily; he was acting; it surprised Laurie to see that he could do it so well. More, he looked tired; for the first time since he had gone on night duty there were dark smears under his eyes.

"Sit down, you're giving me a crick in the neck." Straining not to betray himself or to sound unwelcoming, Laurie could feel himself striking a note of appalling heartiness, like a housemaster on sports day. "What a desperate character you are, turning day into night like this. It's only ten to three. What happened?"

"Nothing." Andrew sat down on the grass beside him. "I felt like a walk."

"If I'd known I'd have waited for you. How did you know where to look?"

"I asked Reg Barker, of course. I always do."

"Do you?" He did not add that Reg had never mentioned it. "Have some blackberries." He had picked a leafful on the way.

Andrew ate one and, turning the next one over, said, "I thought you might—I mean, if you'd rather be on your own do tell me. Honestly, I shall quite——"

The lovers of the innocent must protect them above

all from the knowledge of their own cruelty. "You know I never want you to go."

"Well, you did say that as if you meant it."

"Thanks for the few flowers," said Laurie, unable to prevent himself.

"You never do take me seriously, do you?"

Laurie never, perhaps, came nearer to a disastrous self-betrayal than in that moment of almost pure exasperation. It passed, and he perceived that Andrew was almost rigid with embarrassment, as people are who realize that they have let something slip out. "That was only a joke," he added, with the fatal error of timing that destroys all credibility.

"Try sending it to the *New Yorker*. It's too sophisticated for *Punch*." There was a pause.

"Sorry. You were better off with a good book."

"Andrew." There was silence. "Look—what *is* the matter?"

"Nothing." He had been staring before him, his arms around his knees; suddenly he scrambled to his feet. "I think I'll go back to bed. I don't seem fit to be with anyone. Thanks for putting up with me, but I don't see why you should have to. I don't know what's come over me, to make me behave like this."

"Sit down," said Laurie. He had suppressed just in time the hopeless attempt to jump up too. Andrew sat down again: he picked a long, tough stem of grass and pulled it apart. Laurie said, "You want some sleep, that's all." He looked down unseeingly at the book he was still holding. "You're not in half as filthy a mood as I always am if I miss a night."

"Do you often?"

"Not me, I always shout for dope."

Andrew made an irresolute movement, as if to go after all. Perhaps it's better, Laurie thought.

"What were you reading before I interrupted you? Can I see?"

Laurie kept his hand on the book covering the title. In his imagination the pages were printed not with their own paragraphs only, but with all that he himself had brought to them: it seemed as though he must be identified and revealed in them, beyond all pretense of detachment, as if they were a diary to which he had committed every secret of his heart.

Andrew moved back looking awkward and constrained, and Laurie suddenly wondered whether he supposed it was something pornographic; after all in a free country there are very few reasons for hiding books. He tossed it over.

Andrew picked it up and said, "I haven't read this one. I thought it was the *Phaedo* for a minute, we did that at school. What's it about?"

Laurie remembered in the nick of time to say, "Well, primarily, it's about the laws of rhetoric."

"Are you interested in rhetoric? If I were asked to choose the least likely person I could think of, it would be you."

"Actually I suppose people read it most for the sample speeches." Andrew waited expectantly. Laurie felt the held-in feeling in his chest easing off. "There are three, but the first is rather a dull one, just put up to be knocked down. Socrates recomposes it as he thinks it ought to be done. Then he decides it ought not to be done at all because it isn't true. So he does another of his own on the same subject."

"What subject?"

"Love." Laurie skimmed as lightly as he could over the most treacherous word in the language. "The first speech sets out to prove that a lover who isn't in love is preferable to one who is. Being less jealous, easier to live with, and generally more civilized."

"It sounds," said Andrew with the maddening intolerance of youth, "hardly worth stating the first time, let alone redoing it."

"Well, maybe, but Socrates' version is quite amusing. And, as a matter of fact, perfectly true. Only as the whole thing hangs on the definition of love, he's able to turn it inside out in the refutation, which is the highlight of the piece. It——"

"Read it to me."

"What? Oh, no. No, I——" It was a moment before he recovered the presence of mind to add, "It's far too long."

"Read as much as you can, then." Andrew lay down

107

on the grass. It could be seen that he was very tired. His voice had the edgy insistence one hears in a child's who has sat up too long.

"No, I should spoil it." It and much more, he thought. To keep Andrew quiet he went on, "It's got the famous myth of the charioteer."

"I don't know it. Go on."

"Well . . ." He paused. It had been part of his mind's furniture for years, but he had never spoken of it to anyone before. "He likens the soul to a charioteer, driving two winged horses harnessed abreast."

"Yes, don't stop."

"Each of the gods has a pair of divine white horses, but the soul only has one. The other" (he smiled to himself; he always remembered this part best) "is black and scruffy, with a thick neck, a flat face, hairy fetlocks, gray bloodshot eyes, and shaggy ears. He's hard of hearing, thick-skinned, and given to bolting whenever he sees something he wants. So the two beasts rarely see eye to eye, but the charioteer has to keep them on the road together. The god driving his well-matched grays is ahead setting the pace; he drives up to a track which encircles the heavens, and is carried around with eternity as it spins, like——"

Andrew, interrupting, said, " 'Like a great ring of pure and endless light.' "

"Yes. Yes, that will be where Vaughan got it, I suppose." Both found themselves with nothing to say. And now, thought Laurie, he will ask at any moment, "But what has all this to do with love?"

In fact, however, he said nothing, but picked up the book itself from the grass, where Laurie had forgotten it. Presently he said without turning around, "You've had this for quite a time, haven't you?"

"Yes, I had it at school."

"And you took it to France with you."

"All too obviously, I'm afraid. I must get it rebound."

"I should like to read it. Will you lend it me?"

"Yes. Of course. I'll let you have it sometime. I'll try and clean it first, or put on a paper cover or something. It's really in too filthy a condition to pass around."

108

Andrew said, his usually clear voice muffled by the position he was lying in, "You needn't for me."

Laurie knew that at this point he should not have allowed another silence to begin. The rustle of a rabbit in the wood echoed like the tread of cattle; the faint sound of a page turning seemed to go through his skin like a cutting edge.

After all it was Andrew who was the first to speak. "Ralph Ross Lanyon."

"What?" said Laurie stupidly.

"It's the name that's written in the book, before yours."

"Yes, I know, what about it?"

"Nothing. I only thought, perhaps, it was a present from someone."

Laurie reached for a cigarette. "What a romantic mind you have," he said from behind his hands. "It came down to me from a chap who was leaving, that's all."

"I only meant," said Andrew stiffly, "that if it's a book you'd rather not lend, or anything, it doesn't matter. I should quite understand."

He coaxed the cigarette alight, carefully. "Just for the record, I've neither seen nor heard anything of Lanyon since the day he left; if I saw him again I probably wouldn't know him, and it's even less likely that he'd know me." He broke off with a vague feeling that he had said more than enough. "Does that cover everything?"

"It should, shouldn't it? A lot of people would just have told me to mind my own business. Don't take any more notice of me." He put the book down, and burrowed his head into his arm as if to sleep. Laurie sat waiting: longing wearily, yet dreading, to be released into loneliness by the coming of this little death. But Andrew's breathing was quick and silent. He turned and looked up. "I wonder—are you very short of cigarettes, could you spare me one?"

"Sorry, I thought you didn't smoke."

"I don't really. I just felt like it. If you're sure you've enough." He didn't move back when he had taken it. "I haven't a match; give me a light from yours." He

109

leaned up on his elbow; his tilted head caught a splinter of light from between the branches. One of the gold birch leaves had fallen in his hair.

Laurie drew on the cigarette; a bright ring ran swiftly up the paper. He watched it burn for a moment; turned and began to lean down; then took the cigarette quickly and handed it at arms' length across. "Thanks," said Andrew. He got his cigarette lighted, gave Laurie's back to him, and turned away. Neither spoke; the faint curls of smoke looked blue against the shadows of the wood behind them.

After a few minutes Andrew stubbed out his cigarette and said, "I think I shall sleep here. It's quieter than the hut. Do you mind?"

"No," said Laurie. "I can't think of any objection."

"I shan't oversleep, so don't bother about me. Just go when you have to go. You won't need to go yet, will you?"

"No. I shan't be going yet."

"Just forget about me. You looked so peaceful before I came disturbing you. Now you can get on with your book as if I weren't here."

In the lane just outside the hospital gate, Laurie came to a standstill. He had thought that a rest would set the knee right, but on the way back it had started at once, and now he had to admit it was worse than it had ever been; it felt as if it had been transfixed with a hot screw. He stood, a little breathless, making up his mind to go on.

"Evening, Odell." It was Major Ferguson, whose approach he hadn't heard. He pulled himself together and saluted. "Good evening, sir."

"What was the trouble just now, Odell? Not still getting pain with that knee, are you?"

"A bit, sir. Only when I walk on it."

"Well, that's what it's for, after all, isn't it? Eh?"

"Yes, sir."

"What treatment are we giving you?"

"I usually have A.P.C. if it gets bad, sir."

"I said treatment, not palliatives. God knows why these things don't get reported to me. Well, we'd better

110

fix you up with some physiotherapy, I think. I'll see about it."

"Thank you, sir."

He had the dimmest idea of what physiotherapy was, feeling sure only that it would take place when he could have been seeing Andrew. But when he met Nurse Adrian in the covered way she said, "I was hoping they'd do something like that. You'll find it's well worth it, even if it does hold up your discharge a little." Then he realized his luck for the first time, and couldn't remember any more of the interview, except for a vague feeling that his happiness had seemed to communicate itself to her. He wondered sometimes why he didn't overhear the other men saying how pretty she was. She was a little coltish, perhaps, and certainly nothing like the star of the Technicolor musical; and he supposed he wasn't much of a judge.

It was just after this that he and Andrew began to fall into the way of meeting in the ward kitchen at night. It began as an accident, and then there seemed no reason why it shouldn't happen again. After Andrew had done a round of the ward and scrubbed the bed-pans, he always went outside to clean the kitchen up. Laurie would lie awake watching quietly till the right moment, then slip out of bed, reach in a matter-of-fact way for his dressing-gown, slippers, and stick, and make his legitimate way to the lavatory. When he got back to the corridor Andrew would be visible near the kitchen door. They were still at the stage of saying, "Oh, hello," in mild surprise, as a tribute to this coincidence.

The Sister used to make herself a pot of tea before she went off duty, and to the stewed remains of this Andrew would add some hot water. Laurie, arriving at first as if he couldn't stay more than a minute, would prop himself against the wooden slab where the chromium water-heater stood, watching Andrew scrub the sink and the draining-boards. They drank the weak, hot, bitter-sweet tea out of thick china mugs, and talked softly. Nurse Sims soon got to know what was happening, but winked at it provided they didn't raise their voices or go on too long. Andrew would spin out

111

the work a little; Laurie could always remember him, afterwards, bending over the slab with an almost stationary dishcloth in his hand. Sometimes he would express himself with it, moving it slowly and absently when he was shy or uncertain, scrubbing it along briskly to mark a point. A lock of hair, steamed limp over the sink, would come down over one eye, and he would push it back with a wet hand, making it limper.

A cockroach scuttled into a crack behind the draining-board; he watched Andrew reach for a tin of Keatings and sprinkle the crack with it. "Does life stop being sacred," he asked, "when it gets down to cockroaches?"

"Well, the Jains don't think so," said Andrew seriously. "But I never know how they meet the fact that our own bodies destroy millions of microorganisms every day, without giving us any alternative to it except suicide. One has to draw the line where one sees it oneself."

"Is that what you call the inner light?"

"If you like, yes."

Faint noises of contracting metal came from the water-heater, behind which in genial warmth and darkness the cockroaches lived. The dressing trolley rattled faintly in the ward. A cricket was chirring somewhere.

"I was trying to remember how old you are," Andrew said. "But I've never asked you."

"Twenty-three last June."

Andrew looked at him and said, in the voice of someone paying a deserved tribute, "I always thought you were older than that."

Laurie didn't think much about it at the time. Afterwards, when he knew more, this was a thing he always remembered about Andrew, that he took for granted one would regard maturity as a thing to be desired.

It was visiting day. Just after lunch the sky clouded over, a cold, bitter wind got up, and within fifteen minutes it had begun to rain. He had lost his greatcoat in the retreat, and had never had another. Chilled and damp in body and mind, he waited outside the gate, half sheltered by a tree which soon began to drip down his neck. With a muddy splashing the bus arrived; dimly he was aware of a dowdy little woman with an umbrella getting off it, along with several others. Then he saw that it was his mother. His bones, rather than his mind, remembered the pretty clothes she had worn last time, the new hat, when the sun had been shining, and Mr. Straike had been there.

"My dear!" he said. "Whyever, on a day like this?"

"I thought I wouldn't bother with a car." He recognized, sinking, her defensive voice. "It *was* rather extravagant, you know, with the buses running so conveniently."

"But we can't just sit in the ward," he said, "and there's nowhere else here to go." The tree, full of rain now, was leaking everywhere with dull heavy drops. Hadn't she cared enough to foresee all this? "Look, I'll just go in and ring for a car now. It's on me; it won't be much, just the one way."

It was in the car that he had meant to talk to his mother; he had lain awake at night thinking up easy, natural openings. She said, "It *is* a shame about the rain, you said in your letter how lovely everything was looking," and he said, "Yes, it will strip a lot of the trees, I expect." And suddenly he knew that this was not, as he had been saying to himself, simply an unlucky day. It was a day dedicated beforehand to a lost cause. Before she had abandoned him, he had begun already to abandon her. He was marked for life, as a growing tree is marked, by the chain that had bound him to her; but the chain was rusting away, leaving only the scar. It was an irony mathematical in its neatness, that in the moment when the pattern of her possession was complete, the gulf of incommunicable things opened between them. Already it was unbridgeable. She would never now, as once he had dreamed, say to him in the silent language of day-to-day, "Tell me nothing; it is enough that no other woman will ever take you from me."

For the first time when they got out of the car she noticed his boot. She was as pleased as if, he thought, it

113

were a supplementary part of himself which, like a lizard, he had cleverly grown.

Sitting in the dowdy, clean mahogany tea-shop, he said, "Mother, you're sure you're going to be happy? Is he"—he looked down at the cloth, he hadn't anticipated this throttling inhibition, this almost physical shame—"is he kind to you, does he look after you properly and all that?"

"Oh, yes, dear, indeed he does. He would never of course dream of saying so, but I feel, one can't help guessing, that in his first marriage he didn't quite get the—well, quite the affection that a man of his kind needs. That, you know, is just between you and me."

"Yes," said Laurie, "of course." There was a thick slab of sawdust-like cake on his plate, yellow, with dates in it. He could not imagine how it had got there.

"Laurie, dear, I do *hope* you've not caught a chill. Is it this damp weather making your knee ache?"

"No, it's just a bit stiff. I was thinking they'll be wanting the table. Shall we go to the cinema?"

The rain had stopped, but the clouds held the heavy damp over everything; above the still-wet pavements the long slow twilight hung like the moist air, unmoving. Limp dead leaves were pasted to the gutters. They sat in the fireless blacked-out station waiting room which smelt of smoke, dust, old varnish, coal, and feet. A heavy red-faced woman with a heavy red-faced little girl sat opposite staring at them with black button eyes, drinking in every word. The train came in; they had just lit the dim blue bulbs which would give light enough to prevent the commission of crimes. "Well, dear—"

"Get well quickly, darling. Look after yourself. Don't go back and sit in damp things, will you. Dear, you must never think that things will be any different. You know. It would upset me terribly, it would spoil everything, if I thought you felt that."

"No, dear, of course. It's just that—if anything goes wrong, if you start to have any doubts about it, send me a wire, or ring. I'll get a pass somehow and come straight over. Promise me."

"But of course there's no . . . Oh, dear, they're shutting the doors now. Goodbye, dear, take care not to catch cold, goodbye."

Reg was on the bus that took him back to the hospital. It had been one of Madge's days. Kindly they inquired after one another's outing and replied that their own had been fine, thanks. Each sensed in the other a certain reservation; each was grateful not to be questioned too nearly. They sat side by side, nursing their so different griefs which were yet the same grief to the inmost heart, unaware of the instinctive comfort they got from their sense of solidarity.

That night in the kitchen Andrew, opening the subject rather shyly since Laurie had not seen fit to do so, said, "I hope it was all right today, when your mother came."

"Yes, thanks," said Laurie. "Yes, it was quite all right." But lest Andrew should feel snubbed or hurt he produced a few limp platitudes, which Andrew went through the form of accepting as real. It was a sad little session; but he could feel Andrew thinking as he thought, that tomorrow it would be all right.

But next morning the Sister said, "Odell, look after this carefully, won't you, and give it to the Sister of the department as soon as you arrive."

"Where?" asked Laurie. The pain was as sharp and sudden as a bullet, but there wasn't any comeback. A war was on, he had been transferred somewhere else, so what? The war giveth and the war taketh away. Andrew would be in bed by now, sleeping; who would take him a message? Derek, of course. "When am I leaving, Sister, today?"

"Now you know quite—surely I told you about all this yesterday?"

"No, Sister. I went out."

"Oh. Oh, yes, so you did. Well, you're to go into Bridstow twice a week for electrical treatment at the City Hospital. Tuesdays, that's this afternoon, and Fridays. Now don't lose this card, whatever you do."

The relief was almost too much: he wanted to laugh stupidly aloud. When he remembered that for the second evening running he couldn't meet Andrew in Limbo, it seemed by contrast a trifle.

Bridstow had had some more raids since his last call there. The burgher solidity of the city was interrupted by large irrelevant open spaces, in some of which bulldozers were flattening the rubble out. At the City Hospital he had only to wait an hour, which was better than his expectations. Upstairs a brisk gentlewoman took him in hand as bracingly as if he had been a Girl Guide, and applied damp compresses, with electric wires involved in them, to his leg. Rhythmic waves of pins-and-needles followed, which, to his surprise, were pleasant and soothing after a time. At intervals Miss Haliburton returned to the couch where he lay, kneaded his muscles comfortingly, and talked dogs. She bred several varieties, and before long Laurie felt as unself-conscious under her ministrations as if he had been one of them. He left the hospital with an hour in hand before his bus went.

It wasn't worth going to a cinema, and he didn't feel like drinking alone; he thought he would walk a little to see the sights, while the knee felt so good. But he had only got as far as the cathedral green when the air raid sirens went.

It was broad daylight; on current form, it should be no more than a reconnaissance raid, delayed probably by cloud earlier in the day. He walked on among the pathetic little Home Guard trenches on the green. It was a beautiful afternoon.

"Everyone in the shelter. Come along, ladies, bring your knitting, nice and cozy inside. This way, sonny, mind how you go on the steps."

Laurie became aware of a sandbagged cave and a fatherly person in a white tin hat. At that time they were still rounding up people in the streets and shepherding them into the shelters willy-nilly; but, living in the country, Laurie had forgotten. He said, "It's all right, thanks, I'll see how it goes."

"Sorry, son, everyone in the shelter, that's the drill. Come along, now, you've had enough to be going on with, won't hurt *you* to take it easy."

Laurie observed that the warden was over sixty; he had the ribbons of the Military Medal and the Mons

116

Star. "Have a heart, Sergeant, I've only got a short pass."

A thin sputter of gunfire sounded from somewhere near the river. "She'll wait for you," the warden said. "Don't waste time, lad, I've got a job to do."

A voice behind Laurie said, "You can't have this one, warden. He's a patient of mine, due for treatment. I'll be responsible for him."

The warden said, as one who washes his hands of a nuisance, "Okay, you're the doctor," and walked away. Laurie remained, confronted by the young man with the white eyelashes, who had been the target for his rather erratic humor some weeks ago during Major Ferguson's round. He had told himself, at the time, that someday one of these little jokes of his would come home to roost.

"Well," he said, "thanks very much."

"Happy to oblige. I gathered you didn't want to waste half an hour down there." His tone was quite conventional. Hanging unspoken between them, and clearly understood, were the words, "Your move."

A false but powerful sense of destiny attends those decisions which seem to be demanded of us without warning, but which we have in reality been maturing within ourselves. Laurie answered not from the loneliness of his emotions, but from the long solitude of his thoughts. Some instinct of his recognized, in this cautious and discreet person, one who had escaped from solitude, whose private shifts had given place to a traditional defense-system. Somewhere behind him was the comforting solidarity of a group.

Laurie said, lightly, "Well, I suppose if I look about this city I might find something a bit more entertaining than a hole in the ground."

"Why not?" said the young man. "We'll all get there in due course without all these rehearsals. It won't be anything."

"There it goes." It was a single plane, flying very high. "What a flap about nothing."

The young man said, "You're a patient of Ferguson's, aren't you, at the E.M.S. hospital?"

"Yes. I think I've seen you there, haven't I?"

"I thought I remembered you from somewhere. You won't know my name: Sandy Reid. I'm not a doctor yet, by the way." In the midst of an almost timid friendliness, there was something hard and wary about the way he said this. Laurie noticed it with slight distaste, but didn't pause to consider it. He introduced himself. The young man said in a semifacetious American voice, "Glad to know you, Laurie," and then, after a tiny pause, "How about a drink?"

The All Clear went just as they reached the pub. It was a large one, nastily modernized at vast expense. The chromium stools, the plastic leather, the sham parquet floor, and the fluorescent lighting which made everyone look jaundiced, caused him to expect that the beer too would turn out to be a chemical synthetic. A radio, slightly off the beam, was running like a leaky tap. He overbore Sandy's protests and bought the drinks, intending to leave before another round.

This was not the first time he had touched the fringe he was touching now. He knew the techniques of mild evasion and casual escape. Though the Charles episode had been disillusioning, he hadn't given up hope of finding himself clubbable after all. This time, he had briefly thought the right moment had come. But, after all, no: and after all, it was no one's business but his own.

"It's a bit tatty," said Sandy Reid, as the drinks came over the ebonoid bar, "but one runs into people here."

"Oh, yes?" said Laurie politely. "I suppose you can never get far from the hospital, in any case."

"Actually I've got some quite civilized digs just up the hill, with a friend of mine." He added, with a circumspect kind of pride, "We've been together more than a year now."

"Oh? Good." He saw Sandy eying him, anxiously expectant, under his eyelids; they were rather pink, reminding Laurie of white mice. Having been unhappy most of the day, he now found an unkind pleasure in being equivocal and elusive. "Do you have much trouble getting digs here? They tell me Oxford's teeming like a Calcutta slum."

118

Sandy's face had fallen, but not despairingly. He had probably had some practice in distinguishing between ignorance and reserve. "Oh, you're from Oxford. I'm at the local joint. Then you know Charles Fosticue, I expect."

"Only by name," said Laurie with prompt firmness. He gave thanks to his own instincts of self-preservation. "I used to see a good deal of Pat Dean; do you know him? He married a girl from Somerville last year."

Stalemate had now been reached. Applying himself more briskly to his beer, Laurie decided to say that there wasn't another bus if he missed this one.

"Not," Sandy was saying (he had evidently decided to resurvey the terrain), "that I ever knew Charlie Fosticue at all well. I just mentioned him because he's the sort of type everyone meets once. I've run into Vic Tamley now and again. Rather a pleasant person, I thought."

"Yes, I heard someone say so, I forget who."

"I thought you might know him, he seemed rather your type. Drink up, while there's a lull in the rush."

"Thanks, but I shall really have to get cracking to catch the bus."

"Oh, hell, no, you've only been here five minutes. Don't forget I saved you from rubbing knees with sixty-five typists in the shelter. Try old and bitter this time, the local old's quite good." The barman had collected the glasses while he was speaking. Laurie resigned himself to five minutes more.

There was a permanent air of improvisation, he thought, about Sandy Reid. He had clearly now abandoned what hopes of Laurie he might have had, but was loath to let him go. Perhaps the tenacity came only from boredom. He had a manner it would be too strong to call restless, a chronic but trivial kind of expectation. He looked often at the door, but when he was greeted by a couple of men as they entered, he gave them an offhand nod and turned away.

Someone turned up the radio. A brassy-lunged female sang of rainbows. Her vibrato was excruciating; Laurie made a vinegar face. Sandy replied with another, which expressed a subtly different kind of distaste;

119

he must have thought that this was what Laurie had meant, and now Laurie himself was uncertain. Their eyes met in an indefinite kind of acknowledgment.

"Look here," said Sandy, "we're having a few people in for drinks tonight. It's Alec's birthday, he's my friend I was telling you about. Why don't you come along?" After the faintest pause he added, with more directness than he had so far used, "Can't offer you any girls, I'm afraid. If you mind that?"

"Not in the least." So much seemed only fair. "But unless I catch this bus I'll be for it. Thanks all the same, I'd have liked to."

"Oh, well, but if that's all I'm sure we can fix it. Someone will run you back. Let's think . . ."

Laurie for his part was thinking that this was what came of brushing people off with too soft a brush. It was a fault of his. Evidently he would have to use a hard one. "No, thanks very much, but——"

"You can count on someone with a car, definitely. If Bim can't make it there's still Theo Sumner, or Ralph Lanyon, or——"

"*Who* did you say?"

"Oh, d'you know Ralph Lanyon?" Sandy brightened. Now, he seemed to say, we're getting somewhere.

"Not for years." He had a dazed feeling of having fallen through a crack in time. "I expect it's someone different."

"Unusual name, after all. R.N.V.R. type; in armed trawlers, I think he was. He got wounded in the hand during the Dunkirk show and lost a couple of fingers. Now he's doing a hush-hush technical course, radio or something. Well, there you are. That settles it, you'll have to come along now."

As if he had been drifting in uncertainly eddying water, and felt the sudden, authoritative pull of an ocean current, Laurie said easily and clearly, "Well, if you can do with me. Thanks very much."

6

I'T'S a mausoleum," said Sandy at the front door. "All you can say is, the proportions are good."

Laurie said something about Italian influence. He could recall few doors which he had felt such reluctance to enter.

They had been separated in the bus, which had saved conversation. All kinds of little things came suddenly back to him; but most of all he remembered the term after Lanyon had gone. Over and over, during those first months, Laurie had relived the scene in the study, guarding it with fierce secrecy as a savage guards a magic word. Now he felt strands and fibers of Lanyon twitching in his mind where he had not recognized them before, and realized the source of those standards which had supplemented his mother's in those parts of his life where she could not go.

He knew that he didn't want to submit any of this to daylight. Lanyon's survival belonged only between the worn leather covers of the *Phaedrus*. The only firm fact about him now was that he was a friend of Sandy's. It was madness to have come.

The bus had halted and an old woman was getting out. It would wait for her; for him too, if he wanted to escape. Sandy wasn't looking; he reached for his stick. But it would be a lout's trick, he thought; and this distaste gave pretext enough to his divided mind. He sat back again, and the next stop was theirs.

The house was tall and narrow, in a massive late Palladian terrace of Bath stone. As they crossed the threshold, Laurie agreed that the proportions were good.

Inside it looked, like many others in that old once-wealthy suburb, as if it had been lived in for thirty years by a Lord Mayor's widow. It looked uneasy now, turned into a respectable tenement full of transients in a time of flux. They crossed the hall with its thick red and blue Turkey carpet. On the half-landing a huge stained-glass window was half blocked-out with paint, half curtained with an army blanket; there was a cigarette burn on the white-painted tread of one of the stairs.

The first landing had a mahogany tallboy, the second a half-acre engraving of Victoria and Albert at the Crystal Palace. Sandy said, "I'm frightfully sorry about all these stairs."

"It's good practice for me. Sorry to be so slow." There were no stairs at the hospital and he hadn't expected it to be so bad. He took his time. He wasn't going to waste his strength impressing Sandy Reid.

At the top of the next flight he saw, still set in the newel-post, the hinges of the wicket gate which, fifty years since perhaps, had guarded the nursery floor. Voices and laughter came from a door beyond it. Sandy said, "Here we are."

Laurie's first glance around the room told him only that Lanyon was not there; he felt a dull flat relaxation, which he took for relief. Several introductions went through his ears unheard. He roused himself in time to identify Alec, his other host: a dark, narrow-headed, nearly good-looking young civilian, whose calling didn't need guesswork; he looked already much more like a doctor than Sandy did, or like a better doctor perhaps. He talked like one, coolly, throwing all his good lines away. Sandy treated him, rather ostentatiously, like a lovable dreamer to be bossed and protected. The first few minutes were enough to give Laurie all this.

The other dozen or so faces had closed in a little; he became aware that the conversation had a poised, tentative feel. The unspoken query in the air became as unmistakable to him as a shout. Deciding that it was no business of his to resolve it, he threw the onus on Sandy by the simple means of asking to go and wash. As he crossed the landing, he heard Sandy's voice on a rising note: ". . . my dear, *right* across the ward in the middle of the teaching round, as bold as brass, no possible error, it made me feel quite shy. Goodness *knows* why he won't drop a hairpin now, the silly boy."

Returning, Laurie began to take in the room. It contained a big white-painted cupboard (the toy cupboard, he thought at once) and an old-fashioned nannie's rocking chair. There were also two divans covered with hessian and strewn with bright cotton cushions; a couple of modern Swedish chairs; one or two charming little pieces in old walnut; various poufs; a wooden black boy holding an ashtray; and a crayon drawing, literal and earnestly dull, of a young sailor's head. Across the lower half of the big windows, rusty but still thick and strong, the nursery bars remained protectively fixed.

He had heard, as he came in from the doorway, the conversation swerve awkwardly. He was acutely conscious of his limp, of the lowness of the divans and poufs which would exhibit his stiff knee when he sat and when he rose. He recognized Sandy's changed voice which he had heard from the landing: it was the voice of Charles's friends. Suddenly he imagined Lanyon frisking in and speaking like that. With a trapped feeling he saw Alec coming up carrying a whisky and soda.

"I believe it's your birthday? Many happy returns."

"Thank you. Do sit down; try this one." It was one of the Swedish chairs, with helpful arms. Alec poised himself on the edge of a table and said, "You're a friend of Ralph's, I hear."

"Well, I can't honestly claim that. He was Head of the School when I was in the fifths, and we've never even met since he left. If he remembers me at all it'll only be because he's got a good memory for faces; or used to have."

"Oh, he still has. Is your drink all right?"

"Yes, thanks, fine. I rather feel, really, that I've come here under false pretenses." He was quite sure Alec had subtlety enough to interpret that.

"So far," said Alec, "you seem to me very lacking in pretenses." It struck Laurie that he would be formidable in a consulting room someday. "Oh, by the way, I don't know whether you get a kind of functional deafness during introductions, like me? I never got your name properly; was it—er Hazell, or——?"

"*Christ!*" said Laurie, nearly spilling his drink. "No, it wasn't."

"I really do apologize. I thought not, but I just want-

123

ed to exclude the possibility before Ralph got here. Evidently, from your strong reaction, you were there the term he was expelled?"

Laurie put down his drink and said, in the formal voice of open hostility, "Lanyon left the term he was due to leave. There was nothing else to it, as far as I know."

"I'm sorry. But Ralph makes so little secret of it; everyone in our own set knows. And I suppose you struck me as not being a mischievous person."

Laurie felt his anger go cold on him. Under a score of surface differences, and accompanied no doubt by many basic ones, he recognized a speaker of his own language; another solitary still making his own maps, his few certainties gripped with a rather desperate strength. "I didn't mean to be cagey," he said. "Lanyon was a very good Head and generally liked, and I suppose that's what one mostly remembers. Of course you must know much more about him than I do."

"Don't apologize," said Alec, "I liked it." He had a smile of unexpected decision and charm. "And what *is* your name, if you'll forgive my unmannerly persistence?"

"Oh, sorry. It's Odell. I don't think he'll remember me, you know."

Alec looked up. His dark eyes had a peering, shortsighted look. "Odell?" he said.

"Without the apostrophe, if it matters. Needless to say I got called Spud just the same."

"Yes," said Alec. "Yes, I expect so." His characteristic alertness seemed lost; he stared in silence. "You say you don't think Ralph will remember you?"

"Well, I suppose he might dimly." Laurie himself was remembering with sharpening clearness: the green paint in the corridor, the torn books in the basket, the silver pencil. "But I should hardly think so; he had a good deal else to think about, after all."

"You never knew he brought you back from Dunkirk, then?"

"What?" said Laurie dully. His brain refused to yield him the least response. His memories had been

124

healing; he could recall nothing of that journey with any clearness now.

"You didn't recognize him?"

"No. I can't have seen him, even. I think I passed out, you see, most of the way."

"Yes, of course. Apparently he picked up some kind of impression that you knew him. At least, I remember him saying he wrote to you afterwards; but of course he hadn't much to go on. Evidently there was muddle, because the letter came back 'Died of Wounds.' And from the state you were in when he saw you, it didn't seem unlikely, so he left it there."

"I see. I wondered why you seemed surprised when I told you my name." The shadows of memory were disconnected and meaningless, like the first markings on a negative in the tank. "Fancy his bothering to write to me. That's just like him, you know; he made everyone feel he took a personal interest. He was wounded himself, Sandy says?"

"Yes, that was later. He went back two or three more times for another load. His ship got a direct hit in the end, but they picked him up out of the water. Well, he's late, I hope he's going to turn up. Excuse me, I'd better see how the drinks are doing."

He got up. For the first time, Laurie perceived in his movements a kind of reticent, controlled delicacy, like that of a well-bred woman who is usually aware of making, without vulgar emphasis, the right impression. He collected someone's glass and went over to the table with it, catching Sandy's eye on the way. They met at the table and went through some business with a siphon, and talked discreetly. Laurie heard nothing except the end of a sentence from Sandy: ". . . started out long ago. Does it matter?" The rest was drowned by a conversation going on just behind his chair. "So I said to him, well really at that point I couldn't help saying, 'Well, if that's your attitude, I don't mind telling you I think I've treated you very nicely, and when I say that you know what I mean.' And he did, too. 'I've treated you nicely,' I said, 'and in return you've done nothing but two-time me, and not even with decent people, but with people whom I consider absolute riff-raff. *You*

125

know who I mean.' He knew all right; he looked very silly, I can tell you, when he saw I'd been checking up on him. 'I think you'll go a long way,' I said, 'before you'll find anyone who . . .' "

Oh God, Laurie was thinking, where has it got to? He had left his chair and was now searching for his stick. There it was, fallen flat on the floor; and he knew from past failures that he would have to sit down in the chair again in order to retrieve it without looking ridiculous.

"Looking for this, chum?"

"Thanks," said Laurie. "Yes, I was."

It was a soldier, whom Laurie had till now scarcely had time to notice, though he had been vaguely aware of him as a somewhat incongruous presence. He now said, "You don't mind, do you, chum, if I sit here with you and have a word or two?" and, carefully bringing up a pouf before Laurie could answer, settled himself beside him.

Laurie recognized at once the solemn intensity of drink taken; to go away instantly might start a scene. After a little heavy breathing, the soldier addressed him in the flat accent of the Midlands.

"I reckon you got that packet at Dunkirk. Eh?"

"Yes," said Laurie. "Were you there too?"

"No, I was still doing training. I saw you come in. You got one leg shorter than the other, haven't you?"

"Yes."

"Don't they reckon that'll get no better, then?"

"Probably not."

The soldier leaned forward; he smelled of jasmine hair oil and of beer. "Here," he breathed huskily. "I want to ask you something. You ever been here before?"

"No. Have you?"

"It don't matter about me. Look, when you come in here, I took a liking to you. That's what I'm like, always have been, first impressions is what I go by; and when I see you come in limping on that stick, I thought, 'That lad stopped a packet at Dunkirk and they didn't ought to have brought him. That's not right,' I thought, 'they never ought to have done it.' "

"It's all right. I've only looked in for a drink."

"That's what *you* think, chum. Here, do you know what they are, all this lot here?"

"Don't you worry about me; I'm leaving to catch a bus in a minute." He had missed it, but there was another at nine, and he would sit in a cinema till it was due. He looked around, trying to catch Sandy's eye.

"I know what you think," said the soldier earnestly. "I could see it in your face when you come in. You think being lame like what you are, a girl won't have you. You think to hell with all that. It takes all sorts to make a world, give it a go and look after number one same as we all got to do, that's what you think. Now I'll tell you something."

"Yes," said Laurie. "Excuse me." He gripped the arms of the chair and braced himself to rise. But the door had opened. Sandy was saying, "So *here* you are at last. Come along in, we've got a little surprise for you."

Laurie straightened himself smartly. When he was on his feet and standing still, there wasn't much to notice. In his haste he threw his weight too quickly on his lame leg, so that it was shot through with a violent stab of pain. When the effort of concealing this was over, he saw that Lanyon was already in the room.

He had come alone. Laurie would have known him instantly, anywhere; which is not to say that he had not changed. He was in R.N.V.R. uniform with a lieutenant's rings; and Laurie's first clear thought was that if one had had the sense to notice it, he must have looked like a ship's officer even at school. Now the incipient lines were graven in; against his weathered skin his light hair looked several shades fairer, almost ash-colored. He was still spare and alert-looking, but he held his shoulders more stiffly now. There was time for all this while he stood in the doorway. For Sandy he had a suitable smile which, without being exactly guarded, revealed nothing whatever except good manners: when he turned to Alec, though the transition wasn't crude, Laurie could see that it was Alec on whose account he had come. He had brought him a birthday present, Laurie couldn't see what, and the unwrapping and thanks took a little time. Laurie was glad of it. It had all been more disturbing than he had expected, and it occurred to him for the first time that Lanyon might find his sudden appearance embarrassing, once he remembered who he was.

Alec took some time to admire his present; he was evidently one of those who are generous in the receiving of gifts. It was Sandy who seemed suddenly to grow impatient. He gave Lanyon a shove which turned him half around from the door, and said, in a voice carelessly audible through the room, "And now come over here and see what *we've* got for *you*."

Lanyon stared at this and Laurie saw for the first time his light-blue, wary, sailor's eyes. Above the superficial smile on his mouth, they swept the room as inexpressively as if it had been a doubtful stretch of sea. Laurie got ready: but when they reached him, he forgot after all to say anything or even to smile, since Lanyon did neither: he simply stood there, with his face draining, visibly, of color, till one could see that his mouth and chin were less deeply tanned than the rest of his face, because they suddenly stood out pallid against the darker skin above. His mouth straightened; Laurie knew the expression well, but now it seemed part of a naval uniform, emergency kit. It jerked Laurie out of himself. He took a step forward and said, "Hello. They told me you might be coming." But Lanyon still stared at him in silence, so he added, "Do you remember me? Spud Odell?"

Lanyon came up, and Laurie noticed for the first time the glove on his left hand. He said, so abruptly that he might have been charging Laurie with a disciplinary offense, "I thought you were dead."

"Only temporarily." Laurie thought: I can't have very much imagination, not to have expected this. That day at school must have been the worst in his life, much worse than anything the sea's done to him or even the war; seeing me must be like living it over again. He felt so strongly for Lanyon in this that his nervousness left him. He smiled and said, "Alec's just told me that I owe you for a Channel crossing. Is it true?"

Lanyon said in the same court-martial voice, but rather more slowly, "You knew that."

"No." (It wouldn't have taken much more, Laurie thought, to have made him say, "No, please, Lanyon.") "I hadn't the least idea. I was dead to the world most of the time."

With startling abruptness, Lanyon's face broke into a hard gay smile. "Well, for someone alleged to be unconscious, I must say you did pretty well. Sending me up sky-high in front of a petty officer and a couple of ratings. You'll be telling me you can't remember that now, I suppose?"

Laurie's mouth opened. He stared at the jaw-line from which, now, the pale margin had disappeared. "Oh, my *God*," he said. "*That* wasn't you?"

"You're telling me. I got down into the beard I was mercifully wearing at the time, and pulled it up over my head. Much to my relief, a Stuka came over a few seconds later and machine-gunned us. I was a great deal more frightened of you."

"But . . . God, this is . . . I'd had a lot of morphia, and they gave me another shot just before they embarked us, to stop the bleeding. I remember realizing I was light-headed, even at the time."

"I never quite worked out whether you were thinking, 'Well, well, so that was R. R. Lanyon,' or if it was just a case of 'Oh, Lord, here comes another.' "

"I was off my head. Of course I didn't know you. Christ, you don't suppose if I had——"

"Same old Spud," said Lanyon in a kind of echo of the bright voice he had used before. "I wouldn't have believed it." He took a step back and looked at Laurie, then said, not brightly but with a dull kind of incredulity, "Good God, you haven't changed a bit."

"It was the beard," said Laurie. "That was all. I'd have known you anywhere, but for that."

"Ah, well," Lanyon said smiling again, "we've both got a shock or two coming, I daresay."

It was then that Laurie remembered, for the first time in some minutes, the presence of other people. Alec was hovering, with a couple of drinks, tactfully on the fringe of the conversation. Sandy, less tactful, was drinking in their reunion open-mouthed. There had been so much to say, Laurie had scarcely noticed till now the special phrases casually accepted, the basic assumption on which all their words had made sense. What after all could Lanyon have supposed, finding him here? Well, he thought, Sandy would be satisfied. The hairpin had been dropped.

"Aren't you drinking, Laurie?" Alec said. "Here's yours, Ralph."

"Healths in water are unlucky," said Lanyon, looking at the glass.

"Sorry, I gave you the wrong one. This is yours. Laurie, this do for you?"

Laurie, who had lost his first drink, took it. It was rather strong, but he didn't like now to do anything about it. They drank to Alec's birthday and then Lanyon, turning, said, "Well . . . hello, Laurie. I'll get used to that, I suppose."

They drank. Laurie said, "There's no need to, Spud will do."

"No. Boys will be boys, but heaven defend us from Old Boys. Now I think of it, I never did know your real name. When I was doing the lists sometimes I used to wonder what it was. Odell, L. P. What was the P. for?"

"Patrick."

"Well, I got that one right, anyway. I wish you wouldn't keep looking at me as if I might give you a hundred lines at any moment. For God's sake relax." He stared at his glass, then emptied it with a jerk.

"Sorry. It's all very well for you, but Ralph does feel a bit of a hanging matter."

"That'll pass off, you'll find. Drink up and I'll get you another."

"Not for a minute, thanks."

"How are your drinks?" asked Sandy, who all this time hadn't been far away. "The usual, Ralph? Oh, by the way, I'm afraid I've rather been committing you in your absence. Have you got your car?"

Lanyon's face shut like a door. Laurie had seen him first take in the room with one angry, summarizing glance. "Well," he said, "yes and no."

130

"If you can't, never mind," said Alec easily. "It was just for Laurie. It seems he's got to run for some god-forsaken bus in about five minutes, unless someone can lift him back."

"Oh. I see. Where to, Laurie? Surely, yes, I can do that all right. I thought Claude wanted a taxi for his bit of rent." The soldier was still sitting where Laurie had left him, staring in front of him with a glazed, hazy eye. No one seemed to be taking the slightest notice of him.

Beside the fireplace, opposite the toy cupboard, was a gramophone on which Sandy now put a stack of dance records. Two or three couples stood up. They all danced very seriously and correctly, as if they were in a ballroom.

Lanyon said abruptly, "For God's sake let's sit down, and tell me what's been happening to you." They went over to one of the hessian divans; it was very low, and Laurie hesitated for a moment. Lanyon at once slid a hand under his elbow, and firmly lowered him down. It was smoothly authoritative and unfussy, like hospital. Then he remembered the glove. Lanyon kept the left hand in his pocket most of the time; but it was on his knee now, and Laurie could see that half of it had a padded, artificial look.

"Cigarette?" said Lanyon. Laurie was only just beginning to notice how naturally he did with one hand a great many things for which most people are apt to use both. This is Lanyon, he thought, actually sitting here and lighting my cigarette.

Suddenly Lanyon stared at him and said, "Good God! Don't tell me they saved that leg for you after all?"

This approach to the matter gave Laurie an oddly comfortable and relaxed feeling. "More or less. They've been tinkering with it ever since."

"Well, I think that's a bloody miracle. When I saw you on deck, the only thing I couldn't understand was why they hadn't taken it off back at the dressing station. But they'd lost most of their equipment anyway, I suppose."

"I expect so." For a moment, through the press of

131

their own concerns, there rose between them the shadowy constraint of the beaten army confronting the unbeaten navy, the suppressed withdrawal, the carefully careless tact.

"I'm the one to talk," said Lanyon. "You know I lost my ship."

Something in his voice reminded Laurie for the first time that this was rather more than an incident in which one was liable to be killed.

"I just heard," he said. "I'm sorry. Had you commanded her long?"

"Five and a half months. My first; and my last, of course. In seventeen ninety-eight, missing parts were considered quite amusing, even for admirals, but all that's terribly dated now. Well, it might have been worse; we were on the way out, not coming back. Really, there are some bloody good surgeons about nowadays. You had a great splinter of bone sticking clean through the dressing into the open air. We had some of those big gunshot jobs in the hospital. They seemed to give people hell for months. Does yours?"

"Only off and on. They've sent me in for treatment here, to get it fixed up."

"Why on earth don't you get yourself transferred here altogether? Isn't yours one of these temporary dumps? This place is quite good, or so Alec always says."

"I couldn't do that," said Laurie, with an absurd prick of anxiety. "I only come in twice a week."

"Oh, well," said Lanyon. He picked up their glasses and made for the table, at the last moment noticing that Laurie's was nearly full and putting it back.

While they had been talking, two or three more people had arrived. He realized that a young man, one of the newcomers, was threading among the dancers in a purposeful way, and was plainly making for the place beside him. Just then Lanyon came back. He stood over the young man, quite quietly, with the kind of expression a captain uses on a tipsy passenger he has found exploring the bridge. "Excuse me," he said. The young man flinched like a startled fawn, and hurried away.

132

Lanyon sat down again with what, Laurie supposed, must be his fourth or fifth double. He seemed as self-possessed as if he had been drinking water. His voice had got louder, but so had Laurie's; it was the only way of making oneself heard. Except for two people in a far corner who seemed to be holding hands in dead silence, they were probably the quietest couple in the room.

"I nearly didn't come tonight." Lanyon stared for a moment unseeingly at the dancers, then added circumstantially, "I was working on something and nearly forgot about it."

"I refused twice," said Laurie. "The third time Sandy happened to mention you, or I'd have refused again."

Lanyon's light eyes lifted, sharply, under his straight fair brows. Laurie remembered the look.

"You don't know him well, then?"

"I don't properly speaking know him at all. We knew each other by sight at the hospital. Till we ran into each other this evening, I didn't know his name."

"Oh?" said Lanyon without much expression. "Then which of these people have you met before?"

"Only you."

He hadn't meant to give this simple statement of fact any special significance. For some reason which he couldn't understand it seemed to go on ringing, like glass picking up a note. Alec, he thought, tasting his drink again, was inclined to mix them strong.

"He will drown them," Lanyon said. "Give it me, and I'll tip it out and give you another."

"This one's all right." However, since Lanyon looked impatient he finished it fairly soon. It still embarrassed him to have Lanyon wait on him. He watched him elbowing his way through the dancers, and saw someone snatch the empty glasses from him, and try to make him dance. He refused smiling; then at something the other man said he seemed to grow suddenly angry, and walked sharply off.

He sat down in silence with the two drinks and then, when they had scarcely started them, said, "For God's sake let's get out of here."

133

"Are you due back on duty?"

"I said let's get out, that's all."

"Isn't it a bit early? I shouldn't like to upset Alec, he seems rather nice."

"If it's Alec you want, I'll fetch him for you."

Laurie looked up; he couldn't think of anything to say. Lanyon said, "Sorry, Spud."

He gave the drink in his hand a look of cold irritation, as if someone had planted it on him, and put it up on a bookshelf near by.

"It doesn't matter," Laurie said. "We'll go if you'd rather, I don't mind."

"No, it's his birthday, I suppose there'll be some nonsense with a cake. We'll give it another minute or two."

Someone dancing by leaned out (the dancing had grown a good deal less conventional) and called, "What's he got that I haven't?" Lanyon's reply was swift and explicit; he added, "Go to hell." Turning to Laurie he said, "This party's deteriorating," then, "Are you all right, Spud? You look a bit done in."

The knee had started, but not specially badly; it was rather better than it sometimes was by this time of night. He hadn't been thinking much about it, except as a background like the gramophone. As a rule, he hated to think that other people could notice anything, but, he thought, when most people asked these questions you could see them hoping to God you would say everything was fine, and they needn't do any worrying. Lanyon sounded different: he even made one feel that some real, effective potential was actually being offered. It was absurd, but very comforting.

"I'm all right," he said.

"Yes, I know, you feel like a million dollars. Only I'm going to get you out of this and back to bed." He stood up and held out his hand.

"No, thanks, it isn't anything. I'm not tired. The leg gets up a bit in the evening, but you don't get anywhere taking notice of it."

"Just a minute," said Lanyon. He went out of the room and, when he came back, took the handkerchief from his breast pocket with three tablets in the corner.

He slipped them to Laurie and said, "Try that. Alec gave it me for the toothache once."

Laurie took the tablets. On a sudden impulse he said, "Thank you, Ralph."

Ralph smiled at him. It was an odd smile, with a practiced charm which it was impossible to mistake, and yet with something curiously vulnerable and defensive in it. Laurie felt an inexplicable urgency to be kind, for which he could find no expression.

"What treatment are they giving you?" Ralph reached up absently to the shelf and recovered his drink again. "God, I can see you now, with those filthy bandages black with blood, and the bone sticking out of them. D'you know how I came to find you? I was called to settle an argument on whether you were dead. I was rather busy just then; I remember asking what the hell I was supposed to do about it if you were, and did they think I was Jesus Christ? I didn't come for about five minutes, and by that time you were sufficiently alive to hand me the biggest raspberry in living memory."

"Don't keep telling me that. I was just being funny with myself. I'd have said it to anyone."

"You looked me straight in the eyes and brought it out snap."

"I couldn't tell you from Father Christmas. I don't think I'd remember it at all if someone hadn't told me about it afterwards. I'm only surprised that you recognized me. I can imagine how I looked from seeing the others."

Ralph gave him a narrow, silent look. "As a matter of fact, I recognized you then more quickly than I probably should have at any other time."

Some warning sense made Laurie look up; the dancing was getting spirited, and a couple was gambolling heavily toward him. With a flinching anticipation he saw them about to collide with his leg and tried to get it out of the way. Ralph was quicker: leaning out, he handed-off the dancers with such force that the near one almost fell over, regaining his balance, indignantly, some yards farther on.

"Why the —— can't you look where you're — well

135

going, you ——?" If Laurie had imagined Ralph as a captain before, he now glimpsed him vividly as a first mate. The dancer said, "Well, really, I'm sorry I'm sure, but there's no need to speak to me like *that*." Ralph's only reply was to stare him out; Laurie could hear him working off his protests on his partner half-way around the room.

"Hell," said Ralph, "that settles it, we *will* go." Just then, however, Sandy made an entrance, carrying the cake. Candles were lit and everyone stood around to see Alec blow them out. Sandy watched proudly at his elbow; someone said, "Have you wished?" and Alec paused for a moment, concentrating like a child with shut eyes, before he blew. Watching, Laurie was aware of some inward change in the group about him, a hopefulness, a wistfulness; they looked at the little ritual as though it were an affirmation of something doubtfully promised, or insecurely held, a symbol of stability, of permanence and trust. He thought of the white toy cupboard, the window bars, the place for the gate on the stairs.

Alec's health was drunk. "Happy Birthday" was sung, and the moment of sentiment was over; a reactive rowdiness at once set in. Ralph and Laurie hung about in the middle of the room, waiting to say goodbye, but Alec was telling a story and couldn't be detached at once. It was during this wait that someone came up whom Laurie recognized as the dancer Ralph had sworn at. He smiled at Ralph—he had a smile which looked as if he used it more often than not on people he disliked—and said, "My dear, *what* have you done with Bunny? Couldn't he get away?"

"He's working late," said Ralph. "He'll be along soon, I expect." His voice was extremely cool and steady. There are moments when one is aware of an actor using his technique in social life, and this was a professional manner too, but the profession was different.

"Well, I must say, I *am* relieved. Claude said to me only just now, 'Ralph's arrived on his own, does it *mean* anything?' You know what a bitchy little number *that* one is."

"What am I supposed to do?" asked Ralph calmly. "Bring Claude a duty sheet to show him why we can't all knock off at five?"

"Take my advice, my dear, and don't tell him *any*thing. You know *I* don't tell tales out of school." He looked at Laurie and back to Ralph again, gave a sudden startled giggle, and disappeared into the crowd.

Ralph said, "Alec's a fool to let Sandy bring people like that here." Then he looked straight at Laurie and added, "Bunny's a friend of mine, as I suppose you gathered. We're both working on the same job, more or less."

"That's a bit of luck for you both," Laurie said quickly. At a deep level of irrationality, too stupid to let oneself think about, he felt sore because Ralph hadn't told him before.

Ralph said, "Laurie, would you mind waiting here for a minute or two? I think I ought to make a phone call before I go."

"Of course." There had been something deliberate in Ralph's calling him Laurie again, it put time in remembrance.

The music had started again and the dancing was beginning. Ralph said, "Will you be all right here?" and helped him down on one of the divans against the wall. "You can look after my drink for me; here's yours." He put them down on the floor and, as he stooped, said softly, "Don't go away." It was a quick throwaway, done with great charm and at the same time discarded, as if to say, "You see what nonsense amuses some people." Laurie felt a sadness pressing on him from he did not know where. He smiled and settled his leg and said, "Not going is the thing I do best."

After Ralph had gone he felt suddenly isolated. In the bookshelf behind him he saw a binding he knew. Its schoolroom shabbiness was friendly and he took it down.

Soon cool drafts of air began to reach me; and a few steps farther I came forth into the open borders of the grove, and saw the sea lying blue and sunny to the horizon, and the surf tumbling and tossing its foam along the beach.

I have never seen the sea quiet round Treasure Island. The sun might blaze overhead, the air be without a breath, the surface smooth and blue, but still those great rollers . . .

A young man sat down beside him on the divan and, without any kind of preliminary, said, "Is it a queer book?"

"No," said Laurie.

"Oh," said the young man, on a note of utter deflation. He got up and went away.

. . . but still those great rollers would be running along all the external coast, thundering and thundering by day and night; and I scarce believe there is one spot in the island where a man would be out of earshot of their noise.

A considerable tumult at the door interrupted him. Rising above it a precise, scholarly, drunken voice was singing, "Happy Birthday to You." He looked up to see a man of about fifty-five, impeccably dressed, accompanied by a small crowd of naval ratings. There was a brief and clearly embarrassing exchange on the threshold, while Sandy and Alec eased them out again. The sailors, who were rather less drunk than their host, remained strictly neutral. Behind his shoulders two of them stood like heraldic supporters, one a curly-browed Cretan bull, the other a blank-faced boy of about eighteen. After the door had shut Alec walked over to Laurie, probably for no better reason than that he had happened to catch his eye. On a doctor's note of mild deprecation, he said, "One can't do anything about Harry. He'll get himself murdered, one of these days. We don't see more of him than we can help. I mean, one's prepared to pay one's own piper, but——"

"If one goes *any*where, after all," said Sandy, "one's bound to run into people."

"And you know," said Alec, "he's kind when he's sober. It's his business really, I suppose."

"I suppose," said Laurie. His mind had reverted to the younger sailor's face, with its look of a blank sheet waiting helplessly to be scribbled on.

"I'm glad we got rid of them, though, because Ralph

if he'd got back and found him here would have walked straight out of the place."

Laurie said nothing. With a new and better-informed gratitude, he summoned up remembrance of things past. He was still by all reasonable standards sober, but the gentle glow of his small dose reinforced the feeling which presently, as if by some magic power, seemed to open the door of the room and present him with its object.

Ralph came in looking not altogether happily preoccupied. Then he saw Laurie, and crossed over as if they had been the only two people in the room. "How's the leg? Did that stuff of Alec's work at all?"

Laurie realized with surprise that he hadn't noticed the leg for some ten minutes. He said, "It's marvellous stuff, what was it?"

"Something he gets from the hospital. A couple of drinks don't hurt either, in my experience. Where's mine you were looking after, by the way?"

Sandy came up just then and said, "Hello, Ralph, your *very* favorite person came and you missed him."

"Oh?" said Ralph, in a very even, colorless voice. He looked at Sandy, who began suddenly to rattle away at his little story so fast that it was quite ruined. Ralph gave a laugh which, though irritable, was also relieved. "I wonder why Alec always maintains he's so kindhearted."

"When he's sober, that's all Alec says." Sandy had tried to sound offhand, but a simple, almost brash partisanship sounded behind it.

"That must narrow down his opportunities to about six hours a week."

Alec had joined them in time to say, in his easy muted voice (it was always linked in Laurie's mind with remarks like, "I'll have a look at these sutures, Sister"), "He gets a bit lonely, I think. He always hates the thought of a party breaking up."

"I don't blame him," said Ralph crisply. "It must be tiresome to find that one's broken up along with it."

Alec looked at them with quiet resistance. He was, Laurie thought, a person who hated soft thinking on one hand and intolerance on the other; much of his life

139

must be spent fighting a war on two fronts. "One doesn't know how far he can help himself. Perhaps he can't be different from what he is."

"God," said Ralph, "what are any of us?" His blue eyes stared out with a kind of tired anger. "It's not what one is, it's what one does with it."

"Get your feet on the ground, my dear. People get sick of what they are. They get sick of carrying it. What d'you think dictators and party bosses are for? Or they just pour it down the drain and forget it, like Harry does. Everyone isn't like you, Ralph, trying to carry the world." His eyes met Ralph's for a moment. Laurie saw Sandy turn quickly and walk away.

When they had gone Ralph turned to Laurie. "You don't miss very much, do you?"

"Plenty, I should think." But he knew well enough what Ralph had meant.

"It was more than two years ago. I was running between Avonmouth and Quebec then. It got to a point where I threw up my job and spent a couple of months looking for something ashore. By the end of that time we both knew it would never work anyway. Sandy knows, of course. He's jealous of his own shadow and wasn't too pleased when I pitched up again, but he's not quite such a fool as he looks. He knows we had all our second thoughts at the time and there aren't any more. When people part as friends it's usually past resurrection; this was, anyhow."

Laurie found that none of this was a great surprise to him. Very early on, he had thought that Alec knew too much. He said, "You'd have missed the sea."

"I'll need to get used to that." He flipped idly at the padded fingers of the glove. "Alec formed the opinion that I took too much on myself." Without looking around he picked up his drink and finished it.

A rush of old memories went through Laurie like a pain. "I've never noticed," he said, "that the competition to take things on was as killing as all that."

Ralph stooped down and picked up the book from the floor; he must have seen it when he bent for his drink. Now he turned it over and read the title. "Oh,

Spuddy," he said, laughing and looking away. He got up quickly with the glasses and went over to fill them.

Laurie, who felt a fool, was relieved to see him caught up with a group of new arrivals at the door. As greetings settled down into conversation, however, the thought that he might not come back again was less welcome.

The party had warmed up by this time. A momentary detachment came upon Laurie as he looked on. After some years of muddled thinking on the subject, he suddenly saw quite clearly what it was he had been running away from; why he had refused Sandy's first invitation, and what the trouble had been with Charles. It was also the trouble, he perceived, with nine-tenths of the people here tonight. They were specialists. They had not merely accepted their limitations, as Laurie was ready to accept his, loyal to his humanity if not to his sex, and bringing an extra humility to the hard study of human experience. They had identified themselves with their limitations; they were making a career of them. They had turned from all other reality, and curled up in them snugly, as in a womb.

Trying to form his ideas quickly before he was interrupted again, he found instead that he was staring at Ralph, who was standing in the thick of the crowd, hard and crisp and gay, laughing at someone's dirty story, his battle-scars put neatly out of sight.

He moved impatiently in his seat; he felt angry and useless, and wondered how late he would have to stay. He had a sudden homesick vision of Andrew in the ward kitchen starting to wash up, the brown teapot with the Sister's stewed tea saved on one side.

For the last few minutes two army officers had been sitting at the other end of the divan, punctuating a hot item of gossip with little squeals. Now one of them nudged the other, who raised his eyebrows, coughed, and went away. The first moved, purposefully, nearer.

"He *knew* I wanted him to go, but he gets *daily* cruder. Now quickly tell me all about yourself. Why haven't I seen you here before?"

"I've not been here before." Laurie didn't mind the pink and yellow gold bracelet, which was Cartier and rather beautiful; but he noticed too the eyes, which were hard and shallow, and the soft self-pitying mouth.

"Not? And you don't go to Max's, at least so Claude tells me, *I* don't go, my dear, not my thing at all." With rapid but profuse detail he sketched the private life and eccentricities of the man who had just gone. Laurie listened, fascinated, not believing it but impressed by the inventive fertility. He listened indeed a little too well, for soon the officer was saying, "Well, come along, dear, this seems as good a moment as any to be slipping away. Though what moment wouldn't be good; I do see now what they meant about Sandy's evenings. Whether it's the sight of Alec's true-blue past frowning on the revels like the statue in *Don Giovanni,* though for all that they do tell me, strictly *entre nous*—"

"If you mean Ralph Lanyon," said Laurie, who was beginning to be rather drunk, "he's a friend of mine, I've known him for years."

"*Real*-ly? *No.* Then, my dear, do tell me, is it true that he"—here something in Laurie's face seemed to give him pause—"well, there, fancy. Now before Alec starts to organize intellectual paper games, which can scarcely be ruled out as a possibility, we'll tiptoe off and——"

Feeling suddenly annoyed, Laurie said, "Well, if it's really all right about the wooden leg?"

The officer looked down and noticed the stick for the first time. Laurie watched, smugly, his struggle for equilibrium.

"Sorry," said Ralph. "Thought I should never get away." He lowered himself onto the middle of the divan, coolly forcing the officer to make room. So relieved was Laurie by his arrival that he scarcely noticed it had been proprietary to the point of arrogance. The officer appeared to recognize with delighted surprise someone at the other end of the room. When he had gone Ralph said, "I'd only just realized that was happening, or I'd have got here before."

"I wasn't nervous," said Laurie lightly, reacting to the proprietorship without noticing it.

"I'm sorry if I interrupted anything."

Laurie could not believe that he was expected to

take this seriously. He said, "Do you remember that old red Turkish slipper you used for beating the twirps?"

"Yes," said Ralph, still half frowning. "It was an odd one."

"They argued that a lot. They used to try and remember, before they went in, to look if it was left or right. No one ever did."

"Spud, did I tell you just now you were too good to be true? Stop me if you've heard it, because they tell me I tend to repeat myself when drunk, and I'm about one short of bloody drunk, so kindly correct any such tendency on all occasions. Thank you. I think I might have the other now."

"Aren't you going to drive me back? It's the only way I've got of getting there."

Sounding suddenly stone sober, Ralph said, "Don't worry, Spud, that will be all right." He went off rather stiffly to the drinks table.

Just as he had got back again, someone near the door said in a suppressed voice, "Look, here's Bim." At this announcement Laurie saw a weasellike person, to whom he had not spoken all the evening, looking at him expectantly.

A young flight-lieutenant came in. He was a small man but very handsome, with a tough, steely kind of grace. The high girlish voice with which he greeted his friends was burlesqued and perfunctory, like a carnival vizard held with a flourish a foot away from the face. You felt, and were meant to feel, that he was playing at it. He was like a little fighting-cock, brave, shining, and cruel. He took one swift look around the room, saw Ralph and Laurie, and crossed over to them beautifully, like a dancer walking.

"Ralph, my poor sweet," he crowed shrilly, "what *have* you got there?"

Ralph said quite quietly, "Hello, Bim." He put down his drink and stood up.

Bim cocked his head sideways and glinted up at him. "How many times has Auntie got to tell you? You *must* attend to these things earlier in the evening, while your eye's still in."

Now we'll see something, thought Laurie not without satisfaction.

Ralph looked at Bim quietly for a moment; then he took his arm and said, pleasantly, "Relax, my dear, you're full up with benzedrine and five drinks behind. Come along and get loaded down to your marks, there's a good boy."

Laurie perceived now in all this hard glitter something feverish and taut. Alec had come up, looking unhappy. He said, "Shut up, Ralph, what he wants is bromide and twelve hours' sleep."

"Shut up, both of you," said Bim gaily, shaking off Ralph's hand. "I'll tell you what I want when I want it. Introduce, my dear; it's so unlike you to be the least bit gauche."

Standing behind his shoulder, Alec gave the others a look of warning and apology. "Bim Taylor, Laurie Odell. Laurie and Ralph were at school together; they've just run into each other tonight after not having met for years."

Laurie was the only person not standing, a thing that does not seem awkward till one is tied. Nothing would have induced him to struggle to his feet under those bright satiric eyes, so he lounged defiantly where he was. But something rather odd was happening; Bim had taken a step backwards, wide-eyed, and was staring at him with awe.

"But, my dears, you don't mean this? Not *the* Odell?"

Laurie thought he had seldom heard a more pointless joke and didn't even take the trouble to smile; though, considering much else that had been going on, he couldn't see why Alec should look so embarrassed about it.

"Perhaps," said Bim, "I should have said, 'Not the late Odell?' Well, better late than never, obviously."

The feeling of a dense atmospheric pressure caused Laurie to look around. He saw that Ralph was staring silently, not at Bim but at Alec. Alec opened his mouth to speak, but didn't say anything. There was something pent and helpless about him, though he had not dropped his eyes. Laurie supposed that he must have

144

been gossiping to Bim on the landing before he came in. Ralph's look of shocked contempt was a little excessive, but he could be awkward after a few drinks, as Laurie had seen already.

Bim stood looking at all three of them with a deadly kind of inquisitiveness, the intent irresponsible look a monkey gives to something it is just going to pick up and break. "Have I," he asked, "said anything in any way out of place?"

"Not in the least," said Ralph. Once before Laurie had heard him speak with what might have been called professional finish. It was very much more apparent now. You would have said that he hadn't a care in the world, and that his next words would probably be, "Take your boat stations in an orderly manner, please. There is plenty of room in the boats for everyone."

In fact, however, he said, "I think you *had* better get drunk, Bim. Come along and I'll fix you one of my specials."

"We'll *all* get drunk in a minute," said Bim, looking around with a flashing smile. "But, darlings, if you think I'm going *any*where before I've got the true story of this romantic Odyssey, you must be *mad*." He flicked out a heavy silk handkerchief with a monogram; a gold and platinum identity bracelet caught the light. "It *is* the Odyssey, isn't it? I went to such a ropy school, my dear," he confided to Laurie. "Free expression and no classics, *you*'d have *hated* it. *Is* it the Odyssey? The one where this silly boy goes away for about twenty years, and when he appears again he's so dreadfully gone off that no one knows him except the nurse who . . . oh, excuse me, perhaps we'd better scrub that bit. And the dog took one look, didn't he, and died of shock. And all this while, the poor queen has been knitting and knitting away *madly* in the bedroom, dropping stitches left and right, with suitors camping and screaming all over the house." He smiled at them ingenuously, like a stage undergraduate. "Or is it Shakespeare I'm thinking of all the time?"

Laurie swung himself up on his feet. On the spur of the moment he found a new technique for doing it; it was rather painful, but it looked smooth. With intense pleasure he found himself three inches taller than Bim.

"No," he said. "It's the Odyssey all right. It's the one where the man comes back from the war and finds the flash boys on his pitch, and runs them out."

"Your sentiments do you credit," said Bim raising his eyebrows.

Laurie listened to the internal echo of his own words with incredulous horror. Whatever would Ralph . . .

"Now, you two," said Sandy suddenly. "Paddy-paws, paddy-paws, claws in." A kind of pepper-cloud of facetiousness was flung on them from all sides. It brought Laurie very thoroughly down to earth. He could feel himself shaking with mingled anger, strain, and fatigue; and in jumping up he had wrenched his knee. Stirred by Sandy, the group was changing and breaking up around him. He felt a hard grip on his elbow and, turning, found Ralph saying something to him with anxious insistence; but he had missed it, and now Ralph had vanished in the crowd.

Laurie sat down again, feeling deadly tired. This was his first night out of hospital for months. Looking at his watch he saw that it was after ten; even with a pass he would still have been late. He had better ask Alec where the nearest telephone was; but Alec was talking to Sandy in a corner and it looked as though they were having words. The room was full of new faces; there were some furtive slippings-out, and self-conscious reappearances. Longing to be gone, he lit a cigarette and snatched a few minutes' awkward rest, propped against the wall.

The divan sagged down. He turned to find Alec beside him.

"Laurie, I'm awfully sorry. Do forgive us all. I promised Ralph I'd look after you specially while he was gone."

"Gone?" said Laurie. He looked around. No, of course, he hadn't seen Ralph for some minutes now.

"He won't be long. He's just taking Bim home."

Laurie drew in his breath sharply. He reached down to the floor, and felt for his stick.

"I don't think I'll wait, thanks very much."

146

"When I say home, I only mean to a friend of his who'll look after him and give him a bed. Ralph'll probably be back in about fifteen minutes. It's not far."

"Thanks," said Laurie, "but I won't wait."

"But what about——"

"It's all right, I can get a car."

He could sleep in a shelter somewhere, and get a bus in the morning. He'd have his passes stopped for a month; but, he thought bitterly, there wouldn't be much hardship in that.

"I do wish you wouldn't," said Alec. He sat curled up on the divan looking rather charming and sensitive, and just a little exploiting it. "You see, there's been a slight misunderstanding between Ralph and me just recently, which it won't be easy for me to clear up; I don't want him upset any more if I can help it."

"It doesn't matter in any case. It's been a lovely party; thank you both for asking me."

He started to get up. Alec reached out a surprisingly firm hand and quietly pulled him back.

"The thing about all that was, Bim had just about got to the end, and Ralph happened to be the only person who could do anything with him."

Laurie thought of a good answer to this; but something gave him pause, and he didn't say it.

"It's a shame you couldn't have met Bim a few months ago; well, even a few weeks. He was light relief, you know. Pure Restoration comedy. I don't know how long it is since he averaged more than two or three hours' sleep out of the twenty-four, he's stopped talking about it; they're not supposed to let on how far under strength they are. As a matter of fact, I think Bim's one of two or three people who are still alive of the original squadron a few months back. I've no idea how long a break they've given him now, but I do know it takes a lot of sedative to cancel out a week's benzedrine, especially if you've forgotten how to give it the chance. He can't go on much longer. It's too bad you had to meet him just tonight."

"I shouldn't have taken any notice."

"Oh, my dear, it was just what he was after. If you hadn't played I think he'd have collapsed like a house of cards, and I'd have hated that. He's had a bit of a thing about Ralph for quite a while, but Ralph's always managed to laugh it off successfully, up till tonight."

"Oh," said Laurie. "I see."

"I was sure you would. Just a minute." He got up and took a plate of sandwiches from Sandy, who looked rather sulky about it. "Do have something to eat; I'm going to. Sandy'll cope with the rabble. How long have you been discharged from hospital, by the way? There was such a babel going on when Sandy told me."

"It'll be another week or two, I expect."

"Oh, *God*. No wonder Ralph . . . I thought you were looking tired. What will they do to you when you get back?"

"Oh, nothing much. First offense. I feel fine. I think, you know, that probably I ought to be going. If you'd just tell Ralph that I'm sorry I couldn't wait."

"If it's a matter of time, it'll be quicker to wait for him. He can't be long." He bit into a sandwich, opened it to look inside, and stuck it together again. "I wonder what I put in that one, it's rather good. In case I didn't make this clear, there isn't the slightest reason why Ralph should take any responsibility for Bim, except that he's a person whom responsibility always seems to stick to."

"I suppose he always was."

"It was rather bad luck, his getting beached. Especially as it was a matter of inches, literally. He lost just half a finger too many. Two and a half instead of two. With two he'd probably have got back on the active list again." He opened another sandwich. "A good deal seems to have happened to Ralph at Dunkirk, one way and another."

Just then Sandy came up and said tartly, "Alec, if you could possibly tear yourself away for a moment, Peter and Theo want to say goodbye."

Alec said, with pointed friendliness, "Just a moment, Laurie; I'll be right back." He went and saw off the people who were leaving; immediately after, Laurie saw him get Sandy in a corner and give him what looked like a quiet but concentrated dressing-down.

148

When Sandy began to argue, he silenced him with a look and turned away.

"I've brought you a drink," said Alec, returning. "Don't take any notice of Sandy; he gets little turns, but they don't mean a thing."

Laurie took the unknown mixture and tasted it. It was smooth on the palate and, he guessed, concealed a ferocious kick; but it made him feel, for the moment, better. Alec said, "It's what Ralph calls his special."

"You were going to tell me something. I can't remember what it was now. About Ralph at Dunkirk, or something."

"Oh, yes. Well, on second thoughts, I can't remember what it was either."

"Just as you like."

"Don't be like that about it. It's just—oh, well, nothing, except that Ralph's got a funny idea about me this evening and it seems rather a moment not to add to it. You see, to give you a slightly more intelligible angle on all this, perhaps I ought to explain that Ralph and I at one time saw a good deal more of each other than we do now."

"Yes, he told me."

Alec looked at him without annoyance and said, "Yes, of course. So you'll see how it is that I might know one or two things about Ralph which at the time he told them to me might seem in some degree to be my concern, and which afterwards one would regard as, well, privileged."

"Yes," said Laurie hazily. "Yes, quite." He could feel the potion dissolving his fatigue into a loose-limbed relaxation. He thought that Alec had a pleasant, restful voice.

"So just now my name's mud, which isn't enjoyable, especially as I can do damn-all about it; but I mind more about Ralph, really. Not that I'm anything much now, of course; it's just that so many of Ralph's things have gone, if you understand me."

"What did you put in this drink?"

"Oh. Oh, yes, of course. Don't mind me, just drop off when you feel like it."

149

"No, stay here and talk. I like it. Only Sandy doesn't like it. You know about that?"

"Yes, I know about that. It's not good for him to be let get away with it. He'll be all right. What makes me cross about people like Ralph is the way everyone uses them. Their life gets like one of those ham spy films where they brief the agent and say, 'But remember, one slip and you're on your own.' Take school. I went to a conventional public school and by firmly eluding all responsibility, I managed to get along nicely. Really, it makes me feel quite indignant when I think what must have been put on Ralph; and then, when the crack-up happened, no one was even sorry for him. Except you, of course."

"*Sorry* for him?" Laurie opened his eyes wide; for a moment he struggled awake; he stared at Alec. "I wasn't sorry for him."

Alec looked at him. "I see," he said slowly. "Oh, God, yes, now I see everything."

"I don't know what you mean." He listened to the drag of his own voice and thought, No doubt about that. Drunk. Stinking.

"It doesn't matter," said Alec. "Let it go. No one but a lunatic would shove his oar in here, anyway."

"I think we're both a little bit tight. I am."

"Oh, well, then we know where we are, don't we? *In vino veritas:* alarmingly true, usually, don't you find? It's nice to know you make such a candid and sympathetic drunk; it's reassuring, as far as it goes. Were you very surprised to find that Ralph remembered you after all?"

"He's got a very good memory. Knew everyone's name, all the little twirps, first day of term, everyone."

"Listen, Laurie. Are you listening?"

"Sorry, Alec. You shouldn't have put all that in this drink."

"Oh, well. Can you see Sandy anywhere about?"

"No. Not here. Shall we look?"

"No, he's just being naughty. We must leave him a bit longer or he'll get spoilt. Everyone seems quite happy." The few guests who were left seemed, indeed, to be sufficiently entertaining one another. "Do you think it funny that a person who's been attracted by Ralph should also be attracted by Sandy? Or do you think I'm just not particular, as they say?"

"No, I think you're nice. Funny, but really very nice."

"Too kind, as Florence Nightingale said to Edward the Seventh. Much too kind, I'm afraid. T. E. Lawrence has a rather sad passage about 'complex men who know how sacrifice uplifts the redeemer and casts down the bought.' He doesn't use the word 'complex' flatteringly, and neither do I. Ralph's tragedy is that he's retained through everything a curious innocence about it. I suppose when at last he loses that, the tragedy will be complete."

"Where is he?"

"Oh, hello. I thought you passed out minutes ago. Ralph won't be long."

"Is he all right? You said he's in a spot. You said then—tell me again. Can I do something? Where is he?"

"Not now. Take it easy. He'll be on his way back by this time."

"No, tell me, please, if I can do something. I want to know."

"Not for the moment. It's a pity, as things are, he takes such a functional view of his own existence. He isn't even scrapping himself tragically; just by fits and starts of irritation, like throwing out junk you don't see a use for. I don't suppose, really, there was ever a time when I could have done much about it. Complex man with his mean little instinct of self-preservation. He could get plenty of full-time passengers, God knows, but he despises them. No, I see now the only kind of person who'd offer him some hope of happiness would be someone up to his own strength with the continual patience to go on concealing it. Or, of course, the modesty not to know it, which would mean an innocence comparable in its way with his own."

Laurie, who disliked to feel himself slipping, had been determined to follow every word of this. He opened his heavy eyes.

"Like Bunny?" he said.

151

"*What?*"

"This friend of his. Bunny, isn't it, he said?"

"Oh, dear God. Make yourself comfortable, my dear. Lie down properly and put your feet up; that's the way. I'm not going to bother you any more."

"I'm not so sleepy. When Ralph comes back, if he's in a fix you've got to wake me. No good keep talking about he's in trouble, and not do anything. Ralph was very good to me."

"Was he? Laurie. *Laurie.* Just a minute. It doesn't matter about the rest if you just listen to this. Do you hear?"

"Yes?" Laurie half sat up, rubbing an arm smarting from Alec's wiry strength. "Yes, I can hear. What is it?"

"Stick around Ralph for a bit. Will you? You, not anyone else. That's all. Just stick around."

"That's all right. I won't go away. I'll wait for him here if it takes all night."

Alec looked down at him for a moment, shrugged his shoulders, got up and went over to the group by the fire. Someone said, "Sandy seems to have vanished lately. Is all well?"

"Oh, yes; he's making coffee or something, I expect."

"Well, you *were* having a rather cozy get-together."

"That? I was just carrying out an experiment in sleep-suggestion. They do it in *Brave New World,* with tiny little radios under the pillows."

"I think I should check your results a good long way from Sandy, if I were you. And just possibly from Ralph Lanyon—or am I letting my imagination run away with me?"

Laurie opened his eyes, vaguely. By some biochemical trick, now that he was free to sleep he found that he couldn't. He hung in a suspended half-consciousness. Alec's cocktail couldn't be wearing off so soon; he discovered that he hadn't even finished it. It occurred to him that the drug Ralph had given him, earlier, had been the potent force; that it was passing its peak, and that though he was both torpid and rather drunk, he was neither to the point of incapacity. He would get up

152

as soon as Ralph came back, and give them all a surprise. Ralph would . . .

The door opened. Ralph looked in and, ignoring everyone else in the room, said, "Alec. Can you come for a minute?"

Laurie sat up. He felt dizzy and swayed a little as he got to his feet; but this did not affect at all the strange sharpness which had happened in his mind, like the sudden crystallization of a fluid, as soon as he heard Ralph's voice. Out of all the known and unknown possibilities, he guessed at once what kind of emergency this was.

He was still drunk enough to have lost certain social inhibitions. The discreet murmur of the residual guests (by now there were only four), and their careful noninterference, infected him with no hesitation. Implanted in his mind, at some nonrational level, was the idea that Ralph was in a fix and needed him. He followed Alec out to the landing.

The party had been discreetly lit with a couple of shaded table lamps; by contrast, the naked light from the open door of the bathroom seared the eyes. Ralph ran down the stairs with the brisk neatness of a seaman; Alec holding the banisters swung down in strides and was just behind him. Laurie, arriving last, found them both kneeling over Sandy, who was lying on the bath mat with a dressing-gown thrown over his naked body. He was groaning, and showing the whites of his eyes. Round his left wrist was a tourniquet made of a folded handkerchief, a toothbrush, and a strip torn from a towel. The bath was half full of crimson water.

Alec said nothing. With a feverish but instinctively exact movement, he took Sandy's other wrist and felt the pulse.

Ralph said, "He's all right. I left the bath so that you could see how much he's lost. You can tell in water better than I can."

Alec looked up. "Not more than two pints at the most, I should think. Pulse ninety-six. Sandy!"

Sandy groaned, and turned his face away.

Speaking across him as though he were an inanimate

object Ralph said, "I heard him in here, doing that, as I came upstairs. The door wasn't locked."

Sandy rolled over toward Alec again. "Let me alone," he said in a dying voice. "I want to finish it. Go away." Ralph slapped him lightly across the face and said, "Shut up."

"Please, Ralph," said Alec, "not now. He's feeling ill."

"He's not feeling half as ill as I'd like to make him."

"Go away," said Sandy. "Go away."

Laurie felt sorry for Alec but his sympathies were with Ralph. There was no doubt that Sandy looked a disgusting spectacle, with his pale damp face, his head lolling on the bath mat, his watery eyes upturned. He had thrown off the dressing-gown as he moved, and Ralph with a gesture of distaste twitched it back again. The movement caught Laurie's eye. Suddenly he realized Ralph had taken off his glove; it was the left hand Laurie was looking at.

He had seen so much in hospital that if it had been displayed to him deliberately, in a moment when he had been thinking about it, he would have felt scarcely a qualm except of sympathy; but now, he felt a catch in his stomach. Not only the two last fingers were missing and half the second, but the outermost bone of the hand had gone too, taking with it the margin of the palm and narrowing it by an inch. The effect was strange and clawlike; at the edge, and at the stumps of the fingers, the recently healed flesh was still red and mauve. Ralph was balanced on his heels, his good hand holding the edge of the bath; and it came back to Laurie that he had had beautiful hands, with which he had never made an affected or exhibiting movement; neither coarse nor overfine, full of intelligence and adaptable strength. The one that was left was still the same.

Just as if Laurie had spoken aloud, Ralph's head came up and their eyes met. He said coolly, "Shut the door, Spud."

At the sound of Laurie's name Sandy squirmed around toward Alec, moaning.

"Alec—don't bring *him* here. Oh, how could you? No no, it's too much."

154

"Shut up," said Ralph. "I'll bring the police if you don't behave."

Laurie said, "I'm sorry. I'd better clear out."

"Don't go, Spud," said Ralph. "I might want you." He jerked the chain of the bath-plug and the water started to gurgle out. Suddenly he said in an urgent undertone, "Bolt the door. Don't make a row about it."

Laurie slid the bolt home softly. Next moment the handle turned, persistently, but in a refined, rather furtive way. Laurie knew at once that a woman was doing it. It hadn't struck him before that in an unconverted house the bathroom might be shared. Ralph slammed his right hand flat over Sandy's mouth, cleared his throat raspingly, and gave a loud, aggressively masculine cough. The door-handle went dead, and a fading creak sounded on the stairs.

"That would have been pretty," Ralph said. He removed his hand from Sandy's face and added, "All right, you can start groaning again now."

"We'll have to get him out of this," said Alec.

"You've got something there. Here, you." He shook Sandy's shoulder. "Get up, damn you. You've got to move."

"Don't, Ralph." Alec knelt down beside Sandy and put an arm around his shoulders. "Look, old dear, you'll get pneumonia lying here all wet on the floor. You've got to let us get you to bed. Try and sit up, come on."

There was certainly a good deal of water about. Laurie noticed for the first time—the darkness of the navy cloth had disguised it—that Ralph's uniform was soaking wet from shoulder to knee. It couldn't have been a light job to heave Sandy unaided out of the bath; Laurie was struck forcibly with this while they were trying to persuade the patient onto his feet. Clammy, slippery, and repulsive to the touch, he kept sliding through their hands like a fish and subsiding on the mat again. Laurie saw Ralph open his mouth, shut it after a glance at Alec, and swear to himself soundlessly.

"Sandy," said Alec. He was panting with exertion;

155

his face looked white and strained. "Sandy, *try*. Why can't you get up? What is it?"

"I'm going to die," said Sandy. "Oh, God, I'm going to die." He rolled over and was violently sick on the bath mat.

Ralph let go of him and stood up. Sitting back against the edge of the bath, with his hands in his pockets, he stared down at Sandy silently; then he looked at Alec. Laurie, who was well sobered up by now, had a powerful consciousness that he shouldn't be there, and looked behind the bath for a floorcloth. The smell of steam, blood, vomit, and stale drink was overwhelming.

The silent conversation behind his back ended, or perhaps was cut off by the sounds Sandy was making. Laurie was in time to see Alec take his pulse again. His face had a blotchy, blue-and-yellow look. Ralph said, unemotionally, "He can't possibly have taken anything, as well, I suppose?"

Alec said, "Sandy, have you? Sandy! Sandy, you must tell us. Sandy—please."

Sandy, stark naked after the recent struggle, heaved himself into a Dying Gladiator pose. "What do you care? I shan't tell you." He collapsed again.

"Sandy. Listen to me——"

"No," said Ralph. He pushed Alec on one side, not unkindly but with finality. "Listen to *me*. How much more responsibility do you expect Alec to take for you, you fish-bellied, blackmailing little crap? You're talking to me now. Are you going to tell us what you've taken, or shall I send Spud here to phone the hospital? Well? Take your choice."

Closing his eyes, Sandy murmured, "Only—aspirin. What there was in the bottle."

Ralph looked at Alec. "How much?"

"Not more than a dozen tablets. He must have brought most of it up."

It seemed, indeed, that there was no more to come. They rolled Sandy's limp form off the bath mat, and Laurie swilled it under the tap. Ralph said, "Better give him a tot, I suppose?"

"Not if he's bleeding much. I'll have a look." Alec

156

untwisted the toothbrush from the tourniquet. "Good Lord, Ralph, you put this on tight enough."

"It's supposed to be a tourniquet. Not a bangle."

"My hand's gone dead," moaned Sandy, reviving a little and working his fingers about. A dark red, sluggish bleeding at once started again. Alec stared at the razor cut, drawing his brows together, before he pressed back the pad and put the bandage on.

Ralph said, "Don't tell me, I know. It needs stitching."

"Yes," said Alec. His examination of the wound had been confident and decisive; now suddenly he looked up at Ralph, worried to rags, his resources scattered, a civilized mind put out of gear by an uncivilized situation. "What on earth shall we do, Ralph? I've got nothing here."

"I'll drive you down to the hospital. You can pick the things up there, surely. Spud'll cope with everything here all right; won't you, Spud?"

He smiled at Laurie, briefly. More than anything till now, the smile evoked a host of memories. For that casual accolade, cutthroat little competitions, all the shrewder for being tacit and undiscussed, had gone on all over School. It looked strange in this hole-and-corner, squalid setting, touched still as it was with confident assumptions and open skies.

"Of course I will."

Ralph smiled again, which hadn't happened at school, and said, "Right. Let's heave him into bed and get going."

Alec, however, looked more worried than ever. "The trouble about the hospital is, I might get stuck there."

"How d'you mean, stuck?"

"If the warning goes. I"—he looked down at Sandy, wretchedly—"I'm supposed to be on a casualty team. If there was a raid. Often there's nothing to do, but if I were in the place I couldn't walk out of it." He reached for the dressing-gown and tucked it around Sandy, who was now shivering violently.

Ralph said expressionlessly, "He's on call too, I suppose?"

Alec looked up at him. "Ralph. Have a heart."

"Sorry," said Ralph. Again Laurie felt that he shouldn't be there.

"Look," he said, "before we start getting him out, would you like anything done about the people upstairs? We must have been in here quite a while."

"About eight minutes. Yes, Spud, go and get rid of them, will you?"

As he pulled himself upstairs on the banisters, Laurie found himself foolishly pleased by the fact that Ralph had said simply, "Get rid of them" without offering any directions.

To the guests he offered Alec's apologies: Sandy had passed out and at first they had thought he was just tight, but now Alec had taken his temperature, which was a hundred and two. Alec hoped it was only influenza, but there was a lot of diphtheria about. It was all rather worrying. Luckily the lavatory was well separated from the bathroom and they all knew the way to it.

Ralph and Alec had got Sandy sitting on the bathroom stool, where he looked like a groggy boxer at the ninth round.

"All clear," Laurie said.

"What did you tell them?" Alec's voice was getting increasingly overkeyed. It was Ralph who said, "Good show."

When Sandy had been maneuvered into the bedroom, Laurie went back to clean the bathroom up. On the floor, under the stool, he found Ralph's glove, the padding round and firm, the empty part defining the shape of the truncated hand. He laid it where it had fallen, touching it kindly.

Upstairs they had got Sandy into bed, where he was quietly weeping and holding Alec's hand. Ralph was sitting on the dressing-table smoking, and Alec was saying to him, "But what will you *say*?"

Ralph drew deeply and irritably on his cigarette. "I shall tell him the truth, naturally. Omitting names, and a few other things."

"But, Ralph, supposing he——"

"He's got a right to know he's not being mixed up in an assault case. Take it or leave it, Alec. If you'd rather I drove you to the hospital you've only to say so."

"All right," said Alec, "if you really think so."

"Good enough," said Ralph. He looked up suddenly. "Oh, there you are, Spud. What happened to you, are you all right?"

"Yes, of course. I've been removing clues in the bathroom."

"This boy thinks of everything. Did I leave a glove there?"

"I didn't see one."

While Ralph was fetching it, Laurie turned to Alec to ask if there was anything he could do. At the sound of his voice Sandy's sobs redoubled.

Pretending not to notice this, Alec said, "No, thanks, Laurie. You've been awfully good about all this. I feel——" He looked down at Sandy, who seemed about to have a fit of hysterics, and made a helpless ashamed little gesture. In a changed brisk voice he said, "Ralph thinks the naval surgeon at his Station will let him have some needles and gut without being too difficult. He's just going off to see."

"Oh, good," said Laurie vaguely. He had stopped wondering when he would get back to his own hospital, or what would happen to him. It became evident to him now that this question was distressing Alec to a point where he couldn't talk about it. Laurie wanted to say it was all right and that he mustn't worry; but the presence of Sandy, the original host, was inhibiting. In a minute or so, Laurie would be left alone in the flat with the two of them. Just then, like an answer to prayer, Ralph appeared in the doorway fastening his glove. Laurie stepped forward.

"Can I come with you?"

"Yes," said Ralph. His face was in shadow and Laurie thought how this gave his eyes a grave withdrawn look. "Yes, Spud, do."

On the landing he picked up his cap and his blue stormcoat and said, "It's cold tonight. Haven't you anything warm?"

"I lost it in the wash, like King John. It's not that cold, anyway."

"Why the army doesn't mutiny I never know. Here, Alec, I'm borrowing your burberry and a scarf for Spud. I'll bring them back." He shut the bedroom door with a relieved kind of finality. "And now, before we do anything else, what's the telephone number of your hospital and who do I ask for?"

Laurie told him. Ralph said, "I'll be five minutes. Wait for me in here." Laurie wandered obediently into the sitting room. It had the usual debauched look of rooms after parties, and he remembered that Alec would have all this to cope with alone. He collected the glasses, found the kitchen, and washed them in the sink.

Ralph's voice behind him said, "For Christ's sake, Spud, haven't you had enough tonight? Leave that and come on. I've fixed the nurse."

"How on earth did you do that?"

"She hadn't reported you yet. It seems the Day Sister had the evening off and no one else was sure if you had a pass. The situation now is that I should have had you back in time, but my car was involved in an accident and I've been held up making statements to the police. You weren't in the accident, it was before I arrived, so you needn't know much about it. Come on, let's go."

Outside he had a big battered sports car, belonging to a year when a resemblance to racing cars—a thick leather strap around the bonnet, the extrusion of copper pipes—was still considered smart. In uncertain starlight they fiddled with its rickety and obstructive hood, nipped their fingers, swore, said it wasn't as cold as all that, and gave it up. Ralph warmed up the engine with a noise that outraged the quiet street; the car started, they were away. Now for the first time abruptly conscious of being alone, charged with the events of the evening and no longer able to diffuse themselves in activity or among other people, they were isolated together at the fixed center of the huge, swiftly running night.

For what seemed a long time they drove in silence. Ralph's two gloved hands, resting easily on the wheel, looked like the hands of any other driver; it was only when he had to change the gear, which was worn and

160

cranky, that Laurie felt in the arm and shoulder beside him the tension of concealed strain.

"Warm enough, Spud?"

"Fine."

They drove on. Somewhere a clock struck the last quarter before midnight.

Ralph said, "I suppose I got there about seven-thirty. Four hours."

They had come to a bridge over the river. The ground was high here, the river ran between cliffs. Laurie thought how in peacetime, from here, the town would have lain below them like a starry sky. Now, as the bridge gave gently on its chains in the wind that swept along the gorge, there was only a darkling sense of loneliness and height. Ralph showed a pass to a cloaked shadow. It was like a transit of the Styx.

The road climbed again, through old dark beech-woods. Ralph said out of a long silence, with a quiet and somehow touching simplicity, "What a way to have met."

Threading the long vault of black trees under a slaty glimmer of sky, Laurie felt an almost astral detachment. "Yes," he said, "it was strange. It was like having been lost in a surrealist picture, eyes with iron spikes growing out of them, and dead horses in Paris hats. All done very bright and sharp and looking almost solid. Then something real appears, and it all peels off like wet paper."

Ralph seemed to pause over this for some minutes. "Did it really seem as unlikely to you as that?"

"It does now." He was in a vivid, dreamlike stage of fatigue.

Ralph flipped a cigarette-case onto the seat between them. "Light one for me too, will you?"

Laurie lit two together as he had seen other people do sometimes. When Ralph took it without thanking him it didn't seem brusque, but as if they had been doing this for years.

"In some ways," Ralph said, "it was like meeting during an action. You come out knowing each other a lot too well to begin at the beginning." He paused to settle his cigarette. "And yet, not well enough."

161

Laurie said sleepily, "So one has to go back or go on."

"I'm not good on reversing."

As if to give an unmeant point to his words, they had come to a steep downgrade for which he had to put the car in second. Laurie felt the effort being made to conceal effort, and guessed, now, that he had not been driving again for long and that the gear-lever still hurt his hand. It occurred to Laurie that a large number of drivers in this situation would have let themselves be tempted to go down on the footbrake; but Ralph had always hated anything sloppy.

He said nothing more till he had changed up again, then, as if continuing a quite different conversation: "I think what gets me down most about Sandy is his stupidity. He's lived a year with Alec and still hasn't cottoned on to his—his fanatical claustrophobia. Anyone who tries to put a screw on Alec is playing about with something dangerous. I don't know how far Alec realizes that himself." He stopped talking while he crossed a main road and added, "Some things about him don't alter, much as he's changed."

The bitterness he had kept out of his voice seemed to thread itself under Laurie's skin. Tentatively he said, "He seemed to be worried about something you thought he'd done and he thought he hadn't. I'm afraid I was rather drunk at the time; I don't think he said what it was."

"He knows what he's done. It's not worth talking about." One should have remembered, Laurie thought, that knack of formidable silence. There must however have been a difference of some kind, or Laurie certainly wouldn't have felt that it devolved upon him to break it. He said, "This will have taught Sandy a lesson, anyway."

As if nothing had happened Ralph said, "That's what I thought the first time. Oh, yes, and he gave Alec his solemn word of honor not to do it again."

"What did he do then?"

"Phenacetin, or veganin, or something like that. About half the fatal dose. Alec didn't know that, of course. He was all alone that time, laboring away with

162

emetics and things and nearly going mental. He goes through torments of remorse afterwards. Alec, I mean; not Sandy, of course."

"You know, anyone could have fainted in that bath and been drowned."

"I think that started to occur to him when he heard me passing the door. It was lucky I did—I suppose. I really don't think one should be expected to meet his friends; if Alec wants to put up with them himself, it's his business. I never go there now without wondering whether they'll start turning up in drag."

"In what?" asked Laurie curiously.

He felt that in the near-darkness Ralph turned his head with an almost startled look; he repeated himself, however, without comment.

"Yes, I heard you before, but what does it mean?"

Ralph said, in a slight clear voice which seemed surrounded by a wide margin of stillness, "Don't you know what it means?"

With one of those little jets of irritability which weariness releases, Laurie said, "If I did I wouldn't ask you."

"It means dressed as women." They had come out of the trees upon a straight open stretch between wire fences. Laurie could see easily, with eyes accommodated now to the night, Ralph's face looking ahead with an intent frown at the pale stream of road being swallowed by the car. "Spuddy."

"Yes?"

"What *do* you know?"

"I know about myself."

"Well?" Laurie didn't answer at once, not from reluctance but because he was tired and it took time to think. Ralph said, deliberately, "If you know about yourself, presumably you know about at least one other person."

"There was a man at Oxford. It was all rather silly. He looked a bit like one of the less forceful portraits of Byron. It wasn't so much he himself who attracted me, though up to a point he did. There are always certain people at Oxford who seem to hold a key. I didn't know what I expected he'd let me into, Newstead Abbey by moonlight or something. He kept telling me I was queer, and I'd never heard it called that before and didn't like it. The word, I mean. Shutting you away, somehow; roping you off with a lot of people you don't feel much in common with, half of whom hate the other half anyway, and just keep together so that they can lean up against each other for support. I don't think I've ever tried to put all this into words before; am I talking nonsense?"

With smothered violence Ralph said, "Christ Almighty, no."

"I started to meet his friends. I'd imagined a lot of rather exquisite people it would be hard work getting to know; but they were all horribly eager, and it wasn't because they liked me really, I could tell that. It was more like—have you read a story by Wells called *The Country of the Blind?*"

"Spuddy, there always was something a bit terrifying about you. Well, don't stop, go on."

"That's all. He asked me to a party and I ran away in the middle, and he took it rather personally, so that was that."

"That was that for how long?"

"Well, it was at the end of the summer term, and the war started in the vac."

"Some types seem to have found the war their great opportunity."

"It depends what you're looking for, I suppose. Anyway, learning to soldier was a bit distracting."

Ralph didn't speak for what seemed like some minutes. Then he said, "That'll teach you to chuck the O.T.C.," in an almost absent voice, as though he were making conversation. After another silent interval he asked, "What about women?"

Although women represented just then an absolute nullity in Laurie's emotions, the question itself, the lack of *empressement* in asking it, gave him a free and stimulated feeling; it was a relief from the bonded circle at the party, from the bars at the window and the gate on the stairs. "One," he said.

"No good?"

"Well . . . I didn't like her much as a human being."

164

"D'you need to?"

"Yes, I think I do."

"That complicates it a bit."

Laurie began to say, "Yes, because one can hardly . . ." but Ralph looked too preoccupied and remote, as if a dangerous bit of road was coming. By the time he knew that it wasn't, he too was given up to his own thoughts, which, after he had rehearsed so much of his history, were inevitably of Andrew. Here if anywhere, he thought, was someone to whom he could release the pressure of so much uncommunicated experience, who would inevitably understand. He remembered how after Charles's party, leaning out of his window long into the night, he had thought of Ralph; though it was already years since their brief meeting, the thought had supported him in his isolation. Now there seemed nothing that could not be told; yet something silenced him. It was Andrew's secret too. Besides, it was holy ground: he was honest enough to examine this simplicity, weigh it, and decide not to abandon it. The result was one of those compromises to which people in such a case will sometimes resort.

"When I say there was nothing after I joined the army"—he could feel Ralph almost start; he must have been miles away—"there was a time when I felt very much drawn to someone; but it was impossible from the first."

"In what way impossible?" Ralph had turned the car onto a bad secondary road. He seemed intent on the driving and sounded a little curt.

"He told me, or as good as told me, without knowing it, that he'd no time for that sort of thing. It was obvious without telling, in any case."

"So you let it alone?"

"Yes."

Ralph seemed to come out of himself. With a sudden kindness he said, "It can be hell while it lasts, though, can't it?"

Laurie didn't answer; the assumption of transience hurt him though it was he who had implied it.

Ralph drove on in silence for a few minutes. Then, with what Laurie could feel beforehand as a decision, he said abruptly, "I was caught up once in something like that."

"Yes?" said Laurie, after waiting some time in vain.

"He was a sub of mine. If he'd been a matelot it would have been all right; I could have put it out of my mind because I'd have bloody well had to. But he was round my neck all day. He wanted to learn everything I knew except what I wanted to teach him. Finally it settled itself in the way which, for some reason, I'd been afraid of almost from the start."

Laurie, his mind still on his troubles, said, "He guessed?"

"No. He was killed."

"Oh!" said Laurie involuntarily. Ralph looked at him for a moment, then back to the road again.

"It happened just when the situation was becoming absolutely impossible. The ship was too small, we lived in each other's pockets; I got to know his girl friend nearly as well as I knew him. Charming manners; he never gave you any excuse to brush him off. He was a highly efficient officer, he seemed to like me, he was dead keen on the ship. I tried to get him promoted away, but he was too young. I didn't see how I was ever going to get rid of him, unless I told him why. Something had to happen. When it did, it seemed obvious that I must have made it happen—I feel it still, sometimes."

"Yes, of course. One would know it was impossible and feel it just the same."

"That's a thing you never know when you're commanding. You've had a hand in everything." He laughed quickly and added, "I grew the beard round about then."

"Some things can't be thought about. The more you try to be honest with them, the more they lie to you. I'm only beginning to know that."

"You know a hell of a lot, don't you, Spud; more than you let on."

Laurie attempted no reply. He felt haunted by untold parts of the tale, which came to him like certainties.

"Don't make too much of it," said Ralph, watching the road. "Believe me, it wasn't a romantic story."

"I know. If it had been it would have been easier, in a way."

"Yes. That's an odd thing for someone like you to see."

The next thing Laurie was aware of was the squeak of the brakes.

"Sorry I can't take you in, Spud. It's all red tape, there's nothing here really that wouldn't bore German Intelligence into a coma. I'll be as quick as I can."

Alone in the car beside a high wall topped with wire, Laurie could hear Ralph speaking to a guard, then his feet ringing crisply into the distance, then silence. He dozed lightly, kept from sleeping by the cold. At last he heard Ralph's voice again, with some other man's, coming nearer, milling over the small stuff of people who work together.

"Was it all right?" he asked when Ralph came out alone.

"Yes, he let me have the whole tackle. I found him at a party so he was fairly mellow. The difficulty was getting away. Sorry I've been so long."

He had had another couple of drinks at the party, Laurie thought. It was not extremely obvious, and betrayed itself chiefly in his own consciousness of it. He had become much more taciturn, and drove with elaborate precision, as if he were taking a test.

Laurie was feeling drowsy again. When the car stopped he thought at first that he had slept through to the end of the run. Then he looked around him and saw that Ralph had pulled onto a farm track just off the road.

"I'll have to stop for a minute or two, Spud. I'm sorry."

"What's the matter?" He felt the tilt of the car on the rutted ground and asked, "Had a puncture?"

"No. Just one party too many. I can always tell"— he was speaking with carefully articulated distinctness—"when my reflexes get bitched up. Luckily my inhibitions stay good till a much, oh, very much later stage. Don't give it a thought, Spud. I know when

167

to go on again." He pushed off his cap and slid back in the seat, his head tilted against the folded hood. "You've got the cigarettes."

"Shall I light one for you?"

"Yes."

He smoked in silence for some minutes. Laurie could think of nothing to say.

"I think from now on I shall change over to the system of Saturday night blind, sober all the week."

"It comes cheaper, they say."

"You make me laugh, Spud. This shocks you more than finding me mixed up with Sandy's crowd, doesn't it?"

"Hell, where do you think I've been living?"

"Falling down on an errand of mercy, m-m?"

"Oh, go on, he's not bleeding to death."

"All the same if he was, you might have said; why didn't you?"

"Because I didn't think it."

"You see, Spud, if you will interrupt yourself without previous notice in this arbitrary and irrational manner, you must put up with a bit of disorganization."

"What was that?"

"Don't be unreasonable. I can't keep saying arbitrary and irrational just to please you."

A wash of cold sweet air stirred across them, like an eddy in water. Drawn along the meadows, a belt of mist began to appear in a milky glimmer.

The smoke of their cigarettes was growing visible, lifting almost straight into the sky. Across one of Ralph's temples, where the tilt of his cap had let it bleach in the weather, the hair in this faint light looked silver, and his head like bronze.

"Spud, there's no need for you to keep falling over yourself to be tactful, because it's of no consequence, so you can just as well say. Did you really mean to do it, or not?"

"Mean to do what?"

"Oh, come. You never used to creep out of things."

"I won't out of this if you tell me what it is."

"At Dunkirk. When you sent me up."

"Of course not. I told you."

168

"You looked at me when you said it."

"In the army you somehow don't think of seeing people you know with beards. I just thought 'beard' . . . I daresay it was partly not having died."

"Who's supposed to be drunk, you or me?"

"Well, the thing was that I'd felt rather bad just a while before. I expect it was just seasickness really; but I seem to remember thinking, This is it, I must let go now. Then I woke up and there was this officer with a beard. It was reaction, I think. Street-urchin sort of thing, really."

"God, that's funny." He lay back laughing to himself.

"The chap lying next to me thought it was funny, too."

"That's really all you remember?"

"Yes. What did happen, actually?"

"To see you sitting there saying, 'What did happen?' It's so bloody ridiculous, I can't tell you. Well, now, what happened, yes. I'd just had my pom-pom gunner shot. It was awkward taking the gun just then, my sub had got put out of action the trip before, but there wasn't anyone else so I was stuck with it. I couldn't hit the bastard, he got away. Then up comes Norris with some garbled story, would I tell them if someone was dead. I told him where to go, and then suddenly there was a lull and time on my hands, so I went over. You shouldn't have been there really, the order was no wounded on deck, but we were full up below and we always finished up with a few odd ones. I was picking my way between them when a gingery man with a couple of black eyes seemed to grab me by the ankle. ' 'Ere, sir, Spud 'ere ain't gone is 'e? There's a sailor 'ere keeps sayin' 'e's 'ad it. Don't you let 'em put 'im overboard, sir. I swear I seen 'im breathe.' 'There's no question of doing that,' I said, 'in any case, on a short crossing like this.' Then I looked to see what it was all about, and it was you. Have you got the cigarettes?"

"I shouldn't think you'd have recognized me very easily."

"Now that was the uncanniest thing I've ever seen. You were dead white, of course, and, well, here's a thing you wouldn't know about, but that day, when you knocked at my study door and came in, I suppose what with the awkwardness and one thing and another ... Well, anyway, there you were. No, light it for me, you've got the lighter.

"So I felt your pulse, only I couldn't feel anything except that you were as cold as a corpse, so I opened your tunic or whatever you call those workhouse slops the army wears now—can't you remember any of this?"

"I expect I might have just afterwards. It's all gone now."

"It's funny, that, really damned funny. I felt for your heart and it seemed I could feel something just faintly ticking over; and then you moved a bit. 'Hello, Spud,' I said, 'how are you feeling?' The next man had told me your name so he didn't think anything of my knowing it. I think I said, 'Hold on, Spud, we'll get you home all right,' or something like that. And then you opened your eyes, very deliberately, and seemed to give me a good look up and down. 'Sorry, dearie,' you said, smiling to yourself in a private sort of way. 'Sorry, dearie, some other time.' Then you turned away as if that were about enough. Famous last words." He drew once or twice on the cigarette and added, "I heard you were dead about three weeks later."

"Thank you for writing to me. I wish I'd had the letter."

"There must be some reason why things happen. Something in us must touch them off. Like a magnetic mine."

"I don't know. I always think when you go to war you make yourself over to chance by an act of will."

"You have a peaceful mind, Spuddy."

"You'd be surprised."

"Should I?" There was a long silence. Laurie could hear, deep in the field, the clumsy shifting of a sleepy horse, waking to graze. "Well, life's full of surprises, isn't it?" Suddenly his voice was light and hard, as it had been at the party. He sat up, stretched, put on his cap, switched the ignition on. "Let's see how it goes now."

They talked very little after that. Ralph's contest with the car had developed a certain grimness. There was nothing wrong with his driving, except a persistent impression of something difficult being done for a bet, which kept Laurie on edge all the time. Because of the cold, or his fixed position in the car, or the bad springs, the ache in his knee was turning into a tight cramp. He was anxious not to bother Ralph with any of this; when he could bear it no longer, he dropped the cigarette-case on the floor as an excuse to move about. The knee had stiffened; he chose a moment when Ralph was turning a corner to try and flex it in his hands.

Ralph said, "How long has that been going on?"

"I don't get it."

"Don't insult my intelligence," said Ralph shortly. "Is it very bad?"

"No, it's only seized up on the bearings a bit."

"Whyever didn't you tell me?"

"It just comes and goes again in no time. Sort of muscle spasm."

"You bloody liar. We'll be back in five minutes."

He opened the throttle. Oddly enough, Laurie didn't feel nervous. It was rather as if Ralph were driving himself as well as the car, with an eye on the defects of both.

They were back in four minutes. In the hall Laurie looked up the high well of the stairs and said, "Run up and give the things to Alec, he'll be waiting for them. I'll take my time."

Ralph paused at the stair-foot. In the dim light outside there had been something young and rakish about his profile under the tilted cap. Light destroyed the illusion; he looked worn at the edges, hard and drawn. "God, he can wait another minute. It's such a hell of a climb, Spud. Let me give you a hand."

For the first time he looked uncertain and ineffective. Why, thought Laurie, pain twitching at the nerves of anger, why not accept the obvious fact that he couldn't do anything, and get out of the way? Any fool must see that one couldn't get up there with somebody staring. The mere sight of all that drive and force, poised inde-cisively, was oppressive; he had a feeling that at any moment Ralph would do something high-handed and insufferable, like trying to carry him. He drew back and said uncontrollably, "Oh, do get on, I can't bear being stood over."

"Sorry," said Ralph. He turned and ran upstairs, brisk and straight-backed, as if he were on a companionway.

Alec had got a table set out with sterilized dishes and boiled water and Dettol, on a white cloth. It looked very professional; Laurie saw it through the open door and didn't go in.

Just then Ralph crossed the landing from the kitchen. Each at the same moment began a strained tentative smile, which suddenly gathered kindness and relief. Ralph was going to help Alec with the suturing; he indicated this with an ironic gesture, and disappeared. Laurie lay flat on his face on one of the sitting-room divans; this posture, which always relieved the pain, was a luxury he had been looking forward to.

"Where are you, Spud?" said Ralph's voice outside.

"Here," said Laurie, rolling over. He guessed that Ralph was trying not to take him by surprise.

"Brought you some more dope. One more lot can't hurt."

Laurie took it thankfully. Soon he was sleeping, his head buried in his arms. The smell of strong coffee wove itself into his dreams.

Afterwards he had only the dimmest recollection of Ralph sitting beside him and persuading him to wake up, of getting downstairs again and into the car. He could not remember whether he saw Alec again or whether Ralph asked him the way to the hospital. Wrapped in something rough and warm he sank, as the car ran out into the country, deeper and deeper into sleep. At first his dreams were full of haste and confused emergency; but later they grew easy and idle, till at last the ivory gate opened, and the phantasms of happiness came out, like Arabian genii answering a wish. He was in bed at home; he had had a new operation on his leg, which had put everything right, and his mother was nursing him. There was some special joy in the fact of her presence, some danger past; but even the memory of what this danger had been was healed and smoothed away. When she had said good night she kissed him, very lightly but with more tenderness than she had shown him since he was a child. He was half aware that he dreamed, and was conscious of an extra happiness because, even after this fatal knowledge had touched him, he still felt the kiss as if it were real. To bring her back he began to put out his hand to her; but she had gone, and his own movement woke him. The car had stopped; beyond the shadow of the tree was the gate of the hospital. Ralph was sitting back in the driver's seat, lighting a cigarette.

"Hello, Ralph," said Laurie, smiling at him out of the peace he had just left.

"Hello, Spud. Here we are. Will you be all right going in, or shall I come with you?"

"No, I'll be all right. I feel wonderful now. I've been sound asleep."

"Have you? Good. Oh, I'd better take Alec's burberry. Next time we meet perhaps it won't be in such a madhouse. I'll ring you up. Good night."

The hospital lay flat in staring moonlight. As Laurie walked up the wide asphalt path between the huts, he thought that if he had been demobbed for years, and had looked in as he happened to pass, it couldn't seem more altered and remote. He reached the ward without meeting anyone. In the corridor Nurse Sims swept down on him, and drove him with fierce whispers into the kitchen.

"No one saw you? Here, drink this while it's hot, you look dead on your feet. To think of *you* breaking out like this! Don't you dare go in the ward till you've changed; I'll bring you your pajamas in the bathroom. Night Sister would kill me. When she did her first round I just threw your bed open and she thought you'd gone through. What *have* you been up to? No, don't tell me, it's written all over you. Don't you ever think I'll cover up for you if it happens again. And another thing. Next time you see your friend, you tell him from me that he's a very naughty boy. He's in the navy, *he* ought to know the man on the switchboard always listens in. Who drove you back here? Oh, *did* he?

173

Well, I'm only surprised he didn't come wandering in here, he seems to have cheek enough for anything. I suppose he thought he'd gone a bit *too* far. Well, goodness, I'd have found him a cup of cocoa or something, driving all that way this time of night. You tell him, I'm not such a sourpuss as all that."

As he was creeping up the ward, someone whispered hoarsely, to the effect that his girl would be wanting breakfast in bed. It was Willis, making the first joke Laurie had ever heard from him which seemed inspired, on the whole, by good nature.

No one else was awake. Reg Barker lay in a patch of moonlight which seemed to eat like acid into the thin surface of his sleep, leaving him half exposed to reality; it was like seeing someone sleeping huddled in the cold. There was something unbearably childlike and vulnerable in the bareness of his unprotected face; so he must have lain while his wife looked down at him with boredom, with calculation, with sensual dreams of the new man. Charlot, the white light piercing his brain with some memory of a naked and dead sky, was whimpering in his sleep as he sometimes did, softly, like a dog by the fire. Laurie slid into bed. With a poignancy he had never felt during the half-stupefying agony on the beach, he was beset by a terrible consciousness of the world's ever-renewed, ever-varied, never-dying pain: children and animals without hope in the present moment's eternity; the prisoners of cruel men, the cruel terribly imprisoned in themselves; Alec watching beside Sandy; Ralph quietly struggling with the gear-lever of his last command; tomorrow's air raid victims, the still unknown suffering of the unmeasured years of war. He heard footsteps coming, and turned on his face to hide it and to ease the ache in his leg. Then he knew they weren't the nurse's, and looked up into Andrew's face.

"Andrew!" he whispered. He had forgotten there was anything to hide. To return to the innocence of their love was like returning home. He reached for Andrew's hand as it might be for the hundredth time, as if everything had been accepted and spoken of between them.

Andrew didn't take it away. He returned a friendly

pressure, smiling in the pale light; at a loss and anxious to hide it. Why not, thought Laurie, slipping away into a lonely understanding. He had been behaving very oddly, quite unlike himself; and to someone who had had nothing he must still smell of drink.

"I'm glad you're all right," said Andrew softly. "We had a warning here, so I wondered."

"You shouldn't have worried. A funny thing happened, I'll tell you tomorrow."

"It was a big day for you, meeting your friend again."

Nurse Sims must have said something, then. Suddenly he remembered saying to Andrew in the woods that he and Ralph wouldn't know each other if they met. "What a grapevine this place is. However did you get that?"

"He gave me his name," said Andrew, "when I answered the telephone. Sleep well; good night."

The moonlight shifted silently. Charlot's uneasy sleep had turned to one of his nightmares; he started to fight the bedclothes and to mutter, *"Au secours!"* Kept wakeful by the sound, Laurie saw again the endless interlocking chain of the world's sorrow, and Andrew's face, no longer in the secret orchard, but locked and moving with the chain.

7

So it's officers now, eh?" said Reg. "That run you into something, I reckon. Saloon bar stuff."

"Bit of free. A party at someone's flat."

"Ah. Nice girls?"

"Fine." If only one had notice of these questions, Laurie thought. The answer that seemed to save trouble on the spur of the moment hardly ever did. Sure enough, a few more minutes' cross-examination had involved him in factual accounts of Alec's wife, Ralph's girl friend, and his own partner, for whom he had to supply a service career as well as complexion, clothes, and a name.

He was so tired that he slept all afternoon, a thing he hadn't done since ceasing to be a bed patient; and the strangeness of waking from a sleep so deep that it had drowned the noises of the ward, to altered light and the evening routine, made everything seem even more different than it had before. The twilight struck chilly as he went outside. He experienced for the first time that special dread brought by the first touch of winter to lovers who have nowhere to meet except out of doors.

"You've been catching up with your sleep," said Andrew, smiling in the lane (it was the same spot where Ralph had stopped the car last night). "Now you know how I feel every evening."

"There's Christian charity for you. As a matter of fact I wasn't as drunk last night as you probably thought."

"No?" said Andrew, looking at him amusedly. In sudden panic he paused to drill his disorganized inhibitions. If he hadn't been drunk, then what was supposed to have happened? Dimly he was aware that it wasn't the loose talk at the party which was making him careless now; it was the dark confessional of the car on the long empty road. It seemed to him that there was nothing he couldn't have said, and very little that he hadn't.

"It wasn't the drink," he said lightly, "so much as the dope."

"It sounds quite a party." Andrew didn't appear uncontrollably amused. Unwillingly, Laurie explained.

"It was rather trusting of you to swallow the stuff without even asking what it was. Do you like him as much as you did at school?"

"I don't know." The electrifying pertinence of Andrew's questions seemed always to be taking him off guard. "I never knew him well at school, you know. He still seems a pretty good type to me."

They went up the lane between October hedges draped with flossy swags of old-man's-beard. Laurie was saying to himself that it would soon cease to seem so important, this discovery he had made that, instead

176

of accepting concealment as a permanent condition of his life, he had merely been enduring it.

Andrew said, continuing the almost unbroken conversation, "He seems to have made a great hit with Nurse Sims. I've never seen anyone bridle on the telephone before."

"I hope he didn't overdo it."

"Is he married?"

"No."

"Tell me about him."

For a moment Laurie was attacked by an almost ungovernable impatience; a feeling of the utter waste of time involved in going through the motions of exposition, where no possibility of enlightenment exists. "Well, he was Head of the House two years before me, only he was Head of the School as well——"

"Head of the *School?* He must have been a very democratic one."

"I keep telling you I didn't really know him. I never spoke to him apart from routine till the day he left."

"Yes, I see. When he gave you the Plato?"

"I expect he was having an orgy of giving away everything he couldn't find room to pack."

"It was a nice thing to choose, though. Not what one would give to the first person who came along."

"Well, naturally it pleased me to think so, at the time."

"So then he joined the navy."

"No, the merchant service actually."

"As an apprentice or something?"

"No, as a deck hand, I think. He was keen on adventure, and roughing it, and all that."

"He sounds very strong-minded. Is he doing well?"

"He's had half his hand blown off. They won't give him another ship."

"It must be a bad time for him. A little sad, I expect, to meet someone who'd only known him in the days of his glory."

Laurie tried to look at the intrinsic kindness of this rather than its unconscious cruelty. He said quickly, "Well, he hardly needed to worry about that with me.

Only a few minutes before I met him, I'd found out that he saved my life."

"How?" said Andrew. Laurie saw it then, when it was too late to do anything but go on.

"Well, perhaps that's rather a stagy way of putting it. He commanded the ship that brought me back from Dunkirk, that's all."

"How lucky you found out in time." There was a helpless and painful silence.

One might almost as well, thought Laurie, have said it aloud. Because he did for me what you wouldn't do, I'm alive to be with you now. Here at last, stripped of the secondary things, of motive and praise and blame, were the bare bones of logic, grinning in the sun.

Laurie said urgently, "Look, my dear, we've had all this in principle. Let's be sensible when something concrete turns up. We knew this whole position before we'd even spoken to each other for the first time."

"This isn't the school debating society. This happened to you. Do you think I've got no imagination at all?" He was looking away.

"God, you have to take people for what they are, not for what you expect to get out of them. Why do you suppose I fell"—his tongue stiffened. What had possessed him?—"felt we'd get on together?"

"Laurie, you don't look yourself this evening. Are you feeling all right?"

"Of course I am. Let's go up to the beechwood."

It was warm in Limbo, in the dry mast-filled hollow out of the wind; but it was a close fit for two, and when they had talked for a while and fallen silent, Laurie found himself remembering Ralph's story about the sub-lieutenant. But that had been different. A kind of starter's pistol went off in his head. It said, "Why?"

He knew that he had only asked the question because he had just found out the answer. Ralph's had been a story in which no moral choice existed, only impossibility and a desire excluded by the facts of life. It was Andrew who was the difference.

At once there seemed never to have been a day when he hadn't known this; he looked back with wonder at the times when he had waited, in so much doubt and uncertainty, for Andrew to make himself known. How should he confess what he himself had not discovered? All yesterday evening Laurie had been, consciously and subconsciously, using his eyes, and noticing little things; and now, when he looked at Andrew, it seemed written all over him.

After all, thought Laurie, it wasn't so hard to understand. Too much had been put on the boy too young. The army traditions which, however repudiated, must still have roots in him; the uncompromising ethic he had accepted; the certainty, as war came nearer, of the coming choice which would violate half his nature either way: all this had been for him the anticipated responsibility of manhood. It had been enough: his whole organism had known the impossibility of accepting more. But escape, and unconscious escape most of all, is like a usurer; it heaps up the liability. Andrew's present liability had become more than either half of his divided nature was made to bear. To make him aware of it, thought Laurie quite clearly, would scatter his whole capital of belief in himself. He must never know.

With the tail of his eye he saw Andrew look at him and, respecting his concentration, turn away. Andrew recognized thought as a human activity. He stretched contentedly in the dry beech-mast; almost absently, Laurie moved to settle him more comfortably. Andrew looked up at him. "Hello. How've you been keeping all this time?"

"Oh, well but busy, you know. Sorry."

"It's all right. About the only time you ever get to be alone is when you're with me. I take it as a compliment."

A faint blue mist, which the small morning hours would crystallize into frost, was furring already the dead leaves on the ground. When he got back to the ward Reg said, "That knee packed up, Spud?"

"Not too bad."

"You want to watch it, sitting out these cold evenings. Get the rheumatics in it, that's *all* you need. When do you go for this electric treatment?"

"Tuesday."

"You better be getting the old alibi ready."

"Oh, I shan't want that again."

Beds were tidied, lights put out; in a little spotlit circle at the desk, the Sister gave the Night Nurse the report. When the telephone rang she waited irritably till the day orderly came to the desk. "Oh, well, yes, I suppose so. But tell him he must ask his friend not to do it again, it's very inconvenient."

Laurie was out of bed already, reaching for his dressing-gown. Although he hadn't expected it before tomorrow, still the anticipation had subtly colored, and faintly disturbed, the day.

"Hello, Spuddy. I thought I'd just make sure you hadn't been put back on the danger list, or up for court-martial, or anything."

"No, you fixed that. Everything's fine."

"Is it? Good."

The empty wire crackled faintly. It hadn't occurred to Laurie to have any conversation ready; one always imagined Ralph taking charge. Now, sensing at the other end a tentativeness at least equal to his own, he felt suddenly afraid of drying up. The thought of Ralph ringing off after a few perfunctory commonplaces came to him with a terrible sense of flatness, disappointment, and failure. He hadn't anticipated any of this. However, in the end they talked for nearly ten minutes.

When he got back Reg said, "You look better, Spud. Coming in just now you looked properly cheesed."

"Oh, it just wanted a bit of rest."

Charlot turned his rough curly head on his fixed shoulders. "I think a nice girl ring for you, Spoddi, bit of all right, yes?" He grinned benevolently.

"Not this time, no such luck." He was dismayed to feel that he had blushed violently. But the lights were dim and probably Reg had noticed nothing.

Nurse Sims turned off the radio, and everyone settled down for the night.

"Leg okay now?" whispered Reg.

"Yes, thanks, fine."

"Your officer friend dating you up again?"

"We might have a drink or a meal or something next time I go up."

"Odell, Barker. Lights are out, in case you didn't know it."

She was at the desk for some time, ruling lines in a book. By the time she went outside again he thought Reg was asleep.

"Spud."

"Hello?"

"This officer now. No offense, Spud. But know him well at school? To know what he's like, mean to say?"

"Oh, yes, I think so."

"What I mean, you'd know if he's on the level and that?"

"Good God, yes."

"No offense, I hope, Spud?"

"Of course not. Takes a pal to do your worrying for you." Over the time of Madge's flight, Laurie had learned to talk this language almost without embarrassment, and was relieved to find it still came back to him.

"That's right. How some might look at it, though, worrying's one thing, noseying's another. Got to think of that." He sunk his voice till Laurie had to lean half out of bed to hear it. "Don't mind me, Spud. Interfering with what I don't know nothing about, sticking out my big neck and asking for it, you don't have to tell me. See, Spud, how it is, you done plenty of worrying for me, and I reckon that didn't always come easy, putting yourself in my place. If that don't make sense, forget it. All I want to say—any trouble, any time, don't make no difference if it's not my kind of trouble, not to me it don't, no more'n what it done to you. A pal's a pal the same all the world over. Well, that's the lot, least said soonest mended. Night, Spud."

"Night, Reg. Thanks. God bless."

He lay looking at the ceiling: a number of little things came back to him, starting with the girls in the blackout. He wondered whether Reg had done his own simple addition, or whether someone else, Neames for instance, had totted it up for him. In any case, this was it. It had caught him up. If he hadn't expected it he had been a fool, and the sooner he got used to it now the better.

The soft rattle of the trolley, and the chink of crockery, sounded at the doors. He didn't need to look. He heard the slight noises of things being shifted on the lockers to make room for the mugs. As the homely domestic sounds drew nearer, he thought that the ward was quieter than usual, that no one was saying much.

There had never been a time when he hadn't thought of himself as one of this company the mischance of battle had brought together: one with a secret, as many others had of one sort or another; one with an oddity, but there were plenty of those. Lovell, who had owned a freak-booth that toured the fairs; Jansen, who was three parts colored; Willis; Charlot; Odell, who had started with the handicap of "talking posh." Now in a cold solitude he imagined, everywhere in the shadows, men quietly watching, curious, or mocking, or repelled, according to their kind, but all thanking their Maker for the solidarity that didn't include him. Then he remembered that it wouldn't be he, lying down protected by the shadows and made cautious by self-knowledge, who would entertain them most, but Andrew in his unguarded innocence.

There was nothing to do about it. He couldn't pretend to sleep, for Andrew must have heard him talking to Ralph just now; it would seem like a slap in the face. He couldn't do anything, except behave as if nothing were the matter. The trolley rattled up.

"Hello, Andrew."

"Hello, Laurie. Did we walk too far today?"

"Of course not." He held out his mug. "Thanks."

"I think we did. Have you had your A.P.C.?"

"Yes, thanks. I'm going to sleep now." But Andrew, who had never had a dismissal from him before, didn't recognize one when he heard it.

"There's quite a party going on in our hut tonight. You know Richard on Ward A? He's just got engaged." He was speaking softly, not to disturb the other patients. Something like this happened nearly every night. No doubt it looked very intimate. Andrew had never had a moment's concern about it. That everyone knew they were friends was a thing he took for granted.

"Good show." But he said it too warmly, torn between the longing for Andrew to go and the dread of showing it.

"Yes, it is; you see when the war started he wouldn't ask her, he didn't think it was fair. But she kept on writing, and finally, the other day——"

"Good for her," said Laurie, cutting him off short. Where did he think he was, exposing this naked happiness and trust? It was time he learned to be decent.

Andrew's face changed. One day Laurie had been swishing a stick about, and caught his dog a cracking blow by accident; he had looked incredulous and bewildered, just like this.

Suddenly Laurie thought, Oh, damn the lot of them. He smiled up at Andrew and said, "Tell me all about it in the kitchen."

"No, don't get up tonight, you're tired."

"Oh, wrap it up. Of course I'm coming."

Later, when he had seen Andrew go out from the sluice to the kitchen, he lay looking at the dim face of the clock on the wall. Five minutes, he thought. He had always waited for five minutes, not to make it obvious. He wondered how many people, for how long, had been having a quiet laugh about it.

Five minutes passed. He got out of bed, and put on his slippers; they felt odd and lopsided nowadays, after the boot. He reached for his dressing-gown and his stick. A mattress creaked as someone turned over; the twenty yards between his bed and the door seemed suddenly very long. He would have liked to cover them with a little more speed or a little more grace. No, he thought, it was really too naïve to get so upset about it; one was supposed to carry off this kind of thing with a flick of the wrist and a light laugh which would tell the world one hadn't been trying. Playing at hearties with all these dreary common people; my dear, I'm exhausted, I couldn't have been more bored.

Suddenly, as if the memory had been kept in storage especially for this, he saw with extraordinary vividness Ralph's face against the background of the dismantled study. Ralph had been nineteen. And here was a grown man in wartime making such heavy weather of so little.

Earlier today, during one of the current invasion rumors, Laurie had pictured an English Thermopylae behind the Home Guard roadblocks; amid the last-ditch grimness of this vision there had intruded a vague exhilaration, and he realized that he had imagined Ralph beside him. So, but much more so, it was now, and with this sudden comfort he found he had got to the door, and was outside in the shelter of the corridor.

He would have been glad of a few minutes' pause before going on. But the sound of his step was too individual; already Andrew would have recognized it.

8

"RIGHT, then, about five-fifteen tomorrow. Don't wait about in the street bitching up the knee before we start. Sit in the Out-Patient Department and I'll come for you there."

Laurie began to say, "Do you know where it is?" but remembered in time that Ralph must know the hospital very well. "I'll do that," he said.

"Was this all right, my ringing up again?"

"Yes, Sister's off duty."

"The other men in the ward don't think anything, I suppose?"

"Life's too short to spend flapping about that sort of thing. I shan't be here much longer, anyway."

"What? Sorry, what was that?"

"I said they'll be discharging me, anyway, as soon as this electrical treatment's finished."

"Oh, yes. Of course. How long's that going to be?"

"Discipline would go to pieces if they told us things like that."

It was much colder this evening; but when he got back to bed, he found someone had put a hot-water bottle in it.

"Did you get this, Reg?"

"Nurse Adrian done it." Busily intent on tidying his locker, Reg added, "I reckon that girl's going to miss you, when you go."

He had never referred, even obliquely, to last Friday's conversation; but life had become a tight-rope walk for both of them. Laurie would have given anything to be able to repay Reg's overture with some grateful confidence; Reg himself would have given anything to recall it. Laurie guessed that this forced remark about Nurse Adrian was an invitation to pretend nothing had happened. It was, indeed, the only tolerable solution; he accepted it with relief. "I'm more likely to do the missing. Rodgers must be blind, saying she's got no sex appeal."

Reg accepted the *modus vivendi* with transparent thankfulness. He would never, Laurie knew, have ventured so far into the open if the thing hadn't already been openly discussed.

That day the first breath of winter had reached the shrinking flesh of a continent at war. It had a message for Laurie as well as for the rest. He still hadn't a greatcoat; Dunkirk had been a summer disaster. For the first time that day, walking with Andrew, he had found he couldn't move fast enough to keep warm. Walking patients in the square had thrown blankets or dressing-gowns over their shoulders, or a civilian coat lent by one of the c.o.s.; but to go outside the gates one must be properly dressed. He had got a cramp in his knee almost at once, and they had had to turn back, more than half an hour before the usual time.

Andrew said, "There's a stove in our hut. This time of day there's hardly anyone there."

"Better not. It might make trouble."

"Well, listen, I know what we can do another time. I've got an old carriage-rug from home on my bed, it's enormous. I'll bring that, and we can take it to that dip in the beechwood, and roll ourselves up in it."

Like an actor who dries up on the crucial cue for which the scene is waiting, Laurie could think of absolutely nothing to say. He ordered and implored himself; he could hear, as exactly as the click of a time-fuse, the moment when the pause became remarkable. The impulse to look up was like the impulse people feel to throw themselves off towers, or under trains. He looked up. Andrew was scarlet to the roots of his hair. It was all up, thought Laurie, as suddenly and simply as this, only through a moment's lack of resource. Then he realized that Andrew's embarrassment was acutely social, and that he hadn't had time yet to see beyond it.

"You must think," Laurie managed, "that I've a horrible mind. The trouble is, I've got a pretty good idea what the Staff Sergeant's is like."

"Yes," said Andrew. He swallowed. "Lucky you thought. Sorry."

"That's the army for you."

"I shouldn't really have been as dumb as that, because a boy at my school was actually expelled for it, though most of us didn't know till afterwards."

In spite of himself Laurie had to ask, "What was he like?"

"Not very nice. He used to bully the little boys, and terrify them into doing what he wanted."

"No; he doesn't sound very nice at all."

Andrew said, "Well, if we give it a bit of thought there must be somewhere to go. Never mind, it will probably be much warmer tomorrow."

"Yes. I'm afraid I shan't be here, though."

"Of course. I was forgetting. Will you be back on the six-thirty bus?"

"No, not this time. I've got a pass." He said quickly, "God, it's freezing, isn't it? We'll have to get in. See you tonight." As he limped to the gate he could feel Andrew looking after him, but it was useless to turn back.

Later that evening, it occurred to him that it would be possible to represent Ralph as an object of pity, in a way which would reconcile Andrew at once to the whole situation. Laurie glanced at the idea and at once found it revolting. Since this had been the only thing left to say on the subject, he gave up the attempt to say anything. They tried, in this way and that, to make signals of confidence in each other across the No Man's Land which both avoided.

It was shortly after this that Ralph had telephoned. When Laurie went back to bed, he could tell by Reg's breathing that he wasn't asleep; but neither he, nor anyone else of those who might be awake and watching, made a sound.

Miss Haliburton at the hospital remembered him at once. When she produced from some cache or other a two-months dachshund puppy and let him nurse it, he knew that she had favorites. He usually got on with strong-minded old maids, and it was one of his wry private jokes that they so unawarely waived their misanthropy on his behalf. He found himself confiding not only the life-history of his elderly airedale at home, but how the knee had been behaving and what brought on the pain. She put on a crepe bandage to keep it warm; on the way he had bought a pullover to wear under his uniform, and began to feel under a slightly less medieval servitude to winter. When she had done with him, he went down to wait for Ralph.

The out-patient departments of general hospitals do not conduce to a thoughtless optimism. Beside him a thin, overworked woman described to a very old one the three operations that hadn't cured her trouble; a mentally defective girl appeared, six months pregnant; male syphilitics, with an air of indescribable seediness, were queuing for treatment; there was another queue of skin cases, with dirty bandages and patches of gentian-violet paint. The smell of antiseptics, sick bodies, and old clothes pervaded everything. Amid all this Laurie sat and wondered, with rapidly decreasing confidence in each successive answer, what he was going to do with his life. The surrounding climate of shabbiness, dejection, and failure seemed to subdue all possible futures to itself. It was in the midst of such thoughts that he saw Ralph walk briskly in at the street door.

The contrast was dazzling. His energy and precision stood out among the sick, worried people, slumped on the benches waiting their turn, as bright steel stands out in a heap of scrap iron. His well-fitting, well-pressed uniform would have shone against the dingy clothing, even without the gold on the sleeves. The cleanness of the hospital staff was functional, a reminder of the human ills against which it was directed; Ralph's was personal and aristocratic. In spite of the glove he seemed a

187

foreign visitor here; and as if to emphasize this he was carrying, for show, the other glove of the pair. Watching him come nearer, Laurie realized what a confused memory of the other night he had brought away, for he had thought of Ralph as looking quite five years older than this. Even from across the hall, you could see that his eyes were blue. He raked the benches swiftly and systematically, saw Laurie, smiled, and came forward. The devitalized figures in the gangway seemed to melt out of his path.

"Hello, Spud, am I late, have you been browned off waiting here?"

As they left, nearly all the faces at that end of the hall turned to gaze after them. The looks were not of the kind that Laurie had come to fear just lately. He could feel a wistful envy in them. He had been one of them all with his stick and his white card, and now in a moment he had become a person while they were cases still. Watching these young men meet as if in a street or a hotel, they were downcast or cheered according to their natures by the invasion of life, by Ralph's happiness and the sudden lightening of Laurie's anxious face.

"Too early for a drink," Ralph said. "How about a drive before it gets dark?"

The sun was still up, warm and clear. Ralph headed for the hills, not talking much. Presently they came out at a famous view-spot; parked in it was a closed saloon car with people sitting inside reading magazines. They both laughed. Ralph said, "Can you put up with four counties instead of five?"

Behind them, when he stopped, the crown of the hill rose from a tonsure of trees; below were the patched colors of stubble and roots and grape-purple plowland, streams picked out with thorn and willow, a puff of wool from a toy train, a silver band of Severn water on the horizon. It was a sight, in the autumn of 1940, to evoke special emotions. They were almost silent for some minutes, except perfunctorily to point out some landmark. Laurie had a feeling that the conversation had no need to be filled in with words at every stage.

"I always find," said Ralph presently, "that the fur-

188

ther I go away, the more patriotic I get. Believe it or not, in Adelaide once I had quite a heated argument with some local who spoke lightly of the English public-school system." He blew a puff of smoke into the soft West-country air and added, "I'm not used to doing such a long stretch of home and beauty."

Laurie said, "I don't blame you."

Ralph looked around at him for a moment, then returned to his cigarette. Suddenly he said, "For God's sake, you're not trying to fix me up with a grievance against society, are you? There wouldn't be the least justification for it. All that gives me a pain in the neck." The expression he used was a good deal coarser.

"I should think there'd be plenty of justification."

"Now, Spud, come. You ought to know better than that by this time, with a couple of stripes up too. If you're talking about school, as I suppose you are, I can see of course that you had it all rather sprung on you at the time." He turned to flick his ash out of the car. "But don't tell me it never occurred to you later, when you were a prefect yourself for instance, that people who abuse a position of trust have to be got rid of. At least, I should hope it did."

He's lecturing me, Laurie thought; first with surprise, then in some amusement, till without warning he found himself almost unbearably touched and sad. Collecting himself, he said, "I hardly knew enough to make snap judgments like that, did I?"

A sheet of cirrus cloud was beginning to be flecked on its underside with crimson; the horizon was darkening to blue. Looking away at it, Ralph said, "You must have given me the benefit of every conceivable doubt."

"Well, of course. I had every reason to."

"Nice of you," said Ralph briskly, "but even so it doesn't add up." His head, against the flamboyant sky, looked remote and severe. "I suppose you could make out some sort of case for me, as an individual. But for a pillar of the institution, the only possible justification was never to get found out. I deserved the sack for my judgment of character if for nothing else." He examined some afterthought here, and laughed shortly.

"It was a good job for Hazell his people took him away."

"I'm sure he'd agree with you. He's in Hollywood now, didn't you know?"

"Good God, is he? Who with?"

"Really, Spud! I didn't think you had that much bitchery in you. Of course you're perfectly right." He related Hazell's success story.

In seven years, thought Laurie, every cell in one's body has been replaced, even our memories live in a new brain. That is not the face I saw, and these are not the eyes I saw with. Even our selves are not the same, but only a consequence of the selves we had then. Yet I was there and I am here; and this man, who is sometimes what I remember and sometimes a stranger I met at a party the other day, is also to himself the I who was there: his mind in its different skull has travelled back to a place his living feet never visited; and the pain he felt then he can feel again.

"What is it, Spud?" said Ralph softly.

Laurie remembered the voice from the other day, it was charming and intimate and too experienced and left you in doubt. "I was just thinking about Hazell, and all that."

"Oh, Hazell," said Ralph slowly. That he should have read the words as a question embarrassed Laurie greatly. No one could be expected to talk of such things except to strangers. Strangers are a distorting mirror, and hold things off. But Ralph spoke first, before he could change the subject.

"Hazell was generally underrated, you know. He was really rather a clever little boy. All that Dostoievsky was largely put on: it worked quite well."

"He used to get away with murder." One of Ralph's burnt-straw-colored eyebrows shot up intimidatingly into the peak of his cap. But ancient resentment had suddenly revived, and Laurie faced it out.

Ignoring it, Ralph went on, "Of course, if you took him up at all and seemed sympathetic, he used to play down the idiocy and let his intelligence be glimpsed; not obviously, just so that one felt he'd been given a bit of confidence. Perhaps it really was that, partly. It can't

190

have been quite as calculated as it seems to look back on, I realize that."

"He was easily scared," said Laurie, trying to sound detached.

"The thing was, there was no doubt about him. Obviously, most people at school who get caught up in it are either going through a phase, or merely in the position of cattle who if you don't give them salt will lick it off the ground. I gave a lot of thought to this in my last year; there hadn't been so much time when I was working for Cambridge. It wasn't everybody one felt justified in taking a chance with. Side-tracking them, or something, perhaps; one couldn't know. I used to look round, and try to decide whether there was anyone I could feel as sure about as I did about myself."

The sky was now a great sheet of rose fire, rippled like ebb-tide sands. It would be gone in a matter of minutes; already a long arm of shadow, cast by something on the horizon, was stealing across.

Ralph broke off his thoughts with a visible jerk of impatience, and threw the stub of his cigarette away. Silently Laurie gave him another. Ralph said, "Did it ever strike you about Hazell, at the time?"

"No. I just thought he was a bit bats, I suppose."

"He hated you," said Ralph in a light, cool voice. "Didn't you know why?"

Odd, thought Laurie, that whatever one's contempt for the hater this news is never quite without its sting. "I had awfully little to do with him. Didn't he ever say?"

"I didn't ask him," said Ralph shortly.

"Nobody could imagine afterwards," Laurie ventured presently, "how you managed to meet without getting caught."

"In the prop room mostly. The stage has the most elaborate lighting panel for its size in the British Isles. It was the only thing I knew something about that would get me inside the place. He leaned toward the Old Vic in those days; he used to hint sometimes that I'd saved his genius from being pushed over the thin line into madness. Can you imagine me falling for that?"

Yes, thought Laurie; but he supposed this was the wrong answer.

"I was a fool whichever way you look at it. I must have known really, of course; he was all a mess from cellar to attic. His sexual tendencies were just a minor symptom. He didn't like reality, and he didn't like doing anything for himself that he could get done for him. He had a great talent for being appreciative, of course. Really I think I fell for the corniest gag of the lot, the great *esprit-de-corps* racket. Esprit de corpse, Spud. Every time they try to slip it over on you, just say to yourself, 'The lower they go, the tighter they hang together.' "

"The trouble is, how else are you to meet people you're sure about, if it's only to talk to? After all, it's the way you and I met again."

"I don't forget that, Spud, believe me. No, of course we all have to use the network sometime. Don't let it use you, that's all. Ours isn't a horizontal society, it's a vertical one. Plato, Michelangelo, Sappho, Marlowe; Shakespeare, Leonardo, and Socrates if you count the bisexuals—we can all quote the upper crust. But at the bottom—Spud, believe me, there isn't any bottom. Never forget it. You've no conception, you haven't a clue, how far down it goes."

Laurie almost said that he had picked up one or two clues at the party; but something in Ralph's face told him he would be making a fool of himself, so he kept his mouth shut. Presently he said, "Don't you think it's mostly a matter of how sorry for themselves people are? I mean, whether one wants to be let off everything like a sick child, or—well, one could feel that one owes the race something, rather than the other way. It seems more logical."

"Ah. I might have guessed I've been saving this for the last person who'd need it."

"God, no," said Laurie. "You're wrong there." Ralph made a gentle interrogative noise. "Oh, I don't know. You get a bit tied up, making your own rules and trying to piece it all together."

"Yes, I know." The sky was fading, and the sun going down into a belt of mist. In the valley it was dark already, but up here a thin copper sunlight fell flat on their faces still. "There it is, Spud. When all's said and done, the best way to be independent is to have all you need at home."

Laurie looked away. He had wondered when Ralph was going to mention Bunny. Not to have done so would have seemed unfriendly; yet now it had happened Laurie found that he had no real wish to pursue the subject. He said, "Yes, I suppose it is," but he couldn't put as much feeling into it as he would have liked, and realized his inadequacy when Ralph failed to follow it up. He said, "You never finished telling me about Hazell."

As if he had introduced some irrelevant new subject, Ralph looked vague and drew his brows together. "There isn't much more to tell. What did you want to know?"

Thus confronted with the unspoken question in his mind, Laurie said at once, "Well, nothing specially."

"Unfair to Spud," said Ralph, suddenly laughing. "Sorry." Snapping open his case he said, "Have one of mine," and lit two. With an obscure pleasure, Laurie perceived that this wasn't one of the things in which practice had made him perfect. "I never told you how it ended, did I?"

"Well, no one in their right mind would have thought of asking."

"Why not? Ancient history. Hazell and I fell out on a matter of discipline in the end. By the way, when you said just now that he used to get away with murder, were you in point of fact referring to me?"

"No," said Laurie, losing his nerve. "Of course not."

"Well, he was a responsibility in any House, even Jeepers had the wit to see that. I believe he tried to get rid of him several times, but the Head took the view that he was a plow the School had put its hand to. Anyway, there he was, and one had to use a bit of discretion. Then this began, and at first one seemed to be helping him find his feet and really making something of him. I suppose some of that might even have been genuine. Quite soon he began to be tiresome in various ways, trying to take advantage. I remember I

193

had a long talk with him, explaining in words of one syllable why that would be bad for both of us. When that got nowhere, I told him that the next time he came up to me for a beating, that would be what he'd get. He could see I meant it. I was surprised when he turned up a couple of days later. I thought he was calling my bluff. Perhaps that's what he thought himself. I don't know. Anyway he'd left me no choice. I hated the whole business, I don't know when I've hated anything more, so I got down to it without wasting time. And afterwards I was just about to say, 'Well, that's that, don't let it happen again and now let's forget about it.' And then I realized."

Laurie waited and then said, "He couldn't take it, you mean?"

"Well, no. Just the opposite. If you don't know it doesn't matter."

"Oh," said Laurie. He thought how lightly he would have read all this, stripped of its human reality, in a psychological handbook.

"I think I just stood there and looked at him. Of course one sees if he was like that he couldn't help himself, poor swine. It wasn't the kind of thing I'd ever expected to find myself mixed up in, that's all. I'd have liked to see him dead, so long as I hadn't got to touch him. I suppose he saw it. It may be he went to Jeepers out of revenge, but I don't think so. I think he was scared, and it made him a bit hysterical. He told it reversing the point of the final episode, if you see what I mean. I didn't see very much future in arguing about it."

"God, how little we all knew. How awful for you."

"For him too," said Ralph, "I suppose." For a minute or two he didn't speak, but tapped with his fingers on the top of the car door, a broken rhythm like Morse. "The thing is, sooner or later one has to think it out, one can't just leave it there. I realized afterwards, some time afterwards, a perfectly normal person wouldn't have been so angry. He was sick, after all. But that, really, was it. That was what I had against him. I'd been trying to work up what I was into a kind of religion. I thought I could make out that way. He made me see it as just a part of what *he* was." His hand moved absently over the dashboard; suddenly the narrowed pencil of the masked headlamps shone out into the empty air of the valley, tracing paths of pale vapor in which midges danced like sparks. He swore under his breath and switched them off.

"Well, we have to face that sooner or later, of course." Now that the sudden light had gone it could be felt that the neutrality of twilight was over; it was almost dark. There was a moment of extreme quiet in which the distant shunting of a train, a car on the road behind them, the chirr of a night bird, were like differently colored silences. Ralph said, with a basic simplicity, "You see, Spud, don't you? That was why."

"Yes," said Laurie, "of course I see." He was too much moved to narrow his thoughts down to any one point of the story. He strained for better, more expressive words, which would not come. It was at this moment that the approaching car turned in and parked beside them. Inside it girls' voices were already giving provocative twitters of protest; whispers of giggling reproof pointed out that strangers were present. Ralph switched on the engine and, with carefully managed ease, put in the gear.

They drove for some time in silence. Soon they got down into traffic again; and it was then that he became aware of Ralph's increasing irritability. The small misdoings of other drivers seemed to infuriate him; after keeping up for some miles a profane running commentary, he started to address the offenders direct. Laurie put it down to the gears at first, till it occurred to him that Ralph hadn't had a drink yet this evening. He sat quiet, to avoid attracting the lightning, till a youth on a bicycle wobbled across in front of the car. Ralph pulled up and stayed to deliver a reprimand. For a moment it was funny to see the youth clinging paralyzed to the hedge like a monkey fascinated by a python; but when it was over he could see that Ralph was depressed and angry with himself, so at the next pub they passed he said, "What about stopping for a quick one?"

"No," said Ralph shortly. "Won't be time." He accelerated. About a quarter of a mile on, he said quite

195

pleasantly, "If we're too late, everything fit to eat will be off."

In one of their silent pauses Laurie found himself wishing it were possible, without telling Andrew too much, to get a sensible idea of Ralph into his head. It was the first time he had ever thought of Andrew in terms of criticism, even such gentle criticism as this.

"Usually the food's a bit less filthy here than anywhere." The hotel Ralph stopped at was Edwardian, shabby, clean, and restful. To Laurie's relief, after the third double Ralph made a move to the dining room. By that time he had started to talk again.

"I must say, Spud, you're remarkably well balanced for the offspring of divorce. Quite often being queer is the least of it."

"Well, my mother's pretty well balanced," Laurie began. Then it all came back to him. Ralph looked at his face and said gently, "Come on, Spud." With an awkwardness gradually superseded by relief, Laurie brought it out.

Ralph didn't urge him to see the best in Mr. Straike. He sounded, Ralph said, a bloody-minded old so-and-so. Rather like the first captain he had served under, he added almost as an afterthought. He was an old so-and-so if you like; if he had ever come down off the bridge in a gale someone would undoubtedly have tipped him overboard. But one trip he had taken his old woman along, and she seemed to think he was God's gift, it oozed out all over her. You couldn't account for women.

Laurie found this rough comfort, but did his best not to show it. "I expect it'll work out," he said.

"Have I been unnecessarily brutal, Spud? I'm sorry, I wouldn't know. I'm not much of an authority on family relationships. None of my girl friends went in for that sort of thing, either." He looked at Laurie and laughed. "Come, now, Spuddy, let it go at a raised eyebrow. That stunned expression isn't very flattering."

"I didn't mean——"

"No, but joking apart, you don't want to have written off half the human race at your time of life. I don't mean this unkindly, but perhaps you're having the
196

navel-cord cut in the nick of time. Look at it that way and don't be too upset about it."

There was an odd unexpected relief in this hard handling. "All the same, I doubt if mothers will ever need to lock their daughters up when they see me coming."

"Oh, perhaps not, I didn't mean that so much. It's more an attitude of mind than anything. What I always feel——"

This opened a conversation that went on for most of the meal. Once or twice Ralph would have changed it, but Laurie kept it going, not for the sake of the advice, which he couldn't feel would ever be important to him, but to make Ralph talk about himself. So it turned out, for after dismissing the soup and remarking that they seemed to have used shark's tripes, he said, "I did two years of women, when I first went to sea." He said it very much as sailors say they have done two years in tankers, or two years in sail.

"Did you?" said Laurie. "Why?"

"Oh, for almost every reason except the real one. I'd had rather a sickener of the other side. Once people know about you at sea, they want you to be too obliging. It's not so good in peacetime starting lower deck with the wrong accent and so on. I didn't want to give them anything on me. Besides, when I found I could if I gave my mind to it, I thought I might become naturalized, so to speak. Some people seem to take an inordinate pride in never having made the attempt, but I don't see it myself. I decided I'd give it the two years, anyway."

He broke off to attend to his food. Laurie saw that though he could use the left hand well enough, the padded fingers of the glove were clumsy and got in his way. It was impossible to guess how much he felt all this.

"Did it make any difference?" Laurie asked him.

"Well, yes, it did in a sense, of course. It's bound to do something for one's self-confidence, if nothing else. I think one year would have been enough. Funny thing, you know, it didn't feel at all like going straight. More like trying to cultivate some fashionable vice that never quite becomes a habit. I served out the contract,

197

though. No, let's be honest, I broke out a week short of the time. I happened to meet someone and I'd have been at sea a week later. All I can remember thinking is 'Thank the Lord, back to normal at last.' Well, there it is. Some people make a go of it. I don't think it was a complete waste of time, though; it stops one getting too parochial. Now and again I've even had a woman since; I've met one who reminded me of one of the early ones, or something. I don't know why, really. Vanity very likely. You look thoughtful, Spud. Do I sound very unfeeling?"

"No," said Laurie. He felt a fool and looked away.

"Well, I only managed to get along with real bitches, and none of them complained. Good women are definitely not my cup of tea."

This seemed reasonable in the circumstances, and Laurie hardly knew what it was that made him ask why.

"Probably because they're the cruellest of the carnivora. Give me the bloody Nazis, any day."

He had used the voice that closes a subject. Laurie, who had never gone in for forcing people's confidence, thought afterwards that it must have been the gin which had made him behave so uncharacteristically. It did not occur to him that there is a degree of emotional insecurity, in which he had been living for some weeks now, where the need for reassurance can produce almost the same effects as the desire for power. The coffee came and Ralph ordered brandy with it. Laurie led the conversation round in a circle and tried again.

"Well, Spud, you see, I shouldn't have said what I did just now. Don't know why I said it. Cheap and nasty, I've been seeing too much of the wrong people lately. I can't very well tell you after that . . . No, I mean look at it for yourself, once you start passing the buck to the previous generation, where do you step off? I suppose Eve put Cain's nose out of joint by petting his little brother. You can flannel out of anything."

"It doesn't matter. Sometimes it helps to know about other people."

"Well, Christ, it's nothing. It happens every day.

What do you think it is, the secret of Glamis or what? See, now. My mother was a good woman, only she saw something nasty in the woodshed. She couldn't help what she felt about it. *Her* parents were Plymouth Brethren."

"But what did she see?"

"Well, me of course. Oh, waiter, two more brandies. What a flop this story's going to be after the build-up you've given it. She saw me aged six, and the little girl next door aged seven, rather solemnly discussing anatomy. I imagine the same thing's going on at this moment in about five million woodsheds from China to Peru. However, it was apparently the filthiest crime that had ever touched my mother's life. She found it quite hard to talk about, so by the time she'd done, I took away some dim idea that carnal knowledge of women would cause one's limbs to rot and fall off, like leprosy." With an unconscious tic which Laurie had noticed in him once or twice before, he touched as if for reassurance his spotless white collar. "She got my father to do the beating; he told me it was about time I went to school to learn a clean life. Rather horrible precocious child I must have been, I suppose. Finish your brandy, Spud, you're one behind."

Laurie could see that if he wanted more of the story than this, it would be necessary to ask for it. He finished his brandy. "I see now," he said, "that last day at school, why it was you said you were going straight to Southampton."

There was a short pause. Then Ralph said, "Did I? Well, that was what I ought to have done."

After this, Laurie learned without much surprise, soon after, that Ralph had had nothing to do with women since leaving hospital. He offered no comment on this; but it would fit well with his conception of them, Laurie thought, to expect that they would punish him with his deformity.

Suddenly he seemed to remember the text of his earlier sermon, and laughed. "No, all I mean is, Spud, don't have a closed mind about it. I can't remember who those cranks are who say you mustn't think negatively; but they've got something, you know. About the most boring conversation this world affords—and I don't say this lightly, Spud, I've been in ships that took passengers, and sat with them at meals, and still I've heard nothing to touch a bunch of queers trying to prove to each other that the grapes are sour."

"I know what you mean."

"Well, look at Shakespeare's girl friend in the Sonnets, who was probably the bitch of all hell, yet she gives the thing what you might call body."

"Yes, but the thing about Shakespeare is that he was normal plus, not minus."

"Good Lord. Well, if you're prepared to admit *that* without a struggle, I've just been wasting your time. Have a cigarette."

As in this public place they took and lit their own, Laurie found they were exchanging the shadow of a smile, and he couldn't be sure afterwards which of them had smiled first.

"There's always this," Ralph said. "If one hasn't accepted too many limitations, one can pay one's final choice the compliment of——"

"Your brandy, sir," said the waiter.

Shortly after this Ralph looked at his watch and said, "Well, we've got an hour or so in hand; let's go round to my place."

"Surely there won't be time?"

"What? Oh, not the Station, I've got a room in town. Very utilitarian. There's a nice old square outside, but you won't see that for the blackout. Never mind."

The argument over the bill, about which Ralph was inclined at first to be imperious, ended amicably in a draw. Laurie scarcely noticed that his side of the discussion only made sense if they assumed that they were going to see a good deal more of one another.

The house was later than the one where Alec and Sandy lived; probably mid-Victorian. You couldn't say of this one that the proportions were good. It still came within the great period of the town's wealth; Ralph's torch picked out door-frames and banisters hideously carved, but made of solid teak. The landlady had summarily settled the blackout problem by removing the light bulbs from the hall and staircase. It was a narrow

200

house: as one came in one could almost feel the squeeze of the walls. There were two flights of stairs, but Laurie began the climb without misgiving; Miss Haliburton's machine was still doing him good. The first landing was quite dark and silent, without even a crack of light under a door.

"Are you all right, Spud?"

"Yes, fine."

The blackout in the room was still open. Irregular blots of darkness surrounded a tall glimmering rectangle of night sky. From the doorway, Laurie caught an indefinable, strangely familiar and nostalgic smell of shabbiness and simplicity. It was the combination of these two things, so often divorced, that stirred the memory, as much by what was absent as what was there: a positive kind of cleanness which lacked the institutional sour undertaste, a smell of scrubbed wood and beeswax and books.

Ralph's shoulder jutted sharply against the window. "Take a look if you like, but you can't see much."

Laurie came over, feeling his way along a table. They were on the upper side of the square, which sloped with the slope of the town. Beyond the houses opposite, a gray expanse of distance merged into the sky.

"Where are you, Spud?"

"Here." He put out his hand and touched the stiff cold braid on Ralph's moving sleeve.

"You can't see anything. It must have been pretty, when they had the lights."

"I expect it's nice in the daytime."

Laurie narrowed his eyes at the invisible horizon. A curtain, made of some harsh stuff, brushed his hand. He was scarcely aware of it, of what he was looking at. In a flash of recognition, he had identified the smell of the room. It was like school: not like the corridors and classrooms, which smelled of gritty boards and pencil shavings and ink and boys, but like the Head Prefect's study. He might have thought of this sooner, since it had been his own for a year; but just at this moment he didn't feel it as ever having been his. His perceptions, to everything else so dull, were full of this special feeling of the room, and, growing out of it, an intense awareness of Ralph standing close and silent beside him, not in serge and braid but in gray flannel; it seemed to him that he could even feel the cloth again. It all took him suddenly and with bewildering force; his next immediate reaction was a panic fear of having somehow betrayed himself. He had a dim impression that Ralph had made some movement and that this must mean he had noticed something. With Andrew so much on his mind, Laurie had become unreasoningly nervous; he obeyed a chain of reflexes with scarcely an intelligible thought. He turned quickly from the window, said, "Shout when you've done the blackout and I'll do the light," and made for the door. Haste made him clumsy; he collided with a chair and struck it hard with his knee, the wrong one.

It was very bad and seemed to go on for some time; he was only distantly conscious of Ralph speaking to him and couldn't answer; but by the time Ralph had done the blackout and got over to the light, he was able to say, "Sorry. All right now."

"Sit down," said Ralph. He used what Laurie thought of as his court-martial voice. He guided Laurie to an armchair; even at this moment there was some dim reminiscence in the fact that it was the only one in the room. Having settled him there, he stood looking down at him for a moment, then walked sharply across to the cupboard. Laurie had been longing to be let alone, but had had just enough control not to say so. The first white flash of pain had sunk to a red smolder; confusedly he recalled that he had had a silly mood of some kind, which had caused him to go blundering about the room in the dark; but this crude sensation had effaced it, the image of it was gone.

Ralph came up with a glass. "Here. Get this down."

"What is it?"

"Navy rum. Tip it down. It'll fix you up all right. They'd have taken off your leg with it in Nelson's day."

"I wish they bloody well had," said Laurie bitterly. He looked at the glass. "And if I drank that, I should think they could. God, what do you think my head's made of?"

"It's only a double tot. Just enough to make you happy."

The pain now was no worse than it had been several times before. Suddenly Ralph looked touching, standing there in anxious muddled kindness with the rum. "No, it'd make it worse. Tip it back, go on. All I need's three aspirin and some army char."

"Tea?" said Ralph blankly, and then, "Of course, my dear. If the mice haven't had it."

From the bottom of the cupboard he produced a tin kettle. This also must be where the rum had come from, for Laurie could hear him pushing aside some bottles. This must have been one of the servants' rooms when the house was new; the teak joinery didn't reach so high. The cupboard, the shoes, the kettle, would still have been like the study; but the faint clunk of the bottles had snapped the thread of illusion and now it wasn't like school any more.

Ralph had extracted the kettle from the back of the cupboard; he stood up. Mixed with the weakness of physical shock Laurie felt a strange complex of emotions. He said, "You shouldn't let me make such a nuisance of myself."

Ralph came up to the chair, changing the kettle over from his right hand to his left. For a few moments he stood there silent, then he touched Laurie's shoulder. "Spud."

"Yes?" said Laurie, looking up.

Ralph's face changed. He said in his officer's voice, "You damned fool, why didn't you have that drink? You look like death."

"I'd rather have tea."

"Lie down over there." It was an order. He held out his hand; obediently Laurie took it and was lifted up. This, he found, was what he wanted. He felt tired and sick and it was wonderful not to be obliged to think, or to be in charge of himself. Ralph half carried him across the room, taking the weight easily: his face was older than his years, but he moved like an athletic boy in hard training and one remembered then that he was only twenty-six. He pulled the cotton counterpane off the bed and settled Laurie's head on the pillow. Afterwards he folded the counterpane neatly, edges together, not fussily but as if it wouldn't have occurred to him not to do this. He sat down beside Laurie and said, "I think we should look at this knee before you walk on it again."

"Oh, it's all right, I'd feel it if anything had gone."

"You might not. Better let's look. Every ship I've been in for years that hasn't carried a doctor, I've always done this job. I won't hurt you."

"All right," said Laurie relaxing. Suddenly he felt free of it all. It had been taken over. He had been quite long enough in hospital to know that even a surgeon wouldn't swear to anything without X-rays, yet this knowledge seemed curiously irrelevant to his passive trust. He untied his boot and dropped it on the floor, and lay in an irresponsible peace while Ralph undid the bandage, and with an intent grave gentleness manipulated the joint. It was evident that he had some experience and knew what he was looking for. Laurie, who was used to the detached curiosity of doctors, felt something different here: Miss Haliburton had it, but in her it was overlaid with a complex technique, and in becoming mechanically perfect lost something of its nature. In Ralph it was direct and human, as it used to be in the old country bone-setters who came to their trade with nothing but an instinct in their hands of tactile sympathy with pain.

Laurie thought: At school, we were always discussing him. The thing about Lanyon is that he's this, or that. That's how he manages to do that, or this. And all the time no one knew anything.

"You ought to have been a doctor," he said.

"I've only had to cope sometimes when there wasn't anyone better. While I was living with Alec I did try to read up a bit of anatomy and so on; but he told me unqualified people messing about were a menace to society, and of course he was quite right."

"Ralph. If you'd gone up to Cambridge and everything, what were you going to have done?"

"Some sort of geographical survey work, I rather thought. There are quite a few odd corners still left to do."

204

"Yes," said Laurie. "Yes, of course."

By now, he would have fulfilled his destiny. He wouldn't have struggled for it; it would have come to him inevitably from a course of knowing first what needed doing, and doing it rather sooner and more thoroughly than anyone else; from an accumulation of confidence which would have been forced on him by the trust of other people, such as F.R.G.S.s and porters and village priests. His profound happiness in it wouldn't have come often into his conscious mind. He wasn't made to accept his limitations without trying to compensate; being what he was he could only have done it on some such scale as this. He could have worked out his salvation, if they had let him alone; all he had ever asked had been to work his passage. You'd think, after seven years, they might have let him keep his ship, said Laurie to himself; he used the soldier's "they," having been long enough an infantryman to find the disposing powers—Divisional Headquarters, the Government, God—all very remote and hard to isolate one from another.

"I'm not as handy as I used to be," Ralph said. "Excuse bad pun."

"You've got a lot of grip in it, so soon after."

"One has to practice it. Have a rest while I make this tea."

He picked up his glove from the floor. Laurie said, "Don't be silly."

"Oh, I always wear it. Might meet the old woman outside. They told me at the hospital it would harden up quicker if I didn't cover it; but I went into a pub and a tart who'd had a drink or two got it in focus rather suddenly, and shot a foot in the air before she could stop herself. No point in upsetting people."

"All right. But I'm not drunk and I'm not a woman."

"I know," said Ralph at the door. He smiled unexpectedly and charmingly, and went out with the kettle.

Laurie sat up and rebandaged his knee. For the first time he had a feeling of its being no longer in the foreground of his self-portrait. He turned on his face, which as usual did a certain amount of good.

They talk about realism, thought Laurie, burying his face in the blanket, which smelt faintly of the cyanide with which ships are fumigated. As if only the outside were real. This is a very ugly room, and I've sat for my portrait for a handbook on war surgery; I expect Ralph has too. When he comes back, I think I'll tell him about Andrew; I don't know why I haven't done it long ago. I've wished so often I could talk about it to someone who'd know.

The corner of the blanket, which was hanging out, had the label of a shop in Halifax, Nova Scotia. Slipping from under the displaced pillow a pair of pajamas showed, made of the thin silk sold in Indian stores; with instinctive curiosity Laurie fingered its foreign texture. He was lying like this, face forward, when the door opened.

He rolled over quickly, furious with himself for being taken by surprise: he was always careful not to be caught looking, he thought, as if one had been having a good cry. To remove all suspicion of this he began at once to say, "I was just looking at your pajamas." At the moment of reaching the end of the sentence, he took in the fact that it wasn't Ralph.

He hadn't a moment's doubt of who it must be. The situation wasn't one which would easily yield to words: it could only depend on the kind of person Bunny was, so he looked to see. But it was impossible to notice anything about him, initially, except his conspicuous good looks and the confidence that went with them; it was like trying to read something printed on a bright surface which dazzled the eye. He did not, however, appear angry, and this at once seemed to Laurie like a gesture of prodigality from someone who can well afford it; he had a moment of feeling rather dejected and down-at-heel, before remembering to be glad that Ralph had done as well for himself as this.

Bunny stood easily just inside the door with his hands in his pockets; he looked thoughtful, and this gave his boyish face a certain pathos as if he were carrying a burden beyond his years. This grave moment gave to the smile that followed an irresistible sincerity.

"Now don't tell me who you are. I know I'm right. Laurie Odell."

"Yes. You're Bunny, aren't you? Ralph was telling me."

"Oh, was he? It's all very well for him to keep telling people about each other and never to let them meet." He came in and sat on the edge of the table, swinging one leg. "I hear you've been having a pretty tough time in hospital. I'm so sorry."

"It's not much nowadays. A rest soon fixes it." He leaned down and reached for his boot. At the back of his mind hovered a feeling that Bunny was taking it almost too well. In his place, Laurie thought, he himself wouldn't have guaranteed to be charming at a moment's notice. But then, he reflected, in Bunny's place, one would feel pretty solid; it would take more than that to shake one. Ralph had said something: that the best way of being independent was to have all you needed at home. This easy and careless trust; not like Sandy; it was heartening to know that it did actually happen.

"Is Ralph anywhere about?" Bunny was asking. "I wonder I didn't meet him on the stairs."

"He can't be far. He went to put on the kettle for some tea."

"For some *what?*" asked Bunny, staring. Laurie had no time to be analytical or to put a name on the hard flippancy in the smiling eyes. "Well, well, that's definitely a new one for old Ralph. Now me, I'm a proper old auntie for the stuff. Up at the Station we're always ... Oh, hello, sweetie. Here I am back after all, with my gay evening in ruins."

The door had been open, so Ralph must have heard their voices as he crossed the landing. He stood in the doorway with a cool, cheerful look, and nodded at Bunny as if he had half expected him.

"Why, hello, Bunny, what happened to the party?"

"My dear, I couldn't be more furious. I'll swear by anything you like that Binky told me it was today. Now he says it's tomorrow. He was rushing out somewhere and didn't even stop to offer me a drink. Never mind, I shall have some of your delicious tea, instead."

207

Ralph said, "Here's the aspirin," and added, "I was downstairs getting some milk." It had a certain note, not of apology, of giving an explanation which one owes. He was carrying the milk in a little gray aluminum jug; he must have been to the basement to beg it from the landlady. Laurie felt foolish because he hadn't anticipated this difficulty. "You shouldn't have bothered, I don't mind it without."

"I do, though," said Bunny boyishly. He got up. "Well, dears, why on earth are we all sitting about up here?" He spoke as if it were something temporary done in preoccupation, like loitering in the hall or kitchen. "Come along downstairs and get comfortable, and we'll have it out of proper cups and saucers, like ladies and gentlemen." He gave Ralph a flashing smile and added, "I bet you were going to give it him in a toothglass, weren't you?"

Ralph said, "We'll come if you've got some fresh tea. I don't trust this lot." His manner was very light and easy; it had been like this during the first part of Sandy's party. He put out the light and they groped their way across the landing to the stairs. About halfway down, Ralph said, "All right, Spud?" and put an arm quickly around his shoulders, as if to steady him. The gesture had a helpless, almost a childish tenderness, like that of a small boy who has got his little brother into a scrape. But there below was Bunny's room, and he was hospitably waving them in.

It was hard to believe one was in the same building. The room had been, one could say, interior-decorated. There was a single picture, which was vorticist of a kind and had patently been chosen to match the color scheme. A large number of glossy magazines were strewn about; but such books as could be seen looked as if people had left them behind and never missed them. The furniture was very low, with that overstated lounginess which rarely turns out to be physically comfortable. It was all very bright and sleek, and had the look of being kept under dust-sheets except when open to the public.

Bunny threw open a glittering cocktail cabinet lined with looking-glass; this seemed to be an automatic gesture like switching on the radio, which he did at the same time. Talking brightly against it, he went to a cupboard and got out a red-and black tea set. Ralph walked over to the radio and, without permission or apology, switched it off.

"Oh, *you*," said Bunny coquettishly. He arranged cups on a gold lacquer tray. "It's *so* nice to meet a fellow addict. Sit here, Laurie, then you'll have this little table." The chair seats were a few inches off the ground and there was nothing to do with one's legs but stick them straight out before one. Laurie settled himself, feeling conspicuous and vulnerable. Ralph hovered uncertainly for a few seconds, and then took the next chair.

Bunny held up a tea tin and shook it playfully. He looked at Ralph, who was lighting a cigarette and seemed not to notice.

"I should think that old kettle of yours must be boiling madly. Run along, do, sweetie, my tongue's hanging out."

It is possible, in a very low chair, to adopt a posture which makes getting up look like a physical impossibility. Ralph had settled himself like this, his legs crossed and extended, his hands in his pockets, the cigarette tilted at the corner of his mouth.

"No. You're the tea expert. You make it." One might have called his manner a colorless extract of decision.

Laurie saw their eyes meet. Although he had brought to this occasion a number of preconceived ideas, he was too keenly interested to let his powers of observation sleep. He knew at once that the air of a cozy family bickering was a thin façade, that Bunny had had a surprise and was only beginning, yet, to be angry. Ralph lounged in the chair, giving him the straight look which hadn't changed essentially in all the years that Laurie remembered. It would be odd if by this time Bunny weren't equally used to it; yet, seeing these two men in uniform confronting one another, Laurie had a suspicion that he wasn't used to it at all, that finding the challenge suddenly removed into the field of man to man, he felt something like outrage, as if Ralph had won on a foul.

He carried it off, however, quite well, making as he got up a whimsical face at Laurie and murmuring, "You see? Just an Eastern slave." He had after all, thought Laurie, met a difficult situation, just now, in a civilized manner, and in the matter of the kettle Ralph was demonstrably in the wrong. In any case, thought Laurie, it wasn't his business. Now that he was alone with Ralph he felt a dead weight of constraint; the glossy magazines made him think of a dentist's waiting room. After nearly a minute's silence Ralph said awkwardly, "Bunny's fixed himself up nicely down here. I'm a dead loss at interiors and all that myself."

"Me too." He suspected that Ralph wished without disloyalty to disclaim the standard of taste around him. A leisured view of the room yielded so many awful little superfluities, so many whimsies and naughty-naughties, tassels and bits of chrome, that one recalled one's gaze shamefaced as if one had exposed the straits of the poor. Laurie remembered the room upstairs: the absence of all loose ornament, the mantelpiece firmly packed with books, the little shelf fixed to the wall over the bed; the smell of scrubbing-soap, the wood and brass polished as a seaman, not a landlady, does it; the single eighteenth-century color print of a frigate under all sail. As tactfully as he could, he said, "I expect he likes to feel as unnautical as possible when he isn't at sea."

"Bunny isn't a sailor." Just for a moment, before he covered it, Laurie saw that he had wanted to laugh. "He's attached to the navy for instructional purposes in this thing we're doing. He was in the same sort of line commercially, before the war."

"Oh. Does he instruct you?" Laurie found he resented it deeply. Then it struck him that Ralph might take it for a cheap joke. But Ralph said simply, "He did at first. I've moved up to another class now." It was just then that Bunny came in with the tea.

For some time Laurie had been telling himself there was nothing remarkable about the smooth cool surface Ralph had presented ever since Bunny appeared: the more he felt, the less would be on display; you could be certain of that, Laurie thought. Now, however, he stopped snubbing his own instincts; he knew that all wasn't well in this household, though, no doubt, the flaw was passing and trivial; he had blundered in at a delicate moment, and almost certainly complicated whatever trouble there was. In some anxiety he waited for Bunny to speak.

Bunny only surveyed the tray with his head on one side, and the naïve boyish look of one who will surely turn out to have forgotten something, but hopes for the best. "Well, now! Who's going to be mother and pour out?" He put the tray at Laurie's elbow and smiled confidingly. "Miss Odell?"

Laurie said equably, "All right, if you like." A course of Charles's friends had inured him to this kind of humor. He began putting milk in the cups. When he reached the third Ralph said, "Not for me, thanks," and went over to the cocktail cabinet, where he got himself a pink gin.

Laurie poured out for Bunny and himself. In the lower ranks of the army, brewing tea has few feminine associations; to an ex-merchant seaman, he thought, the joke wasn't likely to be excruciating either. Probably it was this which had irritated Ralph. He had come back with his drink and Laurie found himself thinking of him with vague perturbation. Imagining him ideally happy with Bunny had had a peaceful kind of remoteness. Now, as soon as one began wondering what could be wrong and why, one began to have new and disturbing thoughts and to resent Bunny more than was reasonable. Laurie got exasperated with himself and revolted against emotion altogether. With a decision which his habitual fear of boring people made rare in him, he embarked on a conversation about the war.

Ralph flung himself into it with transparent relief, and displayed a grasp of naval strategy which was practical and lively, if not profound. Used as Laurie was to considering the prospect of invasion in terms of what was to be done about the Germans when they arrived, he found it stimulating to be rapped smartly over the knuckles for assuming that they could arrive at all.

211

At the back of Ralph's mind, he suspected, was the thought that an emergency on this scale might get him on the bridge of a fighting ship; but they didn't discuss it. The conversation, begun as an expedient, soon became absorbing to both of them; some minutes of it passed before Laurie realized the fact that it was a dialogue. He looked up to see Bunny absorbed in his own reflections; not resentful it seemed but resigned, like someone who is used to not being considered much.

For the first time, Laurie admitted to himself that it was a mistake to have come. In anyone he had liked and trusted less, he would have suspected by this time that he was being used to bring Bunny to heel. But it was simple enough, he thought; Ralph had felt bored and depressed, perhaps because Bunny had arranged to go to a party without him, and had wanted someone to talk to and pass the time. And why not?

Just then he saw Bunny glance at Ralph's glass which he had just emptied, pick it up, and refill it. Laurie watched the process out of the tail of his eye; the tot of gin was very small, the bitters helped to color it, the rest came from the water-jug. It shed quite a new and different light on Bunny, and made Laurie resolve to be very tactful indeed.

Just after this, the doorbell rang and Bunny went to answer it. Ralph applied himself to his drink in silence. Laurie had wondered whether he would take the opportunity of making it up to strength, but he was too preoccupied to notice anything.

The callers were Alec and Sandy. Laurie felt very awkward; but it was made clear to him at once by both that a new leaf had been turned and that his name was on it. It was the first time Laurie had observed them both together; he realized quite soon that Sandy regarded Alec as belonging to a superior order of beings, and was childishly proud of him. Perhaps it was admiration that caused him to commit such violent assaults on Alec's emotions, as a small child will pummel an adult, not believing that it can really hurt him. As for Alec, one would have supposed that he and Bunny were the best of friends. Laurie thought this reasonable but decided that he himself would never have been

212

equal to it. Tea things were swept away and Bunny dispensed drinks; he went on looking after Ralph's glass as before, choosing moments when his attention was divided. Certainly it made one look at the pink mirror coffee tables with a gentler eye.

For the last few minutes, Ralph had been watching Alec, not talking much. Suddenly he said, "Has something happened?"

"Yes," said Alec. "It's Bim. I thought, as we were passing . . . I wasn't sure if you'd heard."

Ralph said "No." He stared at the glass in his hand, and drank as if it were a routine duty he was absently carrying out. "No, I'd not heard. How was it?"

"Over Calais somewhere. He was seen to hit the ground; he hadn't bailed out. There seems no doubt about it."

Ralph didn't speak. It was Bunny who said gently, "Poor old Bim. I ran into him only the other day. It seems like a few hours."

"He had a long life," said Sandy, "as it's going now." Laurie could see that he was really distressed; his face was sharpened with it. Today he and Alec seemed closer and their friendship no longer unlikely. They reminisced together for a few minutes about Bim.

Bunny said, in the same gentle sickroom voice, "You met him, didn't you, Laurie? At Alec's the other night?"

"Yes. Only for a few moments."

"No, of course I remember, he didn't stay long. You swept him off, didn't you, Ralph, to get some rest?"

Ralph said abruptly and rather loudly, "Well, someone had to. He was ill. He ought to have been in hospital."

"Oh, I *know*," said Bunny earnestly. Seeing Ralph about to get another drink, he took his glass and gave him one. "I remember you saying, Alec, if Ralph hadn't taken over, Bim would have folded up in a couple of hours. It seems like fate, doesn't it?"

"No," said Alec in his clinical voice, "I didn't say so. I've had training enough not to make that sort of cocksure prognosis."

Staring at Bunny and forgetting to care if anyone noticed it, Laurie thought: How stupid he is; how does Ralph bear it? Of course he's very good-looking, and I suppose ... "I suppose," he said, "the skies over Britain are full just now of fighter pilots who ought to be in nursing homes if they had their rights."

"I'm surprised, really, they hadn't grounded him," Bunny said. "I expect they would have if he'd gone round the bend any further. What do *you* think, Alec?"

"I'll save him the trouble of telling you," said Ralph. His face had a heavy stiffness and his voice had gone flat and hard. "He thinks untrained people should mind their own —— business, don't you, Alec?"

Laurie looked at him puzzled. If it hadn't been so clearly impossible—for the last three gins Bunny had given him would hardly have added up to one good double—one would have sworn he was getting drunk.

Alec didn't rise to it. He had brownish eyelids with long dark lashes, under which his eyes slid around to look at Bunny for a moment. He spoke however to Ralph, with pleasant detachment. "Not in this instance, my dear. At least, I can assure you, you did precisely what I should have done if I'd had any influence with Bim, which I didn't."

"Well," said Ralph, "it seems that night he knew what he needed better than anyone else did. Too bad he got pushed around." He gave Bunny his glass and said, "Not so much bloody bitters this time, Boo."

Boo, thought Laurie. He looked at Ralph, who was beginning to have a fixed stare when he was not actually speaking. Boo. Well, good God, what business is it supposed to be of mine? He looked at his watch and got up.

"It's on the half-landing," said Ralph, rousing himself.

"Yes, I know, but I won't come up again, I'll have to catch my bus. Don't get up, it's all right."

Ralph said, "What in blazes are you talking about? I'm driving you home." He stared at Laurie as if he had been insulted and were waiting for an apology.

How *can* he be drunk? thought Laurie. I could take what he's had myself and hardly feel it. He replied calmingly that of course Ralph wasn't to turn out and that the bus went to the door.

"Sit down," said Ralph, "and don't talk crap. I'm driving you home and that's the end of it."

Laurie hesitated. As he did so, Bunny caught his eye and said, "Don't worry, Laurie; it'll be all right." He sounded both kindly and confident. After all, thought Laurie, he should know.

On his way to the half-landing, where he retreated for a brief escape from all the tension upstairs, he knew that he was relieved not to be going yet. He hadn't realized, till it came to the moment of saying goodbye, how much he had hated leaving Ralph after this news; in this awful flash room it was like abandoning him in a strange town or in a desert. One had to keep reminding onself how very far from strange to him it really was, and that he wasn't alone, either.

When Laurie got back, they were all discussing a recent blackmail case. Sandy and Alec had met someone who knew the victim, and had all the details, which were sordid enough. Remembering long discussions at Oxford, Laurie remarked that the present state of the law seemed to encourage that sort of thing; it was unenforceable, and merely created racketeers.

"I agree," said Alec. "You could add that it gives the relatively balanced type, who makes some effort to become an integrated personality, a quite false sense of solidarity with advanced psychopaths whom, if they weren't all driven underground together, he wouldn't even meet." He caught Sandy's eye fixed on him reverently, and, as if he were giving way to a suppressed irritation, added, "Not that I can feel much pity for anyone who'll submit to blackmail, myself."

Sandy said at once, "No, really, that's a bit sweeping, Alec. What about his job, what about dependents, what if his mother's got a weak heart and the news will kill her? It's not like you to be so rigid."

"Oh, Sandy, we've been over this *so* often. It's a matter of what your self-respect's worth to you, that's all. Isn't that so, Ralph? In the first place, I didn't choose to be what I am, it was determined when I wasn't in a position to exercise any choice and without my knowing what was happening. I've submitted to psychoanalysis; it cured my stutter for me, which was very useful as far as it went. All right. I might still be a social menace, like a child-killer, and have to be dealt with whether I was responsible or not. But I don't admit that I'm a social menace. I think that probably we're all part of nature's remedy for a state of gross overpopulation, and I don't see how we're a worse remedy than modern war, which from all I hear in certain quarters has hardly begun. Anyway, here we are, heaven knows how many thousand of us, since there's never been a census. I'm not prepared to accept a standard which puts the whole of my emotional life on the plane of immorality. I've never involved a normal person or a minor or anyone who wasn't in a position to exercise a free choice. I'm not prepared to let myself be classified with dope-peddlers and prostitutes. Criminals are blackmailed. I'm not a criminal. I'm ready to go to some degree of trouble, if necessary, to make that point."

Sandy looked quickly around the room for applause. "I only mean," he said, "that you can't always know what other people are up against. Of course, if normal sex were ever made illegal, you'd get decent married couples meeting each other in brothels and dives and getting tarred with the same brush."

Ralph stirred, in what seemed a sudden uncontrollable annoyance. "Well, for Christ's sake, don't let's make blasted ostriches of ourselves. Anyone would think, to hear you and Alec talk, that being normal was immaterial, like whether you like your eggs scrambled or fried."

"I didn't say that," said Alec temperately.

"That's how you expect to be treated. Even civilized people had better hang on to a few biological instincts." He had had to slow himself down to manage the last sentence without stumbling.

"It's time they learned to be a bit more tolerant," Sandy said.

"They've got children and they want grandchildren. Make you sick, the dirty bastards. So what? They've learned to leave us in peace unless we make public ex-

216

hibitions of ourselves, but that's not enough, you start to expect a medal. Hell, can't we even face the simple fact that if our fathers had been like us, we wouldn't have been born?"

"Well, I don't know," said Laurie. "In Athens we could have been."

"Good old Spud," said Ralph slowly and distinctly. "You'll get yourself lynched if you don't look out." He leaned forward and tapped Laurie solemnly on the knee. "A lot of bull is talked about Greece by people who'd just have been a dirty laugh there. Not you, Spuddy. I'm not talking about you. You'd have got by."

Alec shot a glance at Bunny and said swiftly, "Yes, well, we know under the social system the women were illiterates in semi-purdah, and most of the men were bisexual from choice. Hence Socrates, though probably not Plato. I think that supports my argument rather than yours." His concern for the debate had something perfunctory about it.

"All right," said Ralph rather thickly. "They were tolerant in Greece and it worked. But, Christ, there was something a bit different to tolerate. There was a standard; they showed the normal citizen something. There was Aris——" He stuck on the name; either he couldn't pronounce it or he didn't remember it. He looked at Laurie, as if he were issuing an order.

"Aristogeiton," Laurie said.

"And the Sacred Band. In fact they took on the obligations of men in their friendships instead of looking for bluebirds in a fun-fair; and if they didn't, they bloody well weren't tolerated, and a good job too."

Laurie didn't realize how completely Bunny had been forgotten until he moved. He had been sitting on a tartan divan with his patient left-out look, as if a group of mathematicians had overlooked his presence and started to discuss relativity. Laurie had had enough of this and hadn't glanced at him again. Now he got up gracefully and took away the glass with which Ralph had been tapping for emphasis on the arm of his chair.

"You'll break it." He smiled brightly across at Laurie. "I bet he handed you out some canings at school, didn't he?"

217

"About the usual number," said Laurie, rather coldly.

Bunny put his head on one side and looked down at Ralph with an indulgent smile. "It did something to him, you know. Scratch old Ralph after a couple of drinks, and you'll find an unfrocked scoutmaster."

Laurie was certain afterwards that if he had had one more drink himself at the time when Bunny said this, he would have got to his feet and struck him. As it was, he was just sober enough to notice Alec looking at him, which brought him to himself. He sat upright in his chair, which wasn't easy, since it seemed designed for patients under general anesthesia, and looked Bunny in the face.

"We didn't have a scout troop actually," he said. "But I think it's quite good. It keeps boys off the streets. Did you ever join one?"

Oh, God, he thought, that was a bit much. He saw Sandy try to catch Alec's eye and Alec pretend not to notice; he saw Ralph frowning in forced concentration as if he knew something ought to be dealt with. He looked at Bunny again.

"I should think I did," said Bunny genially. "I was prepared every minute, but it turned out a terrible flop."

He spoke as if he had missed the point; but Laurie had seen his face at the moment of impact. While Alec and Sandy hurried to pad the conversation with gossip, Laurie thought: He took that because he couldn't think of a comeback he felt would be smart enough. That's what he wants more than anything; cleverness, making things go his way. And he's just clever enough to suspect sometimes that he's fundamentally stupid, and it limits even his malice. That must be most frustrating. I suppose Ralph sees the best of him when they're alone.

It was at this point that the air-raid sirens went.

There were the usual sounds of weary and resigned irritation. Bunny went to the window to fix a dubious bit of blackout; a warden shouted at him from the street for showing a light; there was some moving about in search of a drawing-pin. Laurie bumped the cocktail cabinet and slopped over the cut-glass water-jug, and returned to mop it up with his handkerchief. As he was about to put this back in his pocket something arrested him; he brought it out again and sniffed it. Bunny was at the window, and didn't see.

Ralph heaved on his chair-arms, and got to his feet. "Well, Spud," he said, "time we were getting you home."

Bunny came over. In his gentlest voice he said, "Ralph, my dear, really and truly I *don't* think you ought to drive."

"Now look," said Ralph, "I've only——" He frowned again, as if he were trying to remember something.

"Yes, we know all about that." Bunny's cozy voice seemed addressed to an engagingly naughty child. "Just you take a little nap till I get home. I'll see after Laurie."

Laurie said to Ralph, "It's all right. Don't worry." Ralph took hold of the back of the chair to steady himself, and stared at him with his eyes narrowed, as if he were a bright light. Laurie went up to him. "I enjoyed this evening. Thanks for everything." It didn't matter any longer what Bunny thought.

"It's a pleasure, Spud, any time," said Ralph, speaking carefully and rather pompously. "Bunny's right, you know. Bad show, I'm sorry. Comes of mixing them. I shouldn't have had that rum upstairs."

"You didn't have any rum," Laurie said. He didn't care whether Bunny heard him or not.

"That's what I thought too," said Ralph, nodding solemnly. "Only goes to show." He sat down again; this time he looked as if he wouldn't get up so easily. Just then the guns began, crackling and pattering at the other end of the town. Laurie looked around at Bunny. Evidently it would be necessary to speak to him sooner or later.

"You'd better forget about driving me back. You'll have to get back to the Station, won't you?"

"Oh, no," said Bunny soothingly. "That's all right, I'm not on duty."

"Won't you want to run Ralph over?"

"Ralph?" Bunny smiled as if something whimsical

219

had been said. "He's only on a course. He isn't responsible for anything."

Laurie's hand clenched itself in his pocket; his fingers met in the wet twist of handkerchief he had used to mop the cocktail shelf. Ralph's eyelids were dropping, he was just in the pose for which the chair had been designed. Laurie said to Alec, "Will you be here?"

"We're on casualty tonight. We ought to be on our way now. I'm sorry." His eyes met Laurie's in a look of open understanding. "I shouldn't worry, it can't be helped, you know. Well, thanks for the drink, Bunny. Good night."

Laurie wondered, as the door shut on them, what their first words would be when they were alone. There was a thump; the bombs had started. He walked back to Ralph's chair.

"I'm not going," he said. "Not till this is over."

"Push off, Spud," said Ralph drowsily. "I'm going to sleep." He shut his eyes again.

Laurie walked around him. He wasn't going to speak to Bunny across him as if he didn't count. "We can't," he said evenly, "just leave him here. What if the house gets a stick of incendiaries?"

Bunny spread his hands in a vaguely mystic gesture, committing them all to the will of Allah.

Laurie breathed sharply through his nose. *"Christ——"*

He turned at a sound behind him. Ralph had picked himself up from the chair. He stood with his feet apart and his hands dug in his pockets, swaying slightly as if he were giving with a moving deck.

"What in hell's all this nonsense about? Stop flapping, Spud, and don't be such a bloody nuisance."

"All right." He could feel Bunny watching at his elbow. "Try and stay awake till you see how it goes."

"See how what goes? What's eating you, for God's sake?"

"There's a raid on." As he spoke he heard a bracket of bombs go down; it was like heavy feet running a step or two.

"All right, Spud, all right." He stood there frowning, as if the raid were an obstruction which Laurie had called into being. Suddenly he narrowed his eyes tightly; something came into them, it seemed from an indestructible strong-point far behind. "Look after yourself. I'll be ringing you. God bless."

"God bless," said Laurie, meaning it. The last thing he saw of the room was Ralph settling back in the chair again. As he went out, he saw Bunny go back and take the lighted cigarette out of Ralph's hand. He's thinking of his nice carpet, Laurie thought.

They went down without speaking. Laurie heard the dot-and-carry sound of his own feet on the stair-treads, and imagined Bunny in the hall below, hidden by the darkness, standing and listening to it.

Outside in the street Bunny said, "We'll have to use old Ralph's car, I've lent someone mine this evening."

They got into the car, which Bunny started with a patronizing kind of carelessness. The guns were still going and a lot of search-lights were out; the streets were almost empty, till they came to one where a house lay half across the road with a rescue squad working, and they had to go another way.

Laurie thought: Andrew wouldn't judge too quickly. Andrew would say you should get free of yourself and try to understand. For example: Bunny had gone to a good deal of trouble, which only made sense if one assumed that he was much fonder of Ralph than he seemed. It was true that his methods had not been aristocratic; but he had probably had a very unhappy childhood, or something. Very likely he tormented himself as much as Sandy did, but hid it better.

A bomb came down, not very near, somewhere behind them. Laurie thought of Ralph asleep in the deep tilted chair and wondered if it had been close enough to rouse him: but this did not further the effort to understand Bunny.

"I'm afraid this is rather a way for you." To say he was sorry Bunny had had to turn out would have been too much.

"Oh, no, I adore driving at night, don't you? Before the war I had one of those huge spotlights on my Riley. It made everything look madly dramatic, just like a color film. People used to look so funny blinking and

221

staring in it, like fish in a tank. You'd love the Riley. I had her done specially, a sort of bronze, with cream upholstery. If I'd only known, I wouldn't have lent her tonight. I hate doing it really, but this boy helped me out of a rather awkward predicament and saved a lot of unpleasantness, so one could hardly refuse. Of course, it *would* be tonight. Never mind, you must try her another time."

"Thanks," said Laurie reluctantly. One could hardly pick a quarrel in the face of this unexpected civility, unless one had decided never to see Ralph again. After all, he thought, people were patchy; Ralph, who was no fool, had found something in Bunny to love; and there was always the risk of investing one's snobbery with moral sanctions.

"Most of the excitement seems to be the other side of town. We'll be out in the country in a minute, then you'll have to begin showing me the way. I didn't mean to seem callous about Ralph, just now. I just happen to know that the old dear practically never passes out flat, no matter what he has; and that hag downstairs would wake him at a pinch. She adores him, you know, she thinks he's a wicked romantic sailor; it would kill you, honestly, to see the way he plays up to her, and she's such a dim draggle-tailed old thing, Christmas in the orphanage I always call it. My dear, I said, one dark night you'll find you've given her so much self-respect, if that's what you call it, that she'll nip up the stairs and into bed with you and then you'll be sorry. He got so annoyed, I think that must have really happened to him somewhere or other. There's a lot of funny little kinks about old Ralph."

"Yes?" said Laurie, whose attention had wandered; he had been watching Bunny drive. Unable to stand it any longer in silence, he said, "You'll only make the gears worse than they are, slamming them like that."

"Oh, my *dear,* the whole bus is just a Palladium turn. I think it originally went by steam, and they modernized it at great expense about 1920. Have you *seen* it in daylight?"

"Yes."

The thing that always astonishes me is to find the

222

lever inside at all, and not sticking out of the mudguard in a brass casing."

"Ralph seems to manage it pretty well, considering what he's got left of that hand. It must be a bit of an effort for him."

"Oh, but you know he adores effort, it's his thing. He thinks comfort's absolutely decadent. Now, I'm not a bit like that myself."

"No," Laurie said.

"The great thing, *I* think, is for everyone to be happy. What I always say is, life's so simple really, if you don't complicate it. It's just a matter of live and let live, don't you think so?"

"For God's sake, do put the clutch in properly when you're changing down. If you grind them like that they'll soon be jamming all the time."

"It's all such a nonsense," said Bunny petulantly. "Well, this is the *very* last time I lend the Riley."

Laurie's hatred faded in spite of him. His mind groped over the personality beside him seeking something to grip on, and everything that had seemed salient resolved itself into a deficiency. He was too tired to be choice with words: Common, he thought inadequately. I thought after Dunkirk that would never mean anything again. How does he keep all this from Ralph?

They were out in the country; the sounds of the raid behind were muted by distance. Less warmly than he would have spoken to a chauffeur, Laurie showed Bunny the way.

"Oh, yes, I know. You're an awfully reserved person, aren't you?"

"I'm afraid I've never thought about it."

"I get terribly bored with people who are just on the surface. They never give you any surprises, do they? That was the thing that first attracted me to Ralph, you know. He didn't put everything in the shop window. Now, of course, I know him inside out, and it's not that I'm not terribly fond of him, but—well, I wouldn't tell just anyone this, but it's different telling you——"

Laurie had to speak twice before he succeeded in interrupting. "I'm sorry; but if you don't mind, I'd rather not hear about all this."

"I wouldn't have told you," said Bunny in a hurt, sincere voice, "without a very good reason."

Laurie said abruptly, "Well, you can tell me this, then. Why did you do it?"

"Well, really, my dear, I was more or less swept off my feet. Between ourselves . . ."

"Tonight, I mean. You gave him about five neat gins straight off. It was in the water-jug."

"Goodness, you *are* observant, aren't you? Or is it an old trick in the army too?"

"I wouldn't know, I'm not an officer."

"Of course, it doesn't work with everybody. If I'd tried it on you, you'd have spotted it straight away. But with hard-drinking types like old Ralph, who've got one or two on board already——"

"I asked why you did it, that's all."

Bunny stopped the car.

"You awful boy," he said. "You *do* believe in playing hard to get."

It was probably for not more than a second that Laurie was paralyzed by sheer incredulity. It seemed far too long. Though Bunny hadn't got beyond the arm flung along the back of the seat and the deep intimate gaze, Laurie felt already a nauseous anticipation of contact.

"Look," he said, "shall we get something straight? I don't like you. I don't like you in any possible way that one person could like another." He paused for breath. When he remembered everything it didn't seem enough. "If you were the last human being left alive, I'd sooner——" The phrase with which he finished took him by surprise. It was what Reg had said to the girls in the blackout. Laurie had never supposed that a time would come when he would use it with satisfaction.

"My, my," said Bunny. "Aren't we butch?"

Laurie thought, That got through.

"In that case," said Bunny. He leaned over and snapped at the catch of the door. "I should hate to force my company on anyone who felt like that about it. Good night."

Something primitive stirred in Laurie, as in a solitary

224

man beset by the creatures of a swamp or forest. "Oh, no," he said.

"I shouldn't take that tone, if I were you."

This, thought Laurie, is what he doesn't tell everyone. The practiced inflection had held many chapters of inadvertent autobiography.

"You know," he said, "Ralph's going to wake up before long and ring the hospital to see I got back all right. If I haven't, what do you expect me to do tomorrow? Back up your story?"

"Why, you little——"

"Yes, all right. You've bought this. It's not even your car. You're a volunteer for this job. You went to a lot of bother to drive me back. Now you damned well drive me."

The pain jumped in his knee; he was shaking a little, but not to notice in the dark. He waited.

"Well," said Bunny, *"please* don't let's have a scene about it in the middle of the road."

He let in the clutch.

As the car ran on through the cold sweet autumn night, Laurie thought, All that was an impromptu. It wasn't a deep-laid scheme or anything. He's just a chancer.

With a cold barren weariness that quenched the dry glow of anger, he thought, What can you do about these people? The terrible thing is, there are such a lot of them. There are so many, they expect to meet each other wherever they go.

Not wicked, he thought: that's not the word, that's sentimentality. These are just runts. Souls with congenitally short necks and receding brows. They don't sin in the sight of heaven and feel despair: they only throw away lighted cigarettes on Exmoor, and go on holiday leaving the cat to starve, and drive on after accidents without stopping. A wicked man nowadays can set millions of them in motion, and when he's gone howling mad from looking at his own face, they'll be marching still with their mouths open and their hands hanging by their knees, on and on and on. ... No, Andrew wouldn't like that.

When they got to the hospital, Bunny said, "I suppose you won't be able to run to Ralph fast enough with all this."

"You're afraid of him, really, aren't you?"

"Don't make me laugh," said Bunny shrilly. "He never caned *me* at school."

"No," said Laurie. "Quite." He got out of the car. "Don't worry; I shall never mention you to Ralph again if it's possible to avoid it. He's a friend of mine. It's a good old English word and I'm using it in the literal sense, if that conveys anything to you at all. Good night."

He got back to the ward within seven minutes of the time limit; but Andrew, he found, had finished his work and left.

He had got to see Andrew. He felt a need more imperative than any he had experienced in the keenest crisis of personal love. He wanted to recover his belief in the human status.

The late-pass men who had got off the last bus were still having cocoa in the kitchen; fairly drunk, but sober enough to be solemnly careful of the Night Nurse's modesty, simmering with the things they had to tell when she had gone. As the door shut behind her, out it came. Laurie didn't wait. It was no longer supposed, he thought, to be anything to do with him. He knew where Andrew would be: in the next ward, washing up and cleaning the kitchen. There were two night orderlies for four wards. He walked to the outer door; Nurse Sims came out from the linen room as he reached it.

"Odell! Whatever on earth do you think *you're* up to?"

"Oh, sorry, Nurse." He wasn't in the least embarrassed, only occupied with the certainty that he would do what he had determined. "I've got to speak to Andrew Raynes for a moment. You don't mind, do you? I won't be long."

"Well, really, I don't know. I suppose you've got enough sense not to let Sister see you. Don't be there all night, then, will you? What a pair you two are. I always call you David and Jonathan."

Ward A kitchen was just the same as the one in Ward B, except that all the fittings were on the opposite

226

sides, which gave one a feeling of stepping through the looking-glass. Andrew was at the sink with the taps running; their noise covered the sound of Laurie's approach. Moving quietly, he got without being seen almost to Andrew's elbow. You could tell it was his second lot of washing-up; his hands were red, the front of his hair was loose and limp. He had the look of hard concentration which Laurie recognized as his substitute for worry. Yes, Laurie thought with inexpressible comfort, Andrew was solid. One could imagine oneself being involved with him in utter disagreement, in exasperation even; but one would never chip the facing and find rubble behind. There was a number of demands one could never make on him; but perhaps this, which he had given unasked and unknowing, was in the end the best of all.

"A penny for your thoughts," Laurie said.

"Why, Laurie!" His look of startled happiness gave Laurie a sense of sudden inadequacy; there was more joy here than his tossed mind was capable of receiving. "Where did you come from?"

"I didn't want to turn in without saying good night."

"I thought by the time I could get back you'd be asleep." He was holding a dish in his hand; he stared at it, smiled, and put it aside. "Is this all right? Don't get yourself crimed whatever you do."

"Nurse Sims said I could. She says she always calls us David and Jonathan."

"Does she? How nice. Did you have a good time?"

"The first part was all right. It got a bit boring later; too many people."

"How's Ralph?"

"He got a bit bored too." It was a silhouette of trouble, flat now and unreal.

Laurie picked up a tea-towel and they began drying the things together.

"Did they tell you?" said Andrew. "Is that why you came?"

"Tell me what?" The moment's security dissolved; the secret wilderness crept back again, in which no good could be assumed of the unknown.

"You just came," said Andrew, as if a natural trust

227

had been confirmed. "You don't know about Dave, then?"

"No, is he ill or something?" His treacherous imagination formed a picture of Andrew spending days at Dave's bedside, claimed by an older loyalty.

"I hope not, though it's enough to make him. They sent for him to London. Cynthia's been killed."

"Is that his sister?"

Andrew stared at him. "But have I never—surely I—Cynthia's his wife."

"His——!" Laurie realized after a moment that stupefaction was a lame response. "I'm most terribly sorry. Was it in a raid?"

"Yes." He stared at the cup he was rubbing, and added, "Dave's got to identify her."

"God, I'm sorry."

"She was older than Dave. She must have been sixty at least."

"Have they got any children?"

"They had one who died, and after that she couldn't. Sometimes I wonder if that's why Dave's always been so kind to me."

Laurie polished the china, thankful that with Andrew it was always possible to be silent.

"I know the same thing's happening all over the world," said Andrew. "But I keep thinking about him. He'll have to go to some gray mortuary and look at whatever there is, and then fill up forms, and when he's done that someone will read what he's written and say probably, as they did to another c.o. I knew in similar circumstances—no, he wouldn't want me to tell anyone, even without the name."

"Dave's big enough to take that," said Laurie helplessly. Yes, he thought, I'm the one who was such good form just now at the gate. And worst of all I can feel the cold draft around my inferiority complex because I learn that he isn't one of us.

He stayed for another five minutes or so, to the limit of Nurse Sims's estimated patience. Shortly before he left he said, "I say, Andrew. Do you believe in the proposition that all men are created equal?"

"Not in the fact. Of course not. It would be a bit like

228

believing in a flat earth, wouldn't it? But I believe in the proposition right enough. It's what you might call the working hypothesis of Christianity."

"Simple, isn't it, after all?" He himself was unsure whether he spoke in irony or not.

The All Clear sounded after he was back in bed. For a little while he lay awake, without quite owning to himself what he was waiting for. He hadn't really supposed for a moment that Ralph would ring. It had been good enough to scare Bunny.

"Can't you sleep, Odell? Is it the leg?"

"It's not too bad, Nurse, thanks. I wouldn't mind some A.P.C. next time you're passing."

The telephone was silent. Laurie thought, He's been in hospital himself, he knows what an uproar it makes if it rings late. Sensible of him really. Of course, he's probably still asleep. Bunny will just come in and——

"Oh, thank you, Nurse. No, I'll be fine. I'll drop off in a minute."

The All Clear was a long time going. I wonder what it was like back there. If anything happened to him, there'd be no one to tell me.

9

"HERE, Spud."

"Hello," said Laurie, peering into the bathroom from which Reg's voice had come.

"Thought I recognized your step. Have to listen for it now. Just a bit heavy on the one foot, that's all."

"Want any help?" asked Laurie, coming in. Reg hadn't needed any since the days of the airplane splint, but he had heard from Madge that morning and Laurie had seen his face as he read the letter.

"That's it," said Reg. He shut the bathroom door. They sat down on the large wooden board which, placed over the bath, made a table for scrubbing mackintoshes. Their embarrassment was enhanced by the precarious nature of their privacy. Laurie said, "Let's have a fag on it," and then, "I suppose I can guess."

"No prizes offered," said Reg with bitterness.

"It's a damned shame," Laurie said.

For a moment they were linked in a vague nostalgic coziness. Then Reg cleared his throat, and consciousness fell between them. Laurie said, "Same chap again?"

"That's right. Offered her a job in his business now. Cooked meats and fish bar. Edgware way."

"Not much future in that. Can't you stop her?"

"Well, see, Spud, that's it. Don't hardly like to ask, but can you lend me seventeen and a tanner till next month?"

"I could." As a matter of fact he was very short. "But what about asking the Major? Urgent private affairs?"

"Won't wait till tomorrow," said Reg, staring at the wooden bath mat. Laurie realized he hadn't been told everything.

"French leave?" he said.

"I had about enough, Spud. I'm going today and fix it."

Laurie looked at his face. "With this chap, you mean?"

"I'm going to fix it. Never mind the rest."

Laurie took another look. The glasshouse, he thought, if nothing worse. Absurdly, the fact that he couldn't spare the money kept obscuring his judgment; he felt he was being mean.

He said, "Reg, honestly. I wouldn't do it."

Reg leaned rather elaborately across the bath to throw his ash into the space behind. "Well, Spud, maybe not. It's all according, see what I mean?"

His face was crimson. Laurie saw what he meant.

He was overcome by a sudden, stifling claustrophobia. Charles's and Sandy's friends had tried to lock the door on him from inside. Now Reg was doing it from out in the street. There was a difference: he liked Reg much better.

"Look, Reg, I'm not taking that."

Reg stared at him in mute horror. "What you mean, Spud? Not taking me up wrong, I hope?"

"And what a hope. Not bloody likely. Now look,

Reg, there's nothing fancy about this, I know what you feel, like anyone else. It's people that matter; if not, what are you worrying about, what's Madge got that you can't have for a bob against the railings? You care about someone and they let you down. It can happen to anyone; where's the difference?" As soon as he had said it he knew that it wasn't a hundred per cent honest argument, and perhaps didn't deserve to succeed.

"That's right," said Reg slowly. "That's true enough, Spud, you got something there. Forget what I said. Half silly with worry, that's what."

"I know." He considered. No, he thought; Reg is the sort that prison would do something to forever, and she isn't worth it. "Trouble is, Reg, now I think, I doubt if I've got seventeen and six, till I hear from home. I spent a bit in town."

"That's all right, Spud. Forget it." To his surprise he saw a struggling respect fighting the disappointment in Reg's face. "You hang on to that. Got to be independent. Make 'em think all the more of you."

Suddenly Laurie got it. Christ, he said to himself, has Reg really been thinking . . . But he won and it was Reg who dropped his eyes. "Hell, Reg, what do you think I am?"

"You're okay, Spud." He knew it wasn't the apology Reg minded, it was the exposure. "Knew that all along. Shoving my oar in. No offense meant, honest to God."

At least, he thought, one could do something for Reg out of this ephemeral ascendancy. "Tell you what. Leave it for today. It can't make all that difference." He couldn't help that, and Reg hadn't spirit enough to resent it. "I'm going to do a bit of thinking. Okay?"

"Okay, then." Laurie knew he had rushed Reg into this, chiefly by terror of what he might say next. They got up from the bath cover. Laurie stood holding the door, to make sure it didn't swing back against Reg's arm. Reg cleared his throat. He hung back. " 'S okay, Spud. Shan't be a minute."

Reg's prudery being what it was, there might have been many reasons for this; but this time something arrested Laurie and illumination struck him. Oh, no, but no, he thought in helpless protest: it really was, at last,

231

too much; suddenly it collapsed into an outrageous joke. He stood in the doorway and rocked with laughter. "But it's——" he gasped. He gazed at Reg and imagined him creeping coyly out after a discreet delay, like a *femme galante* at a house party. It was excruciating.

Reg was grinning sheepishly. He looked curiously comforted and relieved.

Laurie leaned in at the door. "I shouldn't worry, Reg. If you like, I'll give you a certificate."

The post office was only ten minutes down the road. He pulled a telegraph form from the string-tied pad. Reg had had a couple of leaves in between operations; Laurie had written and forwarded letters, and knew the address by heart.

"Your husband's condition grave please come immediately." He signed it with the name of the hospital; Madge wouldn't notice a thing like that.

An hour or two later, when it was too late to undo all this, he did what he had known he must, and went to warn the Sister. He would have thought poorly of her if she hadn't been angry. "I've never known a patient take such a thing upon himself, never in all my years of nursing. Perhaps you'll pay more attention to Major Ferguson in the morning. You've been here too long and you've got thoroughly above yourself."

"Yes, Sister. I'm sorry."

Luckily it was in the Staff Nurse's duty period that Ralph rang up.

When the message came through he hesitated, wondering whether to send word by someone that he had just gone out. He hadn't expected to hear from Ralph again.

On the morning after their last meeting Ralph had telephoned. They had been evasively facetious till it had stuck in both their throats; Ralph had approached the question of next Tuesday with awkward casualness; Laurie had said that he was sorry, this time he would have to get back. Ralph had taken it very quietly; there was no way of knowing what Bunny's story had been. Now, to know that he had rung again, and was waiting, was full of excitement and inevitability, like a suspense story with a happy ending; but, he thought, still hesitating by his bed, there could be nothing but sadness in these perfunctory gestures of farewell. Involuntarily he felt at the leg-pocket of his battle-dress; he had got into the way of keeping the *Phaedrus* there again, as he had in the south coast training camp and afterwards in France. Now it no longer stood for something rounded off and complete, but for confusion and uncertainty and pain and compassion, and all the tangle of man's morality. And yet, he thought again, it was for such a world that it had been written.

"Hello, Ralph. I'm sorry I kept you waiting."

"Just a minute," Ralph said. Laurie heard the telephone laid down, and a sound like a door shutting. "Sorry, all right now. Well, Spud, how are you?"

"Fine." Yes, he thought, it was going to be that kind of conversation. "How about you?"

"Fine. Look, Spud, will it be all right if I pick you up this afternoon after the treatment, and run you back? I'd like to have a word with you, and that way it won't hold you up. One can't say much on this line."

"Of course. Thanks very much." Bunny must have kept his story for a day or two, cooking. Now, it seemed, Ralph had decided to have it out. It would have to be got through. . . . "Odell. Lanyon wants you in his study after prayers."

He said, "I'll wait on the same bench as I did before."

"Good." There was a short pause. "There'll be no one else coming."

"All right." It must certainly be trouble. "Five-fifteen, then. Goodbye."

"Spud, just a minute."

"Yes?"

"Don't worry about anything." The line went dead.

Before he left for Bridstow, he wrote a letter. It was for Madge, and was ostensibly an apology for the trouble he had given her. He wrote it with the incident of the Wurlitzer request program held steadfastly before his eyes. Afterwards he read it over to himself, with a kind of fascinated nausea. The thought that Madge might not destroy it, that it might continue to exist, even, by way of ultimate horror, that she might show it to the Major, who would accept it as a fair sample of his style—all this crept in his stomach and in the hair on his neck. The secret of its peculiar gruesomeness was that it wasn't pure invention. Under the shaming sentimentality, the awful all-jolly-good-sorts-together, it was quite sincere.

He stuck it down quickly before he had time to dilute it, and gave it to the Sister when he went to catch his bus. She glared at him; but she had made herself his accomplice. She hadn't told Reg anything.

Miss Haliburton's puppy was noticeably bigger. The department was rather less busy than last week and she spent more time with him, asking questions about the leg. Something he said, which hadn't seemed to him of the slightest significance, seemed to excite her. She whipped him out of the apparatus, put the boot on his bare foot and leg, and made him walk around the cubicle. To his extreme embarrassment she got down and, as he moved, followed on hands and knees; it was like being investigated by an Old English sheepdog. The bare leg with the boot on it already seemed to him pure Salvador Dali; he felt that, even for hospital, the macabre was being overstressed. He could hear her tut-tutting under her breath. The puppy waddled beside her, breathing eagerly.

"Who made this?" she barked suddenly. He presumed that it wasn't the leg to which she was referring, and replied that it had been made by a small man with cross eyes and thick glasses, whose name he didn't know.

Miss Haliburton called a senior student to her, and made a speech. ". . . everything so slapdash. No conscience about their work. Look at it, Miss Cardew. Look at this rotation here. Put your hand on the peroneus. (Just walk a few steps again, Odell.) There, feel that. And when the boy gets pain, first they give him aspirin three times a day and then they order faradism. Really, sometimes one despairs. How *does* a government like that expect to win a war?" Almost before he knew what was happening, she had him out of the boot again, drew lines on it with chalk, and, to his

234

alarm, handed it over to a deliberate old character with a walrus mustache, who poked it with a blunt pencil, explained why he wouldn't be able to make a right job of it, and took it away.

"You'll have to have a new one, of course," she said as he was watching it vanish. "But this will help meanwhile."

At first he could think of nothing but the delay. It was nearly five-fifteen already; he felt he could bear anything except that Ralph should think he had run out on him, with things as they were; and he knew hospital too well to suppose there was any possibility of sending a message. It was only gradually that he began to understand what she was still trying to tell him. Hope trickled slowly, through a half-choked channel, into his mind. Pain had become as inevitable to him in these last weeks as any of the body's natural demands, differing from them in being insatiable. Even now he wouldn't trust himself to anticipation, but he remembered to thank her.

"Don't thank me, my dear boy; I'm saving myself trouble in the long run. Now this bit of intense treatment we're starting will really do something for you. Ah, here's Arthur. Now we'll see."

It was after five-thirty. He was almost too worried to notice what Arthur had done to the boot, which was largely a matter of altering the tilt of the thickened sole. It felt odd for the first moment, then very quickly seemed natural. He thanked everyone again and escaped.

When he couldn't see Ralph anywhere in the hall, a wave of such misery struck him that he stood stockstill where he was, saying to himself stubbornly that it wasn't true. He looked around again, refusing the facts, and, as if created by his act of will, Ralph was there after all. He was sitting on one of the benches, his back turned, listening attentively to what looked like a long story from a very old man. When Laurie had approached within a couple of yards he saw him, smiled, and motioned him to wait. Laurie heard him say at the end, "Well, sir, I can see I've missed a lot not shipping with you. I've enjoyed this very much."

He fell into step beside Laurie, telling him, as if they hadn't been separated for more than an hour, the old man's story: the start in sail, the wool-clipper, the Chinese pirates, the torpedoing in 1917. Out of the tail of his eye Laurie saw the ancient captain, a stocky figure in a shiny old blue suit, look after Ralph with an old man's sour approval, before settling down again to his long wait.

"Thanks for waiting. I was afraid you'd write me off."

"Good Lord, I know hospital. I shouldn't have started worrying for another hour. Did they tell you anything?"

"Yes, as a matter of fact, this time they did." He explained about the boot; he was getting used to the feel of it now, and it did begin to seem more comfortable than before. Ralph listened carefully and at the end said, "Nothing else?"

"Well, not yet." This reserve reminded Laurie of the caution he had urged upon himself. "They wouldn't say much more till they've seen how it works."

"Good luck to it, anyhow." They had got to the car. When they were in, he hesitated a moment. "I suppose you've not got time for a quick turn round the Downs?"

"Oh, I think so."

Ralph drove in silence through the pink stone streets, took a half-turn around the Downs, and pulled off the road at the spot where cars stop to admire the gorge. Twilight was falling and no other cars were there. The steep side of the gorge with its sheer faces was out of sight below them: opposite were wooded slopes, with a scoop of quarry. The ebb-tide river flowed sluggishly at the bottom, a muddy threat between two long slopes of slime.

"It's all right, Spud. I told you, there's nothing to worry about."

"I wasn't worrying."

"I brought you up here to tell you a bit of news, just in case it makes any difference to anything. Bunny's gone."

What had he done? With what clumsiness had he

236

floundered in other people's complex and dimly comprehended business? Playing for time, he asked, "Has he been posted?"

"Oh, no," said Ralph coolly. "As a matter of fact he hasn't even left his room. I can hardly expect him to, seeing what he's spent on the fittings. I shall find another myself, as soon as I can. Still, he's gone, in a manner of speaking."

"Ralph, I—I'm most terribly sorry."

"Sorry? Don't be ridiculous."

"You mean it's my fault. There doesn't seem very much to say. Except that I'd give anything for it not to have happened."

"Oh, come, Spud, don't make yourself out a bigger fool than you are. Bunny was a long hangover after a short drunk. Far too long."

The relief of this was at first enormous. Then he wondered what, exactly, had happened, and whether it hadn't made Ralph a good deal more unhappy than he cared to admit. "I'm glad if that's how it is."

"By the way," Ralph said in an almost impersonal voice, "I owe you an apology for last time."

"If you mean about driving me back, you don't. I can tell you now." With more satisfaction than he liked to admit to himself, he explained about the water-jug.

"Good God, what a corny one to have fallen for." He laughed, but Laurie already felt ashamed. He lit cigarettes in silence and for a minute or so neither spoke.

"I have a feeling," Ralph said presently, "that a few other apologies may also be due. He did actually deliver you at the hospital, I suppose?"

"Oh, yes."

"I know I wasn't very discreet that evening; did he make a scene about it?"

"No."

"Something happened. All right, never mind; I expect it was embarrassing enough without being cross-examined on it." Laurie let this go, hoping he would drop it. He did in fact fall silent for a couple of minutes. Just as Laurie had opened his mouth to change the subject, he said abruptly, "Look, Spud, this is

237

shooting blind, but he didn't try anything else on, by any chance, did he?"

Laurie had been thinking, the moment before, that after all some partings are only final for the first forty-eight hours; provided, that is, that no one interferes. Now neither truth nor lying seemed quite justified. In his irresolution he waited too long.

"Well," said Ralph. "I see." He spoke with a curious, precise flatness; he sounded almost bored. Yes, Laurie thought: all that about a short drunk is what he'd like to feel now. God, there's no need to rub his face in it.

"It wasn't serious, you know. I think it was just a sort of experiment to see how one would behave."

After a pause Ralph said, in the same colorless and exactly pitched voice, "I suppose it's all for the best that I didn't know this sooner." He took the cigarette out of his mouth, examined it, and put it back again. Speaking now conversationally, he remarked, "We began with a minor disagreement, and one thing led to another."

"Yes?" Laurie said. He was feeling that he had managed badly. Knowing Bunny, one could have been sure that the showdown hadn't been as complete as Ralph imagined, and that all sorts of things could still come out.

"Well, Spud, there it is. You saw enough for yourself: there's no point in prettying it over. About all I can say is that I never told myself many lies about it; and whether that's a recommendation or not depends on the point of view. Main thing is, it's finished. Do you feel like believing that?"

"If you say so, of course." And now, he thought, perhaps it really is my fault. No one who knew so little had the right to do this.

Ralph turned and adjusted the windscreen wiper, which was out of true and took him some minutes. Still fidgeting with it, he said, "Well, now, about this appointment of yours. I don't know how urgent it is. I thought possibly you might just be feeling you'd seen enough of my domestic *ménage*. If I'm wrong, or if
238

you still feel the same way about it, let it go and we'll be on our way."

"Oh," said Laurie. He had completely forgotten. Ralph's eye caught his and all at once they were smiling. "Well, I've not got a late pass, but it's no more urgent than that. ... I did rather feel he and I might get in each other's hair if we met again."

"He's on duty this evening, so you won't do that. How long have we?"

"If you can lift me back, about an hour and a half."

"Come on, then, let's go."

The strict room was wearing a half-smile of hospitality; there was a cloth on the table, and a plate of sandwiches bought ready cut and sealed in wax paper. There was something comforting to Laurie in the matter-of-fact way Ralph made no bones about having expected him. There was a feeling of being looked after, a feeling almost of home. Ralph mixed a couple of drinks, lifted his glass, and seemed to hesitate. In the end he just said, "Happy days."

"Happy days," said Laurie smiling. If only he had got a late pass he could have kept Ralph company for the rest of the evening. At a time like this one would remember little things that had been harmless and happy and which one expected always to remember with pleasure, and they would seem to look at one with a sneer. Laurie would have worked hard to make himself good company, if that had been necessary, but in fact they had plenty to talk about and the meal was quite gay. When they were washing up and making coffee in the little hole of a kitchen, Ralph said, looking up from his plate and tea-towel, "This is better, isn't it, Spud?"

"Yes," said Laurie, "of course it is." If only he hadn't outstayed his pass so recently. He hated the thought of leaving Ralph alone.

The popping blue gas fire had warmed to a spreading glow. Beyond the hooded reading lamp's small orbit it touched the room with dusky gold and rose. Laurie sat as he was bidden in the armchair; he had learned to accept such things simply, like the old. Ralph, curled easily on the old hooked-wool rug, would have looked incongruous there to no one, probably, except to Laurie, who found ancient habits of precedence still haunting his mind. The senior studies at school had had gas fires. He looked down at Ralph; except for being seen from the wrong angle, he, too, in this mellowing dimness seemed very little changed. He had nice hair, Laurie thought; it still had that freshly washed look, and the neat cut was the same. Fine, light, and straight, it had a kind of innocence; it would be pleasant to touch. Then he remembered how this thought had come to him seven years ago, at the moment when Ralph was saying goodbye to him.

He said, "Do you still like your toast done thin and crisp? I feel I ought to be making it."

Ralph looked up, his face turning from the light. In the deep shadow it could only be seen that he was smiling; his face was a dark brightness edged with fire.

"What do you know about it? You never fagged for me. I say, Spud."

"Yes?"

"I've got a bit of good news I've been saving up for you. When you hear it officially, don't forget to look surprised."

"Of course I won't." He couldn't imagine what it could possibly be and fell back into a trusting blankness. Perhaps a new secret weapon was about to appear which would end the war in a week. "Well, come on, what is it?"

"I rather thought they'd have told you today. As a matter of fact, Alec's been pulling a few strings for you. He's rather a pet of the old girl who does your massage." (So it was that, Laurie thought, which had started her on the boot. Suddenly he noticed that the leg hadn't begun aching yet; he was about to communicate this good news, but Ralph hadn't finished.) "She thought you ought to be coming oftener, and she takes a dim view of E.M.S. hospitals anyway; so she put the recommendation straight in. They're going to transfer you to the hospital here in a day or two. That'll be better, won't it?"

Laurie didn't answer the question, because he hadn't heard it. The first shock was too great either for protest or disguise. He sat for many long seconds, fixed in the dull astonishment and slow comprehension of a mortal wound, his face naked and forgotten in the light of the fire.

He became aware presently of something outside the shell of his own pain. Ralph was kneeling beside the chair, gripping his arm and staring at him. He tried to get his face in order.

"Spud. What's wrong?"

"Nothing," said Laurie stupidly. He put the back of his hand across his eyes; the light felt too bright. "I expect it's gone through by now." Dimly he knew that this was unkind, perhaps more; but he had been injured beyond his strength and had to struggle with himself to keep from being much more cruel than this.

There was a long silence after he had spoken. Then Ralph said, with the crudity of deep feeling, "You've got someone there."

"Yes," Laurie said. Voices came through the shell now; kindness and loyalty tapped remindingly on the walls. He said dully, "But you couldn't have known that."

"I could have thought."

Ralph's face was still turned from the light, but it ran along his shoulder and arm and caught the edge of his glove, and Laurie, for whom everything was etched as hard and sharp as silverpoint, saw that the padded fingers had become oddly separate in their limpness, quite dissociated from the rest of the hand. "You've been there since June, and you——Christ Almighty, I should think anybody could have thought of it."

"I meant to have told you last time." Laurie spoke with apology; he felt exhibited now and ashamed. "I was going to tell you here, but there were too many people."

Ralph said in a neat, quiet voice, "That's been the trouble, hasn't it? Too many people."

He should have asked me first, thought Laurie. It was all beginning now to burn down into his imagination: he could fill with their lost content the stolen days. He'd only met me twice; why should he assume that I'd told him everything? He takes too much on himself; he acts like God.

With all this, he gave no sign of what he thought; for the near presence of great anguish touched some instinct in him, though he was too confused to recognize it except as a phantasm projected on his surroundings by his own pain.

"It was my fault. I ought to have told you. I talked so much, I told you everything but that. I didn't talk like a person who's keeping something back."

"For God's sake why should you?" Ralph looked down and seemed to notice the clenched hand in the limp glove; there was a kind of distaste in the movement with which he straightened it. "Some people never learn, and it seems I'm one of them."

"Don't," said Laurie, "please." In the shadows he could feel, more than see, Ralph's eyes looking into his. "It's not like you think. It wouldn't have been any good, ever."

Ralph said, "The first night we met, in the car. You said something about this."

"Not really. I talked as if it were years ago. It *is* my fault, you see."

"Of course you talked as if it were years ago. So would anyone who—God, you hardly knew me. Just because I've been spending my time with a lot of nattering queens—you even told me, and I had to do this to you."

"Look, Ralph, this had to happen quite soon. It's better to get it over with."

Ralph said, looking down at his hands, "Like dying tomorrow instead of next week."

"Not only like that. It's been getting risky. You see, he—I think he quite likes me, and he mustn't ever know. It would spoil his life, and there's no need. I wonder if this wasn't meant to happen. One gives oneself away without meaning to. It's much more important he should be all right."

He became aware of Ralph staring at him. He couldn't see the eyes, except as curved reflecting surfaces in a mask of darkness. "Spud, for God's sake. Stop it. It's like a ghost."

242

"What?" asked Laurie, confused.

"Nothing. Sorry. Well, tell me about him, who is he, what's he like? Well, come on."

"Oh, he"—Laurie stared into the fire—"he's——"

"Well," said Ralph, his voice suddenly gentle, "he's a soldier, I suppose?"

"No. No, he works there. He's a Quaker; a c.o."

Ralph said, "Jesus Christ."

"If you met him, you'd understand."

"Yes, of course. I'm sorry, Spud. You don't get anything like that at sea."

"His name's Andrew. Andrew Raynes."

"That's a nice name."

"He's younger than I am, quite a bit."

"Yes. I mean, is he?"

"He's fair, with gray eyes. . . . I'm sorry I've not got a photograph to show you."

"You must bring one another day."

"The thing about him is, he wouldn't know how to run away from it."

"That's always a thing," said Ralph, in a gentle dead voice. "It makes one feel responsible, doesn't it?"

"Yes, that's just it. That's just how I do feel. There's no one I could talk about this to, except you."

"Thank you," said Ralph. "What about another drink?" He got up and reached for the gin bottle. He still kept his back turned to the fire.

"Yes, I'd like one, please." Now that the half-seen eyes were no longer there he could bring it out more easily. "You see, when I say there's no one else I could have told about it, I meant . . . Those people the other night, for instance. Anything goes. They'd never see it. There was something you did for me once. I expect you'll have forgotten long ago; but it made all the difference. I just wanted to tell you." He groped in the leg-pocket of his battle-dress, found what he wanted, and held it out. "Do you remember? You gave me this."

It must be true, he thought, that Ralph had forgotten; for he stared at it dumbly, almost stupidly, and only reached out to take it just as Laurie was about to put it away again. He carried it over to the table and held it under the shaded reading lamp, standing up so that the light only fell on his hands and on the book. Suddenly Laurie remembered what it had looked like that day in the study, crisp and clean and nearly new. The pool of light was small, but bright and hard: it picked out the bloodstain and the rubbed edges, and the rough whitened patch from the sea. He said, "I'm sorry I've not looked after it better."

"Well," said Ralph with his back turned, "after all, seven years." He put the book down on the table and looked abruptly at his watch. "Look, Spud, I'm sorry, I have to phone the Station now. There's a man I have to give a message to. It's all right. I shan't be long."

Laurie began to say something, but he had caught up his cap and gone; a few moments later came the slam of the front door, and quick feet on a frosty pavement. Almost as soon as he had gone Laurie noticed the blue topcoat still lying on the bed; but now that he was alone, his own disaster seemed to fill the world, and no one was Ralph's keeper.

To escape from thought, which told him nothing except that he must bear it, he took down the book nearest to his hand and opened it where it fell apart. He read: *... and there shall we see adventures, for so is Our Lord's will. And when they came thither, they found the ship rich enough, but they found neither man nor woman therein. But they found in the end of the ship two fair letters written, which said a dreadful word and a marvellous: Thou man, which shall enter into this ship, beware thou be in steadfast belief, for I am Faith, and therefore beware how thou enterest, for an thou fail I shall not help thee.*

He could take in no more of it; he sat with the open book on his knees and the last sentence ringing in his head like an unanswered bell.

It must have been fifteen minutes or so later when Ralph came back. To Laurie it seemed much more. At first it had been a relief no longer to consider anyone's feelings but his own; to rest his head in his hands, to be silent. He hardly knew at what point solitude passed into loneliness, and he began to listen for the sound of the door. Footsteps approached and seemed for a moment to be familiar, and came near and were a stranger's and died away. It was strange, he thought, but true, that even after this catastrophic blunder the instinct still persisted to confide in Ralph and look to him for comfort. Anger was futile and no longer even a relief; it seemed now just a wretched mischance for both of them. His own secretiveness, and Ralph's weakness for running other people's lives, had conjoined like adverse stars. Laurie remembered the story of Bim and thought, Poor old Ralph, he does have bad luck.

It was at this point that he heard Ralph coming upstairs; the door opened a second or two later.

It must be a cold night, thought Laurie; not because Ralph looked cold, but because he had clearly been going fast to keep warm, and now, coming in again, he had the bright unfocused eyes and the slight strangeness that people have who suddenly emerge from darkness wide awake. He had turned up the collar of his jacket and forgotten to turn it down again; his eyes were extraordinarily blue. He looked sharp-edged rather than blurred, with a frosty sparkle, a flash of the night about him; he stood in the doorway a little out of breath, narrowing his blue eyes against the soft light as if it were dazzling, and looking at the room as a man might who after a long absence expects to find changes here and there. He was at all times compact and neat, but now there was more than this, a kind of diamond concentration, so that his unconscious pause on the threshold was brilliantly arresting, like a skillfully produced entrance in a play.

It was a striking reversal, for Laurie, of the mood it had interrupted. If he had remembered his pity, it would have embarrassed him; but he had at once forgotten. First he was simply glad to see Ralph back; and then, as he looked again, there was a sharp stirring of some very old, romantic memory; perhaps of some book illustration he had known as a young boy, of which his very first glimpse of Ralph at school had reminded him before he had even known his name. So strong was this sense of the past that his own feeling, caught up in it, seemed like a memory. He stood looking at Ralph in startled admiration, moved by a dream of mystery and of command, and at the back of his mind was a thought that he wanted this moment not to end and that it was ending. Even as he formed it, Ralph came forward from the doorway into the room.

The first telephone box he came to hadn't been working, he said. He was sorry he had been so long.

Laurie said, "You've been running."

"It's cold."

"You don't need this now, anyway." He turned down the collar of Ralph's jacket.

"Oh, thanks. Yes."

They looked at each other. But their thoughts were set, deeply gripped in the situation that already obsessed them, and which seemed to them as hard and unyielding as stone; they were not aware of having altered it in any way. Laurie's instinct hid what it had felt, for just then his heart would have rejected it as an outrage. As for Ralph, he had had a trying half-hour, and his perceptions were strained; it cannot be supposed he had subtlety enough to guess that a moment of black courage had given him power unasked, when he had only been seeking strength.

He got a pair of ivory brushes out of the cupboard (Laurie saw how characteristically clean they were) and polished his light hair to its usual smoothness; then he came back to the table, poured a couple of drinks, and said, "We'll have to be going soon."

"Shall we?" He had fancied it was earlier; the thought of breaking the news to Andrew dragged at his heart.

"Not for a bit," said Ralph. "It's all right."

They drank in silence for a minute or two. Laurie said, "I think what I really want is to get drunk."

"How drunk?" asked Ralph practically. "Blind?"

"I suppose so."

"You can sleep here if you want."

"I only meant I'd like to. I've got to be back tonight."

Ralph poured some more tonic in Laurie's glass. "I

246

suppose you spend hours talking about life and death and God, don't you?"

"What makes you think that?"

"Well," said Ralph, not unkindly, "the alternatives are limited, I gather."

"By the time you've done a few months in an E.M.S. hospital, you can do with someone to talk to."

"You sometimes can even on a freighter. It's funny we've been within a few miles of each other for months without knowing, isn't it?"

"Yes, it is. I wish we had."

"You're being almost inhumanly forbearing about all this, Spud; but let's face it, you'll never really forgive me, will you?"

"I told you about that. In the end you've probably done me an even better turn than you thought you had."

"Poor old Spud. Does he tell you why his girls are different from all other girls?"

"No. You see, that's really the hard part."

Ralph looked up. "No girls?"

"No, none." He met Ralph's eye and said, "Yes, I think so. He's almost told me; but he doesn't understand what he says."

Ralph finished his drink and folded his arms on the table.

"Well, for God's sake, then, if that's all, why don't you tell him?"

"Have you ever met any Quakers?"

"Not that I remember. Would he think you were Satan incarnate?"

"It isn't that," said Laurie, appealingly. Ralph seemed suddenly shut away and he felt it like an absence. "It would spoil everything for him. He would never do anything about it, and—well, you see, he—he's an affectionate sort of boy. He's gone through life so far being fond of one person after another and it seems always to have made him happy. Knowing would poison all that for him, it would never be the same."

Ralph took another drink. "Well, Spuddy, it's your life. Will he mind you going away?"

"Yes, he will."

"As much as you?"

"Oh, well . . . He will mind, though."

"If he's honest with himself, when it comes to the point he'll know. Why do you want to help him tell himself lies?"

"I don't. It means something different to him, that's all."

"Different my foot. Don't fool yourself, Spud. He'll come back in a year or two and tell you all about his boy friend. That one's a classic, didn't you know?"

Laurie hadn't believed he could ever have felt so lonely with Ralph in the same room. He said, "Once you wouldn't have talked like that."

Ralph looked at him across the table. For one extraordinary second he seemed about to throw back his head and laugh.

"Wouldn't I? Well, in the meantime I've been around."

So strong was Laurie's sense of solitude that for a few moments he stared past the lighted table into the shadows without any self-consciousness, as if physically he were alone.

"Spud."

It wasn't the voice that roused him, but Ralph's hand closing over his on the table. "Spud, cheer up. Come along now, snap out of it."

He swallowed and said, "It's all right."

Ralph got up and went over to the window, standing as if the blackout weren't up and he could see out.

"You stick to it, Spud, and don't worry. You don't want to let people hand you these smart lines of talk. They pick it up at parties and it gets to be a habit and most of the time it doesn't mean a thing."

"Didn't it?"

"Oh, come, be your age. For God's sake, what does it matter to you what I meant?"

"It does, that's all. I can't imagine there ever being a time when it wouldn't."

There was a little silence. Then Ralph said, quite quietly and simply, "Of course I didn't mean it. It was just a line of talk. Forget all about it."

248

After this, there was a retreat into commonplaces; then presently Ralph began to talk about the sea. They had returned to the fire, but this time Laurie wouldn't take the armchair. The rug was comfortable to lie on, sprawling with his chin in his fists. He lay there, getting heavy with the heat and the residual fumes of the gas fire.

"... I said, 'I'm sorry, senhor, but I shipped with you as a passenger to Beira, and I'm not prepared to navigate for you under conditions like that: either your mate's mad or he isn't; if he isn't, you don't need me, and if he is, you'll have to put him under restraint even if he is your brother-in-law, because I can't do with him under my feet in the chartroom weeping and praying and playing about with knives.' So finally he ..."

As he lay listening, Laurie's whole being seemed to relax in a sigh of mysterious contentment. Even the day's disaster withdrew into a distance where it was known rather than felt. All the tangles of his life seemed looser and easier to resolve. He didn't want to take his mind from the story, or disturb with analysis this fragile happiness and security, which were what one might feel if some legend, dear to one's childhood but long abandoned, were marvellously proved true.

"... these big ocean-going dhows that come over from Arabia with the monsoon. They have a high carved poop like a caravel, and a raked-up bowsprit. There were a lot of them coming into the Old Harbor the way they do, covered in tassels and pennants with the crews singing and dancing on the decks, and beating drums and gongs. Just after we'd passed them ..."

The strange feeling of fulfillment touched Laurie again; suddenly he remembered and understood. In the weeks of that summer holiday seven years before, after he had read the *Phaedrus* by the stream in the wood, he had gone for long walks alone, and, returning, sat in the evening by a September fire, so silent and enclosed that more than once his mother had asked if he was well. It was of this that he had been dreaming.

Involuntarily he moved his hands so that they covered his face, as the dream came back in all the high

249

colors of boyhood: his own room with the fire he had, as a rule, only on the first day of the holidays, furnished as he had thought, then, he would want it when he was older; the flickering light on leather and books; and Ralph's face at nineteen. In the dream there had always been a pause in which he had looked up and said, "Next time you go away, I'm going with you"; and Ralph, who hadn't had a first name in those days, had looked down all the same and answered, "Of course."

". . . She was the filthiest ship I ever set foot in, garbage trodden into the decks, Indian kids piddling in the scuppers, the officer on watch was drunk, and the stink was something you could hardly . . ."

Laurie took his hands from his face and looked up: at the room, the blackout curtains fastened with safety-pins; at the padded fingers of the glove lying on Ralph's knee; he could feel in his lame leg the pull of the cobbled muscles, and in his heart the bruise that couldn't be forgotten for long. Life is cruel, he thought; leaving out war and all that wholesale stuff, human life is essentially cruel. Sometimes you can feel a smile. The Greeks felt it. Apollo Loxias at Delphi smiling in the smoke behind the oracle, and saying, "But I don't mean what you mean."

". . . came tearing up to say it was typhoid they had on board, as if that were something astonishing."

"Yes?" said Laurie. A part of his mind, which had never lost touch with the story, had become aware of a pause. "Yes, go on, what happened then?"

"Oh, of course that put us all into quarantine, so I missed the job with Union Castle after all. Spud, you shouldn't lie down flat like that in front of a gas fire, you'll fill yourself up with carbon monoxide or whatever it is. Are you all right?"

"Yes. Of course I am."

"Because we'll have to go now, or you'll be late back."

Laurie began to get up, turning himself into a sitting position and catching hold of the chair-arm to pull on. He sat there for a moment, his head beside Ralph's knees, and this sharp sense of life's cruelty trembling in

250

him like an arrow that has just struck. "It was such a good story; you might finish it."

"There isn't much more, and there's not time anyway. I thought you'd dropped off."

"I could have listened all night. Most people get muddled and have to keep going back."

"I used to keep a notebook and write all that sort of nonsense down. Look at the time, we'll have to get a move on."

"I wish I'd got a late pass tonight. I wish I could stay."

Ralph put the good hand on his shoulder and sat looking down at him with his brows drawn together. "Poor old Spud, what a hell of a day you've had." He rose smartly to his feet and helped Laurie up.

Just as they were starting, he said, "By the way, how about some aspirin?"

"What for?" Laurie asked.

"Why, for the leg, of course."

"My God," said Laurie incredulously. "It hasn't started. I'd forgotten it."

"Well," said Ralph briskly, "that's one of your troubles on the way out."

He turned off the light and the fire and they began to grope their way down the dark staircase. They had crossed the landing and begun on the lower flight and Ralph was guiding him a little around the turn of the stairs, when suddenly a round white eye of light leaped out, almost in their faces. It held them blinking for a moment and disappeared. There was a pause of complete silence, then a soft laugh.

Later on, it struck Laurie as odd that it should have affected him so strongly. Earlier in the year, he had spent a number of hours lying, helpless and in pain, exposed to the efforts of people openly trying to encompass his death. It was ludicrous to have one's hair lifted by a mere giggle in the dark.

Ralph said in a cold empty voice, "Good night, Bunny."

There was a brushing sound against the wall and a whiff of scent. The laugh came again, from the landing above them now.

"Good night, boys. You sillies not to have waited. It's *madly* unlucky to pass on the stairs."

10

THE office was different by artificial light. Major Ferguson had taken off his white coat and was sitting in uniform, to look more disciplinary. It only made him look like a doctor dressed as an officer. He stood Laurie at ease and fixed him with a calculated stare, at the same time tapping unconsciously with a pencil on a pair of prominent front teeth.

"Well, Odell. This is pretty disgraceful business. Uhm?"

"Sir."

"Got to deal with this now, I'm operating all tomorrow. It's a serious matter."

"Yes, sir."

"We've taken a good deal of trouble with you one way and another. We don't expect you to start setting the place by the ears as soon as you're able to get about."

"No, sir. I'm sorry."

"Do you know what you've done? In effect you've forged an army order. Don't you realize that's a court-martial offense?"

"I see, sir."

"As this is an E.M.S. hospital, the position's slightly less cut-and-dried than it would be in a military one, fortunately for you. But use your common sense, man. If every relative a hospital sent for knew it might be a hoax, imagine the position. You can't monkey about with these life-and-death services, it isn't in the public interest. D'you understand?"

"I'm sorry, sir; yes."

"Now I've had this man dragging his wife in here to beg you off, tears and intimate family histories and the Lord knows what. Did you know that?"

"No, sir."

"Well, he insists you've kept him from desertion and

manslaughter. What you've kept her from isn't gone into, and it's a matter of opinion I should say. However, in view of all this I'm not dealing with you as severely as I should have done otherwise. All passes stopped for a month."

"Yes, sir."

"Of course, if you're transferred to a civil hospital before that, then it'll lapse and you'll be luckier than you deserve, uhm?"

"Thank you, sir."

"Uhm. What are you going to do with yourself when we discharge you, eh?"

"I've a year to go at Oxford, sir. After that I don't know."

Major Ferguson passed a hand back over his bald crown to the occipito-parietal line where the hair began. He supposed that before the war was over, and still more afterwards, he was often going to hear that tone of voice. "Uhm, well, a year to look round in, uhm? All right, you can get back to your ward, Odell."

Reg, in pajamas and dressing-gown, was waiting for him in the dark quadrangle between the huts.

"Just slipped out. Had to find out the damage. How'd it go?"

"Fine, thanks to you. You mad with me, Reg?"

"Ah, shove it. Never had a pal what'd go that far for me. Fact."

"So long as it worked."

"I'll tell you something, Spud. She cried. Cried like a child. Never forget it, long as I live."

"Did she think you were dying?"

"She was over that. It was your letter done it."

"Oh, said Laurie inadequately. With a cold crawling of the bowels he reviewed it, held now by the lapse of time shudderingly at arms' length.

" 'Let's have it, girl,' I said, 'and I'll take it to the Major. There won't be no trouble if he reads this.' But no, she wouldn't. 'I never had such a beautiful letter written to me,' she says, 'never. If you'd have written me a few like that things would have been a lot different,' she said to me, 'and I'm not giving it you for strangers to poke their nose in. I'd rather see the Major and tell him what's what myself.' And that's what she done."

"Well, do thank her for me when you write."

"She's stopping the night. Stopping at the Feathers. We'll have a day out tomorrow, like old times."

"That's fine."

They had got to the ward. Nurse Sims, scuttling through the outer corridor, acknowledged Laurie absently. His experienced instincts picked up at once the sense of emergency, even before he saw her go into the side ward and shut the door quickly after her. A blurred, crazy-sounding mutter was going on inside. He turned to Reg. "It's not operating day; who's that?"

" 'S okay, Spud." Reg looked away and spoke with spurious cheerfulness. "Old Charlot had a bit of an upset. Shell-shock or some job. I dunno."

"Charlot?" The muttering had got louder now and he could hear it quite easily through the door. He said with the idiocy of helpless protest, "But he was all right this morning. I *talked* to him."

"That's right. I missed the start of it with Madge coming. Some of them reckon it was the bomb, but——"

"Bomb?" Fear for Andrew slid between his ribs. "Anyone hurt?"

"Nah, nothing to it. Some flipping Jerry on the run. Far end of that field there; broke the odd window in Ward D. No, if you ask me, I reckon it was this mobile gun. New issue, quick-firing job, shells come clipped on a belt, noisy bastard it is. Seems they brought it right up the lane here, silly muckers; might have been in the ward by the sound, Purvis says. See, when the bomb dropped, old Charlot took it same as anyone. But soon as they heard the first burst from this gun, he shouted out something in French, and heaved himself clean off the bed. Machine-gunned them in the boats, didn't they, when he stopped his packet? Well, done up in all that plaster, you can see how heavy he'd fall."

"God, yes."

"Must have hit his head; been like this ever since."

"It might only be concussion."

"That's it," said Reg helpfully. Nurse Sims came out,

looked at them as nurses do when they find patients discussing other patients, and told them sharply to hurry up and get into bed. When she had gone Reg said, "Your pal Andrew's got a nice job tonight. Got to sit in there and see he don't do it again."

Perhaps he wouldn't see Andrew all night, then. He thought that this is what always happens when one's anticipations are overkeyed. As he passed the door he could hear Andrew's voice, delivering some reassurance in careful schoolroom French, and then the mutter again.

For more than an hour Laurie lay wide awake beside the flat empty bed from the side ward which had been put in Charlot's place. At last, from a change of light in the corridor outside, he knew that the side ward door had opened. He got on his dressing-gown hastily and slipped out. It was remarkable how quickly he had ceased to care very much whether people were noticing, and tonight he didn't think about it at all.

Andrew was standing in the open doorway, looking out. Without any greeting he said quickly, "Oh, Laurie, good, it's you. Will you stay with him for a minute and keep him as quiet as you can? I've got to get some clean things and I don't like to leave him."

Laurie said, "Yes, of course." He had never seen Andrew like this before; but then he had never seen Andrew with any urgent responsibility on his hands. At any other time Laurie would have found it interesting. But he had longed to unburden his heart; this concentration of Andrew's seemed to make common cause with the indifference of circumstance. Laurie walked into the side ward feeling the kind of resentment which, in people too fair to justify it, refuses to confess its own existence.

The injured man was lying with his head resting on a towel; Laurie realized that he had vomited on the sheet and pillow, and that was why Andrew needed clean things. Charlot's eyes were open; he looked exhausted, yet painfully, mechanically alert. His eyes moved toward Laurie, but they were flickering, and it was impossible to know whether he recognized anyone or not. As Laurie looked down, all of a sudden he forgot his

255

own troubles. Simple and unself-conscious as he was, still Charlot had turned like any other man his chosen face to his fellows; now, dreaming awake and revealing his dreams, he was more unprotected than in his sleep. One saw him naked in fear, or in need, and though the objects of these feelings were illusion, still it seemed not decent to spy on him. He had begun to talk again, but in so dull and blurred a way that probably even a speaker of his own patois would have made nothing of it. His thick chin, firm at other times, looked heavy and flaccid on the pillow, his mouth was half open, his lips crusted and dry.

Just then he lifted his arm gropingly, and fumbled at the wall as if he were searching for something to pull himself up on. Laurie settled him back. *"Eh bien, Charlot,"* he said experimentally. "Hello, cock. Look, it's Spud."

Charlot grabbed clumsily at his wrist and muttered something excitedly, like a warning or appeal. Laurie said, *"Tranquillise-toi, mon vieux, regarde alors, tu es ici avec moi."*

The man on the bed opened wide his oxlike brown eyes and his fingers tightened. Weeks of inactivity had softened the calluses on his big hands, but their grip was still something to remember. Just then the door opened and he let go. Laurie rubbed his bruised hand. "Did he hurt you?" Andrew asked.

"No, it's all right. I'll help you fix the bed."

"Would you really? Nurse Sims is sure to be busy." He stood looking at Charlot, in his intentness oddly austere; then, as if fully aware of Laurie for the first time, "No, of course you mustn't, you're always in pain by this time of night."

"No. They've fixed that." Just as Andrew looked up, Charlot started to move about. He seemed suddenly terrified; his blunt hands dragged and scrabbled at his plaster jacket. Andrew said, "He's forgotten what it is, he thinks he's been tied up or something. *Du calme, Charlot, personne ne vous fera mal."* But it was only when Laurie spoke that Charlot turned his head. Laurie loosened his hands from the plaster and he was quiet again. "You're the only one he seems to recognize," Andrew said.

"He didn't know any English at all when he first came. I suppose he got used to my voice."

"I'd better just see if Nurse Sims wants to come." He went out again, leaving the enamel bowl and the linen beside the bed. Laurie got out the soap from the locker and started to wash Charlot's face and hands. He gave no trouble, except that once he tried to raise himself up and muttered with great urgency something about heading for shoal water. Laurie did not know even in English the expert reassurance; suddenly he imagined Ralph walking briskly in, speaking to Charlot in his officer's voice and, when he had got him quiet, laying a hand on his forehead.

Andrew came back to say that Nurse Sims was doing a dressing behind screens, so they began work on Charlot together, changing his pajama jacket and the soiled bed-linen. From the far side of the bed Laurie could see, whenever he looked up, Andrew's bent head ringed with soft light from the shaded lamp on the locker. It made a gold blur around the edges of his hair. It was as if, thought Laurie, one were idealizing in memory someone already lost.

Suddenly for the first time he felt the parting to come as implicit in them from the moment of their first meeting. He wanted to reject this: if he could talk to Andrew, he thought, it would be exorcised. But it wouldn't be easy, or even decent now. While Andrew was taking the dirty things to the sluice Laurie looked down at the bed again, and listened to the clockwork breathing. During his months in hospital he had seen death's approach several times. Just then, waking from a moment of stupor, Charlot plucked at his sleeve and spoke his name.

"*Qu'est-ce que tu as, Charlot?*" said Laurie helplessly. His emotions refracted from his own concerns focused in an intense point of compassion like the center of a burning-glass. Charlot's almost animal state gave him the feeling one can have with a dying dog, that one is being trusted like God and is going to fail.

"Can you hear what he wants?" asked Andrew anxiously at the door.

"Not when you're talking." He had never snapped at Andrew in his life. "Sorry." They bent to listen together; but this seemed to frighten Charlot, who tried to push them back with a waving arm. Laurie said, "There's no point in our both hanging over him. It only puts him off."

Andrew withdrew obediently and stood back against the wall. Laurie sat down by Charlot on the edge of the bed and took his hand. His speech had become more jerky and agitated, and was not quite incoherent; he seemed to be begging for something. Andrew tried him with the bed-bottle, but he pushed it away, and, turning toward Laurie, seemed to look for a few minutes straight into his face. Laurie leaned over him and stroked his coarse, curly hair. *"Qu'est-ce que tu voudrais, dis-le moi, je t'écoute;* look, it's me."

"Spoddi," said Charlot thickly. Laurie felt his hand stir and tighten. His eyes had stopped wandering; Laurie could have sworn he knew whom he was talking to. Of his next few words it was possible to recognize several; Laurie heard the name of some French curé and the words *péché mortel.* His heart contracted. All other thoughts were swamped by the idea that Charlot had struggled to the surface for a moment, had looked into his face and made this appeal to him alone. He turned to Andrew and said, "He wants a priest."

For a moment there was no answer, and Laurie realized that just then Andrew had been entirely away from him.

Sometimes when they were sitting quietly somewhere out of doors, Andrew would withdraw into himself, and Laurie, without any wish to interrupt him, used to sit silent, watching him with admiration and love. Now suddenly he felt alone and excluded. The sudden pain mixed itself with the pity he had been feeling for Charlot before. He felt urgent and desperate, without understanding the nature of what he felt.

Andrew said, "I'll tell Nurse. We must ring for Father James." He looked once more at Charlot and went quietly out of the room.

258

Charlot's face had slackened and grown heavy; even his eyes did not move. When Laurie squeezed his hand he murmured something faintly. Andrew had said, while they were changing the sheet, that a brain specialist was coming out to look at him in the morning; he might have to go to Bridstow for an operation. With luck Father James would get there in time to see him first. But before long, even if he was still alive, he would have receded out of Father James's reach. He had only asked, Laurie thought, for this one thing.

Just then Andrew came back into the room and said, "We can't get through to the presbytery. I suppose the wire's been bombed somewhere; they said try again in two hours."

"That's a long time."

Andrew looked at him quickly. "Nurse is coming as soon as she's got a minute."

"It's always later than one thinks."

Andrew looked at his face, and after a second or two said slowly, "You've heard something, haven't you? You've got your discharge, you're going away."

"Never mind all that now." He did not know why he spoke so curtly. On the way, he had planned all kinds of gentle ways of breaking the news. He saw the startled grief on Andrew's face, and, without letting it come clearly into his mind, felt a secret primitive satisfaction; insecurity wants always to make its mark. But his concern for Charlot, which was perfectly real, allowed him to lose sight of all this quickly.

"We'll talk later on," he said. "Look, Andrew, we must do something about this while it's still some use. He's forgotten who you are. If I tell him you're a priest it will be all right."

The unhappiness in Andrew's face gave way to a blank, flat bewilderment. He looked at Laurie as if expecting him to say he hadn't meant it. Laurie only waited impatiently. At last Andrew said, "But of course we can't do that."

Laurie knew that he had expected Andrew to say this. His desperation, compounded of more pressures than one, at once began turning to anger.

"Oh, God. What difference does it make? He can't

259

talk sense anyway. Just so he can go feeling it's all right."

"You know we can't do it," Andrew said. He stared at Laurie with a lost, exploring look.

Laurie had a reasonless but terrible feeling of having been discovered and condemned. He tried to push it away, but his mind still felt shocked, bleeding, and raw. "But you don't believe those church things matter. So long as what he feels is right. You've always said so. It isn't much to do for him."

Andrew said, as if he hardly knew now what words would be simple enough, "But it's not what we believe. He's a Catholic. You know what that means as well as I do."

"It's my responsibility," Laurie said, "suppose anyone's chalking it up." He met defiantly Andrew's straight gray eyes. "Not his. Or yours, if that's how you feel."

"It's a responsibility neither of us has any right whatever to take." Andrew's face had set with decision; Laurie felt that it had hardened against him. "He's a human being. When he was himself he chose this creed. Now he's ill and doesn't know the difference, we can't possibly deceive him. Laurie, you *must* see that." There was appeal in his face. Laurie felt he was being asked to deny not only this, but everything. With a sudden stab of nostalgia he thought, Ralph would have understood.

"You're pretty hard, aren't you?" he said.

Andrew had read in Laurie's eyes the will to hurt, his altered face showed it. It showed too that he knew he was being punished partly for what he was and believed. He said, "That doesn't mean anything. A thing's right or it isn't."

"How simple," Laurie said.

Their eyes met and Laurie felt for an instant that a knowledge had passed between them so fundamental that the special fact, which had seemed so significant all this time, was only a trivial detail of it, unnoticed as yet. Andrew said earnestly, but without the smallest wavering of decision, "Don't you see, some things are too important to be tampered with for any reason at all."

260

A kind of *déjà entendu* twitched at Laurie's mind; then he remembered Major Ferguson. The thought made him angrier and more injured; but he still felt himself to be moved only on Charlot's behalf. Andrew was standing very straight. As on rare occasions before, his blood was showing in him; in his gray hospital-orderly's coat he looked more like a soldier than Laurie did in his battle-dress. He was distinct and separate and far away, and strikingly good-looking.

"For God's sake," said Laurie, even now remembering not to raise his voice, "don't stand there like St. Sebastian full of arrows, thinking of nothing but your own bloody principles. When you care about people you can't always be so choosy. Go outside, then, and keep yourself clean. I'll manage here. Charlot and I understand each other."

What he had said came home to him only gradually, like the collapse of a wall which starts with a few loose bricks.

Andrew stood where he was. His face had a pinched look, as if he were cold. You could see the bone-structure of character showing, the shape of the winter tree.

"I'm sorry, Andrew. I lost my temper. I didn't mean all that."

"Whatever you meant," said Andrew in a voice of ashes, "I've been given this job to do and I must do it. I can't leave it just for a personal reason."

For a moment, this putting him in his place seemed to Laurie the last affront. He felt he would say anything to revenge himself and only delayed to make the telling choice; but this was not true, he was losing time by putting aside one weapon after another as too base to use, shocked by what he had used already. During this interval he recovered part of his reason and saw Andrew freshly, as he stood.

With an increase of effort which left him with a drained, almost empty look, Andrew said, "I know you only wanted to help him; I realize that."

"Andrew, I must have gone off my head. I can't think how I—I'm sorry."

There was an oxygen cylinder standing in the corner; it was the stiff, seized-up one that couldn't be used,

261

kept here out of the way. Andrew went over to it and picked up the spanner, turned it about in his hands for a moment, then suddenly fitted it to the cylinder head and gave it a violent wrench. The gas hissed like an angry snake; he wrenched the spanner back again and shut it off.

"That's all right," he said. He looked at his hands; there were deep crimson weals across his palms. "This thing works after all." He hung the spanner back.

"Yes, does it?" Andrew's face at the moment of attacking the cylinder had been something of a revelation. "Look, I was wrong about that." He was only just starting to realize how wrong. It occurred to him too for the first time that Charlot's mind might have been wandering back to some confession five or fifteen years old. "I'm sorry, Andrew."

They were interrupted by a guttural sound from the bed. As they turned, Charlot, who had been quite quiet, began to have a kind of epileptic fit. They held his head away from the wall while he jerked like a huge, grotesque marionette; even the legs moved, which had not moved for so long. When it was over he sank into a deep, heavily relaxed unconsciousness; his face was dark, one side of his mouth sagged, his breathing was loud and very slow. They spoke to him, touched him, dug their fingers into his arms. He made no response at all.

They looked at each other. Andrew said, "I'll go and get Nurse."

She arrived this time in a matter of seconds. When she turned away from the bed the first thing she said was, "Odell, what are you doing here? Go back to bed at once." She watched him out of the room; there was no chance to make peace with Andrew even by a look.

In the ward he found half the men awake and asking what had been going on. Some were grumbling because they needed this or that and there was no orderly. Laurie went around and got them what they wanted as well as he could. After a while the talking died down; he heard the voices of doctors arriving outside, of Major Ferguson's assistant using the telephone, and, about half an hour later, of an ambulance driving up. Then suddenly everything was quiet again; Nurse Sims came in and sat down at the desk, looking all around with suspicion as if trying to guess what they had been up to while she had been gone.

The night deepened and grew cold, the local air-raid siren went, and the darkness tightened like stretched gauze. Once the mobile gun was heard stuttering in the distance. Andrew came in at last, his work outside done, and made a round of the patients, most of whom were by now asleep. He reached Laurie's bed, stood by the locker and looked down, trying after the bright light outside to see if Laurie was awake. Laurie slid out a hand and touched his wrist. "What happened?" he asked softly.

"They've taken him to the big hospital for a decompression." He paused and added, "They don't think he'll make it." Laurie, whose eyes were at home in the darkness, saw clearly the strain in his face.

He whispered, "See you in the kitchen after she gets back from her meal."

It was eleven-fifty. Ten minutes later Nurse Sims went out, and Andrew, whom this left in charge of the ward, sat down as usual at the desk. Soon Laurie felt he had been lying forever watching the hand of the clock crawl and the dusky light on Andrew's bent head. At last Nurse Sims came back again. Laurie gave it a couple of minutes and went out.

Andrew was getting ready a little tray for Nurse's coffee. Laurie had never met him in the kitchen quite so late. The cracking of the hot pipes sounded enormous, and the throb of a single plane overhead widened in great spreading rings like a pebble dropped in a still pool. A silence as wide as the night sky closed them in, and all the world's sleep lay heavy over them. Laurie was aching with weariness; his eyes felt dry, and his face drawn with it.

"I had to see you," he said. "You know I—you can't go on feeling—no, I mean it, Andrew, you must believe I do."

"You shouldn't have stayed awake," said Andrew in a flat kind voice. "You look terribly tired." He got

263

some milk from the refrigerator and filled a cup with it. "Would you rather have it hot?"

"No, thanks, this is fine." He drank it mechanically, watching Andrew. "Look, just because that happened after what I said to you—it was a filthy thing to say and when I said it I knew it wasn't true. I just got emotional and lost my grip."

Andrew smiled at him, and for an instant he had the illusion of looking at someone older than himself. "You'd take back what happened, too, wouldn't you, if you could?"

"That makes no difference." He hadn't realized how Andrew's certainties, including those he didn't believe himself to share, had knit themselves into his cosmos. Now to see them shaken was not pathetic but terrible. "I was wrong, of course. It was a thing Charlot wouldn't have wanted done, if he'd understood."

"I know," said Andrew. "I didn't mean that." He looked straight in front of him. "It was about me you were right."

"God, no, Andrew, I wasn't. I wasn't even trying to be. I was just bitching you because—well, I was in a mood, and one thing and another. I can't tell you. Just take my word."

"Everything that was actually done for him," said Andrew slowly, "was done by you. I couldn't think beyond what not to do. If I . . . if my mind had been where it should have been, I'd have known what ought to be done, something would have come to me."

"That was my fault too."

"No. No, it wasn't your fault."

"Look, Andrew. I ought to know. I do this kind of thing. I get steamed up about things that happen to people till I've got to do something or burst, and if it turns out to do more harm than good, hell, what's the odds, it did good to me. At school for instance. A man—one of the boys I mean, was going to be sacked, and because I liked him I took for granted he couldn't have done it, and I was all set to have raised hell and involved a lot of other people. And all the time he'd done it after all."

264

Andrew, who had listened intently, said, "It must have been rather horrible finding out."

Laurie said quickly, "I didn't. He told me himself, to keep me out of trouble."

"Oh." There was a pause; then Andrew looked up. "What was it? What had he done?"

Laurie had not thought of this question. "I don't think I ought to tell you that."

"No, of course. Sorry." Andrew looked away. Laurie saw too late that there was no good reason not to tell, unless the person concerned was one whom Andrew knew of. After a few moments' silence Andrew picked up the tray. "I must take Nurse her coffee, she'll be wondering."

"I'll wait for you."

"No, don't. You look done up. Go and get some sleep."

"I'd rather wait. There won't be very much longer."

Andrew turned, the tray of coffee in his hand, and looked at it blindly as if he had to get rid of it but couldn't think how.

"Take that first," Laurie said. "Don't worry, it's all right." Andrew went out quickly.

When he got back, Laurie explained about the transfer, leaving it to be inferred that he had heard of it at the other hospital. He wouldn't be far away, he told Andrew; after he was discharged he could often come over, he could stay at some farm. . . . Andrew said at intervals suitable things: that it was a good thing they had noticed the boot, and so on. It didn't take them long to get through all this.

"I've never known this place without you," Andrew said. "We got here at night, you know it was quite dark, and in the morning, before I'd been working half an hour, we met."

"We never did get that record of the oboe concerto, in the end."

Andrew attempted to smile. "No. So now it will be one of those tunes that people have."

"Don't talk like that. As if we——"

After a pause Andrew said, "This doesn't seem very—very sensible. Other people aren't like this."

265

"That doesn't make any difference."

"No."

"You'll have Dave back in a day or two."

"Dave? . . . I heard from him today. He's working in the East End, he wants to stay there."

Like most people, Laurie had heard more about the blitz than the papers were printing. "Does he have to do that?"

"He can go where he likes, he's years over military age. It's because of Cynthia, I know." Andrew gave him a strange bewildered look and added, "I know how he feels. No, that must sound stupid. I mean I——"

"Yes," said Laurie. "Yes, it's all right."

"How is it that—I've often liked people enough to talk to them, but—things I'd feel a fool saying to anyone else in the world—I don't always tell you, one doesn't of course, but I always feel I could and you'd know what they meant better than I do."

"I don't suppose so," said Laurie roughly. "It's just that you know I like you. People who—oh, well, anyway."

"Only you keep things to yourself sometimes. Well, of course. It's just a way you look with it. 'No, he couldn't take that.' You oughtn't to think of me as a person whose head has to be stuck in a bag. That ought to be the last thing, if you see what I mean." When Laurie didn't answer, he said with difficulty, "It makes me feel, in a way, jealous, without knowing what of."

Laurie looked up and said deliberately, "You needn't ever feel that."

For a moment their eyes met, then Andrew went over to the sink where there were a few things left from making coffee. He picked up a jug and looked at it. "You see, the fact that I could say a thing like that to you, and you . . . One shouldn't waste time analyzing oneself with the world in the state it is. I try not to. But things happen that one can't completely . . . It's all right when I'm with you. I don't have the feeling of being different, then."

"Don't have it on your mind," said Laurie unevenly. At this moment, he could feel nothing in himself from which Andrew ought to be protected. With a simplicity

266

which this knowledge made to seem quite natural, he leaned over and kissed him. Even when he had done it he felt no reaction or self-reproach. It was as if it had happened before and they both remembered.

Just at this moment, when Andrew was looking up with a kind of strangeness which was only the threshold of some feeling not yet formed, they heard a sound in the doorway. It was as impossible not to spring apart as to keep the eye open against flying grit. Nurse Sims said, "May I have a teaspoon, please?" Her voice was a tone louder than is usual on night duty, and had an unfamiliar formality.

Andrew said, "Oh. I'm sorry." He brought out a handful of spoons from the box, dropped two, picked them up from the floor, nearly handed her one of them instead of a clean one, and said "Sorry" again. She walked rapidly to the door, half turned without looking around, and said, "I think you'd better be going back to bed now, Odell." Afterwards he didn't know whether he had answered her or not. When she went out, she shut the door behind her. They had left it ajar, as they always did.

They were alone together; for Laurie it was like a parachute jump in which he felt for the cord in vain. After what, perhaps, was really only a matter of seconds, he said, "Oh, hell. I never get away with anything." Andrew didn't look around. "I only once ever cried at the theater, and in a flash the curtain was down and they'd turned on every light in the house."

Andrew turned with a resolute smile. "She must have some peculiar ideas now about the way we spend our time in here."

"Oh, I don't think she more than felt an atmosphere, as they say." He had the feeling of carrying out some brutal operation without anesthetics.

"You'll have to go now, or she'll have kittens any minute."

Laurie could see Andrew copying his manner, trustfully, as if quite without resource of his own. "You've got something there, I shouldn't wonder." Suddenly the All Clear went, strident in the silence. "My God, was there a warning on? I didn't know."

"Sleep well," said Andrew. Laurie saw him searching for words, or perhaps for the meaning of whatever words he had found. Better not to wait.

"Don't worry. Good night."

At the end of the ward Nurse Sims was sitting at the table. She had got her sewing out, and she didn't look up.

It was bad luck on her, Laurie thought. She hadn't wanted to know. She much preferred everything to be nice. You would never have heard her commenting unkindly on one of those quiet boys, a bit shy with girls, or one of those clever women, the tailor-made type, a bit independent with men. It took all sorts to make a world. As for people like *that*, them one would only hear of, never meet. They belonged, like sawn-up corpses, to the exotic land of the Sunday papers. Even now, almost certainly, she wouldn't report what she had seen, partly because it would embarrass her too much, but chiefly because she still wouldn't fully commit herself to having talked and worked with, and even liked, people like that. She would rather consign them to some indeterminate limbo of people who were no longer nice but not fully classified; people who were a bit morbid, or had something unhealthy about them.

Limbo, he thought, remembering the apples shining across the stream, and the day of separation coming nearer and nearer, till it would be now.

The A.P.C. had worn off and the familiar gimlet was boring into his knee. He turned and lay with his face in the darkness of his folded arms, feeling as if he had gone away already and were among strangers, alone.

In the end, however, the pain must have eased or fatigue overcome it, for he slept deeply, and when he began to dream, it was about none of the things which had filled his mind when he fell asleep. It was a vivid dream, and too direct to fascinate an analyst. After he woke he thought it surprising; but he knew that at the time it had been full of familiar recognition, and that he had seemed to come home to it all with longing and deep release, after an unbearably long absence which must never be allowed to happen again. It was the kind of thing one can make a joke of next morning, if one can find some uninhibited friend to listen: but that would be impossible for some days, and in any case one could hardly relate such a dream to the person concerned in it.

He slept again after, and in the morning he only remembered it dimly. Soon it was put out of his mind altogether, for he heard from his mother by the morning post. Canon Rosslow, the lifelong friend of Mr. Straike, had been appointed to a colonial see suddenly vacated by death; and as it was unthinkable that anyone else should officiate at the wedding, it had been arranged that this should take place by special license the following week. She had applied in writing to the hospital, asking that Laurie should be given a couple of nights' leave of absence, in view of the special occasion.

11

NEXT day Major Ferguson sent for Laurie, and told him that he was to be transferred the day after tomorrow. He added that he had written to the matron, enclosing Mrs. Odell's letter, and he didn't fancy she would make any difficulties.

This ended Laurie's hopes that the transfer would supply him with some kind of alibi. There was no way out of it now; he would have to go. Remembering in time, he thanked Major Ferguson for his kindness in arranging it.

He had, as a matter of fact, fully expected to be transferred that day. He had keyed himself up to it, at a pitch which could not be maintained for long. He was still unsophisticated enough to feel shocked when he found that the reprieve gave him feelings of anticlimax, exhaustion, and dismay. Andrew was in bed, he had arranged with Derek to call him if Laurie had to go. Laurie sent him a message with the news, so that he could sleep.

The rest of the day stretched before him, a long aimless blank. He loafed out by himself and ran into Nurse Adrian, who was off duty, in the lane. She seemed as

much at a loose end as he, and they walked on together. It was a keen, gray day with an edgy wind; the
dead leaves, crisp and hard, were being scoured along
the road with a gritty rattle. She remarked on the ease
with which he was walking and said the treatment must
be doing good.

"Too much," he said. "It's made them ambitious.
But Sister's told you, of course."

"No. Do you mean you're being transferred?"

"Yes, on Monday. It's a bit of an uprooting all
around, one way and another. My mother's being married next week, too."

She asked one or two questions; she didn't seem
bored or perfunctory but as if she actually wanted to
know. Because of the thoughts that occupied the foreground of his mind, this seemed unbelievably generous
of her. Even the passing illusion that he had struck roots
somewhere, and would be missed, was comforting, especially from a woman. Women still stood to him for
background and stability, as they do to children, because they had never stood for anything more.

Presently she said, "Will you live at home when
you're discharged?"

"Well, I don't suppose so."

"Where are you going, then?"

So much had happened lately that the question had
not presented itself, till now, as something close at
hand. "Quite honestly," he said, "I haven't the least
idea."

In fact, he thought, he would have to start planning
immediately. His exhibition covered his fees at Oxford,
and he had still nearly four hundred and fifty pounds
in the bank, the bulk of a legacy from his grandmother
which had come to him at twenty-one, and which he
had hardly drawn on because of the war. For the time,
at least, he could live anywhere; term didn't start for a
couple of months. He would find some place where
Andrew could go easily on his day off, try to catch up
with his reading. At this point he became aware that
Nurse Adrian was scrambling through her pockets in a
quiet panic. He stopped walking at once and said,
"Have you lost something?"

"Only my handkerchief." She sniffed fiercely. "I'm so sorry ... have you ... could you ... it's the cold wind."

"It's only a hospital one with a hole in it. It's not even clean, very." He fished it out in some embarrassment and held it out to her. It was only then he realized she was in tears.

He stood transfixed with the discovery, wondering what could have happened to her. Had she had bad news from home? Suddenly, in a flash of horrified intuition, he knew.

What on earth was he going to do? Better not take any notice, unless she said something or made a noise. She wouldn't want to attract attention. But how to get away? A sharp gust of wind tore through a gap in the hedge; it caught the handkerchief out of her hand and whirled it away down the lane behind them. Instinctively he started to run after it, felt the stiff drag of his leg, and stopped. She had gasped at finding her face exposed, run like the wind, and snatched up the handkerchief from the bank. Now she had her back to him, so that he shouldn't see her mopping her eyes. Oddly enough, it was the leg, and not being able to run, that settled it for him: the total sum of helplessness and ineffectuality was too much to bear. He remembered how kind she had always been. Walking firmly up to her, he put his arm around her and said, "Here, what is all this?"

As she didn't answer, he took the handkerchief from her and dabbed her eyes with it. At this she gave a hiccup of hysterical laughter, and buried her face on his shoulder. It was virtually impossible now not to embrace her with both arms and he did so. There they were, and he felt as much shock and bewilderment as if he had waked up to find himself stretched in the road after a street accident. Now he must think what to do next. Without a notion of the answer he asked himself what the orthodox procedure would have been: to ignore the whole thing and make conversation; seduce her (there was nowhere to go and the wind was full of dead leaves and grit); tell her he was secretly married; talk her out of it? He supposed though that in more orthodox circles all this wouldn't have arisen, because he would be engaged to her by now. She was the kind of girl you could quite easily imagine attracting men, if their tastes were a cut above the pin-up level: why, he himself, even, found it easy to forgive her for placing him in this ghastly predicament; and he stroked her hair. It was nice hair, fair, fine, and nearly straight, straighter than Andrew's and lighter. Nearly as straight as Ralph's, he thought, running it through his fingers; how odd, what an extraordinary coincidence. He put his cheek against it and shut his eyes.

She was gulping into his neck, like a schoolgirl, and muttering something about being ridiculous and that he wasn't to take any notice. Even his inexperience could perceive her complete physical naïveté. She was sexually backward as is scarcely any female creature except the English girl of a certain upbringing: nothing she wanted was clear to her but love. It was a need which Laurie felt just now as intolerably poignant; where a more specific approach would have alarmed and repelled him, this found out the crack in his defenses. He could no more have kept from kissing her than he could have kicked a lost puppy back into the street.

Her mouth was soft and cool, and didn't taste of tears as her cheek had done. He felt it almost unmoving against his, in a kind of contemplative wonder. How different from the girl in London, four years ago. All at once he was horrified by his own feckless sentimentality. In a muddled tenderness born of remorse, inextricably mixed with the fear of being found out and with a more generous impulse to protect her from the insult of his pity, he pulled her closer and kissed her again.

"Don't," she sobbed, "oh, please. This is awful, how could I? What shall I do?"

"What's awful? Don't be silly. It's all right."

Her hair felt young and beautifully clean, like washed silk; he had laid her head back on his shoulder so as to reach it again. He remembered something Charles had said and thought what hysterical nonsense it was; there was nothing so terrifying about her. In fact . . .

What's the matter with me? he thought. At first he

272

wouldn't admit to himself that it was happening: it was disruptive, undermining all the established decencies and securities of his life. Then suddenly he felt delighted with himself. After this nothing would ever be exactly the same, one's limitations would never seem quite so irrevocably fixed. At this moment she linked her arms around his neck and for the first time kissed him of her own accord. He saw her face; it brought him down to earth with a jolt. He remembered now who it was that was paying for all this.

"Stop being so nice to me," she whispered. "Please stop, it only makes it worse."

"I can't help it either." Indeed, he was having to remind himself that she was very young, and mustn't be frightened. The gratitude he felt to her confused him; unable to resist expressing it along the line of least resistance, he knew at the same time that he was already beginning to exploit her, and that this was only the first of many excuses with which he would be able to furnish himself, if and when he wished. She knew nothing, she had scarcely even preconceptions; he had only to find himself the right kind of emotional pose, which as she trusted him wouldn't be difficult, and he could make use of her to almost any extent. She would be very useful, invaluable indeed, and after all, it was what she wanted.

"It's all right," she said. "I'll soon get over it. Please don't think I'm trying to let you in for anything."

"For God's sake. Don't talk like that." He looked up; in the distance a couple of men were approaching. He steered her through the nearest gate into a field with Alderney cows in it. A high hedge shut off the wind; there was a pile of sawed logs to sit on. He had already put his arm around her to keep out the cold, and it would have been unkind to take it away again. He sat there trying to find something to say and suddenly thought, If I asked her to marry me, she would.

She doesn't think me different, except as the person one loves is always different. No one need ever think that again. I could tell her the truth sometime perhaps. If I put it nicely she wouldn't know what it really meant. She'd probably think it very romantic. Or perhaps she need never know at all.

One would have to be tactful, not let her think she'd rushed one into it. Perhaps one could say . . .

Just then she moved away from him and leaned out and pulled at a loose flake of bark on one of the logs. With her shoulder turned to him, she said, "I know what it is. I know why you're being so sweet about it. It's because you know how I'm feeling. You couldn't be like this if you weren't in love with someone else."

He took her hand. "Yes. Life's rather hell, isn't it? If things could possibly be different, it would be you."

She squeezed his fingers and said, "I think I've guessed there was someone, all the time. How terrible to have so little self-control: this must have been the most dreadfully embarrassing thing that ever happened to you in your whole life. I could just about jump in the sea."

"Not embarrassing. Or, well, it depends what you mean." He put his arm hard around her waist. "I nearly behaved very badly, you know." He was afraid this must sound impossibly naïve, and was greatly relieved to see that it had impressed her. Although he was ashamed to find himself capable of detachment at a moment when she was very unhappy, still he couldn't help being aware that the memory of having tempted a man, and shaken his fidelity, would not come amiss to her in future dealings with life. She was sweet, he thought.

"I suppose people are always telling you what nice hair you have."

"It's terrible now. There isn't a decent hairdresser for miles. I've given it up, I just wash it under the tap."

"Don't have it permed or messed about. It's nice. May I kiss you again?"

But the shift in their combined weight caused the pile of logs to roll apart, and they went sprawling. It was the kind of accident in which people can be quite badly hurt; when they had picked themselves up unscathed except for some nettle stings, they were both so generally shaken that they collapsed into weak laugh-

274

ter. This, and hunting for dock leaves, offered a rescu-
ing anticlimax; both of them were thankful.

In the lane she said, "I oughtn't to ask—but why
doesn't she ever come to see you?"

For some reason he was quite unprepared for this. It
was poverty of invention, rather than sublety, which
made him say, "Well, the thing is, as far as she knows,
we're nothing more than friends. I've never told her.
She—she isn't free, you see, and she wouldn't think it
was right."

"I *am* sorry." Transparently, this grown-up situation
caused her to look at him with new eyes; he felt both a
fool and a fraud. "I do hope it will come right for you
both someday."

"I don't suppose so, really," he said, and slanted-off
the conversation. They were both young enough to be
capable of solemn abstract discussion about love; and
in this way, with its pleasantly painful stirring of the
emotions, they made their way back to the turning
where hospital people who had been walking out
used to part discreetly. As they neared it, he knew that
he didn't want her to go. Now that he wasn't going on
with it, he began to idealize what might have been, and
to soften the deceits and the dangers. "Would you mind
if I wrote to you, sometime? I don't want us to lose
touch with each other."

"Oh, what nonsense, of course not. You're just taking on something that's going to be nothing but a burden to you, because you want to cheer me up."

"No. You've made a great difference, more than I
can explain. I shall never forget you."

She said, "If you mean that, of course I should love
you to write," and he saw her look away to hide her
sudden hope. For a moment he felt guilty; but after she
had gone, he realized that, in the deep essentials, he
had meant what she had believed him to mean.

When he got back to the ward, Charlot's empty bed
seemed to dominate it like a grave. There was no sign
of Reg. Madge was still here and they were spending
the day together. Neames was there, and one or two
new men he hardly knew and didn't much care for. His

solitude seemed all the more insistent because this time he had bought it for himself.

In the asphalt walk he was drawn into conversation by Willis, of all people. Laurie couldn't remember having ever before had speech with him alone. It emerged that he had got his discharge for the same day as Laurie's transfer. He was going to Roehampton, to be trained to use an artificial hand and to learn a trade; he had been an unskilled builder's laborer before the war. He seemed quite cheerful about his future. The real surprise came a few minutes later: Willis was engaged. The girl was an evacuee who worked at one of the farms. They had been walking out for some time and this morning, on getting the news, he had "got it fixed up regular." Laurie realized that it was weeks since he had paid anything but the most perfunctory attention to Willis; in the interval there had been a considerable change. Suddenly he said, "You wait till young Derek hears about Shirl and me. This'll shake him, not half."

"Pal of yours?" asked Laurie, concealing his astonishment with some care.

"Comes from down our street, Derek. We bought our groceries off his dad. Ain't you heard, then? Come up and told me. He was bright at school, see, got scholarships, that's how he comes to talk posh. Nothing toffee-nosed about him, though. Reads me his mum's letters with all the home news, every week regular."

"Good show," said Laurie. He thought of Derek's little refinements, of the kind to have been fiercely instilled and as fiercely cherished.

They had exhausted for the moment their store of communicable thoughts, and were strolling mutely, when Reg came up the path from the gates, Madge hooked to his arm.

Laurie was delighted to see him. They wouldn't see much more of one another; there was a lot to talk about. Reg's last X-ray had been a good one; he would be discharged too before long. Already they were full of plans for a celebration before Reg went back to his unit again. Seeing him approach between the huts, Laurie felt that this at least was solid. It had stood everything and there had never been any cheating.

276

Reg must have brought Madge back here to get the bus for the station. Laurie waved to them; Reg waved back and steered Madge over.

Willis, of course, was news. He shifted from leg to leg under the rain of congratulations. The jests with which he strove to cover his coyness got progressively lewder: Reg was obliged before long to cough. Madge parried apology with an indulgent giggle, anxious to show herself no spoilsport, without stepping down from the pedestal on which Reg had chivalrously placed her. She turned to Laurie, and tapped him skittishly on the chest with a brown paper parcel she was carrying, much as an eighteenth-century lady would have used a fan.

"Now then, Spud, own up. Don't you tell me *you've* not had a finger in this, because I shan't believe you."

"Help *him?*" said Laurie, keeping the party going. It was his first meeting with Madge since the letter, but he had been comfortably sure that she wouldn't refer to it with Willis there. "That'll be the day." This was meant to turn the spotlight on Willis again.

"Oh, go on with you. We all know who's the Cupid around here, don't we, boys?"

Willis guffawed obligingly. It was evident that he was ready to take Cupid on trust, as he did, probably, one word in ten of most conversations he heard. Reg's appreciation was a little more guarded. He could be seen going through vague motions of a "Well, time we were off" kind. But Madge was well away, you could see the wit gathering like wind in a sail.

"Tell you what, Spud. What price that for a career? One of these bits in the fashion magazines, let Lady Vera solve your troubles. I can just see you sitting in some posh office with three secretaries all worked to death and the fan-mail rolling in. Onlookers see most of the game; that's right, Reg, isn't it?"

Laurie was only moderately embarrassed; he thought it was an accident. Then he saw Reg's face turning brick-red, and knew that it wasn't.

He looked around at them: Madge brassing over a sudden misgiving; Willis, who had clearly decided that he knew now what Cupid meant; Reg with the same fatuous, stupefied look of injury that Samson probably wore when, in the cold dawn after the bedtime confidences, he first ran a hand over his clipped head. For a moment Laurie saw them all fixed like a row of grotesques, looking at him. He said, "It's an idea. Well, goodbye," and walked away toward the hospital, without looking back.

Before he had even turned the corner, after only a few seconds, he knew it was all up now. He and Reg had had it. Reg would never get over this, they would never be able to face one another alone again. By coolness, humor, and address at the crucial moment it was just possible that Reg could have been rescued. Laurie hadn't been equal to it, and that was that.

Back in the ward, the afternoon routine of bed-tidying was going on; Nurse Adrian and Derek were doing it together. He straightened his own bed quickly and went out again. He still thought them two very nice people, but they seemed a long way off and nothing much to do with him.

Outside the village post office the door of the red telephone box swung ajar. It had a comforting, inviting look. The search for Ralph cost him one and sixpence before their conversation began; and when it did, Ralph opened with the phrase which meant, by arrangement, that he wasn't alone. They only talked for a couple of minutes, idle stuff to be overheard. But when Laurie came out again, he felt rather less like a citizen of nowhere.

12

THE ward looked about thirty feet high. The walls were painted brown for the first seven or eight feet. In the middle stood a towering cast-iron stove of Gothic design. The nurses, intent on mysterious tasks, wore the old-style uniform, tall starched caps, stiff aprons, black stockings and shoes. The Sister, who seemed to have been measured for the ward, stood about six feet in flat heels. Her belt was massively clasped with silver, there was a flat rigid bow under her chin. Laurie and Andrew stood in the doorway, looking at each other. Andrew said, "I'd better not come in."

He had worked, with much trouble, his night off for last night so as to come with Laurie today. Laurie had known it would be like this, and would far rather have seen him on duty in the ward as usual; but he had lacked the heart to say so. It had all been, he thought, like the kind of deathbed one hopes not to have; going on too long, one's nearest and dearest doing the right thing with dreadful conscientiousness and stifling guiltily their prayers for the end. He didn't know which had been worse, Reg's painful flux of talk or Andrew's helpless dumbness. Nurse Adrian had lost her nerve at the last, and hidden.

As they faltered at the door, the tall Sister suddenly strode forward. "Are you the new admission?" she asked accusingly. In the end he didn't even see Andrew go.

They showed him his bed. On one side was a terribly ill-looking boy of nine or ten, propped high on a mound of pillows; on the other, a very old man who seemed to spend nearly all day having things done to him behind screens. After the afternoon's massage and electrical treatment, the day stretched ahead empty. Laurie realized that if he had persuaded Andrew to stay on, they could have spent most of it together. But it was better like this. He knew it as he lay, later, looking up into the dusty recesses of the ceiling, isolated by the strangeness of the place, in a pause of unlooked-for peace and rest. The first lap of the race was over, not without victory. Words sounded in his mind like winged hoof-beats: "... *it sinks down in the midst of heaven, and returns to its own home. And there the charioteer leads his horses to the manger, and puts ambrosia before them, with nectar for their drink. Such is the life of the gods.*"

"Hello," said an infinitely distant voice. "What's your name?"

Laurie perceived that it came from the next bed, and it was its faintness, rather than his abstraction, which

279

had made it sound remote. Two hollow, inquisitive brown eyes had opened in the boy's blue-white face. Laurie said, "It's Spud, what's yours?"

"Mervyn. Did you get hurt in a raid, or in the war?"

"In France. Have you been stopping a bomb or something?"

"No. I just had an appendix and it burst. Isn't it a swiz? I say, did you come back from Dunkirk in one of those boats?"

"Just a minute. When was this operation?"

"Middle of last night. But I've stopped being sick now." He had talked himself out of breath already.

"I tell you what; take it easy today and get some sleep, and I'll tell you about the boats in the morning."

"You be here in the morning?" he asked suspiciously. He looked like a boy with few illusions.

"Yes, of course I shall."

"Swear?"

"On my solemn oath."

"Okay, good enough." He shut his eyes.

Laurie tried to recapture his private happiness; but a few minutes later a nurse appeared with a letter which had preceded him. It was from his mother. At school, and even at Oxford, she had always sent a letter ahead to welcome him. Touched, he opened it, to find it full of detailed plans for the wedding.

He had only attended two weddings in his life, one as a page of four, the other at Oxford in the first days of the war, a rush affair of close friends wearing their everyday clothes. Now for the first time it started coming home to him: the Best Man, the reception, the archaic vestiges of sacrifice, of capture, and of sale. Great Uncle Edward was coming to give away the bride; she was afraid it would be too much for him, but he had said no, they were a small family and Raymond would have wished it. Raymond was his mother's only brother, who had been killed at Gallipoli. Mrs. Trevor had written again about the house, and——

"Corporal Odell."

Laurie nearly sat at attention and said, "Sir?" But it was the six-foot Sister standing over him.

"These have been left for you." She laid a couple of

280

new novels on the bed. Her voice was somberly reserved. Perhaps she had sampled them and considered them immoral, thought Laurie rather wildly, perhaps she didn't think N.C.O's ought to be able to read. When she had gone he opened them and found the note inside.

The last time he had seen a page of Ralph's writing it had been pinned to the House notice-board. In those days it had been rather precociously formed; it hadn't changed very much since. The lines straight, the letters slanted a little and pressed on the down-stroke, it had under its regularity a kind of suppressed impatience; one could see how it had been conditioned by the necessity of transmitting vital information, making permanent records, issuing instructions which must not be misunderstood. It was a curiously stiff, shy letter, boyishly conventional, even at times boyishly facetious. There were three more pages and he wondered however Ralph had filled them. He turned over and read, "I was in a pub yesterday when a Pole and a Welshman had a row." As soon as it became impersonal the letter came to life. The writing had got almost practiced; it had a genuine, natural feel. He remembered Ralph saying, "I used to keep a notebook and write all that nonsense down."

Something caught his eye. He looked up. The boy in the next bed had thrown all his covers off and swung a leg over the side. He was only wearing a pajama jacket.

"Here," said Laurie, "what goes on? You don't get up, do you?"

The boy muttered something about just going outside. Laurie saw he was delirious. All his operation sutures must still be in. Laurie jumped out of bed and eased him back again. The child muttered vaguely and wound his arms around Laurie's neck. He had no idea where he was or who was with him. His hair and skin had a weak, sickly smell.

"What's this? What are you doing with this patient?"

The Sister stood over him like a hanging judge. Laurie felt a lurch inside him. Had Major Ferguson heard

281

something and written? Was he never to get away from it?

"He was getting out of bed, Sister. I'm sorry."

"You must call a nurse, Corporal, if you see a patient needing attention—NURSE EVANS!" It was just the note he had been trying in secret to acquire when he had expected to be promoted sergeant. "Come here, Nurse Evans. Do you know that while you were frittering away your time, this boy with peritonitis would have been out of bed if he hadn't been put back by another patient who hasn't been more than a few hours in the ward? You must do better than this, Nurse Evans, I assure you. Now give that boy what he was looking for, and get on with your work."

He didn't sleep much; the ward was taking in emergencies that week. Two arrived in the night, followed by doctors and relatives and theater trolleys. The boy Mervyn, however, slept well, and by morning had made one of those dramatic improvements peculiar to children. He had taken a shine to Laurie and wouldn't let him alone. After lunch he demanded the Dunkirk story. Laurie stuck to the sea part, since not much of the land events seemed edifying to youth. You couldn't be vague on your facts. He was a bright, sharp boy, and seemed to have lived with people who regarded lying to children as the natural means of keeping them quiet. The more he wanted to trust you, the sharper he got.

"A lot of this," Laurie explained painstakingly, "I don't remember myself, I heard about it later."

"Who told you?"

"The man who was commanding the ship told me most of it."

"The captain did?" Sad suspicion darkened the hollow eyes. "Go on. You're a corporal."

"Yes, but we were at school together."

"You and the captain?" He sighed and sagged on the pillow. "Oh, yeah?"

"Yeah," said Laurie, reaching the end of his resources. Shortly after, a snuffling, meanly respectable woman came to visit the boy. When he was taken ill she had told him that he wouldn't have to stay in hospital and that she would be back in a few minutes to fetch him home; now she had come with more lies to explain it. The boy listened apathetically; once his eyes slid around to Laurie with a vague unformed hope. But it was time for massage; he had to leave them to it.

Miss Haliburton had sold her dachshund puppy; but she had brought another, a bull-terrier this time. It gave Laurie a pink wink; the other eye had a black patch like a bruiser's. It took to Laurie with fervor, and tried to get inside his blouse. Arthur measured him for the new boot.

It was falling dark. The landings and corridors were lit with blue electric bulbs. His ward was in the oldest part of the hospital; everything was huge and dingy, with dust-trapping Victorian joinery. Before him rose the steps to the ward, a dim gaunt sweep of worn stone. He measured it with his eye and stepped forward.

"Hi, Spud. Wait below there, I'll come down."

Brisk firm feet rang on the steps; Ralph ran down smiling. It was like the sight of something green on a burnt moor. Laurie knew that his face showed it. Ralph took his arm in a quick hard grip and let go again. Laurie said, "God, it's nice to see you."

Ralph said with his swift smile, "Poor old Spud, don't you like the view? Who's that lunatic, Alec lent me the book once, couldn't read above half of it—chap called Kafka. This is just the setup."

"Or an old German film. There's nowhere to sit. She won't have anyone in the ward out of visiting hours."

"I know where we can go," Ralph said. "I used to know this place once like the back of my hand." He steered Laurie around a corner into a short, dimly lit passage which smelt of beeswax. "Have a pew."

There was in fact a large yellow pitch-pine pew beside them, stacked with hymn books. They were in the outer lobby of the hospital chapel. They sat down. The place, angled back from the corridor and almost dark, had the nostalgic smell of truancy and escape, like lumber attics and the shut-off wings of old houses. They talked softly, almost in whispers.

When Laurie thanked him for the books, Ralph said, "I didn't come last night, I thought you'd be set-

283

tling in." Laurie realized that he had thought Andrew would be there.

"I didn't get here till late." It was, he realized, only a simple way of not mentioning Andrew directly. Laurie still would not let his mind cross the borders of half-knowledge. It was just one thing and another; but it wasn't possible to talk to Ralph about Andrew any more.

Ralph said, "You'll know the ropes by tomorrow; ring me up and we'll try to have supper out."

"I can't tomorrow; I'm going home."

"Home?" said Ralph sharply. "Oh—the wedding. I'd forgotten that was so soon. It won't be a mad riot for you, Spud."

"Well, it's only one day in a lifetime, I suppose."

"Spud, is—anybody going with you?"

"Good God, no."

"Why, would you hate that?"

"I hadn't thought."

"I'll go with you if you like."

Laurie was a moment taking it in. Ralph said, more formally, "I mean, of course, if it wouldn't annoy your mother, your bringing a stranger along." Laurie remembered then that his social contacts must have been unconventional for a good many years.

"Good Lord, Mother would love it; you'd probably ruin the wedding for old Straike. But I think I'd better go on my own. You couldn't get away, anyhow."

"Oh, yes, I could work thirty-six hours." His voice dropped half a tone. "Would you like it, Spud?"

At that moment, someone in the corridor shut a door, or switched off a light, plunging them into almost total darkness.

Taking him unaware, the extinction of light filled Laurie with a deep and warm relief. He could see dimly the silhouette of Ralph's head, quite near, against a faint loom of light from the passage. Everything was going to be taken care of; there was no need to say anything. Then, as if he were waking from sleep, he knew why it was that he mustn't take Ralph with him.

Collecting himself, he searched among his old good reasons for excuse. "I don't think I ought to settle

284

down to being sorry for myself, taking people with me for moral support and so on. You'd hate it, too, the relatives are bound to be hell, especially his. I expect I'd better just take it straight. Sometimes things are easier if there isn't anyone to know how you're feeling." In a voice he tried to keep quite unchanged, he added, "Especially if it's something you ought not to feel."

There was a little silence. Laurie said to himself, It's just a state I'm in. It's just because of the wedding, and leaving Andrew, and being alone in this awful place. It needn't mean anything if I don't let it.

"Spuddy. You mustn't worry the way you do."

The voice was kind; but there was more than kindness in it. It struck the sounding-board of Laurie's loneliness and his will died. Ralph's arm was lying along the back of the pew, but he didn't move it. Laurie could just feel his shoulder and that was all.

"You mustn't get so upset about what you feel, Spud. No one's a hundred per cent consistent all the time. We might like to be. We can plan our lives along certain lines. But you know, there's no future in screwing down all the pressure valves and smashing in the gauge. You can do it for a bit and then something goes. Sometimes it gets so that the only thing is just to say, 'That's what I'd like to feel twenty-four hours a day; but, the hell with it, this is how I feel now.'"

Laurie didn't try to speak. In the pause they heard, half muffled by walls and distance, the thin crying of a child.

Ralph said softly, "Things can happen. It's not in the blueprint, perhaps. Perhaps it isn't for ever. But a person who knows you will understand that. No one's going to hold it against you afterwards."

"I know, Ralph. It's all right." What does that mean, he thought; it doesn't mean anything. He had known it was necessary to start talking. After a moment he said, "Ralph, I—I don't really want to go alone. But I think I ought to."

Ralph's voice didn't alter. He stayed just as he was. "Do, then, Spud, if that's how you feel. It wouldn't be good to make up your mind for you now." For a moment Laurie sensed a deep undeclared reserve of confidence, glanced at, considered in the light of experience, and returned to store. "If you feel like company you can ring me up. Ring this number." With sight better attuned than Laurie's to the darkness, he got out a pad and scribbled across it: Laurie wondered what more he had been able to see. He tore out the leaf and offered it. Their hands touched. Ralph said, "You mustn't worry any more, Spud. There's nothing difficult or complicated or anything. I'm there when you want me. That's all."

After a moment Laurie said, "Ralph, you're too good to people. I'm not worth your taking trouble over. Whatever happened, I never could be worth it."

"What a silly boy you are." He spoke as if someone were flirting with him at a party. Outlined in the doorway, Laurie saw him get to his feet. "I was forgetting, they have supper at some ungodly hour here, about a quarter to six. If you don't go now you'll miss it."

As Laurie got up he found he was levering himself on a pile of hymn books; some almost submerged tactile memory remarked, *Ancient and Modern,* not *Songs of Praise.*

As they parted at the ward door Ralph said, "You've not lost that telephone number, have you, Spud?"

"No," said Laurie. "It's here."

"Good. Don't worry. God bless."

He was just in time to catch the supper trolley. Going back to bed with his mug and plate, he found the boy Mervyn being fed by a nurse with a feeding-cup.

"Hello, Spud."

"Hello, son, feeling better?"

"Look. There's a navy officer in the door there, waving to you." As Laurie turned, Ralph gave a valedictory wave and smile and vanished. Mervyn said, "Who's he?"

"A friend I was at school with. He was at Dunkirk too."

"You don't mean," said Mervyn, "the captain off that ship?"

"Yes." He had quite forgotten the conversation. Now

286

he realized that Mervyn had experienced a miracle of adult integrity. He was gazing after Ralph as if Michael the Archangel had looked in. Well, thought Laurie, that's something anyway.

The rest of the evening he spent writing to Andrew. He had meant to talk about the wedding. But now the whole subject had become so entangled with things which couldn't be told that it confused him, and in the end he didn't dwell on it very much.

In the middle of the night he woke to hear whispers and movement behind the screens of the old man's bed. He knew what had happened, as soon as he saw that the blankets had been thrown on the floor. In the morning there was a flat empty bed, like Charlot's, neatly bisected by the center folds of sheet and counterpane.

He got up and went out some time before his train was due, so that he would have a chance to telephone Andrew before he went off duty. It was wonderful to hear his almost speechless pleasure at recognizing the voice; but considered strictly as a conversation, it was like waving handkerchiefs from a quarter-mile away. Ralph from long practice had always known how to extract humor from the fact that people were overhearing, while at the same time he conveyed with neatness and subtlety almost anything he wished. Laurie could hear Andrew's sense of inadequacy behind every word, and longed to make him feel easier. "I'm in a call box, I can say what I like; I expect you're standing in the middle of all the bathroom traffic, aren't you?"

"Yes, it's about peak hour. I wish——"

"I know. We'll work something out when I come back."

"I hope it won't be too bad. If I'd only thought, perhaps I could have got my night off then, instead, and gone with you."

There was a moment's pause. "I wouldn't have inflicted that on you. You must come up and meet Mother some other time."

"I expect your stepfather might think me rather a bad influence."

"Oh, yes, horrible. If he found Jesus Christ

preaching on the village green, he'd have him arrested for blasphemy inside five minutes."

"Laurie——"

"Sorry. Just a manner of speaking."

"It's not that—I wish I could see you before you go."

It wasn't till Laurie was sitting in the train that he remembered he had left no message for Reg.

He had not been home since his embarkation leave; and now, seeing from the gate the small, low house, its thick walls blunted at the edges and smoothed as if by the wear of giant hands, the fifty-year-old cedar floating its dark clouds over the lawn striped from the mower, it seemed impossible that change could touch it all, without or within. To gain this moment he had told his mother not to meet him, as she must be busy, but now it was spoilt for him because in his heart he was deeply hurt that she had taken him at his word. As a last charm to bring back the familiar, he gave the special whistle he used for his dog, and, standing behind the blue spruce at the gate, waited to see old Gyp come pottering stiffly out with his ears cocked. But it was his mother who heard and came out instead.

He had known it would sharpen his sense of loss to see her; but he had been unprepared for the bright defensive flutter, the silliness which came from self-consciousness and her unacknowledged sense of guilt toward him. She was determined to believe that he was losing nothing: it made her overinsistent, demanding of him in everything the role she had allotted him in advance to set her mind at rest.

The house was a last-minute chaos of clothes, luggage, and half-packed crates. He had expected this but hadn't guessed at the desolation. He had forgotten too to expect Aunt Olive, which was foolish; for she lived for others, and her status as the family drudge was guiltily recognized by all its members. She was always overthanked and underloved, having something unco' guid about her which led her always to do a little more than people wanted done. She was really only a cousin

288

of Mrs. Odell's. When Laurie went upstairs for a bath and a moment's quiet, he found her packing his room.

He had known he must do this before he went, but had reckoned on finding it still intact. It looked as if it had been ransacked by gangsters. The divan was stripped, the chair uncovered showing its ancient scars, the cupboard open and all its contents strewed on the floor. Aunt Olive sat beside a wooden tea-chest, surrounded by books which she appeared to be dusting. The *Oxford Book of French Verse* was in her hand, and she was carefully shaking out the pages.

Taking a grip on himself, he thanked her profusely and said that he would finish now, as she must be cold.

"Goodness, *I'm* never still long enough for that! Now you're here I can ask you the little things I wasn't sure about. Now for instance *here*, all these bits of paper and things I've found stuck in books, I thought you'd better see them before I threw them away."

He looked with horror at the heap beside her knees. Some were merely markers, but some were not. He said, "Oh, just burn them."

"No, I'd rather you *looked* first, one never really knows. Now what about this, for instance?"

She held up a bit of cardboard. Next moment he recognized it. It had been cut, not very expertly, from the center of a First Eleven cricket group. The cut had sliced through four out of the five heads in the square. Ralph's was the one in the middle. The picture had been taken a week before he left.

"Aha!" said Aunt Olive. "You see! Raves, *we* used to call them, but I'm sure *you* didn't use such sissy expressions! Now you must look at everything, or goodness knows what precious trophies might go up in smoke."

"I will in a minute. Please don't bother about it."

"Now don't forget. I know what you boys are, you *mean* well, till some other absorbing activity comes along! Now, *this*." She plunged into the mouth of the cupboard, and emerged waving a fencing foil.

Laurie relieved her of it. It was strange to feel it lie so easily in the hand, to feel the body remembering its

289

response as though, at the word, it would still obey as lightly as ever.

Hamlet had been the set play for School Certificate, so following custom the form had enacted it in the autumn term. Laurie had played Laertes. He had had, in those days, the kind of looks you would think of casting for Laertes rather than Horatio, for instance. The School Certificate Shakespeare play was an annual joke, but that year people said that at least the fencing bout had something. Treviss had coached it, and Lanyon had strolled in sometimes during practices to watch. Once Treviss had been sick and he had taken the practice himself. Laurie remembered now, how clearly, the sensation of seeing him walk in at the door instead of Treviss, and pull his jacket off. Once he had taken the foil from Hamlet to demonstrate something in the last passage, and there they were, as Laurie had phrased it to himself at the time, facing one another across the cold steel. After a pass or two Lanyon had broken off and said, "Come along, come along, Odell. You're supposed to know this foil's poisoned: for the Lord's sake fence as if you cared whether you get hit or not." Everyone said that when Lanyon went up to Cambridge he would be sure to fence for the University.

"You see," said Aunt Olive, "it's too long for a packing-case and so *awkward* for a truck. I was wondering what you'd like to do with it?"

"I can't imagine. What would you do with it if you were me?"

He saw her neck go pink between the wisps of hair. He knew he would despise himself later, so added unwillingly in a kinder voice, "Perhaps the scouts could use it in some of their shows."

"Yes, dear." She fidgeted a little, collecting herself. "That *is* a good idea. We must ask your father about it when he comes." She added archly, "Though perhaps we shouldn't say *that* until tomorrow."

After a short interval Laurie said, "I'm so sorry, but I was thinking of taking a bath." After she had gone clucking out, his first action was to throw off all his clothes, with some furious thought of confronting her if she tried to get in again.

Afterwards he flung the things from the cupboard back to see to later, and went through the papers. There was a note from Charles; notes had been one of his accomplishments. Laurie tore it across, and picked up the photograph again.

Even in the first embarrassed glance, he had been aware of making some discovery about it; and now he saw what it was. It had been taken at a moment when Ralph must have got bored by the preliminaries and started thinking of something else; the shutter had caught a moment of preoccupation, of some serious private thought. Now Laurie realized that in the first instant he had recognized in it not Ralph but Andrew. It wasn't really like him, but as a poor likeness it would almost have passed, except for the eyes. Once one began to think of it, one realized that the whole structure of the head was very similar, and the hair, though Ralph's was straighter, grew in much the same way from the brow. Without the picture Laurie would never have thought of it; Ralph had altered, he saw now, more than one supposed.

Staring at the portrait he thought how sometimes, when he looked at Andrew, he had felt glimmerings of a mysterious recognition. He had wondered sometimes, secretly, whether it was possible that they had met in a former life.

It was not till he was brushing his hair that he noticed the black hairpins on the dressing-table. Then he remembered that, since the little house had no spare room, Aunt Olive would be sleeping here tonight, and he on the living-room divan. He, in fact, had invaded her bedroom, not she his; you could say that she had won after all. He could think of nowhere to hide the photograph, so put it in his breast pocket.

There was a number of odd jobs still to be done about the place, and he was thankful for the occupation. Once or twice at odd moments he went into the garden to look for Gyp, but he hadn't come back. He was an independent dog and often went for miles by himself, ratting and rabbiting, though not so much in

291

the last few years since he had got rheumatic. Laurie thought to himself that when he went looking for digs, the first thing must be to make some arrangements for Gyp. His mother, though kindness itself, wasn't good with dogs and never trained him at all; and it would be just like Straike, Laurie thought, to expect the poor old thing to learn new rules like a puppy and crack down on him when he was slow and confused. Anyway, just for once, sleeping downstairs tonight one could have him in, even if he did smell a bit. He didn't fidget, or conduct violent flea-hunts in the small hours. He was so glad to be there, the thought of it seemed to last him all night.

It was just after tea, when Laurie had persuaded his mother to have one of her rare cigarettes, that, without knocking, Mr. Straike walked in.

Laurie hadn't believed it could happen. He knew they mustn't meet on the wedding morning, and his wishes, rather than his reason, had covered this evening with the same immunity. He sat fixed with his cigarette in his hand, without the wit to rise, for some instants; at once he sensed that this was just what Mr. Straike would have expected of his normal manners. He got up; but now his mother (having first put out her cigarette with a shy guilty look) had got up first, and Mr. Straike was kissing her warmly.

For a moment Laurie felt he was being subjected to an obscene outrage which would be recognized as such anywhere in the civilized world. He waited for his mother to protest and remind Mr. Straike that he was there. Then he saw Aunt Olive looking sentimental, and understood that it would go on happening, probably, for years, and that when it stopped he ought to be sorry.

His mother sat down with a pretty, flattered look; Mr. Straike, pressed, accepted tea. He then devoted himself for several minutes to Laurie, making himself emphatically pleasant. Laurie looked at the raw, red hand, close to his mother's on the table; it was like a rough thumb rubbing a wound. He felt that none of this was really addressed to him. He imagined Mr. Straike saying, "Observe how I am being nice to your

292

ill-mannered, sulky, and (I suspect) neurotic son. It is for your sake I am doing this so much against the grain. I trust it is appreciated."

"No doubt you're enjoying the, hrrm, relative lenities of civil hospital routine?"

"Well, they seem rather strong on discipline so far. After all they're the regulars, in a way."

"Ah, yes, I do seem to remember at the other place there were certain signs of improvisation." (The teacups, Laurie thought.) "In fact, I well recall saying to your mother in the train that if conchies *must* be employed to wait upon war casualties, possibly in the hope of arousing some vestigial sense of shame, they might at least be kept where they need not affront the eye, in suitable activities such as scrubbing latrines, and so on."

A bright spinning anger seemed to press outward against Laurie's temples and eyes. He felt light, as in the first stage of drink. He said coolly, "How did you guess? When I met my best friend he was doing that very thing."

Mr. Straike said, "Urhm," and decided not to see the point. "Then no doubt *his* reaction to their arrival was 'For this relief, much thanks.' " It was a tactical error; it gave the enemy time.

"Oh, well," said Laurie pleasantly, "we all reacted to their arrival, of course. But actually, we found persecuting Christians awfully overrated. Perhaps we needed lions or something. Perhaps we ought to have tried burning them alive. Perhaps we just needed to be civilians and not soldiers. I wouldn't know."

Mr. Straike wore his dog-collars large; but the creased red skin of his neck had become tinged with purple, and Laurie saw a large Adam's apple surface twice.

"Laurie, my *dear*."

He turned at the sound of her voice, suddenly shaken as if after physical violence. Anger might have toughened and braced him; but he saw something worse, a cloudy misgiving. He knew that by her own standards she was fully committed, and would be quite unequal in any case to the ordeal of escape; that if he urged it on her she would deny with conviction that any such thought had touched her mind. They sat looking at each other across the used tea things, gagged and helpless. Laurie got to his feet.

"I'm sorry," he said with difficulty. "We got to know these chaps and like them. I oughtn't to have been rude about it. Will you excuse me, Mother? I'll just go out and look for Gyp." As he got to the door he thought his mother called after him; but he pretended not to hear.

It was twilight. He walked up behind the house to the warren, needing his stick but thinking that if you were with a dog, a stick didn't show. He gave his special whistle and called, "Come on, boy, come on."

It was lonely and quiet on the warren, in the lee of the firs. The colonnades opened into deep tunnels of dusk, till over a rise he saw a lake of gold sky and a lace of birches.

> *Childe Maurice hunted the silver wood,*
> *He whistled and he sang,*
> *"I think I see the woman coming*
> *That I have lovéd lang."*

He had known *Childe Maurice* by heart for years. The tale of this young outlaw, the hidden love-child whom his stepfather murdered, taking him for the lover instead of the son, had always gripped Laurie's imagination. He had never wondered why.

He could not find Gyp, and the unfamiliar jerk of walking downhill made his leg ache. When he got back the blackout was up, and his mother waiting for him in the porch. As soon as they had looked at each other, he knew what it was she had to say.

"Mother. Where's Gyp?"

"Laurie darling. Oh, dear, I *am* sorry. It was dreadful of me not to have told you before."

He stared at her, stonily. Part of him refused it entirely; the rest said bitterly that she should have no help with this.

"Where is he? It's late. It's his dinnertime. Do you know where he is?"

294

"Darling." She had only looked at him for a moment. "Poor old dog. You know, he was . . ."

Laurie walked past her, through the hall to the corner under the turn of the stairs. The basket was gone. There was only a large crate labelled GLASS WITH CARE.

He turned around. "What did he die of? You didn't tell me he was sick."

His mother tucked in her lower lip, and he saw that she was beginning to have a sense of injury. "Dear, one doesn't write worrying letters to people in hospital."

"But Gyp was mine. He was my dog." Like a child he said helplessly, "He was a birthday present, he belonged to me."

"Dear, of course I know, but you've not been home for a long time" (Gyp must have noticed that too, Laurie thought), "and we had to do what we thought best."

"*We?*"

"Laurie," said his mother with grieved gentle dignity, "you're not trying to make me unhappy, are you?"

"He wasn't sick at all, was he? You had him put down." She didn't answer. "He was all right when I was here. You had him put down because that——" Carefully he said, "because that man didn't want to be bothered with him."

Now he knew that in his absence she had been reviewing the scene at the tea-table and protecting herself against its meaning. "Laurie, dear, I know you're upset, but that is a very unfair, unkind thing to say."

"I'm sorry. I shouldn't like to be unkind." He must have known, Laurie thought. Dogs always do. He must have wondered what it was he'd done.

"Laurie!" He must have been staring through her.

He said, "You would never have done this before. Did you decide he'd be better off that way?"

He saw her eyes, frightened behind their anger as she recognized what she had hidden from herself. "Mother——"

"Aha! So *there* you both are!" Aunt Olive came tripping out of the kitchen, a fall of fine pearl-gray trailing from her arm.

"Oh, Olive, dear, how good of you. Did it need

295

pressing again?" He saw that this intolerable interruption had come to her as a rescue.

"Mother, please could we——"

"Later, dear, not just now. Look at poor Olive doing everything by herself. Be a dear boy and just see if there's room in there for the air-twist glasses."

He got out the case from the recess under the stairs, remembering how he had trained Gyp to sleep there when he was three months old. The first night he had cried a good deal, but Laurie had known it wouldn't do to give in to him and fetch him upstairs. He had gone down himself, wrapped in his eiderdown, and Mrs. Timmings had found them both asleep there in the morning; but of course, he had only been at his prep school then.

Afterwards he made up the living-room divan for himself. Sometimes on cold nights he used to take off the mattress and put it by the fire, but nowadays it was firelight or ventilation. On his embarkation leave, he had looked around his room thinking he would probably never sleep there again; but he had guessed the wrong reason.

Soon after, his mother came in. He must be good to her, he thought, as if she were going into hospital with something worse than she knew. He found some sherry and they sat down to village gossip by the fire. It wasn't, he thought, an ill wind for everyone; for she would make a good vicar's wife if she were allowed to get on with it, unintrusive and kind. She was happy to find that he had stopped being difficult; they chatted quite gaily till, remembering something he had meant to ask before, he said, "By the way, Mother, what are you doing about the house?"

"Well, dear, really! You don't mean to say that you've not written to the Trevors *yet*? It's not fair, you know, to be unbusinesslike with friends, and they depend on it so much. As you didn't write back about it, I naturally assumed you'd no objection."

"Me? Whyever should they mind what I think?"

"Laurie! Didn't you *read* my letter? Surely you do know this house belongs to you now?"

As she spoke it began to come back to him. It had

been fifteen years ago, and he had forgotten with the deep forgetfulness which is not an accident. He had been just old enough to understand that it would be in the nature of things for him to outlive her; his grandfather's death had been a terrible reminder of her mortality. He had thrown his arms round her and said, "But you're not going to die or get married, so you'll have it for ever."

Now he didn't know what he felt. For the present it was an empty possession; even if war regulations had allowed him to keep it as a weekend place, he couldn't easily have used it with the vicarage a quarter-mile off. But it was something of his own, a fragment of the past that couldn't utterly be snatched away. No one could cut down the damson or the cedar. "I'll write straight away," he said when they had discussed the business. "I'm sorry I left it."

He was writing the letter when Aunt Olive, who had answered the telephone, snatched pencil and paper and began to take down a wire, her manner becoming tinged with gloomy importance.

"I'll read it you word for word." She cleared her throat. " 'Sharp attack last night doctor vetoes travel very sincere regrets and heartfelt wishes for your happiness Edward Lethbridge.' "

"Oh!" said Mrs. Odell. "Oh, *dear*. I was so afraid . . . I asked him if he really felt equal to it, but after what he said about Raymond . . . Besides——"

Laurie said, "I'm sorry he's ill." His wits moved slowly. Aunt Olive gave him a bright, nonreproachful look.

"Well, how lucky it is, isn't it, that you're here and able to step into the breach!"

Without quite looking at either of them, his mother said, "Of course I know it's *considered* correct, but perhaps . . ."

Yes, he had read that part of the letter. He remembered now why Great-Uncle Edward had been so important. As soon as he became capable of thought again, he realized that there was, in fact, nobody else now.

"Would you like me to give you away, Mother? Unless someone's coming who'd be better?"

"Who could be, darling? I know it's rather sudden for you; it's because we're such a small family. At least," she said, in the comfortable voice with which she had smoothed the minor crises of his schooldays, "you won't have to worry about clothes."

"I wish I could have put up a pip for you."

"Darling, everyone can see why it was you didn't have time for that."

Yes, he thought, of course. He tried to remember how long the aisle was. It was quite a big church. "It won't look too good. I mean I'm awkward to walk with, rather."

"I shan't find you awkward." She got up from her chair and kissed him. "We must let Mrs. Joyce know about Uncle Edward at once; she was putting him up."

"I'll go," he said; but it ended with the two women going together. The house was quite near, Mrs. Joyce buoyant and reassuring.

There was still the big cupboard in his room to be cleared for the Trevors. If he didn't do it tonight, he would have to come back to the empty house tomorrow. It could be dealt with quite simply by throwing everything away.

He got a dust-sheet and began tossing things into it. It was something of a massacre, for he had eliminated the rubbish when he joined the army, with the idea of sparing his mother a depressing job if he got killed; what was left had all had value for him as little as a year ago. When he came to the fencing foil again, he thought it wouldn't hurt to leave this in the bottom of the cupboard; it took up almost no room, and the Trevors wouldn't fuss. Then he remembered that out of all that was here, this was the thing he had least occasion to keep.

He was sitting awkwardly on the floor, doing the kind of job for which it is natural to kneel, or squat on the heels. Suddenly he felt run to a standstill under the accumulated weight of the day's wretchedness. He struggled to his feet, the foil still in his hand, its lightness coaxing his wrist and the heavy boot dragging at his foot. The guard rang dully as he let it fall.

Laertes, you but dally, I pray you pass with your best violence; I am afear'd you make a wanton of me. . . .

Laurie walked over to the window-seat. The curtains were gone, only the blackout stuff was left. He went and switched off the light. Now the night sky glimmered behind the damson-tree, and as his eyes cleared of dazzle, the stars appeared.

"You mustn't worry any more, Spud."

There would be frost soon on the pane. Laurie pressed his forehead to the icy glass and shut his eyes. He didn't know why memories which had lain with his mind's lumber for so many years, waking no more than a dim nostalgia, should return now to charge the present with so unbearable a weight of longing. On a stricken field littered with the abandoned trophies of his lifetime, he remembered a victory which had once seemed beyond the furthest reach of the most secret aspiration. But he only said to himself that he must have someone to talk to.

He put on the light and looked at his watch. His mother had only been gone fifteen minutes. Mrs. Joyce was a great gossip; half an hour would be the least.

He went down to the telephone, called Trunks, and waited. There might be a raid on somewhere, he thought, it might take an hour. He found he had got hold of a loose bit of trimming on the chair-arm and was pulling it off.

He had made it a personal call; he didn't want to hear voice after voice saying that Mr. Lanyon couldn't be found. There were women's voices outside, already, at the gate. But they were village voices, and passed on.

"Have they answered yet?"

"No. Will you try again, please, it's urgent."

"The line has been busy but I am trying to connect you." A bit of wire many miles off crackled and whispered.

"Hello, Spud."

Laurie's heart jerked violently, then steadied like a car settling into top gear.

"Hello, Ralph. How on earth did you know it would be me?"

"Never mind. Where are you speaking from?"

"Home."

"Well, Spud, how is it? Not madly gay?"

"Well, so-so. Everyone's out; back any minute, I expect."

"Spud, relax. Forget it's a telephone. We're on our own. Loosen up, and tell me about it. House packed up?"

"Yes; I've been doing my room."

"How long had you lived there?"

"About fourteen years."

"God. Oh, Spud, about the dog. If you want to bring him away, I think I can fix him up at the Station for a bit."

"Thanks. I expect he'd have liked it. He's been liquidated, only they forgot to tell me."

"What? What happened?"

"He was getting on a bit. I had him all the time I was at school. He was eleven."

"Spuddy. I'm very sorry."

"I'd rather have seen to it myself, that's all. You can give them sleeping pills first, then they don't know."

"What time is this wedding?"

"Two."

"Village church, I suppose?"

"Yes. It's his church. Great-Uncle Edward's had an attack, so he won't be coming."

"Oh? Your mother very upset?"

"Well, he was giving her away. It's a good job I'm here, isn't it?"

"*What?* Oh, no, Spud, nonsense. No, they can't make you do that."

"No one's actually making me. But it's hardly a job you can hand over to the churchwarden, when it comes to the point."

"Spud, why the hell didn't you let me come with you?"

"I can't think, now."

Almost as he spoke, he heard the sound of the front door shutting, and voices in the hall.

"Spud, can you hear me?"

"Sorry, here comes the family."

"All right, Spud. Don't worry, good night. I'll be seeing you."

Laurie started to say "I'll be back by——" But the line had died.

A few minutes later, he remembered the unfinished job upstairs. But it was almost suppertime. In the end he bundled everything back in the cupboard again. It would have to be tomorrow, after all. He hadn't meant to take the second night's leave if he could catch the four-forty; but if he missed it, it couldn't be helped.

At ten o'clock, Aunt Olive remarked on the busy day they had had; told Mrs. Odell that she *must* have an early night; then blushed a congested dark red and changed the conversation. After this Laurie and his mother sat up for another twenty minutes, painfully discussing family friends and the war news. Aunt Olive seemed anxious to leave them together; but they both clung to her company, which must have pleased her, Laurie thought.

Later, when he was ready for bed, he raked out the fire, and opened the blackout. The stars looked frosty; it was too early for the moon. It would have been cheerful to keep in the fire, pull up the mattress to it and read; but his mother would have been shocked to find no windows open, when she came down to say good night.

When he heard her, he got up from the bed where he had been sitting and moved out into the room. She walked straight on toward the bed and did not see him until he spoke.

"Not in bed yet, dear?" On any other night she would have said "I came to tuck you up," but tonight she didn't say it. She felt his dressing-gown and said, "This is so thin, darling, don't catch cold."

He put his arm around her waist and kissed her, trying to think of absolutely nothing. "God bless you, Mother dear. Be very happy."

"Laurie darling; you must . . . you *will* try to get on with him, won't you?"

"Yes. Of course."

301

"All these years, all the time you were little, I've thought of no one but you."

"I know, dearest. Of course, I know."

"You must never repeat this to anyone, but Colonel Ramsay asked me to marry him, when you were at school. But I didn't like the idea of giving you a stepfather when you were just at the difficult age. Now I'm not young any more; and next year, or the year after, when you want to get married, I should be all alone."

"Mother. I don't want to get married. If that's all, I . . . I don't think I'll ever want to. It's just something I feel. If you don't want to go through with it, I . . ."

"*Darling,* but of *course* I do! Whatever put such an idea into your head? At this stage, too."

"Sorry, dear. It's only that . . ."

"You must never say such a thing to me again, it's not kind, it's very silly indeed."

"I'm sorry. I didn't really mean it."

"I don't suppose you remember your father, now?"

"A bit here and there. Not very well."

"I wasn't unhappy with him, you know, till I found out how he was deceiving me. You know, dear, a woman gets, well, used to being married. I haven't told you, but sometimes I've been rather lonely."

Once she had come to see him in hospital, before the bone infection had gone down. He had been in great pain but hadn't wanted to tell her; he had lain watching the clock when she wasn't looking, and praying silently, "Go away. Please go away." He withdrew his arm, now, gently and as if by accident, and said, "Well, you be happy, dear, God knows you deserve it."

"I'll have your room all ready for you; all your things, and the books put out."

"I'll have to stay somewhere near a library, for a bit. You can't read much in hospital. Don't unpack the books yet, I might have to send for them."

"Don't stay away too long, darling." He felt that she had dreaded his early arrival in her heart, and was relieved.

He said, "There's going to be a frost tonight," hoping that she would go. He had used his leg a good deal, doing odd jobs and climbing the hill; even with the altered boot it had been too much.

"Laurie, darling. Don't go quite away from me."

There was space behind him, he could turn his back to the little light there was; he had been right not to stay in bed, trapped against the wall. "If ever you need me," he said, "ever, wherever I am."

"But, darling, I shall always need you, just the same as ever." He had made her doubts too articulate; she would escape from him now. "What am I doing," she cried, "keeping you up in the cold, just out of hospital? Good night, darling, we shall all be so busy tomorrow, try to sleep well. Good night."

The light from the door grew narrow behind her, turning to a strip, to a line, to a memory drawn on a slab of darkness. Now he could see that the faint glimmer they had been standing in came partly also from the stars.

In the old days, if one slept downstairs, after the house was quiet Gyp would get cautiously out of his basket, and one would hear his claws on the flags in the hall. He would put his nose to the crack under the door, and make a faint whistly snuffle till it was opened. For a big dog, he took up very little room.

Laurie fell asleep between two and three in the morning. The moon had risen by then, and frost was growing up the window-glass, opening pointed leaves and flowers to the light.

For the last hour he had tried to think of nothing, and in the end had almost succeeded. But nature abhors a vacuum, and it was impossible to empty the mind entirely. So at last he thought of what was next to nothing, the recollection of a dream, which tomorrow need not be remembered. A cold pool of moonlight trickled over to where he lay; but by then he was out of reach, his eyes pressed down on the pillow, and one arm thrown over it in a gesture which, even in the relaxation of sleep, looked abrupt and possessive.

In the morning, as soon as he was awake, it became increasingly like getting ready for a general inspection, except that he himself had been promoted to C.S.M.

Almost before he had time to brush himself down, his mother was being dressed by Aunt Olive and people were arriving. Relations whom he felt he had seen quite recently, and who seemed to him very little changed, exclaimed with wonder at not finding him still a school-boy. Others asked him if he was on leave. Suddenly they all began disappearing; in what seemed no time at all the house was empty even of Aunt Olive; there was only a stray caterer's man arguing with Mrs. Timmings, and then the car was at the door. Hurrying upstairs he nearly fell, recovered with his heart in his mouth, pre-cipitated himself into his mother's room after a per-functory knock, and came face to face with her in her wedding dress.

"How do I look, darling?"

"You look lovely. Everyone who doesn't know will think I'm your brother."

For a moment united as one, each was silently beg-ging the other, "Take it quickly, take it lightly, God forbid we should go through that again."

Softly and musically, the clock in the hall struck two. Time is, time was, time is past.

"We must go." She made a little movement toward her ivory-and-gold prayer-book.

"No," he said. "You have to keep him waiting."

Her hand in its pearl-gray glove, resting on his arm, looked small and naïvely formal, the hand of a Du Maurier child who has watched fans and trains from the top of the stairs.

". . . not by any to be enterprised, not taken in hand, unadvisedly, lightly, or wantonly . . ."

Laurie gazed at the line of little gray buttons that ran down the back of his mother's dress. He was glad, after all, that he had come, that circumstances had presented him with no excuse. She had needed him, a thing which in his hurt pride and abandonment he had forgotten to expect. He couldn't think, indeed, how she would have managed without him.

". . . and, forsaking all others, keep thee only to her, as long as ye both shall live?"

304

In a round, announcing voice, Mr. Straike said, "I will."

The full realization of his physical presence hit Laurie like a blow. He stared at the floor and reminded himself that he was in church. But church had become a smell of hassocks and furnace coke and, ubiquitously, of Mr. Straike. It was an extension of him.

"Wilt thou obey and serve him, love, honor, and . . ."

Oh, God, make her say no.

"I will."

He heard Aunt Olive behind him give a satisfied sigh.

"Who giveth this woman to be married to this man?"

"I do," Laurie said. Now that it had come he could feel nothing at all, except a proud determination to do it properly. He took a measured pace forward and handed his mother to Canon Rosslow to hand to Mr. Straike. He fell a pace back again. With a dry, empty relief, he realized that this was all. He had spoken his line; he could get back into the chorus. There was his place ready for him, beside Aunt Olive in the corner of the front pew. He moved toward it.

Aunt Olive put away her handkerchief, and seemed to cross an invisible threshold to festivity. The moment the psalm had started she nudged him and whispered, "Beautiful."

She had been very kind to his mother. He nodded sociably.

"You did *very* well, *most* correct and dignified."

He made a deprecating face, and applied himself to his prayer-book; but she was touching his arm.

"Just look *quickly,* dear, and tell me who——"

He looked quickly, being sure that she wouldn't let him alone till he did. It was a big church, and the bride's friends sat with plenty of elbow-room. The parishioners, with the modesty of country people, had left several empty pews in the middle. Laurie had no trouble in following Aunt Olive's eye to the stranger in the seventh row.

He was singing from the book, standing very straight and correctly, as if he were at ship's prayers, and not

305

looking about him. But he must have felt Laurie turn, for their eyes met at once. Ralph's narrowed in a brief smile, then returned to the page. Laurie became aware of Aunt Olive's expectancy; he whispered, "Friend of mine."

"*Very* nice," said Aunt Olive, nodding vigorously.

The psalm ended. Laurie, who would never pray on his knees again, leaned forward and covered his face.

". . . and forgive us our trespasses," muttered the congregation; a drowsy, absent-minded sound like the sound of scuffling feet. Laurie looked down through his fingers at a piece of oak smoothed by the hands of six generations, and, the terms of his self-deceit forgotten, thought, I ought not to have sent for him. He knew that he had refused to expect this result, only because that would permit him to make it certain.

Having accepted this knowledge, he allowed it almost at once to drift out of sight. There is much anodyne to a painful thought in mere lack of concentration. He said to himself, as far as he said anything plainly, that Ralph was here now, that it was more than kind of him to have come, that to be glad to see him was only common decency. Beyond this moment, the future was still free and undetermined.

Canon Rosslow had what is slanderously called the Oxford accent. He made the Homily sound like a piece of respectable cant. Laurie found it all slipping by him like Monday morning chapel at school. Everything he was capable of feeling about this event had been exhausted; he was empty, waiting only for something different to happen. He was, though he didn't know this, in the state which at funerals inspires the wake.

It was over. The bride and groom were on their way to the vestry. Remembering his duty, he got up and followed them.

He signed the register and kissed his mother. As if she were covered with an impalpable veil, he could feel only that he was kissing a bride. He saw Mr. Straike advancing and wondered for one dislocated minute whether he would expect to be kissed too. But all was well, Mr. Straike gave him a manly handclasp, two hands to Laurie's one. Soon they were all going back into the church again, and the organ was playing his mother and her husband down the aisle.

He knew he ought to follow, and did so at first; but the organist had set a good cracking pace, and Mr. Straike couldn't be expected to remember. The best man, though thirty years Laurie's senior, had a better turn of speed. People were coming out of the pews and he slid into the stream. He wasn't much held up by civilities, for everyone was hurrying to see the departure outside. Ralph was waiting for him just inside the pew.

"Ralph! How did you manage it?" Admitting the wish but not the expectation, he struck a compromise by which Ralph would not be hurt, nor he himself wholly committed; but he did not think of it like this.

The bridal couple vanished through the west door. Ralph looked him in the eyes and smiled. Someone was here now for whom he came first: it was like a well in the desert.

"Don't bother about me," Ralph said, "you've got people to see to out there. Get along and get on with it. I'll follow the crowd."

"It's only just down the road. I'll walk with you."

"Don't be silly," said Ralph briskly. "You've got to be there ahead; you're the host, he isn't. Get a move on, I'll see you presently."

There had been photographs outside for the county paper; so no one had missed him. When he walked into the village hall, he knew that his mother's new life had begun already. If she had been marrying anyone else, the reception would have been at the George. The boards felt gritty underfoot, there were notices about the Guides and the Mothers' Union. The venerable hired waiters looked like lay helpers at a Sunday-school tea. All this, of course, set the parochial note in which everything centered upon the vicar.

Some Straike relatives had arrived. They seemed to Laurie rather hard-eyed, the kind of people one envisages quarrelling over wills, and their overconventionality struck him as faintly vulgar. He stood close to his mother, observing how much bigger Mr. Straike's family was than theirs. Seeing Aunt Olive appear in a travelling coat (he remembered now that she had to get an early train) he decided she was a great deal nicer than any of them. He fussed over her and found her food. In the midst of all this Ralph walked in.

He must have waited till now when the bride and groom had ceased to receive at the door, hoping to be inconspicuous; but in a gathering where the younger element was mostly in the forties, his entrance had drawn eyes from all over the room. He looked around for Laurie and went over to him at once. With the tail of his eye, Laurie saw that Mr. Straike had noticed.

You would have thought that an introduction to Aunt Olive was the one thing Ralph had been hoping for. Laurie remembered suddenly a remark of Bunny's about Christmas in the orphanage; but he didn't want to think about Bunny any more.

It would be untrue to say that Aunt Olive had grown suddenly pretty, because women who employ no make-up miss it at such moments, and it inhibits them; but her self-esteem had climbed steeply. Suddenly she gave an arch little squeak of discovery and delight. "I know!" she cried. "I couldn't think *where* I'd seen you! Now I remember!"

Ralph's charming smile became just a little less casual. He said, as if he wanted to get in first, "I expect you saw me somewhere about the place at school." As he spoke, he looked around to see who was in earshot, but so unobtrusively that even Laurie only just noticed it.

"School!" cried Aunt Olive in triumph. "I *was* right!" This time no one interrupted her. She turned to Laurie. "Your mother always tells me what a memory for faces I have. *He's* the boy in the photograph!"

She must have taken the short silence that followed as a tribute to her gifts, for she smiled radiantly.

In the next few minutes, before she left, Laurie had time to think. It had been obvious to him from the first that Andrew couldn't have come here without the risk of being exposed to insult. It must, he thought, be a symptom of the way his generation had been torn from its roots, that he hadn't till now perceived the risk to Ralph.

The Head and the staff had tried, naturally, to hush his expulsion up. It was possible, though unlikely, that they even thought they had succeeded. The fact was, of course, that Hazell's hysterical confidences had made it the most resounding scandal in the history of the School. The sensation had been proportionate to Ralph's immense, and rather romantic, prestige; and it was a certainty that there hadn't been a single boy, down to the lowest and most friendless fag, who hadn't known at least something about it.

Although Laurie still felt very close to these events, it was in a purely inward and personal way. Externally, seven years was half a lifetime. He had grown in them from a boy to a man; he had met pain and fear, love and death; his comrades had been men for whom his old world had not at any time existed. Now, looking at the guests around him who had been adults longer than he had been alive, he saw that for most of them seven years must be only the other day. It was unlikely that Ralph hadn't thought of it. The people who are vulnerable to these things are less absent-minded about them.

When Aunt Olive had gone Ralph lifted one eyebrow, smiled at Laurie, and murmured, "Whew!"

"You've not had a drink yet." Laurie gave him one, and as they drank tried to thank him in a glance; but the glance didn't turn out exactly as he had meant. He said quickly, "Come along and meet my mother." As they went he saw, for the second time, Mr. Straike turning from his conversation with Canon Rosslow to eye Ralph with curiosity.

If you knew as much as Laurie had learned by now, you might perhaps get as far as a speculation about Ralph; but even then you wouldn't be sure. He had reviewed his own weaknesses early in life, and with untender determination trained them as one bends a tree; the resolution this had demanded had stamped his face with most of the lineaments of strength. The fastidious severity of his dress and carriage hid, no doubt, a personal vanity by no means extinct; but it had the air of a fine, unconscious arrogance. Laurie, as he walked beside him up the hall, was looking at Mr. Straike and thinking, He'd have liked to be the one who brought him here, to put me in my place. Too bad he belongs to me.

At the last moment, Laurie's mother was caught up by friends, and Mr. Straike came to meet them instead.

The next few minutes did Laurie a world of good. He discovered at once that Ralph hadn't lost the famous manner; perhaps if one had known him well one might have detected a crease or two and a whiff of moth-balls; but it was more than good enough for Mr. Straike. "By the greatest good luck we happened to run into each other at Dunkirk" (he made it sound rather cosmopolitan, like Shepheard's or the Long Bar at Shanghai), "so we were able to pick up the threads again."

"Now I think of it," said Mr. Straike suddenly, "I can't recall that I ever asked your mother the name of your House, Laurence. Very remiss of me."

"Stuart's," Laurie said. It had been Stuart's when he first went there.

"Stuart's, Stuart's. That has some association for me. Wait, I have it. That's the House that was taken over by a school contemporary of my own, dear old Mumps Jepson. Surely that would be within your time?"

"Yes. Mr. Jepson took it over when I was fairly senior, but you know how the old name sticks." Almost unconsciously, he had closed his shoulder up to Ralph's as if they were in battle.

"Ah, interesting. I wonder what impression he made on you. Poor old Mumps, he was something of a hypochondriac; I remember thinking he had scarcely the requisite—hrm—guts for the job. We've lost touch, I'm afraid. But I did meet him, at an Old Boys' Dinner, if I remember, a year or two after he took up his appointment; he was very full then of his trials and his responsibilities, very full indeed. Would it be in '33? It might even have been in '35." He looked at Ralph again. "I'm afraid I heard your name very imperfectly; Langham, did you say?"

There was a short and, for Laurie, terrifying pause. He didn't look at Mr. Straike because he had, in a sense, forgotten about him; and he did not look around because he dared not, for he had felt the finger of some past evasion touch Ralph and dim him, like a quick smudge.

"No," said Ralph. "It's Lanyon."

"M-m, no. I fancy it would be a little after your——"

"Laurie, darling." It was the measure of Laurie's feelings that he had been unaware of his mother's arrival. For the last ten minutes people had been assuring her of her happiness; she had had a glass of champagne; she was expanding like a rose in a warm room. "This *is* delightful. How *could* you not tell me that you'd asked *the* R. R. Lanyon to come? Were you keeping him as a surprise?"

"Yes," said Laurie, "as a matter of fact I was." He presented him.

"Well, my dear boy—because I shall never think of you as more than eighteen even when you're an admiral—you mustn't laugh at me, but, really, I can hardly believe you're true, it's like meeting a unicorn. Of course, I know it's all worlds away now to both of you, but to me it seems yesterday when Laurie used to bring home legends about you, just like my generation with the Prince of Wales."

"You must let him live it down," said Ralph, "after all this time."

"Hrm," said Mr. Straike. "Lucy, my dear . . ." Laurie realized that the healths were about to begin.

His response for the bride was one of the things that had kept him awake till the small hours. But now he had forgotten all about it, and came to it fresh, with a suddenly revived self-confidence. While the guests were still clapping, and his mother looking at him with pride, he was wondering already whether Ralph had thought it was all right.

Few men were there and no other young ones; he and Ralph were kept busy. For ten or fifteen minutes they scarcely met. There was probably no moment of this time when, if he had been asked where Ralph was, he couldn't have given the answer without looking. At last somebody broke a folding chair. With an air of conscientious helpfulness, Laurie went over to the corner where it was and tinkered about with it. Ralph

311

came up and steadied the chair for him, and they bent over the brown varnished wood with their backs to the room.

"This is what you're looking for." Ralph handed him a wing nut from the floor. Laurie couldn't answer. He had heard in Ralph's voice that secret overtone only half of which is created by the one who speaks, the other half by the one who listens, and which says in any language, "By and by all these people will have gone."

After a while, Laurie said, "This is a hell of a party for you to drive all this way for."

"I'm sorry about that just now, Spud. I only hope nothing serious comes of it."

"*You're* sorry?" Laurie looked up. There were still people fairly near; he only looked for a moment.

"I should have said it was Langham. What if he runs into Jeepers again before he forgets? You'll be the one to get the backwash."

"So I ought to be."

"No, I shouldn't have done it. It was just a rather tarty bit of exhibitionism, really."

Laurie looked at the nut in his hand and slid it unseeingly over the worn screw. "You know why you did it. Because I wanted you to."

When Ralph spoke again it was so quietly that no one else could have heard at all; but he only said, "Did you?"

Laurie fixed the nut to an unworn scrap of thread at the bottom, and heard the soft wood crunch faintly. Staring down at it, he said, "Yes."

"Laurence, my dear boy, if I may make a suggestion."

Laurie knew that in the moments of Mr. Straike's approach they had been silent; he clung to this certainty, and quite soon was able to look around.

Later, while he was perambulating with sausage rolls, it occurred to him to wonder why Mr. Straike called him Laurence with such determination, when he must long have known that no one else did so. He realized that in Mr. Straike's considered opinion Laurie was a sissy name, such as would be wished by a woman on a fatherless boy. He was being rechristened as a bracer. With this thought, he looked around for his mother, and couldn't find her. She had gone to change into her going-away things.

For a moment he thought of following her home, so that he could say goodbye to her alone. But if she had wanted it, he thought, she would have told him where she was going; and he oughtn't to leave the guests for so long. He gave up the idea, with a relief for which these reasons seemed enough. The house he had inherited was waiting for him. It wasn't fitting any longer that he should encounter her in it.

At the other side of the hall Ralph had stopped to talk to a girl. She was a Straike guest, a Wren in uniform. Looking at his face, Laurie could tell that he was talking service shop with a conventional garnish of sex which he had found to be expected. They both seemed to be enjoying it. For a moment Laurie felt sharply jealous; but almost at once the feeling became unreal, and he went on watching Ralph with a tolerance in which pleasure was barely concealed. The girl had become a shadowy figure to him, a demonstrator of something in which she had no rights.

He had a sudden memory, heightened and colored by his present emotions, of how at Alec's party he had watched Ralph standing in the crowd, and had felt his essential isolation. He had been like a solitary outpost standing fast in a rout. He had courage, the catalyst without which pride and truth cannot combine. Almost all the others had sold out truth for vanity; or, in the more fashionable phrase, they had flaming inferiority complexes. But Ralph had been willing to lay on his pride the burden of self-knowledge, and carry it with his shoulders straight. How has he managed all these years, thought Laurie; where has he gone, who has he talked to? But now voices at the door were telling his mother how charming she looked, and almost at once someone was crying, "The car's here!"

The grape-purple feather on the little hat tickled Laurie's cheek, he smelt the fragile bloom of powder and violets; then she seemed carried away from him as if he had been trying to hold her against a river flowing

313

strongly to sea. Voices laughed and called, the noise of the rapids; the car vanished, swirled away around the bend of the stream.

He had a feeling, not of grief, but of absolute full stop and aimlessness. He turned, and Ralph was beside him.

For a moment so short that it was over almost as their eyes met, Ralph looked at him with great tenderness, understanding, and reassurance; then said with cheerful conventionality, "Come over here and talk to Babs Whitely, she says you don't know each other yet."

He steered Laurie over to the girl and plunged him into the thick of a conversation. She was amusing, full of little party tricks which repetition might make tiresome, but which were diverting the first time. They all had some more champagne. They were the only people there under thirty, and all in uniform; unconsciously they reacted to their elders' reflected image of them, young, brave, and gay. Ralph had taken Babs's measure quickly; she was unexacting in spite of her façade, with that display of bawdiness on safe occasions often found in women who are not highly sexed, but long to be taken for rakes. As the champagne took effect one could see that she was very good-natured, and liked men, as some people say of dogs, in their place. Laurie reflected that if it hadn't been for Ralph he would have run away from her.

When she left them, in a cloud of warm nebulous resolves to meet again, the party was breaking up at the edges, though a hard clinging core remained. As they returned to their duties, Laurie said, in one of those flashes of high illumination which champagne produces, "Ralph, you're much more briefed up on all this than I am. You've been at a wedding before."

"Well," said Ralph calmly, "I've been a best man four times in various parts of the world. It's previous experience they seem to go for, before good references."

"How long do people usually go on staying?"

"It depends. All night in some places." Laurie gazed at him blankly, then saw the smile under his lashes. There was a brief and rather breathless pause. "Don't you know when the mainline trains go?" said Ralph lightly. "That should give you a clue."

In fact, the London contingent was moving already; the party for the down train would have to go in half an hour. It would be a decisive exodus; the rest who had come by car would hardly outstay it. He told Ralph all this, explaining it carefully. At the end Ralph, who had listened with a kind but searching look, said, "Spuddy. What have you had to eat today?"

"Oh, breakfast and everything."

"Yes, but what did you actually eat?"

When it was put in this way, Laurie wasn't sure. Ralph said, "Well, come and eat now, you're getting tight."

He had been feeling a little strange, but light and clear, not like a recognizable phase of drink. As they stood by the deserted buffet Ralph said, "How's the leg holding out?"

"Oh, it's fine."

"Tell me if you want to rest and I'll fix it."

"There's nothing you can't fix, is there?"

"It's time someone started to look after you."

"Is it?" He felt subtle and rarefied. He looked up.

"Spud," said Ralph softly, "you're drunk. Be careful."

They held one another's eyes for a moment, not having meant to.

Perhaps it was only instinct that made Laurie look around, perhaps it was a movement on the edge of his visual field. At the far end of the buffet, one of the decrepit waiters had appeared. Laurie's gaze travelled out from Ralph's face to meet a cold, flat, withdrawing eye, glaucous and sunken, the eye of yesterday's fish rejected by this morning's buyers, wrinkling on the slab. The face could still be read, as it were, between the lines; faint traces were left in it of a mincing, petulant kind of good looks. The glance, so quickly caught away, lingered on like a smell; it had been a glance of classification. Laurie sensed, without comprehending, the dull application of unspeakable terms of reference; the motiveless calculation proceeding, a broken

315

mechanism jogged on its dump by a passing foot. His eyes, flinching away, met Ralph's retreating too.

There was a moment's uncertain pause; then Laurie moved nearer to Ralph, as he had with Mr. Straike. They had a very small island to defend, he thought, a very isolated position.

Going back into circulation, he met people's good intentions as well as he could. A bride was by definition happy, a stepson not; the balance of proper sentiment was, as he had already found out, too much for most of them. Usually they asked him what he was going to do, in the evident hope that he would produce some fortunate prospect, which would relieve them at once of their concern. Just as it seemed that all this would go on forever, the train party moved off, drawing the lesser bodies cometlike in its tail. He and Ralph were left alone with the gritty wooden hall, the broken meats, the head waiter bowing over the tip, and two spare magnums of champagne. He gave one to the waiters, and they went out and put the other in the car.

It was a soft, damp evening, smelling of black rotten leaves and wood smoke. As they got out at the gate, the scent of the cedar came to meet them. They had hardly spoken, except when Laurie showed Ralph the way.

Leaving the lit hall, it had seemed quite dark outside; but now the clouds had opened, and dusk was discovered looking its last from the depths of the sky. You could see the yellow bronze of the lichen on the roof, the iron lace of the porch threaded with the winter thorns of the roses. Along a crack in the blackout a pulse of firelight was beating. The cedar stretched its great dark hands in the gesture of a wizard commanding sleep.

Ralph said, "So this is your house."

"Yes. It's been mine for four hours, now. . . . It looks different."

Ralph stood looking in silence, and then said quietly, "It couldn't be different."

They went up the path together, not speaking till Ralph said, "You'll keep this place?"

"If I can."

"You must. It goes with you. It would be bad luck to sell it."

Laurie turned, under the black floating planes of the cedar. "Do you believe in luck?"

"I'm a sailor," Ralph said.

Laurie knew he must have slept, because the fire was dying. Once or twice they had dozed before, but not for long; they had opened their eyes at the dry fall of the settling embers, and thrown into the last flames a handful of fir cones, or some of the sawn spruce trimmings from the stack. Now, under a delicate husk of ash, one drowsy red eye was left which only the dark made visible. He lay for a while sleepily staring into it. It was growing cold, but he was warm enough; and it seemed that if he didn't move, time would stop also and nothing else need ever exist but this. But sleep ebbed away from him, as little to be commanded as the tide, and he felt how the bright fire, burning so long in a closed room, had drunk up the air. He rolled softly off the edge of the mattress onto the hearth rug, got up, and opened the blackout of the nearest window. Swinging the casement back, he tasted the quick air of the night that moves toward daybreak, piercingly cold and sweet. Everything was drowned in that remote, secret, and solitary moonlight which, rising late on a world already empty, will not set but be extinguished by the dawn. The moon would linger, a pale spent wafer, in the blue morning sky.

To Laurie's eyes, sensitized by almost perfect darkness, the room behind him seemed now to be only in twilight, patched with white shafts almost as clear as day. In one of these Ralph was lying face upward, his fair hair falling back from his forehead, his arm relaxed and empty. He looked marmoreally calm, as if he had died with his mind at rest.

Stealthily the cold silent night slid around Laurie its noose of solitude. But it was only he who was alone. Ralph lay quiet with the image he had created, the beloved and desired, for whom nothing was good enough, of whom nothing was demanded but to trust and receive.

It can be good to be given what you want; it can be better, in the end, never to have it proved to you that this was what you wanted. But Laurie was unhappy with this thought and pushed it away, for Ralph had been very kind to him. He looked at the upturned face and saw how in sleep it did not sag, but held its strength in a kind of innocent pride. He had asked for nothing, except to give everything. He had made no claims. He had offered all he had, as simply as a cigarette or a drink, for a palliative of present pain. He had been single-hearted; and he slept in peace. It was only Laurie who was awake.

He hadn't been asked to take any responsibility. He need not accept the knowledge that he had moved to this with instinctive purpose, as animals move toward water over miles of bush. It seemed to him now that he had exploited even the loss of his mother to get, without taking the blame for it, what he must long have been desiring. If his wishes had not been fulfilled with such experienced intuition, he need never, perhaps, have been certain what they were. Now he knew, and must go on knowing.

But that was only the part that concerned himself.

His hunger for compensation, once indulged, had driven him to the insistent egoism of an unwanted child demanding reassurance. Not satisfied with the sufficient evidence of his senses, he had longed to prove that he wasn't receiving only kindness; he needed the affirmation of power. At some stage of a broken midnight conversation, he had said, "I've often had a feeling that there's nowhere I really belong." He had hardly known himself what he wanted; but Ralph had said, without a moment's hesitation, "You belong with me. As long as we're both alive, this will always be your place before anyone else's. That's a promise." His voice had been free of emotion, almost businesslike. He might have been speaking to his lawyer about his will.

For a moment, it had sobered Laurie into self-knowledge; conquest is intoxicating, but a gift makes you think. Ralph had been concerned to notice him thinking, so early in the night, with the empty room upstairs. It hadn't taken Ralph long to put a stop to that.

318

He had considerable skill and experience, and his heart was in it.

Now he slept in the deep peace of valor and sacrifice; and Laurie, only half understanding the reproaches of his own nature, thought gropingly: I wanted someone to follow, I wanted him to be brave. But he wants to be brave for me too; and no one can do that.

Facing at last, in the lunar stillness, the thought he had been so long in flight from, he knew that Andrew wouldn't have tried to do it. Andrew was the only one who hadn't believed that one could be rescued from all one's troubles by being taken out of oneself. He had a certain natural instinct for the hard logic of love.

Outside, in the bleaching lye of the moonlight, washed of their distracting colors, the shapes of things burned in archetypal truth. Laurie stood casting his long shadow on the room behind him, silent in a grief and wonder too deep for tears, that life was so divided and irreconcilable, and the good so implacably the enemy of the best.

He felt that his body had grown bitterly cold, and wondered how he had ignored its protests for so long. Returning by the track of the moonlight, he lay down again. Ralph had turned on his side, his closed eyes still smoothed by sleep. Turned by the light to the color of some pale palladian metal, the fair hair, which Laurie had seen for so long only in order and discipline, lay tumbled like a boy's. A secret thrill of triumph, none the less strong for being mixed with gentler things, drew Laurie irresistibly; he reached out stealthily and touched it. When he moved away, Ralph's eyes had opened. They were smiling, and with fear Laurie saw in how deep a happiness, too silent and too deep, eating like rust the core of his defenses.

From some great distance, thin and archaic and perilous, the first cock-crow sounded.

13

IN the morning, before they left, they packed Laurie's room together.

It had been Ralph who had awakened in time, alert and resourceful, and while Laurie was still dizzy with sleep had stage-managed the house to look as if he had slept upstairs. He had straightened the living room and removed the champagne glasses and the rest of the debris, and made tea and waked Laurie with it and asked him how soon he was expecting the woman to come and clean. Now they were packing the things from the cupboard; or, rather, Ralph had organized by rapid stages a system under which he packed, while Laurie only sorted things and gave directions. The cupboard was emptying, the trunk nearly full. Ralph broke off what he was saying in a convulsive yawn; in sudden catlike relaxation he lay back on the carpet where he had been sitting, stretched, folded his arms behind his head, and looked up at Laurie, smiling.

"You've done all the work," Laurie said.

Ralph made a little movement of the head as if to shake it wouldn't be worth the trouble, and went on looking at Laurie under his lashes, a long contented reminiscent look, not demanding an answer.

Because he had brought no spare white shirt he was working in an old flannel one of Laurie's, with the neck open and sleeves rolled. Laurie had got into mufti too, partly for the sake of the few hours' comfort and partly from vanity. He was surprised to discover how much he felt the difference. The fact was that their service conditioning had kept the rank-badges on their uniforms somewhere under the surface of their consciousness; it had echoed the old difference of age which, significant in the teens, can become almost meaningless in the twenties. Reflecting on this, Laurie supposed it was because that was what both of them had really wanted.

Lying there relaxed and dishevelled, with his cloudy

unguarded smile, Ralph seemed to him suddenly for the first time as young as himself. Through the open shirt showed a spearhead of tan which, more than a year after he had last worn tropical whites, was still burned into his fair skin. Laurie thought again that he was built like the hero of a boy's adventure story: strong-looking, but not with the set look of a man's strength; the hollows over the collar-bones and in the pit of the throat had still the softened edges of youth. One could imagine him, Laurie thought, stripped to the waist in all the classic situations, fishing in lagoons or pinioned bravely defiant to a tree. He longed to give him something, to help him with something, to be depended on for a moment. Just then, without moving, Ralph said, "Are you thinking about me?"

"Yes," said Laurie with affection. "I was thinking you look like Jack in *The Coral Island*. There was a picture of him sticking an oar in a shark's mouth."

Ralph appeared to wake up. "He'd be taking a chance if it was a fair-sized shark. It would probably bite it straight through. The teeth work like a double saw; I've seen a man's leg taken off above the knee, snap, like that."

As his mind had moved back to the memory his face had changed; he looked not like the boy in the frontispiece, but like a competent ship's officer describing an unpleasant fatality, no more exotic than a street accident, which has put him in mind of a certain harbor, of this man or that. Laurie felt young and amateurish again. His own spell of action had been so brief, before the tide of retreat swept back his unit to the beach and the ships, that now, as if he had had some control over these events, he felt he had set out to prove himself, only to come to grief and be igominiously rescued. Ralph was saying, ". . . but the deep-water channel at Mombasa's the worst, they breed around there."

He stretched again, lazy, easy, and confident. His left arm was flung out across the carpet and his mutilated hand, uncovered, lay as idly as he would have let it if it had been whole. Laurie had never seen him quite forget it before. When the glove was off he used often to maneuver it out of sight when he thought the movement wouldn't be noticed; and when he didn't, you could feel him preventing himself by an act of will. There was something trustful and touching in this undefended surrender of it; it gave Laurie, for the moment, what he felt to be the most solid happiness he had known among so much contradictory emotion.

Ralph meanwhile had sunk back into his reverie, resuming thoughts to which the sharks had been a pedestrian interruption. Now, as if suddenly he felt himself too highly charged with happiness to bear it in silence, he took a deep breath and said, "Spuddy!" making a statement of it, than which no more needs to be said.

"Hello, Ralph," said Laurie, smiling back. But soon afterwards he moved away and found himself work among the litter that was left. He felt that overanxiety which hides an unconfessed resistance and sometimes brings about the thing it fears; watching Ralph working again, and using the hand with its taut one-finger grip, he felt for the first time that it could get on his nerves.

Ralph had found the fencing foil, now as always the awkward object left over till the end. He got to his feet with it in a pliant spring, balanced it for an instant to feel the length and weight, and flicked it in a quick pass. Laurie saw and remembered how his wrist and forearm looked like an extension of the steel. He glanced at the hacked guard, and suddenly said, "This must be the one you used in *Hamlet,* isn't it?"

"Yes. I never thought you'd remember that."

"You didn't?"

"I was a rotten Laertes, anyway."

Ralph smiled to himself. "Well, I wouldn't exactly say you were a *good* Laertes. You were a very nice Laertes, though. 'It was never like this at Sandhurst, what have I done to get mixed up with this awful crowd?'"

"Was I really like that?"

"I suspected not. That was the secret of its charm."

"You're making half this up."

"But you know," said Ralph, dropping the foil, "there was one moment, just at the end, when you were dying. Quite suddenly it had something. I remember it

322

still. I was sitting in the second row, or was it the third, anyway quite near. 'Exchange forgiveness with me, noble Hamlet.' I don't know, it just seemed to get me. I knew then why I was such a bastard to you that time I came down to coach the duel, when Hugh was in the sicker."

Impulsively Laurie said, "You wouldn't like it, would you?" He picked up the foil by the blade and offered Ralph the hilt.

"Thank you, Spuddy. I should love it." He received it with affection, but, instinctively, in a trained and expert grip. As the blade left Laurie's hand, of a sudden it all smote him with a ruinous significance; he felt in his own gesture the ancient symbol of the surrendered sword. His nature had suffered a self-discovery, a swing off its old center of balance, stranger to him and less foreseen than he had allowed Ralph to know. For a moment an instinctive hostility must have shown in his eyes.

Ralph tossed the foil away, and said quickly, "Spud!"

"What's up?" said Laurie smiling. "It's all right." He was glad that Ralph had read in his face only the passing envy of a cripple for a man who can fence.

Ralph said, "We've about finished here. I wish I could have seen this room with your things in it."

Laurie started to tell him how it used to look; but in the middle he was overtaken by a longing to compensate Ralph for what he felt as a latent treachery, mixed with a simpler and more direct emotion. He said, "Sit in that chair for a moment, will you?"

Ralph dropped into it and said, "Well? What for?" Sliding along the floor to the place beside him, Laurie said, "Only because that's where you always used to sit."

After a pause Ralph said in a stilled listening voice, "Is that the truth?"

"Yes. But not the whole truth." He threw his arm across Ralph's knees.

For what seemed a long time, perhaps several minutes, they sat in silence. He could feel Ralph touching his hair with that intuitive pleasantness which, it seemed, couldn't go wrong. The desire to be needed was basic in his make-up; it had developed in him a high degree of accomplishment and tact. He had, thought Laurie, the power good advertising is supposed to have of creating demands which had not been aware of themselves before. But when he spoke Laurie realized that all this had been absent and instinctive while his mind was elsewhere. "This room, the one I've moved to, I've only taken it for a month."

"You didn't tell me you'd moved."

"I travel light, you know, it doesn't take me long. It's full of velvet curtains and Turkey carpets and stuffy junk, but it's got a telephone, that's why I took it. It's just somewhere to be while we look around. What do you give it till you're out—about a month?"

"They haven't told me anything. I haven't a clue."

It was true, but he knew he would have said it, anyway. The first note of organization had given him a feeling of constriction, almost of panic.

"Never mind," Ralph said. "I'll go ahead, anyhow. If I find something soon, it will give us all the longer to fix up and get comfortable. You know, this trunk we're packing will go on the car easily, and I expect we can get in some more, I'll look in a minute. I can store it all at the Station, there's a . . ." His voice ran on, effortlessly efficient, disposing of everything. Laurie realized that in another few minutes he would want to start loading the car.

"But, Ralph, I'll be going up to Oxford in a few weeks. You'd be stuck with a flat for more than six months of the year."

"Oh, no, we can let a room to someone at the local university in term-time, if we need to. I've got everything taped."

Laurie realized that in every way he had bought this.

Ralph scratched up softly the short hair at the nape of his neck, causing an involuntary shiver like a stroked cat's. "Spud," he said gently, "are you worrying again?"

Laurie looked up, helplessly aware that he was leaving this for Ralph to cope with as he had, it seemed, left everything else.

"Surely, Spud, you didn't think I was going to be

324

difficult, did you? I mean, that was the understanding I came in on. I wouldn't double-cross you like that."

Laurie waited, feeling sure that this must be quite simple and that he had been stupid not to have followed it.

"If you want to see this boy when he's got a free day that's fair enough; you don't have to tell me about it. Unless you need someone to talk to. I can take it either way; for me it's worth it. Nothing to worry about there, is there?"

All Laurie could find to say was, "Ralph, do you mind if I think a minute?"

"What for?" Ralph's fingers moved, producing the shiver again.

What for, indeed, Laurie wondered. They had stepped across a narrow frontier and had become strangers speaking different tongues.

"I suppose," he said, feeling like a man making signs across some valley too wide for the voice to cross, "I suppose I love both of you too much. It would pull me in half. I couldn't live that way. And if I could myself, I couldn't do it to him."

Ralph had drawn his brows together. He looked, not resentful, but as if he felt some physical pain which mustn't be allowed to confuse his mind. "But you're living that way now, and it's been all right. And with things as they are, I can't see how he's losing anything."

Laurie began to look up; but his eyes came first to the torn left hand on the chair-arm, and it was as if Ralph had been speaking of something like that when he had said "I can't see." Seven years was a long time, after all, and something had gone.

Everything he had promised, he would not fail faithfully to perform. It would cost him something; he knew that he would suffer; but he wasn't accustomed to give up his aims out of a fear of being hurt, and, in any case, he would remind himself that it wouldn't be for long. Laurie realized now that, from the moment when Ralph had learned that this was a love without physical bond, he had thought of it as something not quite real. As far as he believed in it at all, he thought of Laurie

325

with compassion, as the victim of an infatuation whose object couldn't or wouldn't return it, who must endure the sickness till it could be cured by time and by a more generous lover. He was touched by it, as a grown man is by the pains of calf-love. Laurie remembered how he always said "this boy," on a certain inflection, faintly indulgent; it would have been patronage in someone a little less kind. As far as he was concerned, Andrew was someone by whom Laurie had been refused. If one had tried to make him see such a relationship as a bond of mutual love with valid claims, that would be too much, he would feel, for anyone to swallow; it would seem to him the reduction to absurdity of romantic daydreams, something not far removed from autoerotic fantasy, which he would probably have called morbid outright in someone he didn't love.

None the less, having been once convinced that Laurie felt like this, he would be quixotically generous; yes, even on the rare occasions when he believed in a rival made of flesh and blood. It would appeal to his honor to keep the compact, to his pride to behave at such times especially well, to his instinct for sacrifice to console Laurie undemandingly, without letting his feelings appear. But most of the time, Laurie thought, he would be like a man who without interference allows his wife to practice some obscure religion he doesn't believe in, because they were married on that understanding. Laurie had a sudden impossible vision of Ralph packing him off efficiently to see Andrew, looking up his trains, lending him a raincoat, reminding him not to walk about and strain his knee, and, when he got home, laying on some special supper to cheer him up.

With the steady confidence of someone nursing a fever which under the right treatment is running its normal course, Ralph would wait for the symptoms to subside. For he had not only courage, but the faith that moves mountains; and, besides, possession is nine points of the law.

"You know," he was saying now, "it's funny, when I saw you at Dunkirk your hair still seemed quite red, but it was only because your face was so white. It's gone like a horse chestnut when you find it in your pocket next year. Conker color."

"Do you mind?"

"Spud: it half kills me to see you making yourself unhappy like this. It doesn't make sense even, not now. Why do you do it?"

"But, you see, it's . . . well, apart from anything else, what would I tell him? People don't meet without talking about what they're doing and where they're living, and how they like it, and things like that. I couldn't talk to him for hours knowing that he was telling me the truth and I was just stringing him along with lies."

"But how much of the truth have you ever been able to tell him?"

"That's not the same."

"Why tell him lies, at that? You can say you're sharing a flat with me. Or do you suspect him of knowing more about these things than he makes out?"

"It isn't that. It's . . . well, I should be different. He'd feel at once that something was wrong."

"Wrong?" From his control Laurie knew that this had suddenly and deeply hurt him. "You didn't behave last night as if you thought it was wrong."

"Not wrong like that. Wrong between him and me."

"You half meant the other, though."

"No, I swear not. There's another thing too. He'd know we were great friends, at least, and he might get the idea that I'd passed him up because he's a c.o.; he thinks already that at heart I'd rather have someone who'd fought."

"Surely not. Who'd be that unreasonable?"

Laurie looked at his face. He understood the effort Ralph must have been making all this time, not to betray the truth which had at last slipped out.

"You despise him, don't you?"

After a pause Ralph said, "Oh, I believe he's sincere. I'd back you to spot a phony quicker than most."

"He has the guts all right. Only he thinks that's a side-issue, because what really matters is whether he's right or wrong. I couldn't bear him to think I was ratting on him."

"But," said Ralph, "he *is* wrong, so then what?"

327

There was a silence. He said in a different voice, "You don't feel any doubt on that point, do you?"

"Yes. When I'm with him, sometimes I do."

"Really, Spud," said Ralph quietly. "At a time like this."

He spoke as one rebukes a child who is old enough to see with what dangerous irresponsibility he has been behaving. He had talked often about the war, never about the feelings he had brought to it. Laurie had supposed that his bitterness at his forced inaction had been chiefly for the waste of his own powers. Now, looking at his face, one could see that this wasn't so; and there was nothing more to say.

"You see, Spuddy, my dear," said Ralph, speaking with great kindness and with care that Laurie shouldn't be hurt, "you have a very sweet nature, really, and you let it ride you a bit sometimes. You say this boy has guts, but what you're trying to do for him is to keep him like a mid-Victorian virgin in a world of illusion where he doesn't know he's alive. He mustn't be told he's a passenger when human decency's fighting for survival, in case it upsets his religion. He mustn't be told he's a queer, in case he has to do a bit of hard thinking and make up his mind. He mustn't know you're in love with him, in case he feels he can't go on having his cake and eating it. If he amounts to anything, he won't really want to be let off being human. And if he does want it, then he isn't worth all this, Spud. I'm sorry, but there it is."

"But——" As soon as he started he knew it was no good. He could have said that Andrew was essentially more realistic and less sentimental than Ralph himself. He wanted so say, "But he does know that I love him, and I know he loves me." But as soon as his mind formed words around these things, he saw that they could only hurt Ralph for nothing without enlightening him at all. "It isn't quite like that. I mean, Christianity on weekdays isn't really such a soft option. I believe enough in him to feel I'd like to help him be what he wants to be. Not hinder, anyway."

"Anyone can see that you weren't brought up in a Christian home."

Ralph's face had altered. It looked impenetrable, and no longer even kind. He had taken his hand away and had begun to tap Morse on the arm of the chair.

Laurie paid scant attention to the actual words. He had heard behind them the voice of an unknown boy who wasn't Jack in *The Coral Island*. As if it were possible to reach into the past, he took hold of the restless hand that was tapping the chair-arm and said, "I don't think that's how it was meant to be."

"Well, anyway, that's how it comes. The pagans did recognize our existence, at least. They even allowed us a few standards and a bit of human dignity, just like real people."

He was silent for a moment, frowning; but it was in concentration more than anger, for the hardness had gone from his eyes. Looking out across Laurie's head he said slowly, as if the words were being salvaged from deep water, " 'If a city or an army could be made up only of lovers and their beloved, it would excel all others. For they would refrain from everything shameful, rivalling one another in honor; and men like these, fighting at each other's side, might well conquer the world. For the lover would rather be seen by anyone than by his beloved, flying or throwing away his arms; rather he would be ready a thousand times to die.' "

Laurie couldn't say anything. He had neither the power nor the wish to hide what he felt.

"It's only since it's been made impossible that it's been made so damned easy. It's got like prohibition, with the bums and crooks making fortunes out of hooch, everyone who might have had a palate losing it, nobody caring how you hold your liquor, you've been smart enough if you get it at all. You can't make good wine in a bathtub in the cellar, you need sun and rain and fresh air, you need a pride in the job you can tell the world about. Only you can live without drink if you have to, but you can't live without love."

Laurie said, "I know," and then a little later, "Ralph, I've got to be alone for a bit, after I get back, and make up my mind about things."

"Why? You'll only get all tensed up again like you were before. I know what you're like without me there; you'll get into this morbid state when you think if you want something, then you shouldn't have it."

"No; I've got to find out what it is I really want. You said something once, it was at Sandy's party; you said it isn't what you are, it's what you do with it."

"At a party? Christ, I must have been stinking."

"And just now in a different way you said it again. And it's true, of course, and that's how it is. I know what I am and I've got to think what to do with it. You're not angry, are you?"

"No," said Ralph quite quietly. "I'm not angry. But don't be gone too long."

Laurie knew, from a closeness that already seemed inevitable, what it was that he was resolving not to say.

"I won't see Andrew again either, until I've decided something; that's only fair."

"Do what you feel, Spud. I wouldn't have asked you, you know that."

"No, I promise I won't." As soon as it was out of his mouth he knew he had been wrong. The feeling of justice had been an illusion, he had felt only the emotion of tenderness for Ralph's pain, and a sentiment, strong but confused, born of all they had shared together, which had made him yield easily to a boyish sense of fair play and had blunted his adult perceptions. There was no real parallel between seeing Ralph and seeing Andrew; for Andrew's cause was more than his own cause, and if he argued it, it would only be by the fact of being himself.

But it was done now; and as they were changing and collecting their things to leave, he felt that he wouldn't recall his promise if he could. He couldn't have borne to deliver Ralph so coolly to the pains of jealousy: at least he could be saved the tension and bitterness of feeling that everything was being won back from him in his absence by someone on the spot. Laurie thought: Yes, if we must part altogether that will be different, a clean cut, finis, the end. But with this thought in his mind he looked around the living room, at the swept hearth, the divan reassembled under its covers against the wall; and a memory, which had been imperceptibly transforming itself into an anticipation, gave a long sigh of protest and whispered, "Never again?"

14

IN the bed where the old man had died there was another one, who seemed to be having the same treatment for the same disease, and talked much more about it, his monologue from behind the screens making them, indeed, almost redundant. But the boy Mervyn was delighted at Laurie's return, and he was glad that at the last moment he hadn't forgotten.

"Here; I've brought you something for tea."

"Coo. What a super birthday cake."

"Wedding."

"Go on. You been and got married?" Good manners struggled with disesteem in his face; it was a much better color, mauve-pink instead of blue.

"No—my mother has." He could say it, he found, as if it were years ago, as indeed it seemed.

"No kidding, Spud?" He considered Laurie gravely, then said, with a mature kind of tact, "Have an acid drop."

"Thanks very much. You look better."

"I've been having the Wonder Drug. Honest. The doctor said. What sort of a night did you have last night?"

"What did you say?"

"I said what sort of a night did you have. You look kind of tired. I thought you might have had a noisy one, like what we had here."

"Oh. Was there a raid?"

"Was there a *raid*? We had an incendiary right on the roof. One of the doctors put it out."

"Did he? Good show."

"I reckon, with the moon like it is now, we'll have another tonight, don't you?"

"Oh, I don't know. Probably not." He realized now that the child was a little too bright and cocky to be quite true. "If there is, we'll just have to tell each other the story of our lives to pass the time, eh?"

"Bags you tell yours first, then."

Laurie got into bed and, opening a book, tried to think quietly behind its screen. Soon it fell from his hand and, with the clatter of the ward work all around him, he slept like the dead. Later with the noise his dreams grew restless; he thought he was back at Dunkirk, but this time responsible for everything, so that he had to crawl about the beach dragging his broken leg. He heard his name being called, but he couldn't go any faster; he muttered, "All right, I'm coming, all right."

"Easy does it. It's only me."

He started awake; the lights were on and the blackout up; a doctor in a white coat was standing by his bed. He blinked and saw that it was Alec.

"I can't really stop. I've got to assist with an emergency in ten minutes, but I couldn't leave you in here any longer without saying hello." He pulled out the stool from under the bed and sat down, looking just as all the housemen did when they came to take patients' histories; one half expected him to bring out a patella hammer or a stethoscope. He chatted vaguely about his work, and how to keep on the right side of the Sister; it was all rather dim and dutiful, and Laurie, who was still muzzy with sleep, began to wish he'd go. But he got out the X-rays from the box on the bed-rail, and started holding them up to the light. Laurie was used to seeing doctors enthralled by this pastime; but after saying, "Good Lord, you were lucky with that callus," Alec became a little absent. He glanced over his shoulder, dropped his voice, and said, "I ran into Ralph for a minute today, just after he left you here."

"Oh, yes, did you?" He didn't feel in a state to deal with it, and hoped his face had given nothing away. The reserves which Ralph had broken down felt, in reaction, shy and raw at the approach of anyone else.

Alec looked around for a moment under his brown eyelids, with his disarming throw-away smile. "I didn't keep him. He was looking incandescent and elevated, like a candle burning at both ends." After a faintly hes-

332

itant pause, he added, "Don't keep him on a string too long, he hasn't the temperament."

Laurie didn't answer. He was violently embarrassed and, in any case, could think of nothing to say. Alec looked at the X-ray again.

"He hasn't been talking. But I know him pretty well."

"Yes," said Laurie. "Of course. I hear you got it quite heavy here last night."

Alec gave him another swift neutral glance. "We've had worse. Sandy got a third-degree burn on the arm from an incendiary, picking it up with a coal shovel. It's making us very short on Casualty. Well, I must go. See you sometime."

Laurie shut his eyes again, to protect himself from conversation. He felt oppressed and dejected. He didn't blame Ralph, at least not consciously. As if a few threads of contact still linked them like the streamers that cling to departing ships, he felt what must have happened: Alec had offered felicitations, Ralph, out of sensitiveness or superstition, had been driven to qualify them a little. As Alec had remarked, they had known each other very well. Laurie wondered whether he had had time to give the news to Sandy yet.

Through the blanket he had pulled around his ears he could hear the evening mouth-washes being poured out. Muffled like this, the clink and splash and talk sounded like party noises. He could imagine the party conversation as well. "Goodness, where have you *been*, you're *weeks* behind. Why, that's deader than the Alec affair. Bunny's with Peter now and Ralph's with this Laurie boy. No, you wouldn't have, he's new, Sandy picked him up in the street originally; he's the boy Sandy and Alec had that row about. Funny boy, a cripple, awkward about mixing. However, Ralph's *madly* in love with him at the moment. I thought *everyone* knew."

You don't get away from it, thought Laurie; once you're really in, you never get away. You get swept along the road with the refugees, till you find you've been carried through the gates without noticing, and

333

you're behind the wire for the duration. The closed shop. *Nous autres.*

It would never be like that with Andrew, he thought. Talking in the hospital kitchen at night, they had felt special only in their happiness, and separate only in their human identities. How good it would be to see him now! At least one could write; and getting down into the bedclothes, he spent comfortingly in this way the next half-hour. It was not till he reread it that he realized how far it was falsified by what had been left out, and by that time it was too late to write it again, without missing the early morning post.

He was asleep when the sirens went. Used at the other hospital not to associate their sound with very much urgency, his subconscious mind dismissed it and let him sleep on. But the guns were linked with other memories, and waked him at once; the bombs began a few minutes later.

The other patients said at first that it wasn't as bad as last night; then they seemed to decide that comparisons were odious, and made no more. Laurie remembered how in France, before he was wounded, he had begun to get his second wind, helped by the stimulus of action and the comradeship around him. It hadn't been so good lying passively on the beach with the Stukas coming over, after one had had a sample already; but the morphia had helped most of the time. It had been light, too. Hearing two old gaffers joking together on the other side of the ward, he realized he was much more frightened than they were; and he remembered with shame Ralph, who hadn't been too drunk that night to know what he was doing, falling asleep in Bunny's deep chair. When he had set the wheels moving for Laurie's transfer from the country, he would scarcely have considered small inconveniences like this. Accustomed to communicate his own courage to those around him, no doubt he believed most people to be braver than they really were.

"Spud. You awake?"

"Hello," said Laurie, sitting up. "Yes, I am, but I didn't think you were. Do they still wake you up at two for the Wonder Drug?"

"No, only ten now. But it's a bit noisy to sleep, isn't it?"

Indeed, no one was attempting to do so, and the nurses had sensibly decided that it was better to keep the patients cheerful than quiet. But children will sleep through almost anything, and Mervyn's stillness had been deceptive. He looked feverish, Laurie thought, and it would be partly that which was making him shiver. Laurie lit himself a cigarette, and got up.

"Let's talk instead. I'll come and sit on your bed to save shouting. Just let me put my boot on, in case the nurses want me to do anything."

They had an acid drop, and later Mervyn had a draw at Laurie's cigarette. It would probably, Laurie thought, with these associations, make a nonsmoker of him for life.

When one of the windows blew in, Mervyn said, without removing his cold fingers from Laurie's hand, "I suppose this isn't nearly as bad as Dunkirk, is it?"

"Well, not for me, because I can get about now. You're fixed more like I was then."

"If I had to walk would my stomach burst open?"

"I doubt it; but I could carry you."

"I weigh six stone eleven."

"Yes, I could manage that."

After a long awkward pause, as if he were making up his mind to confess to something, Mervyn said, "My Aunt Edie's house was hit by a bomb, week before last."

"Oh, bad luck. Was she all right?"

"No, she was killed. And Uncle Ted, and Mr. Robbins that lived with them, and their dog, he was called Smoky, he was half a spaniel. And the baby."

"That's too bad. I'm having another cigarette; want to light it? Watch out Nurse isn't looking."

This time it made him cough; they transferred the cigarette in guilty haste.

"Mum said Aunt Edie and Uncle Ted had gone to Canada, she said not to go round there because there was bad people come to live in the house. Only one of the boys at school said, that lives in their street. So I went and the lady next door told me."

335

"Oh," said Laurie helplessly. "I see." A descending bomb whistled loudly. He leaned across the child, but the windows only rattled this time. Mervyn said, "Is it right you can't hear the one that hits you?"

"That's what they say. You're all slipping down the bed, it's bad for the stitches." He settled his back against the rail, and the boy's head against his shoulder. It felt heavy; if things eased off for even a few minutes he would probably sleep. "Mothers will do it, I can't think why. I suppose they'd sooner think we can't take it than feel we don't need them any more. The more they're fond of you, the worse it seems to be. Only way you can look at it is, women are like that."

"Are they? Is your mum?"

"She used to be. You can't go hurting their feelings about it. The only thing is just to put up with it and think your own thoughts."

The raid was tailing off a little. Two casualties had just been carried in. He wondered if Andrew was safe, and whether Ralph's Station was a target for tonight. He thought that if Mervyn had been five years older one could have tried him with:

> *The sorrows of our proud and angry dust*
> *Are from eternity, and shall not fail.*
> *Bear them we can, and if we can, we must——*

But he looked a little fragile, yet, to shoulder tonight's sky; and besides, he had fallen asleep.

Pressed by the double weight, the bed-rail was boring into Laurie's shoulder; but he didn't want to risk waking the child before the All Clear. For the same reason, he couldn't reach the cigarettes. He had just given up trying when a lit one appeared smoking, under his nose. He looked up. In the subterranean glimmer (almost all the lights had had to be put out, because of the broken window) a small leathery man, who looked like a retired jockey, gave him one of those caustic grins by which some people believe sentiment to be impenetrably concealed. He made a comic shushing gesture, and padded on in his gent's natty dressing-robe to the lavatory.

336

The Night Sister did a round soon afterwards. Laurie saw her with alarm. He was breaking a rule; the nurses had winked at it; now there would be trouble. Sure enough she paused beside him. But she only removed the top pillow from his empty bed, and with a smile slipped it behind his shoulder.

Laurie sat smoking, with the boy's mouse-brown hair under his chin. He felt a warm, kindly solidarity with the Night Sister and the nurses and the horsy little man. It wasn't till some ten minutes later, when he had been half asleep himself, that he even remembered it would have been possible to misunderstand his situation. His neighbors' basic assumptions had been his own. Suddenly he pictured one of Sandy's friends passing by just now; the discreet lifted eyebrow, or snigger, or cough; the not-so-cryptic phrase, meant to pass over the boy's head, which would ensure that there would never again be perfect innocence between them. It wouldn't take so very long for that kind of consciousness to settle under one's skin. We sign the warrant for our own exile, he thought. Self-pity and alibis come after.

It was as if Andrew had walked up and looked at him, and in a moment made everything clear.

For a few minutes, this decision brought him great relief and calm. Then he began to think how he was going to tell Ralph.

He hoped that to sleep on it would help; but perhaps the sleep wasn't long enough, even though he dropped off before the All Clear and had to be steered back in a daze to his own bed. He could write, of course; it would be kinder not only to himself, but probably to Ralph as well; only it wasn't the sort of kindness Ralph would ever understand. Deciding this, he tried to put out of his mind the confusing relief it brought him, and the feeling that an unbearable finality had been made not only less immediate, but in some undefined way less real.

If you wanted an evening out, you waited till Sister was off duty and then had a quiet word with the Staff Nurse. That would be tomorrow. He rang the Station, but they didn't know where Mr. Lanyon was and asked

337

if it was urgent. Thankfully he said no, and left a message. After that he rang Andrew, for he was clear of his promise now and they could arrange to meet. But Derek, who would have fetched him without fuss, wasn't there, only a new silly nurse who didn't know anything. There was a queue for the call box, and he had to leave it till next day.

Alec did not reappear; he worked for a surgeon whose cases went mainly elsewhere, and had seldom any real business in the ward. There wasn't a raid that night; Laurie slept for nearly eight hours, in spite of everything.

In the morning he had his first letter from Andrew. The round young-looking script was deceptive: in writing, Andrew revealed maturities which, in talk, his diffidence often hid. It was a swiftly written, unstudied letter, easy with confidence, the crossings-out light and unconcealing. Near the end Andrew said, "I ought to get over next week with any luck, and we'll find somewhere to talk. The telephone is rather diminishing, isn't it? In a way Morse would be better, because it doesn't pretend to be conversation. I know you felt the same, so don't feel obliged to ring for fear that I'll take umbrage or anything. I ring the lodge every day to ask after you, though, of course, they won't put me through to the ward." Not for the first time, Laurie reflected that Andrew was the realist of them both, or had the courage of his realism perhaps. There was a postscript: "Your bed is still empty. I have got a sense of guilt in advance toward the man they put in it; I don't know when I've resented a perfectly innocent person so much."

When Laurie opened his locker drawer to put the letter away, the first thing he saw was Ralph's note, the one that had come with the books.

He took it out, and opened it. The speculations of his first reading seemed strange to him now. The awkwardness, the reserve, were no longer enigmatic; they were like certain tones in a voice whose every inflection one knows. He put the letter back, thinking, I ought never to forgive myself for this as long as I live.

Ralph's new room was a little nearer the hospital

than the old one. He rang the bell at the strange door, thinking that with its tall squeezed bay windows it was a tight-mouthed sun-shy house, predestined to misery and unhappy leave-takings. But then the dark window opened above his head and Ralph's voice, brisk and warm, said, "Just walk up, Spud. First floor."

The stairs were narrow and rather steep; Ralph must have thought he'd prefer to do them without spectators.

The door of the first-floor front opened as Laurie reached it, and shut behind him. He had meant, in some confused unhistrionic way, to give his entrance a kind of significance which would warn Ralph from the first. Now it seemed unbelievable not to have known it would be like this. To administer a rebuff in this first moment would have been possible, Laurie vaguely supposed, to some other and better person: it wasn't possible to him. In a moment or so, however, Ralph looked at his face and said quietly, "Well, come and sit down."

Laurie had time now to notice the room, which was what the rest of the house would have led him to expect, full of frowsty comfort and solid vulgarity. Ralph had removed all the pictures and ornaments, which had given it the air of a commercial hotel. Where his old room had extended his personality, this flung it back so that all his reality was concentrated in himself.

"You see," he said, "two chairs. Which shall we sit on?"

They were huge overstuffed ones covered in tapestry. Ralph sat on the arm beside him. "All right, Spud, all right. I know this is going to be difficult. Just be quiet for a minute. It's been so long."

It wasn't what Laurie had planned. There had not been time to discover, till now, the sensation of coming home again which is one of the more stable by-products of physical love. One can see sometimes in a crowded railway carriage at night two lovers, lethargic, travel-grimed, and bored, weary beyond the dimmest stirrings of desire, but by instinct comfortably adapting their bodies to cushion and support each other, making a little refuge from the crush while the strangers or even friends around them rub elbows and knees, stiff with apologetic constraint and inward resentment. It was with almost a shock that, after a minute or two, Laurie felt Ralph get up abruptly and move away. He crossed over to the other chair and said, "All right, then, Spud, let's have it. Well, come along, shoot."

Wakened harshly out of the illusion that the conversation which had just taken place had somehow explained everything, Laurie now realized that since the moment of entering the room he had scarcely uttered a word.

Stumblingly, he began saying the things he had planned. But much of it seemed impossible now, much had to be qualified or softened; there was much that he could no longer imagine having ever meant to say. "Ralph, don't ever think it was because I didn't care enough. I——"

"Don't be silly, Spud. I know you love me, and so do you."

Laurie looked up. Ralph's blue eyes were fixed on his face, but not in doubt or entreaty. They were watching him: closely, carefully, with absolute concentration. He understood now how sentimental and unreal had been his picture of Ralph as a passive victim whom his rejection would instantly crush. He was looking into the face of a resolute quick-thinking man used to authority, to measuring other men's strength and asserting his own, to a swift reaction in moments of danger. He stood on the bridge now, going into action: and, as long as Laurie's resolution held, it was he who was the enemy.

"Don't waste time, Spud. It's childish to start an argument about whether we love each other, the moment I go and sit on the other side of the room. Get down to brass tacks. What does all this rigmarole add up to, really? You met me at Sandy's party and you can't forget it. You surely don't still think I went there for the conversation, do you?"

He waited, as if expecting a reply; a disciplinary trick so old and simple that no doubt he was scarcely aware of using it.

"I went because I was on the town, like everyone else in the room. Yes, that includes Alec too, you don't know as much about Alec as you think. Surely Sandy told you it was a queer party before you went there; you knew what it meant?"

"Yes, of course."

"I don't just mean that queers would be there. A queer party: something between a lonely hearts club and an amateur brothel. You expected that, didn't you?"

Much of that evening had been a surprise to Laurie, but he didn't want to sound pious, so he said, "Yes."

"And are you going to tell me you'd have gone yourself if you'd been happy and satisfied, even if you did know I'd be there?"

"Yes. I'd have gone to see you."

"Would you, Spud?" Ralph's face had softened; there was a kind of respect in it too. "After all those years. Yes; I expect you would."

He lit two cigarettes, gave Laurie one, and stood for a while looking down at him in silence.

"I'm not romantic," he began. From his lack of emphasis Laurie saw that he believed this to be true. "When I saw you lying on the deck in all the muck and dunnage, I don't know what I felt, really. You had a two-day beard, you were dirty, you smelt worse than the others because your wound was going bad. I suppose you stood to me for something or other. When you sent me up, I was almost too busy to think about it at the time; but it seemed to sink in later, when I was lying in hospital with nothing to do. So I wrote, because one can't swear to every impression one picks up on a day like that, and I wanted to settle it one way or another. When I heard you were dead, it seemed inevitable, somehow. And after that, so did everything else."

He had spoken in the intent, rather muddled way of a man who is defining his thoughts to himself as he goes along. He had done better for himself, it seemed, than he wanted; for when he saw Laurie's face his own hardened at once.

"Well, that's past history." He added, with the clear colorless decision that told nothing, except that the subject was closed, "You can leave that out of it. None of that could happen again." Laurie remembered suddenly the contempt with which he had gazed down at Sandy on the bathroom floor.

"I wasn't thinking that."

"Well, seeing some of the things you do think . . ." As if it were unnatural for him to meet an emergency except on his feet, he took a quick turn across the room, came back to the hearth, and stood there, poised to move again, looking out across Laurie's head. Laurie could feel how the walls of the room were cramping his eyes. He looked at him, measuring his own resolve against Ralph's courage and his pride, and scarcely realizing that there had been a subtle reorientation. He was feeling now that if he weakened Ralph would respect him less.

Suddenly Ralph smiled, and came back across the room again. As if for the exchange of confidences, he settled himself cozily on the chair-arm. His voice wasn't insistent any longer, but intimate, reassuring, a voice Laurie remembered all too well. "Relax, Spuddy. Don't be so tense. How you like to make things difficult, don't you? We weren't long enough together, that's where the trouble is. Dashing off after a few hours and leaving you to mill over all the reaction and everything by yourself. This bloody war! It won't always be like that. I like you the way you are, Spud; why would I want to make you less yourself? I'm not attracted to people I can push around."

Laurie gathered himself together with a hard, unwilling effort; it felt like dragging oneself up from a warm sea onto a harsh rocky shore. He said, "But you're trying to do it now."

Looking at Ralph's face he saw how quickly the man on the bridge resumed command. "No. You're about to make a decision. I'm putting the facts on which you've to make it."

With painful determination Laurie said, "Half the facts. You don't know the other half."

Ralph was silent for a moment; but his face hardly altered. He said quietly, "That's true; I'm putting the half I know. But I've a right to do that."

"Yes," said Laurie. "I know you have."

"Spud," said Ralph softly, "you break me up when

342

you look like that. What are we fighting over? What nonsense it all is."

"Sometimes I—I wish there were nothing else but this. But——"

"Spud."

"But there is, and if I don't do what seems right to me, it won't be any good in the end."

"And if you do, and it turns out to be wrong, that won't be any good either. I can do with a drink, and I should think you could."

The bottles had become respectable in a fumed-oak sideboard. Laurie realized that a drink was what he needed badly. While Ralph was seeing to it he looked around at the thick Turkey carpet, the crushed-velvet curtains, the coal fire and brass fender, the patent convertible divan. But he had guessed already that Ralph had been sharing the rent of Bunny's room and had added the attic when Bunny's personality got too pervasive; this, no doubt, was costing him less. It was strange how dim, how dead-and-done-with, Bunny seemed.

"Isn't it a fantasy?" said Ralph. "The love-nest of a city councillor, is my guess."

Laurie looked at the room again, and couldn't help laughing. "They called each other Mr. Potter and Miss Smith in bed, like people in an Arno drawing. What were the pictures like?"

Ralph opened the cupboard to show him; the ornaments were there too. In the midst of all the laughing and nonsense Laurie remembered that all this would be ending almost at once; but just then it didn't seem true. They were still laughing when they drifted back to the chair again. The drink had been one of Ralph's more generous doubles; it gave Laurie a feeling not exactly of optimism, for he hadn't had enough to make him silly, but of sentimental living-in-the-moment, a feeling that the future would come fast enough without rushing to meet it. Ralph took his empty glass away and settled beside him. He didn't speak at first. Laurie sat looking into the fire, remembering what it brought back to him, and wondering how it would feel presently to be walking back alone.

"I want to talk to you, Spud. Now just relax, quietly now; you're all fiddle-strings today; haven't you been sleeping? You're only a couple of days away from me, and look at you, all on edge. That's better. The thing with you is, you're too new to it all and you don't know what to be frightened of. I've listened to so many life-histories: I don't know why, I always seem to pitch up when they've had a drink too many, or a knock too many, or something. It's loneliness that rots them, every time. A starving man won't notice a dirty plate. You don't know, Spuddy, I do. When you're settled with someone real you can forget all that. You can afford friends then, I mean friends, people to talk to, like anyone else." He added softly, "You know, we do get along together."

Laurie saw that the time had come: it found him with nothing to say, except, "Why have you made it so hard?" And there was no use in saying that, for Ralph would only reply that he had wanted to make it impossible.

Or one could say, thought Laurie, "I'm sorry, but he comes first and that's all about it," which would have, like a shot fired point-blank, the merit of being unanswerable.

"Spud. I don't ask whether you feel about me what I do about you, it's such a meaningless question, how would you know? But could you bear, really, for us never to see each other again?"

"Don't," said Laurie abruptly. He got up from the chair. Ralph got up too. They faced each other across the heavy fireplace with its brass fender and mahogany overmantel. "I've got to bear it. Don't make it worse. Do you think I'm doing this because I don't feel anything?"

Ralph leaned his elbow on the empty shelf; the blank wood stirred in Laurie a dim memory which, untraced, slid away. "We don't need to tell each other what we feel. You know this is murder for both of us, and you're doing it for nothing."

He looked proud and brave, without the shame and shabbiness of a person who feels himself rejected; he

344

was like someone suffering for a cause in which he believes.

"You'll have plenty of time for the other, Spud, without all this butchery. We'll be separated enough before this war's over, with me still in the navy and you in a job. Let's take what we can, God knows we can't afford to waste it. You don't know how little there is in the world of what we can give each other."

Laurie peered into the cloudy future; he tried to re-create what he had felt last night with the child. He clung to a stubborn loyalty where a vision had been. Ralph, who had not ceased all this time to watch him, spoke in the changed voice of a man who has been following up a thought.

"Tell me something, Spud. Supposing after the war this boy, still not knowing the facts of life, asked you to share digs with him. Would you do it?"

"I haven't thought." The peacetime world had seemed irrecoverably remote, the horizon bounced by months at most. Ralph said, "Well, think now."

Laurie thought of the apple orchard and of Limbo; of the kitchen at night. Amid all this intruded the memory of Charlot's side ward, and the red-shaded light on Andrew's face. Defiantly he said, "Yes, of course I would."

Ralph said, quite gently, "You know, even St. Anthony practiced his austerities in the desert. His temptations came to him in dreams, and he just told them to go to hell. You can do that with a dream; it hasn't any feelings."

Laurie looked at him, meditating who knows what appeal; but he saw at once that there would be no armistice.

Ralph said, "Not that I don't believe in sublimation. I mean, I believe some people have done it. They put it all into climbing mountains, or founding hospitals, or just into prayer. Some say it's all done with will power, and some think it takes a special temperament. What do you think yourself?"

"All right. You needn't say it again. But he means something to me I can't explain: he needs me, I don't know why. And he trusts me. And there it is."

Ralph said steadily, "Trusts you for what? It wouldn't work, Spud. It isn't you he needs, he doesn't know you. He needs someone like himself, who wouldn't have to pretend with him."

Laurie said violently, "How can you tell? You don't know anything about him."

Some instinct was saying that anger would do all he needed, release this intolerable pressure and drug him and give him the impetus to escape. He waited to be angry at what Ralph would say.

But Ralph said, with the greatest quiet and gentleness, "Very well, Spud, if that's your last word. Let's part before we make ourselves any more unhappy. We've got better things to remember. If this is the finish, let's have it now."

He took his arm from the mantelshelf, a slight movement which seemed a gesture of dismissal. Laurie gazed at him, stupidly unprepared. It was like having endured a painful but indecisive illness, and being suddenly told that the end is death.

He took a step forward, for it had always been natural to look to Ralph for help, one would never despair without first having recourse to him. He saw Ralph's straight blue eyes, tenderly and inflexibly watching: the eyes looking at him with love were the eyes of the man on the bridge, who awaits with delicate precision the moment of convergence when he will say, "Open fire."

"Goodbye, then, Ralph. I . . . it doesn't seem . . ." Ralph hadn't moved. It would have to be now. "Goodbye."

"Are you going away just like that?"

Laurie paused in the moment of turning. Ralph looked at him: a kind relenting look, not quite smiling. It said, "Did you really think I would stand aside and see you suffer?"

Laurie stood silent. He didn't want to think, there was too much pain in it; only for a moment, resisting foreknowledge, to stand here waiting, his mind's eyes closed.

"Come here, then," said Ralph with gentle arrogance. "Come and say goodbye to me."

Afterwards he said, "Are you going to be angry with me, Spuddy, as soon as you're alone?"

Laurie shook his head. He didn't want to talk. Ralph mistook his movement in the dark and said, "Yes, you are."

"What do you think I am? I can take my own responsibility."

Ralph said slowly, "You said that to me once before."

"Did I? It's a natural thing to say."

"I'm the one to take it. I know that. Perhaps I was wrong, Spuddy; tell me so if you like. When it came to the last I couldn't help myself, and that's a fact."

"I know. It's all right. Don't talk now."

It was a quiet street. The passing cars were so few that each stirred a transient speculation.

"Spuddy."

"Yes?"

"It's as I said; before you make up your mind about things you have to see how they are."

"I know how they are. I knew before."

"Don't be unhappy, Spud, and blame yourself. I'd rather you blamed me."

"It's not your fault. You thought it would settle something. I knew it wouldn't, but still I——"

"It should settle something, Spud. I think it should."

"It makes it more difficult, that's all."

"You put too much on yourself. You're only human."

"So are we all. So is he."

"Is he? I wouldn't know."

"Don't, Ralph. What's the use?"

A clock struck somewhere. Ralph said, "It's my firewatch tonight, I must go soon."

"Did you have any trouble in the raid?"

"Nothing that wouldn't brush off."

"You never told me."

"Don't worry. We ought to be charmed lives at the moment, God knows. There's only one way of getting death to solve your problems, as a rule."

"Look after yourself."

"Would you care?"

347

"You know."

"Spud, I'd give anything to ease this up for you. Not just for my own sake, though you think that."

"No, I don't. I don't think that, of course."

"You only hurt yourself, you don't know what it does to me. I've been around more than you. If you'd only trust me."

"You can't eat and breathe for me, or live for me. No one can."

"It kills me just to stand watching," Ralph said. "It's not the way I'm made."

15

IT was the tall Sister who brought Laurie the news that he was for discharge in ten days' time. She added that he might go out walking if he wished; making, as he learned later, a virtue of necessity, for his new boot was ready and she had been told that he was to test it.

The next few evenings all merged for him later into a common memory and he thought of them almost as one. They walked for the first hour, usually in the old town by the river, among the ships' chandlers and tattooing shops which looked as if they hadn't changed hands in a couple of centuries, or the steep streets of flaking Adam houses that leaned above the Wells. Then they would drop into some small local for a drink, and join in the talk if it was a talkative pub. If Ralph had had any idea of showing Laurie that he could "pass," he must have forgotten about it almost immediately. Places like this had been the stuff of his daily life too long for him to be conscious of his assimilation. He was more than ever himself when he fell in with some merchant mate or master, picking up the loose-ended gossip of the sea: ". . . They had to fly out a second engineer to Rangoon, and from what I heard when she berthed next to us at Colombo . . ." Sometimes Laurie would feel himself almost forgotten; but in the middle of it Ralph would look at his watch; the blackout would reseal itself behind them; in the dim street he would smile and say, "Let's go home."

When they got in, Ralph would fix the blackout while Laurie got the fire going. Usually they never put on the light at all. As Ralph said, the room looked much better without it.

These nights were dark and clouded. The bombers stayed away, but they would be back. It wasn't a time for rushing to meet one's problems: one puts off mending clothes that may have to be thrown away. Ralph had no problem, only a purpose; but Laurie was living each day as though the world would end tomorrow. Ralph must have known this. He never discussed the future; he never mentioned Andrew; he never tried to make Laurie admit any change of heart. If there was something in this of kindness, and something of common sense, no doubt there was something too of pride. Laurie had no trouble in guessing that scenes of jealousy were relegated in Ralph's mind to a special category, along with bracelets and eye-shadow; he had his private vanities, and was sensitive about them. There was something almost formidably perfect in his manners on this point; but though he didn't touch upon the future, in compensation he talked, and got Laurie to talk, a good deal about the past. All Laurie's most difficult period of self-discovery had been got through alone, except for the unhelpful intrusion of Charles. Though there could be no very useful purpose in telling anyone about it now, there could be a good deal of emotional satisfaction; and Ralph saw to it that there was. After these long retrospective confidences, exchanged under the conditions best suited of all to unreserve, the feeling that they were deeply rooted in each other's lives seemed to Laurie as old as the events they had been reviving.

The boy Mervyn, at whom Ralph had once waved from the ward doorway, had decided to worship him. He never arrived till after visiting hours, so their acquaintance ripened on signals and smiles. It gave satisfaction to Mervyn, however; and there was an understanding that the next time the Sister was out of the way, Ralph should somehow be smuggled in. Meanwhile, Ralph sent him as a present a very old spare copy of the *East Africa Pilot*. Laurie thought it an odd choice; but Ralph had remembered the years of hunger for factual information. Mervyn spent, reverently, his waking hours upon it.

Andrew hadn't written for some days. He had said he would let Laurie know when he could get over. The orderlies' days off were worked out among themselves, and it took a certain amount of shuffling to get a night orderly relieved; Laurie guessed that he must have put off writing from day to day, expecting to hear something definite. The two hospitals were so closely linked that, as Laurie now realized, neither could be bombed without the news travelling around the other in a flash. He had expected Andrew to write oftener; his first letter had been dashed off like a daily journal to be continued very soon. Laurie knew that in other circumstances, this silence would have been a grief to him. Now, because it put off the day when he must write back an account of himself which would be false in every significant thing, he was relieved.

He had reached a point of no return when he could see neither help nor virtue in anticipation. It would cost him his integrity to protect Andrew now; but this didn't present itself to him as a choice, only as a debt he had run up and would have to pay. There was no clean way out; confession would only lift the weight from his own shoulders to Andrew's. It would be impossible for him to know about Laurie now without turning the knowledge on himself.

Staring into the fire, Laurie remembered wishing that his love for Andrew could be divided, leaving only the part Andrew could happily share. The fire, settling, threw up a dim transparent flame; there was a faint resurgence of light on the fair hair beside him. It was a Delphic answer, he thought, to an impossible petition; you could see the smile behind the smoke.

"What is it?" asked Ralph, always at these times instantly aware when Laurie withdrew from a common consciousness to thoughts of his own. He replied only with a violent demonstration of love; and guessed, from a certain quality of comfort and forgiveness in the response, that Ralph had divined the sense of guilt behind it. For Laurie couldn't pretend to himself that even this last loyalty of the heart to Andrew was innocent. It was withheld at the expense of someone who on his side had withheld nothing, and whose need of love was in its kind no less. The idealist and romantic in Ralph, reviving late and left for dead, felt its own wants with the greater urgency; and it had lived too hard, too close to the ground, to be deceived.

It was on the morning of the fifth day that Laurie awoke to a sense of anxiety about Andrew, so fully formed that he must have been reasoning it out in his sleep. He counted the days since Andrew had written. Suddenly Laurie's mind cleared; he knew this silence was utterly uncharacteristic. Andrew was essentially gentle and considerate; if he was having trouble in getting a night off he would write to say so. When he had told Laurie not to telephone, it had been because he had meant to write in any case, instead. Something was wrong.

Laurie looked at the clock. It was half-past five in the morning and still quite dark. The nurses were scurrying about in the busiest rush hour of a busy surgical ward. Less than at any other time of the day was he likely to be missed. He counted his small change, got up, and made his bed. Mervyn, no longer a "heavy dressing" to be done early, was still asleep. Laurie bundled his uniform together, hid it under his dressing-gown, and changed in the bathroom. The quiet empty streets of the city, in which only the first workers were stirring, rang with frost under his feet; he could hear echoed back from the tall buildings on the other side the clump of his thick-soled boot.

He got through from the telephone box very quickly. He could hear the bell ringing in the ward, and tried to picture Andrew hurrying to answer it; but the picture wouldn't form, and when the answering voice came, it wasn't Andrew's.

"Is that Ward B?"

"Yes?"

"Who is that speaking?"

"This is the ward orderly, Roger Curtis." Then, after a pause, "Do you want to inquire for someone?"

It was very cold in the telephone box, which had a

missing pane that let in the wind. Laurie felt his palms filmed with an icy moisture. "Doesn't Andrew Raynes work on Ward B any more?"

"No. Andrew Raynes went to London yesterday."

"To London?" His mind was a blind scramble of conjecture under a cold sky of fear. "Do you know how long he's likely to be away?"

"I'm afraid not." The rather high, pleasant voice paused tentatively; then, "Is that Laurie Odell speaking?"

"Yes. It is. Did Andrew leave a message for me?"

"Not with me; but that will mean he must have written. You've not changed your address lately?"

"No."

"Well, I expect you'll have a letter when the post comes in. I know you're a friend of Andrew's; I'm sure he wouldn't move without letting you know."

"Move?" The cold seemed to have gone through to his bones, not numbly but with a sharp eating pain. "Aren't you expecting him back?"

"Well, not at present, I think. If you don't hear by this morning's post, you could always ring here in the daytime; I haven't his address and I can't leave the ward now, but you could easily get it then."

"Thank you." He rang off.

When he got back the ward seemed just the same, as if it had been fixed in an enchanted sleep through disastrous decades. Mechanically, Laurie undressed again, went into the sluice-room, and with a couple of other walking patients carried out his usual morning job, giving enamel bowls of water to such bed patients as could wash themselves.

The giving out of the patients' mail was one of the Sister's sacred cows. A royal prerogative, it gave way to every more urgent duty but was never delegated. Laurie could remember the letters coming around as late as eleven-thirty. He felt too sick to eat breakfast, though after the early hospital supper he was usually ravenous.

Mervyn, well on toward convalescence, was in the mood when boys are endurable only to one another, entranced with elementary jokes and building on them vast structures of silly elaboration. Laurie lost his temper at last and shut him up. He looked hurt, but not

352

very badly; he knew already that no one keeps a sense of humor much after sixteen.

The letters came around rather earlier than usual, at about a quarter to nine. There were two for him. One was from his mother, a picture postcard of the hotel, her window marked with a cross. The other was from Andrew.

Laurie sat with the unopened letter in his hand, trying to think of somewhere to go. The nurses would be working in the bathroom; there was only one lavatory, never free for long; in a word, there was nowhere. He hid behind yesterday's paper, and opened the letter against the middle page. Andrew's round, young writing stood like an inset on the day's score-card of dead pilots and fallen planes.

Dear Laurie,

Forgive me for not writing before. You will guess why, from what Ralph will have told you, but that's no excuse. I have begun two or three letters, but they weren't honest enough to send. Tomorrow I am going to London to work, which I think you will see is the only logical thing; so I must write today, and I find now that I can. I want you to know ...

"Odell! Do put that paper down, we want to tidy the bed."

"Sorry."

"Sister hates newspapers about. We'll throw it out now if you've done with it."

"No, please. Not yet."

"Well, do have the bed tidy for Mr. Sutcliffe's round."

I want you to know it is true if he says that when I hit him it wasn't even self-defense. There is a belief, which I expect he shares, that a pacifist who has behaved like this must see at once his ideas were wrong. I should have thought there could hardly be a better way of proving they were right. But if that were all I had to tell you, of course I could have written days ago.

Dave says this about temptation, that in itself it is nothing but an opportunity for choice; so it is rather defeatist to feel very guilty about it, as though one were

353

half ready to commit the sin. If I say I have had feelings about you it would have been wrong to act on, you know enough to see what I mean. As a rule it seemed not to matter very much. Often before when I have been fond of people I have got somehow caught up in it all round; but I am such an average person, it must be quite common I thought. With you it was more, sometimes you must have noticed I was difficult; but I got over that and it came to seem more like a smile when one is happy. It is the happiness one thinks about and not the smile. Toward the end I thought you felt the same. I knew I oughtn't to be so glad of this, since it might be my fault, yet often it seemed good, in fact the only thing. Only I found that I couldn't see things so clearly when I was alone, and I should have taken notice of that because it is the real test of everything.

Well, about Ralph. He isn't like I imagined, so I found it hard to picture you and him as great friends. When he told me it was much more than that, I felt—I don't know a better way of expressing this—as if I'd had an anonymous letter. I got one once, after my Board. It is like something from another world, but it has touched you, and the touch is real. So then he said why did I pretend to be shocked when I was only jealous; so that was when I hit him.

He didn't hit me back, he just laughed and walked off. He had a right to. I knew before he was even out of sight that there could be only one reason for what I did. What he had said about me was true. He wanted to see what I would do, I suppose, and I did what he expected. But it taught me something. The thing you want to kill is really in yourself. That is why people become cruel in war, because they are doing what I did.

I don't know what more there is to say, except this: that since one can't refuse to know oneself, and it must have happened eventually, I would rather it was through you than anyone else.

I shall apply to do ambulance work in the line, as soon as such a thing exists again. Meanwhile, London seems the next best. I know what you will think, that I am starting to patch up my self-respect at a rather primitive level. But I find I have to do this before going on. That is another thing about me which had to be faced sometime. I daresay my father would have understood. Anyway, you will.

You will probably be amazed and embarrassed after this

when I ask you to write to me. Not to answer the kind of thing I have been telling you, no one could expect that. It is only this, because I can't see you again and shall often be thinking about you. Will you please tell me yourself that there is nothing in what he said about you and him? Of course I know there isn't. But somehow it has got a hold on me; I can't get it out of my mind. It will be all right as soon as I hear from you. I can get rid of it then and keep the rest. There is much more I should like to say, but now I shall never be able to say it. You know I shall remember you all my life.

Love,
Andrew

He had written an address at the bottom, somewhere in the neighborhood of the docks.

"Spud. I say, Spud. You done with the outside bit of the paper?"

Some mechanical residue in him detached the outer sheet and handed it over.

"Coo, Spud. See about that Hurricane pilot? Spud, you know what, I saw a real ace once. Honest. He came to our school about War Savings. He was wizzo. I say, Spud——"

Confused in his own darkness, Laurie turned to the boy and said as if to a contemporary, "Don't talk to me now."

Mervyn looked from his face to the letter which was showing and said, quite quietly, "Okay, Spud. Sorry." He folded the paper neatly and turned on his other side to read it.

The surgeon of the day came, did a round with his students, and left. Patients relaxed, milled their beds about for comfort, talked to each other across the ward. The stir of activity seemed to release Laurie from a paralysis of the will. He got out of bed, and once more took his clothes out of the locker.

"Going out, Spud?"

Laurie looked at the boy. His thin face was sharply intelligent, loyal, and shy.

"Yes. I've got to, something's happened I have to see about. I shan't be back all day. Don't say anything, will you, or ask them where I am?"

"Okeydoke, I won't talk. Won't she miss you at dinner, though?"

"I can't help that. See you tonight."

He was just in time to get the mid-morning express, and was at Paddington two and a half hours later. So completely had his thoughts absorbed him that he walked almost through the military police, and scarcely realized they had been there till he was in the underground. Perhaps his indifference had bluffed him through, perhaps they had other fish to fry, perhaps they saw his boot and didn't trouble. He got out of the underground in a wide, crowded East End thoroughfare, asked the way and was told to take a tram. It put him off at the end of a long street of smoke-black villas, paired like Siamese twins. Old gray lace curtains framed lean aspidistras in Benares pots; the gardens had starved privet behind twisty cast-iron railings, or little straggly beds of London Pride edged with tile. If you touched the railings your hand came away thick with grime. It was the kind of place where there should have been children playing in the street, but they were mostly gone. The seventh pair of villas had been laid open all down the front, like a child's dollhouse. You could see the dark squares on the wallpaper where the pictures had hung. But these were Nos. 84 and 86, and Laurie was looking for No. 50.

No. 50 had *The Beeches* over the door, engraved elegantly in cement which had once been painted cream. The curtains were casement cloth dyed pink, streakily, at home. There was even an aspidistra, though it looked a little seedy. The door was open. Laurie stepped into the hall. It had an embossed dado with chocolate varnish, and linoleum patterned like parquet and worn into holes, showing the boards. There was a smell of cabbage-water and carbolic soap. He listened; just out of sight, at the back of the house, someone was moving. He had just opened his mouth to call "Andrew!" when a door at the end opened and Dave came out.

"Hello, Laurie." He sounded, as always before, unexcited, attentive, and kind; but he had dropped his voice, and Laurie knew beforehand what he was going to say. "Come in the kitchen, will you, there are people asleep upstairs."

The kitchen was a small dingy room, warm from its black iron range and, it seemed, from the stored vitality of the families whose hub of existence it must have been. A yellow varnished paper on the walls affected wood-graining. The scrubbed table in the middle was covered with clean newspaper, there were rolls of surgical lint and gauze on it, and piles of cut and folded dressings. An iron pot of porridge was simmering on the range, and a big kettle. Dave pulled up an old bentwood chair and said, "Sit down, Laurie, I'm just going to make some tea."

He had always been lean, but lately he had grown much thinner. There were deep furrows in his cheeks, half hidden by the edges of the grizzled beard. He had on a worn leather golf jacket and stained, shabby flannel slacks. He spooned tea from a cocoa-tin into a brown teapot, and tipped the heavy kettle to fill it.

Laurie had had no food today but a cardboardy meat pie at the station. The tea smelt good. Some dim memory stirred in his mind of sitting with the maid in his grandmother's kitchen when he was very small; he felt a sudden nostalgia, piercing and forlorn. He said, "Is Andrew here?"

"Yes," said Dave. "He's asleep with the others. Last night was fairly quiet, but he was still a bit tired, and we may be busy later." He poured out tea in thick white china cups; you could have thought Laurie had dropped in from next door. "Sugar? We've got plenty, Andrew and Tom don't take it."

"Please. I wanted to see him about something rather important. I'm sorry he's tired, but I think he'd rather see me."

"I'll call him presently," said Dave, "if you want him called." He sugared the tea from a Woolworth glass basin. "I've been half expecting you, difficult as it must have been for you to get away."

"I'm absent without leave. I've had a letter from Andrew. I have to see him, there's something I want to explain."

Dave looked at him. "You look worn out," he said simply. He went to the deal dresser, fetched a cloth out

357

of the drawer, spread it on Laurie's end of the table and set a plate and knife.

"Please don't bother," Laurie said. "I couldn't eat anything."

"We've some beef dripping this week. I'm going to make some toast." He got a loaf from the bin, sliced it, and speared the bread on a wire fork. "You can do this one."

Dully, Laurie turned his chair and held the fork to the bars of the range. The glow was comforting; it sheltered his eyes which flinched from being looked at any more. Dave pulled up the other chair and sat down beside him, with his slice of bread on a bent carving fork. They both kept their eyes on the fire, and shifted the toast about, because of the bars.

"Do you ever think," said Dave, "that retribution seems to spread itself very unevenly? It's often seemed so to me. But I think one must take the analogy of the body. A gangrened limb is quite insensitive. Only the living tissues feel pain."

There was a pause, during which a hot coal dropped from the bars onto the hob and bounced down into the ash-pan. Laurie said, "Andrew told you."

"Well, I was rather unfair to him. I didn't warn him I could fill in a certain amount between the lines. I mean, from experience." He added, not defensively, but kindly, as though Laurie had asked for reassurance, "That was a good many years ago."

His toast was crumbling on the fork; he speared it gingerly in a fresh place. "I've felt now and then—if I'm wrong, stop me before I go any further, won't you—that you've had a mistaken idea about my feelings for Andrew." When Laurie said nothing, he went on, "Not that I've any right to resent it. But I've often wished I could set your mind at rest."

Laurie looked at his toast, and turned it over. "I didn't think that, exactly."

"No," said Dave. "I know. Not exactly. I know what you thought and I don't really blame you. Every religious body has a few. With most of them it's woolly thinking, rather than hypocrisy. I had the wool pulled off when I was about Andrew's age, as a matter of fact."

He got up, fetched Laurie's tea from the table and

stood it on the steel fender in reach of his hand. Laurie said, "Thanks," and then, with difficulty, "It might not be a bad thing now for him to know that."

"Well, I told him. He'd have thought of it himself in a short time, of course."

Laurie shifted the toast and said, "Yes, of course. He'd better have someone he can trust to be straight with him."

Dave looked up. "He isn't a fool. You know that better than anyone. He knows why he wasn't told everything, if he wasn't. That's not the sort of thing he has on his mind."

"I know. That's why I came."

"I thought it might be." Dave relieved him of the toast which was beginning to smoke, nicked off a burnt corner, spread it with dripping, salted it, and put the plate on the fender. "Don't let it get cold." While Laurie was eating it he went back to the swabs on the table. Presently he said, "You don't have to worry about me, whatever else you worry about. Do get that into your head, won't you? For a lot of reasons; one of which, a minor one I like to think nowadays, is that Andrew looks just like his mother. Except in character sometimes, I never see Bertie in him at all."

It could be perceived that his youth belonged to a decade when Bertie had sounded charming, even perhaps romantic. He pronounced it Bartie. This trifle had on Laurie the effect of a kind of emotional trigger, and for several minutes he could not speak. Dave continued to fold swabs with the reflex precision of a factory hand who has been carrying out the same process for years. He went on, "As soon as Catherine joined us, it became obvious that Bertie was perfectly normal, except in fastidiousness, so I'd done nothing but make a virtue of necessity after all. With Andrew, I don't know. I mean, I know at the moment of course, but life's made some rather excessive demands on him lately. He may quite well grow out of it. If so, he'll largely have you to thank."

Laurie said, "Not now."

Dave put some finished swabs away in a cardboard hatbox. "You'll know what I'm talking about now better than I do. He came here with some doubt about

359

you which he didn't want to discuss with me or anyone else, and I imagine you've come here partly to resolve it. Of course, if you can give him the answer he wants, you have every right to. Indeed, you should, in spite of the fact that it won't make things any easier for him at first."

Laurie was silent, looking at the fire. At last he said, "I couldn't give him the answer he wants."

He didn't look up. The rhythmic sound of Dave's hands folding the swabs—a pause for adjustment, a light smoothing pat, a moment's pause, and then a flat heavy pat—went on almost unbroken.

Laurie said, "I thought it might make him feel a little better to know that I'm sorry, and that it happened partly because——" He felt his voice about to get out of control, and stopped quickly.

"Of course," Dave said. His lean knotted hands, seamed with work and scrubbing, paused on a half-folded square of gauze. "This is the worst of all my failures."

"Yours?" said Laurie. He contracted his brows vaguely.

"Once or twice I thought of talking to you. I said to myself that you might be as innocent as Andrew was, and my interference might be a disaster to both of you; I couldn't be absolutely sure. So I saved myself a tricky job which would have involved stating my qualifications for taking it on, and I had the pleasure of being right, where Andrew was concerned. But anyone involved in the recoil was just as much my responsibility."

Laurie's stillness had changed and become stony. He said, "I shouldn't waste any worry there, if I were you."

As if he hadn't heard, Dave went on, "I took up the work I do largely to teach myself that sort of thing. As you see, I've not made much headway. Love is indivisible, Bertie said to me once. He'd only been out of the army a few months, but his instincts were better."

Laurie looked up from the empty cup into which he had been staring. "If I don't see Andrew, would you be willing to tell him I came?"

"Yes, of course. You've told me what you came here

to say. I'll tell him that, and anything else you want me to."

The knowledge that he was not going to see Andrew again suddenly came home to Laurie as real. He hadn't believed it while he was speaking.

Dave said, "It's not that I think it would be wicked for you to meet. But you'd both suffer more than now, and no good would come out of it." With a chance inflection which made Laurie able to imagine him as a young man, he added, "He really is awfully tired."

"Yes," said Laurie dully. "He must be. We'd better not wake him."

"When you're on the way back it won't seem so bad. You'll remember it would be all over by then anyway."

"You people are so practical," Laurie said.

Dave got up and came to sit on the kitchen table. His personality could be felt at this distance like something tangible. "There's no need to feel finally cut off. He'll want to hear from you, of course. Write when you feel he'll be needing it, not when you feel you must, and it will be all right. Or if you want to know how he is without writing, you can always write to me."

The room was getting dark. The first twilight was coming already to the long black street, though in the open, probably, it would still seem to be afternoon. Laurie noticed for the first time, hung on pegs at the side of the dresser as herbs are hung in the country, a bunch of gas masks and a cluster of tin hats.

"May I give you my address?" he said. "If he were—ever ill, or anything. If you wouldn't mind."

"Certainly," said Dave, in the matter-of-fact voice he used in the wards. "Write it on this. I'll put it in the file, I won't keep it on me."

While he was doing this Laurie remembered something. He would have liked to say, "I heard about your wife and I'm very sorry." But because of the road by which this thought had come to him, he could not bring himself to say it.

Dave said, "This isn't the day I'd have chosen to give you this advice, Laurie. But don't think of yourself because of all this as necessarily typed and labelled. Some men could make shift, for a time at least, with any woman out of about ninety per cent they meet.

Don't fly to extremes the moment you discover your own needs are more specialized."

Laurie waited, ready to say it after all; but Dave didn't go on, and Laurie realized that his impersonality was in the nature of a human flinching, and that he was willing Laurie not to speak.

"Well, I must go. There's no sense in getting myself crimed my last week in the army, if I can help it."

Dave gave a smile which Laurie recognized as partly one of relief. "Don't try and slip onto the platform by the footbridge, they've been on to that for at least twenty-five years." They both got up. Dave said, "You'd better go out at the back, I think."

The scullery was tiny, there was hardly room for anything but the copper and the sink. The cement floor had been mixed with unsifted earth so that pebbles stood up in it. There were towels hanging by the sink; this must be where everyone washed.

"Thank you for everything," Laurie said. "If you'll tell him . . . you know what to say. Tell him I . . ." As if the sensation had come as a message, he felt something usually too familiar for consciousness, a flat heaviness in a pocket. He got out the book and turned it over in his hand, with the feeling that there was something that needed seeing to. Remembering, he tore out the flyleaf, then got out his pen and wrote Andrew's name on the first page. "Please, will you give him this?"

Dave looked at the lettering on the spine. "You know," he said, "even the most exalted paganism is paganism none the less." He took the book, looking at the scored and salt-stained cover, at the blood. Something came into his face which had been there on the day when Laurie had seen him watching the battle in the air and the falling planes. "Yes," he said. "I'll give it him with your love."

He opened the door. A broom which had been leaning behind it fell with a clatter. They both stood still, listening. There was a sound, muffled by the floor above, of a man yawning; then, more clearly, raised to carry through a party wall, Andrew's voice. "Tom. What time is it?"

Laurie slipped through the door into the scrawny

362

yard. He glanced upward, to ask Dave if the window looked that way. Dave shook his head. Upstairs a sleepy voice talking itself awake said, "Dave's up, good, that means tea." Andrew said, "Someone's with him, I think."

Laurie stood with one foot on the doorstep, perfectly still. He had heard the false casualness of a reviving hope, which dares not be open even with itself. There was a long, long moment of silence before the voices began again. Then, very softly, Laurie said, "While I'm going could you make a noise? He knows my step."

Dave nodded and went over to the sink. In the street a lorry was approaching; that would help too. "Goodbye, Dave."

"Goodbye," Dave said. "God bless you." He spoke as he might have said in the ward, "Here's your blanket"; like a man offering in his hand something solid and real. As Laurie went, he heard him start to clatter the sink with both taps running.

It was not till Laurie had got level with the bombed houses down the street that he became aware of the sheet of paper which, because he couldn't discard it in the house, he was still holding screwed up in his hand. He tossed it away into the road, where it landed in a little heap of rubble and broken glass. On the crumpled edge which was showing he could see ". . . anyon" and just below it ". . . dell."

When he got out into the wide main street it seemed still quite light, but by the time he reached Paddington it was the latter end of dusk, and you could feel everywhere, in voices and footsteps and the sound of the traffic, the faint resonant overtone of a steady anticipation.

16

HE arrived back in the ward just before the night staff came on. The Staff Nurse said, "Oh, there you are, Odell; I suppose you know Sister's absolutely livid with you?"

"Yes, I was afraid of that."

"If you told that child to eat your dinner as well as his own and say you were there, I don't think much of it. When she taxed him with it he got nervous and brought the whole lot up again."

"No, really I didn't. Is he all right?"

"Not much thanks to you. Get to bed now for goodness' sake, if you don't want me to tell her you cut your treatment as well. Luckily for you it's her half day. All I can say is, I hope it was worth it."

Mervyn, flattered by Laurie's concern, waved it away. "It's all right, it was a bit of a waste, but I ate some sweets when I got hungry again, and there was a super pie for supper, I had some more. Did you fix everything okay?"

"Yes, thanks. We'd better stop talking or Nurse won't like it."

"Go on, we've got six minutes yet. I say, Spud, you know what? I had a visitor this evening. I bet you sixpence, come on, I bet you a hundred thousand pounds you don't guess who I had."

"I can't think," said Laurie, coming near to a literal truth just then. "Someone from school?"

"Go on, you're soppy, they come Sundays. Come on, guess. I bet you never do guess. Shall I tell you? Do you give up? Okay, then you owe me a hundred thousand pounds, see? It was Mr. Lanyon. He came right into the ward and said is Sister off duty, so then he asked Nurse if he could see me, and she said, well, don't stay long, only she was busy, see, so he stayed for ages, he told me all about Morse, and he showed me how you sail a dhow, he drew me one, and he gave me my soap and flannel to wash, he stayed right up till they came to make the bed. I bet you'd never have guessed, would you? Would you, Spud? You'd never have guessed if you weren't there he'd come just to see me?"

"No," said Laurie. "Was that all you talked about?"

"Coo, no. We talked for ages." The first bright shine of elation had gone from his voice, and there was half a question in it.

"What about?"

Already the old sharp look was coming back into Mervyn's voice; no clear suspicion, only the knowledge that he was being given at best half a truth. "Only what

364

I was going to do when I leave school, and he asked about you, he asked where you were. So I said I didn't know, you had to see about something on business." He gave the sharp look again, this time a request for approval. Laurie realized that this was some kind of stock answer he had been taught to make at home, perhaps when creditors called. No doubt at the time he had simply told all he knew; this canniness was retrospective. Laurie could feel in himself all the wheels running down in a slack hopeless sense of universal defeat. "I'm glad you had a nice talk."

"Yes, I thought he was super." Laurie sensed, in the pause, a forlorn hope of having everything made right again.

"He tells some good stories, doesn't he? I ought to have left a message for him, but I forgot."

"He said he'd come back tomorrow." A cautious relief quickened in Mervyn's voice. "I say, Spud, did you know, it's Sister's day off tomorrow? Mr. Lanyon didn't know it was, so when I told him, he said he might come and see me again, just for a minute."

"That would be fine. But sometimes he gets orders at short notice. So if you don't see him, don't be upset."

The night nurses were coming in; now there was no need to talk any more. But though the raid that night was a light one and soon over, he was awake till three, with the tight spinning wakefulness of mental exhaustion. Soon after five the lights went on and the day's work began.

The long featureless desert of the morning passed. After dinner he dozed fitfully for about an hour, till it was time to go for his treatment and make his apologies to Miss Haliburton. After that there was nothing to do but think.

At five Laurie slipped out of the ward quietly, and waited at the head of the stairs. In the ward at the bottom someone had just died and the widow was led away crying. For a little while the flagged stone well was empty; then two housemen paused there to exchange a bit of hospital scandal and laugh; a long wait, then a very young nurse hurried away on an errand, rolling down her sleeves and pushing the hair out of her eyes. The next footsteps were Ralph's.

The landing was too near the ward; Laurie went down, and they met on the bend of the stairs. With a kind of horror, he saw that Ralph looked exactly the same. Even now that one knew, there seemed nothing behind his smile but a certain alertness and anxiety, there was nothing to see.

He said, "Hello, Spud. What happened yesterday? If you left a message for me I never got it." Laurie didn't answer; he thought his face would be answer enough. Ralph looked at him again and said, "What's been going on, for God's sake? You look terrible. What's the trouble, Spud, tell me about it."

"I've been to see Andrew," Laurie said, and waited.

Ralph waited too. His face betrayed nothing. If one hadn't known, it would have seemed to show mere bewilderment passing into concern.

Laurie said. "Do you still want to know what the trouble is?"

With an anxious-sounding irritability Ralph said, "Yes, of course I do."

Laurie remained silent; but this time it was because he had been left without words. Ralph's fair brows came down in a straight line. He hadn't even dropped his eyes. He said, slowly, "I suppose you mean he's found out."

Still Laurie stared, unbelieving. It had really seemed to him, till this moment, that he was ready for anything, that not a single illusion about Ralph was left. But he had taken for granted courage in a corner; he had imagined Ralph standing up to this as he had when Mr. Straike had asked him his name.

At first it had seemed not to matter what one said, the thing had been to get it over; but now he felt anger rising in him, pent, aching anger from hidden places, the blind undischarged poison of guilt and conflict and suppressed resistance. He said, "You should know."

"I don't understand. Why?"

After a short pause Laurie said, "Christ!"

"Now look, Spud," said Ralph, suddenly crisp, "this isn't getting us anywhere."

"I've got some good news for you," said Laurie bitterly. "He's gone up to London. You did better than you expected there. He's gone to work in the worst-

bombed place he can find, he thinks he ought to because he hit you. I'm glad you had a good laugh about
it. Are you satisfied now?"

"Hit me?" said Ralph, staring. "Hit *me?*"

Laurie felt physically sick. He knew that this would
have seemed to him really the voice of an innocent person, if any other explanation were possible, if his in-
formant had been anybody in the world but one. His
memories grimaced at him. He said, "Oh, don't be so
cheap."

Ralph stood with his back to the iron banister, his
right hand gripping the rails. His eyes seemed to have
become darker because of the changed color of his
face. He said, presently, speaking slowly and carefully,
"Look, Spud, I'm sorry to say this, I know you're fond
of him; but if that's what he says, he's putting something over on you."

It had only wanted that. Laurie thought of Andrew
on his knees scrubbing the filthy floor, of Willis making
for the bucket, of Mr. Straike, of the whole terrible vul-
nerability of goodness in the world.

"Excuse me." Two theater porters, with a stretcher
and a nurse, had come up below them. They drew
back, mechanically, to opposite sides. The senior porter
said over his shoulder, "These stairs is supposed to be
kept clear."

The interruption had sharpened Laurie's anger, and
the pause had given him time.

"Are you asking me now to take your word against
his? You must have forgotten what people who speak
the truth are like. I know what you are, I've only been
pretending to myself; as far as I'm concerned, this
serves me right. When you wanted me to live with you
and go on seeing him as if nothing had happened, I really knew then. You could be trusted once, you knew
what it was all about, you had it in you; but it's gone
now, you've no feeling for it any more, you're all blunt
at the edges. Won't you ever realize why it is when you
try to run other people's lives you can't do anything but
harm? God, must you go on putting yourself in charge
and smashing everything you don't understand? Like a
drunk trying to mend a watch." He paused for breath.
Ralph stood against the rail in silence. His face had a

367

dead, fixed, stupid look. Laurie had a feeling of total devastation in which all objectives had been destroyed. He said grayly, "I suppose you can't help it by now. Too many Bunnies in your life."

At first Ralph hardly seemed to know he had finished speaking; he stood there, his face curiously stretched and sharpened over the bones, looking half at Laurie and half through him, as people look through a passing stranger when deep in thought. When he spoke it was almost a soliloquy. "Yes," he said. "Yes, very likely."

Laurie said, "You'd better go, they want the stairway kept clear."

A nurse from the ward above came hurrying down the stairs, glanced at Ralph with a flicker of interest, then, touched with discomfort, bustled past them without looking around.

Ralph said, "Yes, I'll be going." He had already moved down a stair, when he paused and looked upward. "Just a moment. When did this happen? This boy, I mean, which day did we meet?"

"How can you talk about it? It was only for you I promised not to see him. And the day I came to tell you, you knew what you'd just done, and you . . . you——"

"Sunday, then, was it?" He paused. "Not that it matters, really, after all. All right, Spud, goodbye, then. I'm sorry; I hope it works out for you sometime. I won't come back. I see now there's a lot of truth in what you've been saying."

Laurie watched the flat white top of his cap as he went down the stairs, slowly at first and then more quickly, moving like a sailor without looking down, his hand—the one in the glove—just touching the rail. He turned the corner at the bottom, and was gone. Laurie waited a little, then went out himself into the street. If he returned to the ward, Mervyn would be sure to ask if Mr. Lanyon was coming.

It was too cold to walk, and he was too tired. In the first cinema he came to, he sat through the meaningless noise of a gangster film. As time passed, and he began to think, he became occupied with the growing strangeness of finding himself so free. As little as three weeks ago, his life had been full of strings: a home, three people he had been tied to. Now he was as free as air, he could go anywhere, it made no difference to anybody.

The film had changed and there was a shot of a girl running with a dog. In the distance she looked like Nurse Adrian, of whom he hadn't thought for days. Now that his life was so uncomplicated, he supposed he might write to her sometime. The thought made a faint tinge of color on the aseptic blankness of freedom. They would reread, as others did, their letters before posting them, measuring carefully their signals of interest and liking, not replying too quickly for fear of seeming to force the pace. Passingly he wondered whether Miss Haliburton had sold the bull-terrier pup yet. At a second meeting, it had seemed to remember him, and its ears were warm.

He left before the end of the film and had something at a snack bar, then went back to the hospital. He had annoyed them sufficiently, he mustn't be late tonight. As he went up the main corridor he thought that he had been living in an enclosed and tiny personal world. These were the real people: this porter propped on an idle trolley having a quick cigarette, this stout, anxious woman hurrying to someone sick enough to be visited out of hours, these two doctors amicably disagreeing as they strode along to the theater; the little knot of nurses coming back from the first supper shift, crying, "Oh, no, she didn't? My dear, what did you do?"

These were the people for whom, after all, he had been fighting. They were the people for whom Andrew was fighting too. He would be one of them from now on.

As he made for his bed, he saw with relief that Mervyn was already asleep.

"Oh, thank goodness, Odell, there you are at last."

He looked around from his open locker, his dressing-gown in his hand. What had he done now? He had got back in good time. It was Sister's day off. He had been so anxious to avoid trouble tonight, and get some sleep.

"Mr. Deacon's been practically living here all evening, trying to get hold of you. I told him you were

369

never back till after eight. I should think if he's rung once he's rung four times. I'd better tell him you're here."

"I'm sorry, Nurse. I didn't know I had to see anyone." He had never heard of Mr. Deacon. This must be some final check before his discharge. It was sure to happen somewhere outside the ward; there seemed no point in undressing. In a few minutes the nurse came back. "Mr. Deacon wants to see you in the doctors' room. Do you know where it is?"

"Yes, thank you." It opened off the landing just outside; sometimes he had seen through the open door an examination couch, a desk, and steel files. The housemaster's study, he thought. He was going on the carpet for having absconded yesterday. It only remained to hope that Mr. Deacon was a civilian. He knocked at the door, which was ajar, and went in.

Mr. Deacon wasn't sitting at the mahogany desk, but on it, his hands behind him gripping the edge. He straightened up as Laurie came in and said, "God, you would choose tonight to go and lose yourself. I've been looking for you since before six." Laurie realized that he had never till now been told Alec's second name.

"What did you want me for?" He would have felt more resentment, except that he noticed Alec looked quite ill. He had the kind of skin which with sickness or strain goes a bruised color around the eyes; his eyelids looked like brown crepe, and his ordinarily pale face had a waxy undertinge.

"Where's Ralph?" he asked. "Did you see him again?"

"Again?" said Laurie. His slowness was self-protective. He had thought that this empty place was all deadened and dull, as one can think with a raw burn till someone takes the dressing off.

With an edgy, fine-drawn impatience Alec said, "After he went at five, did you go after him? When I rang him up, when he took the receiver off, were you with him then?"

"No," Laurie said.

"You had a row, didn't you?"

"I'm sorry, Alec. If you don't mind I'll go back to
370

bed. I thought a doctor wanted me. I'm sorry. Good night."

"Now look," said Alec in a hard casualty-officer's voice, "there's no time for all that now. This is serious. Did you have a row with Ralph over one of the orderly boys at the E.M.S. hospital?"

Laurie found that all the anger in him had gone flat and sour: he could feel nothing but a dull swallow of sickness, even at this. He thought again that Alec looked as if he hadn't slept for days. London had been full of such faces. But now suddenly his dimmed perceptions partly cleared: a vague, premonitory apprehension stirred in him. He said, "That's nothing to do with you."

"Make up your mind about that later. Just listen now. If you've been told that Ralph went to see the boy and had some kind of scene with him, it isn't true. That's all."

"It *must* be true." It disturbed him that Alec's voice hadn't been that of a bland peacemaker, but brittle with the exasperation of a tired man. "It must be true, Andrew told me himself."

"Oh, it's not the boy's fault. He's only young, isn't he? If someone called claiming to be Ralph, why should he doubt it? Only it wasn't Ralph, you see. It was Bunny."

"*Bunny?*" His entrails shrank, heavy and cold. Of course, he thought, of course. The food he had eaten half an hour before lay hard in his stomach, like a meal of wood. "But how could it be Bunny? Why?"

"Oh, use your intelligence, if you ever do use it. Does it *sound* the sort of thing Ralph would do?"

"But he was always saying——" Although he could sense above him an annihilating weight of remorse ready to fall, he couldn't feel it yet, it was pushed out by the grotesque, obscene image of Andrew and Bunny together. "I found it hard to picture you and him as great friends. When he told me it was much more than that——" His hand reached to his pocket as if to touch the letter might alter his almost verbal recollection of it. "It is like something from another world, but it has touched you, and the touch is real."

"Well?" said Alec impatiently. "Now it starts to add up, I suppose."

"But . . . but he didn't know Andrew even existed. I didn't tell Ralph about it till after that. If he knew, then Ralph must have been seeing him all the time. No one else could have told him. That's nearly——" He stopped, recognizing for what they were the bitter lees of jealousy.

"I can guess how he found out. Sit down, can't you; don't stand there passing out on your feet, I've got no time to cope with it."

"I'm not," said Laurie angrily; but he let Alec push him into the patient's chair. It was true that he was feeling sick. Alec sat back on the desk, watching his face irritably.

"I know just what he did, the little sod." He pulled a packet of cigarettes out of his pocket, lit one in a jerky mechanical way without offering them, and drew on it hungrily. "I know, because I've carried the can for him before now. Either he's been reading your letters, if you've written Ralph any, or he's been at his diary again. I know he reads it because once Bim came out with something at a party, and from the way Ralph looked at me, I knew straight away I was the only person he'd ever told. It would have been just my word against Bunny's, and I can't bear these fracas, they make me ill."

Laurie said slowly, "I know when that happened. I was there."

"Oh, God, yes, so you were; of course that was why Ralph was so angry about it. He ought to have left his papers with me, like he did while he was at sea; he trusted me in those days, even after we'd split. The bits he used to show me were just travel stuff, but he always hovered rather, ready to grab it back again, so I assumed he'd committed his soul to it here and there. He'd have lost one lot with his ship, I suppose; but if he began another in hospital, God knows what he put in that." His dark bruised-looking eyes, set in creases of fatigue, stared at Laurie with dislike. He was smoking feverishly, burning the cigarette down one side. "Of course, living in the same house with Bunny, he must have locked things up. I suppose he didn't think to put a Yale on."

It was like getting an anonymous letter, Andrew had said. As a comment on Ralph it might have sounded a little shrill, if the context had not seemed to explain everything. There are drawings which when inverted reveal the features of a new and different face. In a dead voice, its protest mechanical, Laurie said, "How do you know all this?"

"Oh, in the usual way. Toto Phelps and Bunny have been honeymooning for two full weeks now; anyone could have told him Toto's one to get very nasty if he's two-timed, but all these wide boys get swelled head. The crash came yesterday, and Toto couldn't wait to plant the story where it could do most good. He's scared stiff of Ralph, so he came to me."

Laurie sat with his elbows on his knees, his hands pressed to his forehead. Alec twitched out the cigarettes again and lit another from the bent stub of the first which he trod into the rug. "I didn't believe it myself at first. I said to Toto, 'Don't give me that, Bunny's too crude for that Cinquecento stuff.' But Toto says it was more or less handed him on a plate. I gather the final break with Ralph was fairly acrimonious, Ralph wouldn't enlarge on that very much to you, I expect, and he didn't change digs for a week afterwards. Bunny found out all he could in the meantime; well, of course, being Bunny, his first thought was that the thing between you and the orderly boy mightn't be quite what you'd made it look to Ralph. So he went down just in the hope of finding some silly little piece whom he could charm into spilling the beans. Instead of which —well, I've met a few Quakers, I can imagine. And then the moment he introduced himself as a friend of yours, the boy said, 'You must be Ralph Lanyon': the uniform, of course. Well, improvisation is Bunny's middle name. You must have noticed it."

"Yes," said Laurie emptily. "Yes, I know."

"After all, there was nothing to give him away definitely except the hand, and Bunny's always got his hands in his pockets; they were there at the start of the conversation and he remembered not to take out the left one. He must have remembered even when he was

373

hit in the face. If he had any application, he could probably learn to be quite dangerous."

"He was as good as he needed to be," said Laurie bitterly.

"What happened?" asked Alec, as if he didn't expect an answer. "Well, you could have known a couple of hours ago if you'd stayed put. I saw Toto last night; I was going to have told you this morning. But Sandy had one of his bad turns, climbing the walls and threatening what he'd do to himself, and I've been frightened to leave him, to tell you the truth. I had to ring up Dallow to do my jobs for me, and Christ, what I found when I got back." He got up from the table with a nervous jerk; but the room was tiny and there was nowhere to walk to.

"Is Sandy all right?" said Laurie, though he didn't care.

"Oh, yes," said Alec in his flat edgy voice. "I suppose so . . . I've lived my own life to some extent. One can't tell him everything, you know what he is. I've let Bunny get away with little things before now, because of the trouble he could make if he wanted to. Then this blew up, and I thought, No, there's no two ways here, if I pass this it's blackmail. So I did what I always say one should, I told Sandy everything Bunny could have told him. When I got back eventually, after about two hours' sleep, I found one of Harrison's gastrectomies leaking, and they'd buzzed for me three times." He had displaced a pile of report forms on the desk; mechanically he began to straighten them. "I'm due to take my finals next summer. I don't know how I can go on like this."

Laurie had been thinking that Alec always seemed to save his confidences for occasions when one was incapable of taking them in. He said, "You'll be all right, because you're more a doctor than you're a queer."

Alec pushed the forms together and stood up. "You know," he said slowly, "that's the first sensible remark anyone's made to me all day. Let's hope you're right. How could you be such a bloody fool about Ralph? Didn't it even strike you he hadn't a mark on him after this alleged brawl? Bunny's been going around with a split lip for nearly a week, from walking into a lamp-standard in the blackout, *he* said. You don't seem to have given the orderly boy credit for much *élan*. And why should he hit Ralph, anyway? Even if Ralph did put it to him, he'd never put it like that."

"No," said Laurie. Another bit of the letter had come back to him.

"He denied it at first," he said. "And then, in the end, he seemed not to be denying it."

"I suppose he just thought what the hell. Or else ——" Alec smoked in silence for some moments, more evenly now, his hands pushed down into the pockets of his white coat. "Ralph's got a simple mind in some ways, but it follows through. Unlike so many of our fraternity, he's no good at ducking out. It was his doing in this sense, that he was the link. He let in the jungle. About one queer in a thousand has the guts to accept that sort of responsibility, and he's the odd one." He fell silent again, then looked up suddenly. "Just how bad was this row between you?"

Laurie saw Alec summing up his face; there seemed no need to answer.

"Final?" Alec asked. His voice had sharpened.

Laurie got up. "Will it be all right for me to use this telephone? I don't want to leave it till morning."

"He won't answer it. I told you, he took the receiver off the hooks as soon as the bell started. About six-thirty." He looked at his watch. With abrupt decision he sat down at the desk, searched the paper-rack, and got out a form. "You'd better go around there. Yes, for God's sake go around right away. I'll give you a pass. Family affairs, married sister ill. I've no right to do this; never mind, you're not supposed to know that, you'll be covered anyway. Here you are." He blotted the form swiftly and pushed it at Laurie. "I'll see the Night Nurse. I can't help what she thinks. Get on your way and don't loiter. He's not like Sandy, you know."

Laurie took the form. He didn't ask what Alec meant by this uncharacteristic statement of the obvious. He was tired now to the point when he had begun to live on his nerves. He felt he could go on forever, that he would never sleep again.

At the door he said, "I'm sorry you've had this trouble with Sandy because of me."

"If it wasn't you," said Alec unemotionally, "it would be something else. And it wasn't for you, really. Ralph would never let one do anything for him. It was what most of our rows were about." His eyes met Laurie's. Neither had moved, but they were like people at a station who see each other receding and getting small as each departs on his different journey. Alec said, "Walk out through the front door, not the lodge. And get a move on."

In the street outside the hospital, a taxi was unloading its freight of relatives summoned to someone critically ill. Laurie hailed it and got in. The night was black, and bitterly cold.

The drive, from which he had expected a breathing space, seemed over in a moment. He stood on the doorstep, making up his mind to ring. The landlady's radio was on. She was a talker, who had trapped him once or twice in the hall, and he dreaded its happening now. He tried the door; it was unlocked, and he came in quietly. She was rattling away to someone in her room, using the voice she kept for men. Helped by the banisters, he hoisted himself softly up the stairs.

Ralph's door was open and the light was on. Laurie paused at the stair-head. Suddenly he wondered why he was forcing himself on Ralph at all. It seemed formal and meaningless, an expiation important only to himself. What he had done was done. He ought to see to his own punishment; it was clear, from what Alec had said about the telephone, that Ralph wanted nothing of it or of him. Thinking about Ralph as he looked again at the door, he knew suddenly before he reached it that the room was empty.

It looked vividly different, as familiar rooms do after a strong experience. Lying on the bed was a shirt, to Laurie's eye quite clean, which Ralph must just have changed for a still cleaner one. He always used to hurry such things out of sight like guilty secrets; to have found it seemed one more offense against him. He must only have gone out for a few minutes, Laurie thought.

He walked in, across the room and around it; he was at the point of fatigue when delays are intolerable and one tries to abolish them by continuing to make the

376

motions of effort. It was mainly under this taut compulsion to be doing something that, when he found two or three letters on the table stuck down ready for posting, he picked them up to read the envelopes. The top one was for him. For a moment he felt only the relief of his restlessness, that here was something he could be dealing with. By the time he began to have scruples, his finger was already under the flap, and he noticed that the edge was lifting. It had been closed so recently that the gum hadn't quite set. For no good reason this made up his mind for him, and he peeled it open.

Ralph's clear sloped writing was packed in neat sections on a big white sheet from some kind of naval memo-pad. Laurie stood staring at it for a second or two, vaguely aware as he stood by the table of a faint smell which had some incongruous association for him, belonging to some part of his life with which Ralph had had nothing to do. The thought vanished from his mind and he began to read.

Dear Spud,

I am sorry that there seems to be no way of writing to you more quickly than by the post, if one is to avoid people reading it. I should have liked you to know sooner that you are not to blame for this in any way. It was Bunny who interviewed your friend, as I suspected, but that's immaterial. It couldn't have happened but for me, I saw that immediately, so that I have done what you thought in another way. I am telling you this to get it straight between us, because you are bound to find out sooner or later. The real reason I am getting out is that I can see no future for me at sea, and can't fancy myself in a shore job. I have had something of the sort in mind ever since Dunkirk. I swear that is true.

I am sincerely sorry for the harm I have done to you and to this boy. You had the right idea in the first place, knowing yourself best, and I came along and bitched up your life in every way. I can see now that I was wrong even at school; I should either have gone the whole way, which in those days would probably have shocked you and put you against it all, or shut up about it altogether. When I found you remembered, I felt it must have been what I wanted to happen. One may as well face these things.

If it is any satisfaction to you, I paid a call on Bunny

just now and he has been taken to sick bay, with concussion and broken ribs as well as I could judge. He came
around in time to agree it was the blackout once again. I
tripped him into admitting he had been at my private
papers. I shouldn't like you to think I had ever discussed
you or your affairs with him. If you should see Alec, will
you tell him I owe him an apology? He will know what
I mean.

You mustn't go on being upset about this, Spud. I have
never had much time for people who do this kind of thing
as a form of repartee, so if you want to do anything for
me, try not to think of it in that way. The fact of the
matter is that if I hadn't met you again, and had gone on as
I was, I might have drifted past the point where a step of
this kind ought to be taken, and I would rather have it
like this. You did what anyone would in the circumstances.
So don't worry. Just lately I have been happier than I ever
had the right to expect, and as one goes round the world
one sees that happiness is hard to come by and seldom lasts
for long. Good luck to you, Spud. We always agreed that
right, left, or center, it is still necessary to make out as a
human being. I haven't done it but you will. Goodbye.

Ralph

Laurie did not begin to think immediately. He was,
though now he had forgotten this, very tired. He wondered stupidly for a few moments where Ralph meant
to go, and remembered that if he went anywhere at an
hour's notice. it would be as a deserter. The picture of
Ralph on the run had a disturbingly wrong shape.
Laurie turned to the letter again; but, after all, he didn't
read it. He was not halfway through the first paragraph
when he placed the little smell that hung about the table. It belonged to the training depot and the first
months of war. As he bent down it got stronger; he saw
the cleaning rag soaked in gun-oil at the bottom of the
wastepaper basket.

No, he said stupidly; and while his mind was still
inert with refusal, he heard the sound of the radio flow
out through the opened door downstairs, and Ralph's
voice in the hall.

When one checks a fall one is sometimes aware of
the whole complex process as if it were the result of
thought. Laurie pushed the letter back into the enve-

lope, licked the gum again, and with swift accuracy stuck it down. He put it on the table exactly where he had found it, resisting his impulse to hide it under the others; crossed the room, and stood leaning on the mantelshelf looking into the fire. Now he noticed that Ralph had been burning papers, and a book of some kind. A yellow flame was licking through a fissure in the black paper, like a tongue between thin lips.

Some final exchange was going on between Ralph and the landlady in the hall. He heard Ralph's voice, on a note of conventional thanks and apology for giving trouble, moving toward the stairs as he made his escape. It sounded pleasant and easy. Laurie thought that if he had heard it when he first arrived, he would at once have said to himself, "Thank God, everything's all right."

He stood beside the hearth, his arm on the high, empty mantelshelf, waiting, and now Ralph was at the door. He had something in his hand, a little strip of postage stamps. Laurie remembered then that the letters on the table had had no stamps on them. Ralph stood quite still on the threshold for a couple of seconds, then came in and shut the door.

Laurie still didn't know what to say, but now it didn't matter. Instinct told him it was better to wait, not to make speeches. So he only said, "I had to come."

As soon as Ralph was in the room Laurie saw his eyes flick over to the writing-table, where the letters stood beside the telephone. Reassurance seemed to bring him to a standstill. Then he said, abruptly, "Did you try to ring me up, about half-past six?"

"Yes," said Laurie, "but I couldn't get through." He spoke with naturalness and conviction. Indeed, he scarcely knew that he was lying. He felt he was expressing something truer than the facts.

As he said it, he, too, turned to the writing-table. But he was looking at the telephone. Now he realized why he had not noticed it before. There had been nothing to notice. The receiver wasn't off the hooks now. Some time after six-thirty, Ralph must have put it back.

Laurie was unaware, at the time, of doing much more than note this as a material fact. If he had rung later he could have got through; that was all. Ralph's face was bruised on the left cheekbone; it looked rather drawn and sunken, as if he had been ill, but it was set now and gave very little away. What Laurie felt seemed to have its origin only in himself. He wanted it so. Knowledge was cruelty. The moment he had used it, he threw away the discovery he had made, that he had waited at the door of a house without defenses.

He had not thought of this. He had come to take his punishment and, his penance begun, to leave as he had come, alone. That was to have been the beginning. But that was in another country. "Something was wrong with the line," he said.

Ralph didn't move forward. His eyes were dragged down at the corners, as if with lack of sleep; he contracted them strainingly. Behind them, like an almost exhausted runner, his pride seemed to pause, to sway and balance. "What did you ring for?" he said. "I suppose you found out?"

Remorse, even the greatest, has the nature of a debt; if we could only clear the books, we feel that we should be free. But a deep compassion has the nature of love, which keeps no balance sheet; we are no longer our own. So in the presence of this helpless forgiveness, Laurie seemed to himself to be doing only what was nearest in the absence of time to think. There was something here to be done which no one else could do. All the rest would have to be thought about later. He looked Ralph straight in the eyes, believing what he said.

"Afterwards. Alec told me. But I should have come, anyway. I should have had to come back."

Quietly, as night shuts down the uncertain prospect of the road ahead, the wheels sink to stillness in the dust of the halting place, and the reins drop from the driver's loosened hands. Staying each his hunger on what pasture the place affords them, neither the white horse nor the black reproaches his fellow for drawing their master out of the way. They are far, both of them, from home, and lonely, and lengthened by their strife the way has been hard. Now their heads droop side by side till their long manes mingle; and when the voice of the charioteer falls silent they are reconciled for a night in sleep.

380